SCORNED OBSESSION

VICTORIA PAIGE

ISBN: 979-8-9889501-3-4

Editor: Erica Russikoff, Erica Edits
Developmental Editor: Kara Merideth
(Kat's Literary Services)
Proofreader: Judy Zweifel, Judy's Proofreading
Cover Designer: Deranged Doctor Design

Author's Note

The timeline of Scorned Obsession runs in parallel to Scorned Vows. I've taken liberties in renaming the New York Five Families and the Chicago Outfit, creating my own world and rules. This is not a dark romance but is morally gray. It does contain profanity, explicit scenes, and sensitive content.

For a more complete list scan below.

For the good girls who dream to be tarnished
by an obsessed morally gray man.

Prologue

Bianca

"Lose the boyfriend."

My spine stiffened in outrage before I turned to face my stalker, Alessandro "Sandro" Rossi. Never mind that it was my brother Nico's wedding. Lurking at De Lucci gatherings was nothing new to him. He'd made a sport out of it, and he continued to aggravate and confound the hell out of me.

"You're seriously going to do this here?" I snapped.

We were standing a foot apart. If I were any closer, I might smack him on the shoulder, but I was determined that he wasn't even getting that reaction from me. It was time for me to move on from the unhealthy obsession I had with him. Now if only my heart would listen to my head and stop speeding up every time he was near.

"He doesn't deserve you." A muscle pulsed at his stubble-covered jaw. I kept my gaze from wandering over his tux-clad body, but I'd spied him earlier. He was hard to miss when he decided to be seen. His clothes clung to his six-four frame and the formality of the attire did nothing to leash the feral power emanating from its seams.

Challenging Sandro with my eyes wasn't the brightest idea either, because his dark brown eyes saw through any bullshit I threw at him. It also hurt to look at his heartbreakingly handsome face, carved of sharp angles and chiseled to perfection. They belonged to an avenging angel. It suited his profession as a hit man for the mob.

I raised a brow. "And you?"

"Especially not me."

"Then I don't see your point. We've been through this dance a million times, Sandro. Every time I date someone, you and your brutish self show up and scare him away."

"That's why they don't deserve you."

"Oh, and somehow you consider yourself the barometer?" I scoffed. "You're not my father. Nor are you my brother. And newsflash, Sandro, even they don't have a say in who I date nowadays. So what makes you think you do?"

He stepped closer and cupped my cheek in a tender gesture. Even his eyes gentled from their murderous glint earlier. "I care enough."

I jerked my face out of his grasp. "Really?"

"I'm saving myself the trouble of having to kill someone who might hurt you."

I inhaled sharply. I never had proof, and I suspected…but was Sandro finally admitting… I backed away. Goose bumps chased each other all over my skin. "Rest assured that won't happen with Ethan."

"You're playing it safe." His gaze pierced into me. "But will he make you happy?"

"I've been dating Ethan for a month and I assure you, he makes me very happy. I'm sure you've done your research, otherwise you wouldn't be here."

His mouth curved into a semblance of a sneer. "You're into Ivy League investment banker types now?"

"Correction—hedge fund managers," I shot back. "I may like them."

"If he hurts you—"

"That's getting old, *old man.*" The mockery steeping my last two words didn't escape him, and his eyes flared. From irritation? From challenge? Sandro was nine years older than my twenty-three. Not ancient by any means, but old enough to taunt him about our age gap. "You know, sometimes you have to experience hurt before you get a happily ever after. It's called love. Experience its ups and downs and what it takes to love someone with all your heart."

He didn't say anything to this, but his eyes grew guarded. As much as Sandro controlled his facial expressions to a microscopic degree, I'd known him long enough that when his eyes turned flat, he was struggling to hide emotions from me. Whatever. I was sick and tired of his interference and him jerking me around. I didn't understand him anymore. I'd never had a boyfriend that didn't compel him to stick his nose into since I turned nineteen. He was worse than my brothers and Dad combined.

"Now, please, leave me alone."

"You heard my sister," a voice said behind us.

Sandro looked past my shoulder, and his eyes crinkled at the corners. "Lorenzo," he drawled.

I whipped around. My boyfriend, Ethan, stood worriedly beside my youngest brother, Renz. I didn't even have to turn around to see Sandro's smug smile. No boyfriend of mine had ever stood up to the mere presence of Alessandro Rossi.

"Great party," he said. "Give my regards to the bride and groom. I better head back to the club."

I didn't turn to say goodbye, but I knew he'd left.

Renz shot me a sympathetic look before he retreated to the party.

Ethan walked up to me, expression both sheepish and concerned. He had sandy-brown hair and smooth tanned skin. A far cry from the swarthiness that encompassed Sandro with the enticing, dangerous vibe of a modern pirate.

"Are you all right? I didn't really know how to handle all this." He glanced over to where Sandro disappeared. "You seem to know the guy."

"I do."

His brows furrowed. "Old boyfriend?"

"Childhood friend."

"He seems territorial." He fixed his bow tie, drawing attention to the bobbing of his throat. "I didn't want to start a brawl for your honor at Nico's wedding."

Sure. Damn Sandro for his ability to reduce all my boyfriends into shadows not even worthy of following in his wake. I gave him a tight smile. "Let's go inside."

I broke up with Ethan that night. It was hard to respect a man who wouldn't fight for me on his own.

I went home with Mom and Dad to their six-story row house on Tenth Street. My bedroom was on the fifth level, still strewn with unpacked boxes after my graduation. At first, I was excited to look for an apartment in Manhattan, but after this disaster with Ethan, maybe I needed a time-out from the bustling city. I'd always based my ideal man on Sandro, and growing up with the forceful personalities in my family wasn't helping either. Maybe I needed a gentler man. Someone who was anti-Sandro and anti-overbearing.

As I was mulling this over, my gaze fell on a carved wooden

box. Sandro had given it to me after one of his trips to Europe. He made a joke that he'd given me all kinds of shit and it was time to have something to hold them in.

I picked up one of my most treasured gifts. The silver cuff he'd given me for my twelfth birthday. A small crystal was set in the tiny sun overlay made of 14-carat gold. Sunflowers were etched into the bracelet. The silver had faded, and I hadn't polished it in years. It didn't fit my wrist anymore, but that was when I imagined I would marry Alessandro Rossi one day.

Time to get rid of that childhood obsession.

CHAPTER *One*

THREE MONTHS LATER

Sandro

My office vibrated with the pounding music of Club Aristos. Other evenings, I would have tuned it out, but not tonight. Tonight, I found out Bianca was back in New York. She fucking fled to the West Coast the week after her brother's wedding. I had been in a shit mood ever since.

The men in her family frowned at our friendship, but they normally stayed out of our hot-and-cold drama. Every effort to find her was hitting roadblocks that led to one conclusion: She'd assumed a new identity. Bianca left no credit card trails under her name. I lost track of her phone. My investigator reported she wasn't visiting her relatives in LA. The only reason I assumed she was in

California was because she sent me a postcard of the Pacific Ocean. It had a postmark of Malibu.

It said…

Hear that, Sandro?

That's the sound of freedom from your prying eyes.

The brat.

The urge to throw her over my knees and redden that ass had never been so strong. As soon as the image came to my mind, I shoved it away savagely. But it was too late. My cock had thickened beneath my trousers.

Off-limits, I growled to myself. *Bianca is off-limits.*

I glared at my desk's bottom drawer, fighting the desire to rip it off its tracks. A box of things I'd given Bianca was delivered to this club the same day she left New York. I called her, but she had her phone off. I thought she was just in a snit.

Finally, I had stormed Jabbin' Java, and Renz smirked when he saw me. "Don't break anything."

"Where is she?" I snarled.

At my blatant offense, all traces of humor left his face. "Leave her be, Alessandro. Would you give her that?"

Renz De Lucci was only twenty-five, but he had more wisdom than his hot-tempered older brothers. He'd fallen into the De Lucci obsession at eighteen and married his pregnant girlfriend in the midst of a mob war. The obsession was a popular myth in their family. According to Bianca it was like a Cupid's arrow, but instead of love, it was obsession. She had hinted it affected women, too. Well, if she were obsessed with me, then where the fuck was she?

"I care for your sister."

"I know," he replied. "But it's time to let her go."

Every sinew of muscle inside me rejected those words even when logically, if I cared for Bianca at all, he made sense. After I'd determined I wasn't getting any help from him, I gave him a brief nod and left the café that day, but it didn't mean I didn't do what I did best.

I lurked. I stalked. I tried to find clues to where Bianca had gone.

The pounding of the music resurfaced, and I realized I had yanked open the drawer. A carved box sat in its depths, taunting me to lift it. Everything I'd given her over the years was inside it.

She returned it with a note.

I don't need these anymore.

Thank you for looking out for me. I got it from here.

I got it from here? A snarl bubbled up my throat.

She had no clue how I kept the mafia shit from touching her. She was the prized daughter of Cesar De Lucci, for fuck's sake. Her father had many enemies. Many of them swam in the underworld's filth, hiding and afraid of Cesar, but that didn't mean they weren't plotting for the right time to strike. I swam with such scum so I could keep tabs on them. Each time I removed a threat to her, I only became more unworthy.

The blood on my hands was nothing like what she grew up with.

Let her go.

I couldn't. I was forever tied to her, even if she rejected the idea that a protector was all I could be. And the reason I drove all her boyfriends away was because she was safe as long as the De Luccis looked out for her. If she were to marry…

I shut down the line of thinking I wasn't prepared to face.

The door to my office opened, letting in the irritating music of the club. Griselda Scavo stepped in. She was my club manager and former fiancée.

She must have sensed my irritability at the music and quickly closed the door.

"What do you want?"

She raised a brow. "You've been holing up in your office for months."

I pretended to pound on my laptop. On the screen was the report of the last private investigator I hired to find Bianca. "Nothing new there."

"And sometimes you disappear and no one knows where you are."

"Nothing new there either."

"Sandro, now is not the time to bury your head in the sand."

I cast her a disinterested look. "Excuse me?"

"We have a problem."

"We…" I narrowed my eyes. "Elaborate." I leaned back in my chair. As much as I had my focus on Bianca, that didn't mean I couldn't multitask and know when shit was about to hit the fan.

"Gian wants me to marry a capo from the Philly mob."

"And that's my problem, how?" It was a big problem. The Philadelphia mob had been pushing for a firmer alliance with the Rossis. Gian was my cousin, but he was adopted and the only Rossi who wanted to become boss. The rest were wary. After all, two bosses were killed less than two years apart. No one knew exactly what went down, but I did, and I was determined to keep the truth buried.

The Philly mob smelled blood in the water and wanted to move in on our territory.

With Gian as their puppet.

"We used to be engaged," she said.

Of all the fucking reasons Griselda could come up with.

No matter how many times we'd gone over this, she seemed to have amnesia each time she brought it up.

"You broke up with me because I was a bastard son and not the spare heir."

"I wouldn't have minded." Her breath hitched.

"That's a lie and you know it. I never held it against you." I shrugged. "Besides, that's in the past. You were right to break the engagement."

"My parents—"

Oh, fuck no were we going to revisit that shit. "Old news. So, what's the problem now?"

Her eyes widened. "You're okay if the Rossis form an alliance with Philly?"

"That's up to Gian."

Her eyes flashed and she leaned in. "You know what a sadistic bunch of assholes the Philly mob are and with the New York Albanians doing their dirty work, they would make the Rossis look like Boy Scouts."

"I'd like to see them try."

"That's why you need to step up and take over from Gian."

"Not interested."

"I'm pregnant."

It was as if Griselda pulled the pin off a fucking grenade and tossed it on my lap. Foreboding prickled the back of my neck. Was it a dud? What damage would the shrapnel cause? I hadn't decided yet. Griselda and I had a complicated relationship. She was mine once. The doe-eyed, dark-haired beauty of the Scavos, a family that had been linked to the Rossis since the beginning. We'd been engaged at sixteen. She dumped me at eighteen. Love wasn't even a word I associated with her because I didn't know its meaning. It was a word a killer like me never entertained, even with Bianca. Fuck the women in my life. I should exile myself to Tibet and become a monk.

She was staring at me like I had the answer to her problem. "Are you sure?"

She rolled her eyes. "Do you want me to show you the pregnancy test? Or…" She smiled slyly. "Accompany me to the doctor?"

"What exactly are you asking me to do?"

"Tell Gian the baby is yours."

Bianca

I enjoyed traveling in anonymity, but I missed New York. Nico set me up with a fake identity, complete with credit cards and a burner phone. But now I was back to simply being Bianca.

I had come no closer to figuring out a direction in life. Who I was outside my family. I called Mom often just to chat because I felt unmoored on the coast of California. New York had my heart.

I glanced out of Jabbin' Java into the bustle of Hell's Kitchen. I'd been back two days and there was still no sign of my shadow. Or maybe he was around—shadowing. Renz said he had barged into the café and demanded to know where I was. But something my brother told him made Sandro back off. Still, I'd received reports of Sandro doing his sneaky stuff inquiring about me. Sandro stalking was a part of our weird relationship. Admittedly, I'd done my share of stalking too, but I hadn't in the last year. Because my heart was becoming less resilient. Because each time I repaired it, it would get shredded again. Each time I sneaked into Club Aristos to catch a glimpse of Sandro, he disappeared into his office with a woman. Each time I died, because what else would they be doing in there?

Which was exactly why it pissed me off when he scared my boyfriends away in the guise of what was good for me. My pride kept me from storming into his office and doing the same.

So I weaned myself off Sandro, except he kept turning up like a bad penny.

A squeal sounded on my right.

"You're back!" Ivy shrieked.

She rushed toward me. Behind his wife, my brother Nico followed more leisurely. It wasn't that he wasn't excited to see me. Nico and I had met up twice in California. I rose to greet them. From the sheen of sweat still coating their skin, I assumed they had just finished sparring at The Grindhouse boxing gym. Ivy's hair was up in a topknot and she was wearing a white tank and hot-pink track pants. Fashionable as always.

"I'm all sweaty, but you better not care," she announced before wrapping me in a warm, tight hug. A sting of tears burned my eyes, underscoring how much I missed my family.

"I don't," I croaked. "Sorry for missing fashion week. I heard it was another success."

Ivy pulled away. "Bah, we know why you stayed away."

Nico embraced me next. "Welcome back, sis. So have you decided to stay?"

I hadn't let everyone in on my plans yet. "I don't know yet. It seems like everyone has left Manhattan now that I've returned."

"You did surprise us," Nico shot back. "Dad and Mom are on their way back from Italy. Matteo is bummed he couldn't be here, but he and Sera are in Chicago to make sure Luca doesn't have a meltdown."

Sera was the wife of my eldest brother, Matteo. I had antagonistic feelings toward her uncle, Luca. But I felt sorry for his son. "It's Elias's first birthday, right?""

Nico gave a brief nod.

It was hard to put into words the tragedy that had befallen Luca. I didn't want to think that it was all his sins catching up with him. It appeared he hadn't accepted that he'd lost his wife and continued to search for Natalya. Hiring the best hackers and private investigators. Holing himself up at the mansion. In the early days of Natalya's disappearance, the family understood him. But now—what was it, ten months later?—they were beginning to fear for his sanity with his obsessive search for his wife.

He insisted Natalya was not dead.

A shiver went up my spine.

I was actually feeling a smidgen of sympathy for him. Just a smidgen.

"So, what are you guys up to tonight?" I asked.

"Date night," Ivy said. "After I kicked Nico's ass."

"Hey." Nico dragged her into a one-arm hug. "I let you win."

"Riiiight," I said dubiously. Ivy could totally kick Nico's ass. She'd been a practitioner of the martial arts for years.

"Come with us," Ivy said.

"And be the third wheel?" I rolled my eyes. "You guys can't keep your hands off each other in public." They were still in the honeymoon stage for sure, although Sera and Matteo had been married for over a year and behaved the same.

"Bianca can't," Renz called out and walked up to us. "She's helping with deliveries today."

Ivy laughed. "Now that's not the way to get your baby sister to come home and live in New York."

"I don't mind," I replied. "Gives me something to do. I worked in a vineyard restaurant for a few weeks." Besides traveling up and down the coast of California, I picked up short-term jobs to keep myself busy. The objective, after all, was to quit moping over an infuriating man and find out what to do with my life after college. Was he watching from outside right now? Lurking in alleys and dark corners? Sandro never freaked me out, and I drew comfort that someone was watching over me, but I hated that he was doing this selflessly. Why didn't he want more from me?

"You're making the deliveries?" Nico hiked a brow at me.

"I'm tagging along just in case Renz has to double-park and needs someone to move the van. It's where?"

"Brooklyn." Renz checked his watch. "We should leave."

I hugged Ivy and Nico again. "Let's do breakfast tomorrow."

Nico smirked. "Make that lunch. We're going to have a late night."

Ivy shook her head in amusement. I could have sworn her cheeks grew redder, and it wasn't from the workout.

"Gross," I muttered dutifully. But I was secretly tickled by how cute they were. That was the kind of love I wanted.

Thirty minutes later, we were in the thick of rush hour traffic. Renz kept checking the time while cursing at the vehicles in front of us.

Meanwhile, I was busy absorbing the essence of the city I grew up in. Okay, "essence" might be a stretch of what I was trying to reconnect with because I had no intention of inhaling the eau de smog of Manhattan. Did I like the hectic pace? The honking of horns? I spied a rolling cart selling hot dogs. A man in a suit hung around after receiving his order and chatted with the vendor as he served another customer. They appeared to be friends, shooting the shit with each other.

The crush of people in Armani suits, Adidas track pants, and well-worn jeans all blended under the shadows of New York's skyscrapers. A socialite in the latest-model Audi idled beside us. On the other side sat a man in a T-shirt with a baseball cap in a beat-up truck, windows down, while country music blared. The logo of a farm was on the door, and he had probably finished making deliveries to a restaurant touting farm-to-table cuisine that started in California.

I didn't need California. I had everything I loved right here in New York, including family.

Renz sputtered another expletive. "Fucking move! This is not lover's lane." As if to emphasize the point, he blasted his horn. "The light's green, motherfucker."

"Do you always curse this much when you make deliveries?" We De Luccis cursed a lot, including me, but this seemed over the top for Renz.

He flashed me a grin. "Only time I let loose when I'm not around Sam."

I laughed. "Oh, I see." My brother's daughter, Samantha, was almost six years old. "Might I remind you I was around Sam's age when Mom and Dad got summoned to school because I called my classmate an asshole?"

He emitted a deep-chested chuckle. "Yeah, Liz and I are trying to hold off getting those summons for a few more years."

"Losing battle, brother," I quipped. "But…you seem on edge."

Renz ducked his head to check both sides of the intersection before we crossed into Brooklyn. "I detest last-minute orders, but it was a favor for a colleague. Her baker is sick and they need dessert and bread."

"I heard Liz is cooking Irish stew tonight."

"Yeah, Mom's recipe too," Renz muttered.

My mouth watered. "Now my stomach's grumbling." I felt myself getting impatient. "Well, hurry up, then."

Renz snorted, and I didn't complain when he cut in and out of vehicles that were taking their time deciding where to go.

The delivery van finally made a turn into a row of upscale Brooklyn brownstones and slowed to a crawl. "This is the street."

"What number is it?" I asked.

"511."

"This is 480. It should be close," I said. "Look, a car just pulled out."

"I see it."

"You didn't need me after all," I told him as he swerved to claim the spot.

"I appreciate the company of my baby sister," he replied.

"Aw. You missed me."

He switched the car off and turned in his seat to face me. "Everyone missed you. Sam kept asking when her aunt Bianca was coming for a visit. I hated that Sandro drove you away—"

"He didn't," I protested. "I needed a change of scenery."

"All right. Let's talk later. You're staying at my place, right?"

"Try to stop me. I'm gonna get my fill of Liz's stew until you can't roll me out of your apartment."

He barked a laugh and got out of the vehicle.

I rolled down my window and called, "Sure you don't need help?"

"I got this," he hollered back.

Fine. I better check out my new phone. It had a new number that I was going to be more stingy with. I didn't realize how much my identity was tied to a phone number. Maybe because I'd had the same number since I was old enough to have a phone. I set up my apps, promising myself not to download everything cool and clutter this new device. New phone, new me. It was then I looked up.

A couple came into my line of vision.

Sandro?

My gut clenched. Was my mind trying to stamp his image on every man with his build? He was in deep conversation with a dark-haired woman. His date?

The cappuccino I had at the café backed up my throat. I watched them enter the brownstone that Renz went into.

What. The. Hell.

As they reached the bottom of the steps, Sandro put his arm around the woman. I blinked again and squinted. Maybe I was hallucinating and the man wasn't Sandro.

But I would know his hulking silhouette anywhere. He was in all black. He looked good in black. But I hated he had his arm around another woman. The familiar shredding in my chest started.

Before I could stop myself, I snatched the keys and got out of the van. All thoughts about putting Sandro in the rearview mirror evaporated in the face of my resurgent obsession.

The back of my mind was screaming at me to park my ass in the vehicle, but this compulsion to find out who was with Sandro was impossible to ignore. I was going to regret this later. I knew I would. But it seemed one thing I hadn't gotten under control was my impulsiveness when it had anything to do with Sandro Rossi.

I snuck between a narrow alley to get to the back of the brownstone. People were milling around. A big catering truck was parked there, taking over what little space there was in the back. I stared at my attire of black cigarette pants and a Jabbin' Java T-shirt. I could pass for Renz's assistant.

Don't do it. Don't do it.

But it was a losing battle. The compulsion was too strong. Sandro and the woman were like magnets drawing me in, and I was helpless to control my limbs.

I kept my head low as I passed the workers, but someone grabbed me and shoved a catering tray at me.

"Bring this to the kitchen."

A harried-looking woman noticed my shock. She gave me a double take and saw my T-shirt. "Oh, you're with Lorenzo?" She grinned. "Be a sweetheart and help out a bit, would you? I'm kind of short-staffed." She nodded to someone who disappeared into a door. "Follow her."

I hope the smile I gave her wasn't too shocked or excited.

"Okay." This was turning out better than expected. I was still cautious because I spotted men who had *Rossi soldier* stamped on their faces.

Without question, Renz and I had landed in a mafia gathering. Catering staff and arriving guests crowded the hallways. More mafia. I finally recognized some of them, although in my panicking thoughts, I'd forgotten their names except they were top soldiers of the Rossi crime family.

Shit.

I spun around just as their gazes shifted my way. I ran into a room where bottles of wine were being unloaded from boxes.

"Hey, you," the guy with the wine said. He had a slight British accent and looked like another caterer. Maybe a purveyor of fine wine, or a smuggler. "Bring this up."

"But—"

"But nothing. Alessandro Rossi and Griselda just arrived. They're going to toast to the engagement."

"Engagement?" I parroted.

"Yes." He frowned. "Engagement. Alessandro is getting married to Griselda." He leaned in conspiratorially. "Although I hear she's already pregnant, so they want this to go quickly."

There were enough times in my life that made me familiar with the feeling of blood draining from my face. The way you felt like you were stepping into a nightmare, frozen, lightheaded, and with an overwhelming urge to throw up.

The time the Queen Bee in my high school declared at lunch that I gave her boyfriend a blow job in the locker room. It was an outright lie, but the boyfriend didn't deny it.

That time I wasn't sure whether I lost my virginity with consent or not.

And yes, the infamous time I left Harvard and rushed to Club Aristos after I heard Sandro got shot while rescuing Sera. His ex-fiancée, Griselda, blocked my entrance to the club and slammed the door in my face.

Except she wasn't an ex-fiancée now, was she? All those times, I replayed how I would have handled those situations differently. I should have known the woman with Sandro was her, but my mind was in denial.

The man snapped his fingers in front of me. "Hey, are you daft or something?" He stepped back and assessed me. "You have a gorgeous face. You want to earn extra money?"

Don't be a tease, Bianca.

I'm going to be sick. I think I'm tipsy.

Then it'll be more fun. Drunk sex is the best.

Ouch, it's hurting, stop!

I focused back to the present. "Sure, but I don't think…" My chin dipped to my T-shirt.

"No problem. Here, put this on." He handed me a dark apron. "Gian loves pretty waitresses. You know how to pour wine, right? This is expensive stuff."

I called up a smile. "I've served in a pub for years." Despite being born into privilege, Mom always stressed the importance of hard work.

"Pub, eh? Then you'll do just fine." The man seemed to relish me working for him. He was the second person who asked me to help. Well, Renz didn't count. Either I looked like a pushover or I seemed capable.

Desperate people did desperate things.

And I was about to prove it.

CHAPTER *Two*

Bianca

I collared a bottle of wine in each hand. My flash-in-the-pan employer carried a wooden box of top-shelf whiskey. "There's an open bar, but make sure to keep their glasses filled," he said behind me while we made our way up the steps.

Conflicting feelings rattled with each step that brought me closer to the second floor. A part of me wanted Renz to appear and drag me out of here and lecture me for this escapade, while another part of me seethed with righteousness about confronting Sandro. I wanted to sneer in his face. Did he think he was the only one who knew how to stalk? Granted, this was by accident, but I couldn't wait to see the look on his face when he saw me pouring him a glass of wine and congratulating him on his engagement.

I ignored the pressure in my chest. The kind of pressure that made you want to scream into an abyss or ugly cry in a dark corner to ease the pain.

There was no time to dwell on conflicting emotions because when we entered the room where the party was being held, my feet sank in quicksand and I became a statue.

Apparently bravado before and after an idea was different when set in motion.

Quite a few people squinted at me.

One of them was Tommy Scavo. He was Griselda's brother and currently the Rossi underboss. I'd had friendly interactions with him. He was the same age as Sandro but was smooth-shaven and had a lankier build. Whereas Sandro's hair was wavy, Tommy's had tighter curls.

It was wishful thinking that he wouldn't recognize me.

Tommy strode to me directly, a thundercloud on his face.

"Bianca," he whisper-yelled. He gripped my elbow and crowded me into a corner. "What the hell are you doing?"

"I'm about to serve wine."

My faux employer eyed us warily. "You two know each other?"

"Kinda," I squeaked.

"Yes," Tommy shot back with a glare so hard, the other man backed off and disappeared. Turning back to me, he said, "I saw Renz. He's pissed that he didn't know the order was for this. You guys shouldn't be here."

Too late. I was in full-blown stalker mode and determined to get my answers. As long as I'd known Sandro, I wasn't privy to the inner workings of the Rossi crime family. I only knew he was their top enforcer. It appeared he was more involved than I thought. If I had known this, I would have backed off a long time ago. I always thought he was the outcast and the Rossis took advantage of him. But if this gathering was in his honor, then he hadn't been honest with me.

"Hey, Tommy," someone called from across the room. "Stop harassing the wine girl and send her over."

His grip tightened on my arm, but I yanked at my elbow and freed myself. "I have work to do."

I strutted across the room. A few of the men eyed me up and down. I spied Sandro's dark outline out of the corner of my eye, but I refused to look at him.

Yet.

I pasted a smile on my face for the stranger who called me over. "More wine, sir? This is a Barolo vintage 1995 from the Piedmont region."

More men surrounded me. "Okay, you guys need to give me room." I flashed them a fake nervous smile.

"So what's your name?" one of them asked.

"I bet you taste better than this wine."

Wine was the last thing on their minds. They were probably wondering if I was a candidate for mistress.

"Move over, Sergio. Give the lady some room," Tommy growled.

Bodies pushed against me. I could not extend my arms to pour the wine. Air became scarce. Either that or I was panicking, like I'd been thrown into shark-infested waters with a bleeding wound. In this case, it was my bleeding heart.

Just when I thought I was going to let out the scream in my chest, fresh air expanded my lungs.

The bottles disappeared from my hands, and I was staring into Sandro's livid gaze. He used his hulking form and shouldered men aside, or maybe they simply backed off from the vicious hostility emanating from him.

His jaw was clenched. His mouth was trying to form words but failing. He gripped my arms the way Tommy did earlier and then dragged me from the room.

My gaze passed over to Griselda. Her expression was just as furious as Sandro's. That was when I realized she was standing beside the man I knew as Gian. The adopted Rossi. The new boss. I didn't like the speculative gleam in his eyes, like he was already plotting bad things for me.

My legs struggled to match Sandro's long strides.

He hauled me into a living room with pass-throughs on each side. Guests got startled at our abrupt entrance.

"Out," Sandro roared.

The occupants scrambled for the exits.

He let go of my arm and the momentum at which we entered the room had me stumbling a few steps forward.

"What the hell, Sandro?" I shrieked.

"What the hell?" he repeated, as if I had the gall to get pissed off at him. "What the hell," he repeated more softly. And I knew him well enough that he was about to explode. And I was right.

"What the fuck are you doing here?" he roared.

"I came to congratulate you on your engagement." I tilted up my chin. Shocked, how I calmly delivered that line when my knees were knocking against each other. Self-righteous anger simmered inside me, remembering all the years I thought I could steer him away from the Rossis, showing him that their way wasn't the only way. That my family would embrace him and protect him as long as he severed ties with them.

His eyes flickered with an unnamed emotion. Surprise maybe? Or guilt that I knew about the engagement.

"What do you want me to say, Bianca?" He exhaled a resigned sigh. "Thank you?"

"Are they forcing you to marry her?" I asked shakily.

"No." His reply was immediate and my tattered heart started hemorrhaging.

My foolish, foolish heart. I shoved his chest. Angry tears scalded my eyes, but I refused to let them fall. "Then what was that fucked-up game you were playing with me? You scare my boyfriends away and then not want me?" A pained hitch choked those last two words. "You said I deserved better. Help me understand, Sandro. Why marry someone else?"

The last shred of pride kept me from asking, *Why not me?*

"Bianca…" Was that pity in his eyes? I should've turned around and walked away. Left him to the Rossis. It was clear he made his choice.

"Oh, how wonderful that she knows." Griselda strode in.

"Not now, Griselda," he bit out.

"Oh, Sandro." She sidled up to him and clung to his arm. "Sooner or later, she'll find out." The smile she cast me was full of triumph, of satisfaction that in the end she'd won and I was left with heartbreak and humiliation. "It's time to stop indulging her girlish dreams and concentrate on the family we're going to have." She palmed her lower belly, leaving no question what she meant. She was already pregnant. Griselda was having Sandro's baby.

I wanted to throw up.

Sandro stood stiffly, but he didn't object to how Griselda plastered herself to his side in a show of possessiveness. Did I misread his concern for me all these years? Too blinded by my obsession with him, I couldn't see him the way he really saw me.

"Oh, poor baby," Griselda continued. "Sandro cares for you, but you're always going to be like a baby sister to him."

She spelled out what my obsession had kept me from seeing. Sandro remained a silent, brooding mountain beside her, not even trying to contradict her.

"You're right." The grinding in my jaw started to hurt. "Now, can I leave?"

"Not so fast." A new voice joined the conversation, and Gian stepped into the room.

Sandro wiped his face clean of emotions. Griselda grew wary. Tension snaked into the room and coiled around us.

"Bianca De Lucci. Now why is Cesar's youngest here?"

"There was a last-minute change to the catering." It was Tommy who spoke up. "There was a bit of confusion and there was no dessert."

"Oh, I remember now," Gian said in a tone as silky as slime. "Your family owns a café bakery. But…why were you pouring wine, hmmm? Were you hoping to poison the Rossis?"

"That's absolute nonsense. I'm just a business grad trying to find her footing. And if you had the right info on me, you'd know I get into different things. Like I'm helping out at my brother's café right now."

Gian stood beside Sandro. "Is that right? The De Luccis always seemed to be peripherally involved whenever a Rossi boss gets assassinated." He looked at Sandro. "First Frankie, and then Joe."

"That's ridiculous," Sandro cut in, but he didn't offer an explanation.

"I guess we'll never know, but I think if I dig hard enough…"

When Gian passed Sandro and moved closer to me, Sandro's shoulders noticeably stiffened, but Griselda gripped his arm to keep him in place.

"Let her go, Gian," Sandro said, his voice quiet but fierce.

"Or what, Sandro?" Gian mocked. "Your little pet obviously came here for something."

"I told you I just delivered the baked goods, but you were short on serving staff, so I helped. And I wanted to congratulate Sandro on his engagement."

Gian laughed like a hyena. Meanwhile, Sandro was growing more remote, his face darkening, and he was eyeing the back of Gian's head like a piñata. His gaze briefly drifted to mine, but his chin dipped and his eyes scouted the area.

When Gian stopped laughing, he turned to Tommy. "Make sure you educate whoever is screening the service staff for gatherings like this. We're two Rossi bosses down. We need to be more careful, *capisce*?"

Gian's beady eyes returned to me. "Now, what am I going to do with you?"

"You have no choice but to let her go," Sandro gritted.

"Bianca!" Renz's voice shouted behind me. I spun around to see my brother barreling in from the other entrance of the living room.

I stumbled toward him, and he hauled me into his arms. "Are you all right?"

"I'm fine," I cried, my relief crashing over me.

Renz glared over my shoulder. "We're leaving."

"Not so fast," Gian hissed. "How do I know you're not spying?"

Tommy started to say something, but Gian held up his hand and cut him off.

"This was a mistake." Renz started backing away with me, not confirming or denying Gian's accusation.

Sandro's stoic face morphed into one of alarm and anger. He rushed forward and pushed Gian out of the way. I thought he was trying to grab me from Renz.

Everything happened at the same time and in slow motion.

"Put the gun—" Sandro shouted. But then his shout was cut off with a loud cracking sound.

Renz grunted, and we started falling.

"Bianca!" Sandro's anguished roar engulfed the rush in my ears, but my breath deserted me when I landed on top of Renz.

Another blast.

Then chaos erupted.

I scrambled off Renz with my heart lodged in my throat. Tears and disbelief clogged my words and I screamed, "No!"

My brother…

His entire left side was a map of red. I shifted to my knees, paralyzed in terror. "Where are you hit?"

"I dunno," he wheezed. He was dazed, head moving from side to side, his eyes trying to stay open. "Liz…"

"I'm so sorry, I'm so sorry," I sobbed. All my fault. I glanced up and screamed, "Call 911!" Tommy slid to his knees beside me and started ripping Renz's shirt off.

There was a crush of people in the room. Sandro had a man up against the wall, and I spotted another man on the floor.

Everyone was talking at the same time. They were discussing how to clean up this mess. As in, we were the mess. Getting out of here alive was becoming an impossibility.

The stronger odds? Renz could die.

My eyes latched on to the gun that had fallen under an armchair. Without another thought, I scrambled for it and succeeded.

"Bianca," Sandro gritted.

I raised the gun and shot at the ceiling before pointing it at Gian. Several guns pointed at me, but with Renz dying, fear had deserted me.

A thought in my head was on repeat. Renz was bleeding out, and it was all my fault.

"Call 911," I repeated.

"No," Gian sneered.

Sandro grabbed me from behind and divested me of the weapon. I jerked away from him and sank to my knees again in front of Renz, trying not to feel defeated. Trying not to surrender to the fear that Renz would die. Tommy was applying pressure to his chest wound. Blood spilled from Renz's lips.

"We need the doc," Tommy said.

"Already called him," someone said.

I glared at Tommy. "He needs a hospital."

Renz's eyes were barely open, and he groaned, "Sorry, sis."

"Why are you sorry? I was the one who messed up," I choked.

"He needs a hospital," I pleaded with Sandro, my voice cracking, my chest screwing tighter and tighter. It was getting harder to breathe.

He shook his head. "Can't do that."

"If he dies, I'll never forgive you!"

"Excuse me?" Griselda jeered. "You're blaming him when you were the one who crashed our party?"

"Griselda," Sandro growled. "Not now. Not here. Can't you see she's distraught?"

"You always baby her, defend her. Now what do we do with this mess?" She turned on Gian. "You think Cesar De Lucci will let this go?"

"Shut up, Griselda," Sandro snapped.

"She's right." Gian detached from his huddle of soldiers and walked up to Tommy. "What do you think, Tommy? It was one of our men who shot his son, even if Sandro killed him." He glared at Sandro as if saying that was the wrong move and there would be repercussions later. "I don't think he'd take too kindly that we harmed his baby De Luccis."

A round of laughter went around the room. Only Sandro, I, and Tommy were not laughing. I was fuming, but I knew better than to stoke the promise of retaliation from my family.

If Renz dies…

My chest heaved in almighty agony; my throat scraped with burning rage. Thoughts spiraled into a dark place.

There would be no place on earth the Rossi crime family could hide. Dad would exterminate every single one of them, Sandro included. And at this very instant, I didn't care that the boy I adored since childhood was going to rot in hell with them.

An emotion I'd never associated with Sandro surged inside me and I raised my eyes to meet his gaze head-on.

Hatred.

Unadulterated hatred.

The boy I'd been in love with for most of my life was one of *them.*

Whatever Sandro saw on my face disturbed him enough. He was skilled at hiding what he was feeling, but in some ways, I was familiar with his tells. His hand that was at his side, the one not holding a gun, curled and uncurled. He wanted to comfort me, but his arms were the last thing I craved.

I seek atonement.

Because of my obsession with Alessandro Rossi, my brother could die.

I harnessed all my anger and stopped crying. I was a De Lucci. Renz needed me to have my wits about me.

Gian crouched in front of me. "The only way Cesar De Lucci won't come after us is if we form an alliance."

A gripping chill crawled up my spine.

"If you marry me, surely your pop won't kill his son-in-law?"

CHAPTER *Three*

Sandro

In an ideal situation, Gian's brains would be on the wall. I would shoot my way out of here with Bianca in tow. The gangsters present wouldn't dare be in the sights of my gun. Admittedly, there were a few too stupid to live.

But Bianca would never leave Renz. Covered in blood, she speared her venom-filled glare at me, Gian, and every single person in this room. I didn't recognize the woman in front of me and I wanted to roar.

My world was nothing like the morally gray one she lived in.

Mine was pitch black. I swam with the filth of the underworld. The cockroaches.

"Fuck that," Renz gritted out.

"Or do you want me to kill you now?" Gian asked Renz.

My finger feathered the trigger. Gian would be dead before he shot Renz. Griselda clasped my arm, but I recoiled from her touch and stepped away from her.

"I'll do what you want." Bianca's voice cracked. "Just—"

I seethed in silence. *No, Bianca. Fuck, no.* I'd never shot anyone without purpose. My kills were never based on emotion. Cold. Methodical. Words I lived by. I was anything but cold right now. I was anything but methodical at this fucking instant. I exposed my card when I shot the man who shot Renz.

I would kill a Rossi before anyone hurt Bianca.

"Bianca, goddammit," Renz broke off in a groan of pain.

"Shut up and save your energy," she snapped at her brother. She rose like a battered soldier who still had a lot of fight in her. One who was about to make a last stand. She stared down at Gian. "I'll do what you want."

Gian rose to his feet. He wasn't a tall man, five eight at most, but he made up for his height with arrogance and the sickening entitlement he shoved down people's throats to make sure they knew he earned his place in the family. That he earned the Rossi last name, unlike me, I wanted to get rid of it. That was still the plan.

"But my brother gets medical attention right this fucking minute," Bianca continued with steel in her voice.

"Of course." Gian's gloating tone triggered the swoosh of fury in my ears. Marrying Bianca De Lucci was a coup. No one in the mafia dared pursue her for fear of Cesar, but this was a rare advantage. My mind worked furiously on how to get her out of this crisis and it was hitting every roadblock except one.

"And after I marry you, you will return Renz to my family," Bianca continued to negotiate. "Unharmed. Otherwise, I will make you sorry you married me."

"Feisty," Gian said with a malice that sickened me. "I like that."

"Sandro." She addressed me in a monotone voice as if she was reading a manifesto of someone sentenced to death. "If he reneges on his promise and either Renz or I are killed, you will avenge us, yes?"

Gian laughed. "You can't make that request, my dear."

"Sandro is an enforcer, is he not?" Her eyes were still on me, her anger morphing into a chilling stare.

"For the Rossi crime family," Gian said. "He cannot act without my order."

That's where you're wrong, cuz.

I kept my face expressionless. But my whole body thrummed with the urge to act. To yank Bianca out of this nightmare.

"But you put the Rossi crime family at risk if you don't have Renz or me to bargain with." She stared at me. "And as the guardian enforcer, Sandro is acting within his rights to eliminate the risks to the family…meaning you."

A silence fell over the room. I had become an urban legend after I killed the notorious butcher of Toronto at age nineteen. He'd been the biggest threat to our organization. The elders created my title as the "guardian" enforcer—the protector of the family who eliminated anyone who was a danger to us, even a boss or a high-ranking member. They didn't clarify the extent of my powers. When I went away for a year in a Russian prison and didn't crack, the legend only grew. I scoffed at it. No one could really make a direct link to me and my kills. But if it would make Gian second-guess hurting Bianca and Renz, I was gonna play it up.

"She's right."

"And how did she know about the guardian position?" Gian asked. "This is not common knowledge outside our family."

"Who cares!" Bianca snapped. "My brother needs medical attention now."

"Doc is on his way," Tommy said.

"We can't stay here," I said. "This is the first place the De Luccis will look." I ignored the blast of betrayal coming from

Bianca, but Dom and Matteo were out of town. I didn't trust Dom's underboss, and Nico was a hothead.

"You're right," Gian agreed, then grinned at Bianca. "I'll have the marriage license expedited."

Bianca stared at Gian blankly. Lost in the fiasco playing out in front of her, she was bearing all the blame for what happened to her brother. Her skin, once creamy and vibrant, had taken on the grayish pallor of death.

As much as I wanted to reassure her, Bianca needed the enforcer and not her childhood friend.

"We need to move his delivery van," I told Gian. The property owner of this house was a shell company. Given the De Luccis' resources, though, they would connect it with the Rossis in no time. A plan was forming in my head. A path I never imagined taking, but it was the only way.

Hours later, Tommy emerged from his huddle with Gian. "The Brooklyn property is crawling with De Lucci soldiers," he informed me. "Nico is with them."

I'd already switched off my phone with the number the De Luccis knew. Two hours after Renz and Bianca became our prisoners, I received the first text from Nico. Like I suspected, it wouldn't take them long to figure out the Rossis' connection to the house in Brooklyn. Dom texted me next. With my lack of response, they called. The messages became angrier and progressively threatening at my continued silence. And my silence indicated I was involved in their disappearance.

"Keep an eye on what they're doing. Any news on the other De Luccis?"

"No. But Luca is trying to reach us."

Fuck.

The De Luccis were trying to get to us through another channel. One that would be hard to ignore.

"Gian needs to act fast." I needed to act faster. "We don't want to end up on the wrong side of Chicago."

"Gian should have thought about this before he held Lorenzo and Bianca hostage," Tommy muttered.

"You're his underboss. You should've said something."

"He doesn't listen. The power has gone to his head."

"It should have been you," I told him.

Tommy emitted a bitter laugh. "Oh, you mean it should have been you, Sandro? The elders wouldn't want a Scavo in charge. They will always want a Rossi." The elders. Only one elder left and he was acting consigliere—the adviser—for the family since my brother, Frankie, whacked the last one.

"It's time for change," I told him. "The Scavos have been loyal soldiers."

He gave a shrug. Tommy was the one who considered the best interests of the family first. It was through Tommy that I found out that my brother, Frankie, had suggested kidnapping Bianca in retaliation for Matteo stealing Sera from an arranged marriage that would have benefitted the Rossis.

I would kill my own brother to protect Bianca. Luca did it for me. That was the secret Luca and I shared because all witnesses to him shooting my brother were dead.

"I'm going to check on Bianca and Renz."

Tommy smiled faintly. "Good luck with that."

I grunted and made my way through the old house. I wouldn't call it a mansion, but it had eight rooms, and a basement used for interrogations. A lean staff kept it maintained, and it was one of the few properties the other Five Families knew nothing about.

Once Cesar De Lucci landed in Manhattan, war was imminent unless I could head him off before he acted unilaterally and went after us. He operated outside the rules of crime families and had a paramilitary team at his disposal, which he used to police the underworld.

I didn't agree that underworld organizations needed an oversight. Everyone had the right to power. Luca being an example. Had Luca not been related to the De Luccis, Cesar would have gone after him a long time ago. Hypocrite, much? Luca bled power and made deals with the Russians when it suited him. But that power came at a price when he lost his wife. The wolves were circling. They scented a wounded animal. Wounded animals either gave up or fought back.

Luca was fighting back. He was still looking for Natalya.

People thought he was crazy, but I understood his obsession. Because if Bianca disappeared without a trace with no body to prove she was dead, I would scorch the earth looking for her.

Yet, I asked myself, *why? To what end?*

I trudged to the second floor. The ancient steps creaked from decades of use. I was glad Gian was hospitable enough not to stick his bride and her brother in the basement.

Bride.

That word left an acrid taste on my tongue.

I came upon a room with the lock on the outside. I never wanted any part of my fucked-up family to touch her, yet here we were in a more fucked-up situation.

I unlocked the door and stepped inside.

Bianca sat by her brother's bedside, but her eyes focused on me. I wished I could offer comfort, but all I had were the doctor's words.

"Doc said if he makes it through the night, his prognosis is better." I nodded to Renz's sleeping form. "I heard he was belligerent and had to be sedated."

She stared at me for a long time, not speaking. Her condemning gaze weighed heavily on the suffocating silence, but I forced myself to meet it. I could fix this, but everything hinged on her cooperation. The mounting pressure from the De Luccis would lessen if we returned Renz.

"I've never despised a person more than you." Every single word was like a bullet hitting me center mass.

"That's fair," I returned.

She stood, walked around the bed, then stopped in front of me. Jesus, why was she still in her bloody clothes?

"I despise you more than your cousin."

"I understand."

"Did our friendship mean nothing to you?" she asked. Tears rimmed her angry eyes. And I ached to cup her face and wipe them away. But I needed her pissed. To hate me if she must.

"Of course it does, but you never listen, do you? You can't save me. This…" I lowered my voice and threw my arm behind me. "Is my world. This is the sickness that runs in it. You deserve better and it can never be me. Now, do you see why?"

"But you should have tried harder instead of showing me everything to the contrary. You should have showed me what a sick bastard you are. The type to go along and let me marry Gian."

"What would you have me do? Turn everything red? Kill everyone to save you?"

"You could have convinced him to let us go, but your fiancée had to open her big mouth."

"I killed the man who shot your brother. He had every right to shoot Renz." We reviewed the security footage and Bianca's brother overpowered the Rossi goon and knocked him out. "Lucky for us, he wasn't a made man, or Gian would have me removed from the scene. Where would that leave you?"

"Apparently, the same place I am right now. But I wish you could have convinced them to drop Renz off at the hospital."

I crossed my arms because she still couldn't see my dilemma. My worlds were colliding. Protect the Rossi organization and protect Bianca. I didn't know how to do both. Wait, I did. I knew who I would save first, but I needed a plan.

"You overestimate my importance. I'm forever the bastard son of Carmelo Rossi whose only purpose to the Rossi crime family is its assassin."

"Even me? If they tell you to kill me, would you do it? Because I hate your family with all my heart. And if I could burn this place down with everyone in it, including you, it would make me very happy."

"Bianca." Regret roughened the way I said her name. Not because she wanted to kill me, but because I never wanted her to experience such hatred. She had only known love and was spoiled by her family. Seeing her now in bloodied clothes made me want to wage war against my family, but I had to play it smart. Even if it meant Bianca ended up despising me. Maybe that was the only way she would let go of her obsession with me. Maybe she already had.

"Would you kill me if they asked you?" she asked.

How could she say that? This time I couldn't help myself. I erased the distance between us and cupped her cheek. Her multifaceted brown eyes were now dimmed into a brown as dark as mine. "My bullets, my blades, and my fists are meant for everyone else. Never *you*. I would *never* hurt you. I would slit my throat first."

She didn't say anything.

"I'd do it now to prove it to you, but I won't. Right now is when you need me the most."

She stepped back, effectively dislodging my hand from her cheek. I let my arm fall back to my side, yet my fingers itched to touch her.

She held my gaze for a few seconds longer before she walked

back to Renz. "I don't need you anymore, Sandro. I needed you hours ago."

She sat in a chair, elbows propped on the mattress, staring at her brother. "You chose them over me." She shrugged. "I always believed there was hope for you. I was wrong."

Her words should've set me free. Whatever bond we shared broke. Or it had already broken.

She saw the monsters in my family and knew I was one of them.

CHAPTER Four

Bianca

A beautiful creation of lace and exquisite tulle enrobed a body form. A seamstress came in yesterday to take my measurements. I had two days to gird myself for the impending nuptials, but a spiky ball of anxiety was my constant companion. The acid in my gut pushed up my throat. Breathing became a chore. Sand scratched my eyes, and a headache tattooed itself on my skull despite giving in to one of Renz's pain meds.

"This should fit you," a voice said behind me. I turned to Griselda, who couldn't hide how gleeful she was at my predicament. Her whole demeanor screamed, *I win.* Sandro was going to end up with her, after all. But I was in my didn't-give-a-shit-about-Sandro era.

She moved closer and said in a conspiratorial tone, "At least I didn't remind Gian that you are not a virgin."

Once upon a time, if I had known Sandro had reconciled with

Griselda, I would have raised hell because she was the reason I lost my virginity in an unsavory manner.

"You're still a bitch." I pushed out the derogatory word that rarely passed my lips, but these past forty-eight hours seemed like an exception. Everyone around Renz and me were assholes or fuckers or bitches. Talking was a chore in itself because the only person I wanted to listen to was Renz. I resisted getting into my head too much, concentrating on my brother and his unconscious state. After I said my vows to Gian today, Renz would be free.

I tried not to dwell on the upcoming wedding night, although calling this a wedding was a stretch. Another of my girlish dreams ruined because of my obsession with one man. My future was uncertain. Surely, I could file for divorce from Gian after this sham of a marriage. Unless they were going to make me sign some kind of prenuptial agreement. I wouldn't put it past the Rossis.

"Really?" She laughed scornfully. "I'm the bitch? If it wasn't for you, Sandro and I would have been married—"

"You dumped him first," I gritted. "It was only when he became a legendary enforcer that you wanted him back."

"And he wanted me back, but you had to go ruin it. What happened to girl code?"

Griselda and I were each other's ruinations. And guess who was our common denominator again—Sandro.

"Girl code..." It was my turn to emit a short, scornful laugh. "We were not even close to that level, Griselda. I'm the one who's sleep-deprived and you're the delusional one. But let me remind you how you messed with my head."

"Oh, give me a break. You were seventeen; you should have known better."

She walked over to my wedding dress and put her arms around the form, her grin growing wider and more satisfied. "But let's put this behind us..." She let those words hang and touched her flat belly. "We're going to be family."

The idea made me want to hurl. Since captivity, that had been a constant feeling, but I tried to swallow the rancid taste, the bitterness that coated my tongue. I shoved it into the box where I locked down my other feelings for Sandro, tightening them with the chains of my anger.

The sooner this farce of a marriage was over, the better. All I cared about was my brother's freedom.

That he would get to go home to Liz and Sam and get the medical care he should have gotten two days ago.

I thought about Mom and Dad. They must be going out of their minds. Matteo and Sera should have returned by now, too. At one point yesterday, there seemed to be a commotion around the house. I heard men shouting outside, and I thought my family had found us.

But it was really looking like I was marrying Gian Rossi. Once Renz was free, I could wallow in the other heartache that was pushing in.

It had nothing to do with Sandro. Sandro was dead to me.

No, my heartache was being a failure as a daughter.

My heartache was about Dad.

I'd overheard him one day when one of his associates teased him about Sandro being grumpy to everyone else but me. They said we should be engaged.

And Dad said, "Over my dead body will my daughter marry a Rossi."

I got mad at him. I thought he was unfair painting Sandro like the rest of his family. But now I realized my dad had always been right, and I just knew my next torment was because I let him down. All my life, I craved my parents' approval, not because they demanded I do things their way, but because they expected nothing from me. I had only known unconditional love.

I approached the dress form. My icy fingers touched the fabric. My body must still be in a state of shock because all my limbs were stiff and cold. I also hadn't had a proper meal in days, not having any appetite.

"You know what would make this perfect?" I asked Griselda.

"What?"

"Pig's blood." I gave a snort of laughter.

Her brows drew together. "Are you all right?"

But I couldn't stop laughing even when I tasted tears. "All right?" I glared at her with enough force that made her step back. "What is all right about this, Griselda? My brother is sedated to within an inch of killing him. He needed a hospital two days ago." I stomped toward her. "I'm being forced into a marriage with a man I hate." Finally, all the pent-up fury and frustration of the past few days detonated into a maniacal scream. "What is all right about this?"

It did not give me catharsis. I only spiraled deeper into despair.

Rossi soldiers rushed into the room, Sandro and Tommy with them.

"What's going on here?" Sandro demanded.

Griselda rushed to Sandro and dove into him, shrinking away from me as though she were in danger from me. She probably was.

"She's becoming hysterical. Maybe she needs some of those meds they gave her brother."

Sandro shook her hands off. "Fuck off, Griselda."

I laughed harder, wrapping my arms around my stomach. "Is that any way to talk to your fiancée, Sandro?"

His jaw clenched, and his hands descended on my shoulders. "You need to get ready."

"Oh, are you here to make sure I'm going through with this farce of a marriage?"

"Yes."

That one word stabbed me with so much pain, I almost folded over. Tears scalded my eyes and blurred my vision. "Well then, let's make this perfect."

I was going to show them what perfect was.

"You look like the bride of Dracula," Renz croaked from the bed.

I turned away from the mirror. He insisted on sitting up while I went through the motions of getting ready for the ceremony. I'd sent away the makeup crew and told them I could do my own damned hair and makeup.

"Bummer it's not Halloween." I walked to his side. "How are you feeling?"

"Floating…" Even in his morphine-induced haze, I could see the pain in his glazed eyes. His lips were almost white. They'd given him a blood transfusion and had him on an IV. The wound was between his shoulder and upper chest. There was swelling around it, and he was running a low-grade fever. It didn't take a genius to figure out he needed better care, better meds. He would have them tonight. He opened his palm, and I responded by lacing our fingers.

"Stay alive, Smurfette. Don't do anything stupid." He pushed those words out with effort. He winced slightly and cursed before trying to focus on me. "We'll get you out. I swear."

"I know. Don't worry about me."

A knock sounded on the door before Tommy stepped in, dressed in a formal suit and tie.

"Are you here to give me away?"

He gave a slight nod.

"Why not Sandro?" I taunted. "Then this circus would be complete."

"He has to be elsewhere."

"Figures." I didn't know whether I was relieved or hurt, but my feelings about him shouldn't matter now. Dead to me, remember?

Renz's grip tightened. "Say no."

I pried my fingers from his. "It'll be over soon."

"Bianca…" He leaned forward. I wasn't sure if the agony on his face was from his wound or his emotions.

"You're going to tear your stitches." I pushed him gently against the pillows. "Don't make this all for nothing, Renz."

"Damn you." He turned a murderous glare at Tommy. "You're all going to regret this."

"Not your place to threaten us, baby De Lucci," Tommy mocked.

"Don't rile him up." I approached the Rossi underboss.

He scrutinized my face. "You look terrible." He didn't look pissed, he looked amused, and a note of admiration tinged his voice. "Are you making a statement? The boss won't be pleased."

"Does it look like I give a fuck?" I retorted.

Tommy crooked his arm, but I didn't take it and marched ahead, not bothering to look at the mirror on my way out. My hair was a rat's nest. I showered, blew it dry, and tossed it in a topknot. I didn't even bother with the veil. Every single person in the room was going to witness my misery.

I could be vindictive.

People thought I was the amiable Bianca who got along with everyone. I tried to get along with everyone because I was blessed with the best family a girl could have. I didn't lack for love or money, and I tried to put myself in the position of the less fortunate. But make no mistake, I could be as sweet as pie or as scrappy as a junkyard dog when I needed to be. I grew up with three older brothers, and although their tendency was to spoil me, they were still boys. Playful, wicked boys who honed my skills for psychological and physical warfare.

To survive being married to a Rossi and having the backstabbing Griselda as a relative, I had to make a stand now. They would not see a De Lucci cower.

I put on foundation too pale for my skin. I had on red lipstick too harsh for my coloring. Not bothering with concealer, I let my under eyes resemble overstuffed luggage. I overdid the black mascara and liner. My eyes were bloodshot. Renz was right when he said I looked like the bride of Dracula. I certainly felt like it.

Gian Rossi will rue the day he asked me to be his bride.

I didn't know what time it was, but the sun had set and the whole house was lit up with eerie old-world light fixtures. An elaborate crystal chandelier that probably cost hundreds of thousands hung in the middle of the foyer tiled with Carrara marble.

The area crawled with soldiers wearing suits and communicating with comms. One would think they were the Secret Service guarding the president.

"Where's the ceremony going to be held?"

I clutched Tommy's arm as we descended the staircase. As much as throwing myself down the steps to end my misery was an option that crossed my mind, the fighter in me refused to give up.

It was hours closer to my wedding night. If I had a sharp object, would I stab Gian Rossi in the neck before he got the chance to fuck me? I hadn't thought that far yet. What if he tied me up so I couldn't fight him? He should know by now he wasn't getting a meek wife.

As the light in the house grew brighter, my thoughts dimmed. We walked along a narrow hallway lit by elaborate sconces reminiscent of haunted houses. The ones that flickered. The ones that made static sounds. Wood panels and chipped-off paint added to the gloomy atmosphere.

"I don't hear any music." I mocked because the sound of my heels on the flooring sounded too much like a march to my doom. I had to break the rhythm before I crumpled and cried.

"Ah, there wasn't enough time to secure a string quartet."

"Fully booked, huh?"

"The ones we trust," Tommy said. "The family is leerier now after what happened."

"What's the matter? The news of our disappearance making everyone nervous?"

Tommy's non-answer was answer enough. Gian Rossi had bitten off more than he could chew, and it had become a matter of pride.

We arrived at the double doors. I stilled myself. I wasn't going to run. He looked at my hands. "You don't have your bouquet."

I glared at him. "We don't need one for this dark comedy." Griselda brought one into the room earlier. Red roses and baby's breath and ferns. I detested baby's breath and ferns in flower arrangements. They were fillers.

He shook his head and opened the door.

The room appeared sparsely occupied. Rows of foldable chairs. More men in suits and a few women in cocktail dresses were in attendance. I recognized faces from the party two nights ago, but I was shocked to see the man standing at the end of the line.

Sandro. He was standing beside the priest.

"Is he going to be the best man?"

My heart plummeted, past my gut, straight to my feet that refused to budge. Could his betrayal run deeper?

"Come on," Tommy urged, grabbing my arm and whispering in my ear. "Don't fight it, for God's sakes."

My feet inched forward. Lack of sleep, days of despair, and

hours of anxiety were catching up with me. The room was tilting one way and then the other. No. It seemed like the walls had curved over me, shrinking the room. My heart rate skittered.

"Breathe, Bianca. Don't faint now."

I spotted Gian Rossi. He was glaring at me and then at Sandro. He was standing beside a much older gentleman who they referred to as the Blind Don, the elder Rossi, the most revered member of the Rossi crime family. Sandro's uncle. Gian's adoptive father.

It didn't take long for us to get from the door to the front of the room since the space was small, and Tommy, sensing that I was about to bolt, hurried me along. Griselda was standing beside the elder Rossi and several women with perfectly coifed hair. Just like Gian, she was staring daggers at me like she wanted to flay me alive.

What happened? Was I marrying Sandro?

The somberness in the room made it look like a funeral instead of a wedding.

Not a wedding.

A ball-and-chain ceremony.

From across the room, even when Sandro's face was expressionless, I could feel him beseeching me to play along.

The priest stood before us and looked uneasy. He kept patting his forehead as if he was sweating, which reminded me of the dress I was wearing and its high neckline.

Sandro stepped forward, but instead of going straight to me, he stopped by an empty chair and that was when I saw it. A bouquet of sunflowers.

I didn't know whether to hate him or love him for it.

He walked toward me. A trace of a smile on his mouth. "A bride needs a bouquet."

I stared at it. The room was just reduced to Sandro and me. It was a thoughtful gesture but out of place in the scheme of things.

"Bianca…" Sandro said with a warning in his tone.

Murmurings went around the room. He held it out again, so I took it.

I could feel his relief, as well as Tommy's and the priest's. This wasn't over. If Sandro thought he could fix this charade with my favorite flower, he was mistaken. It was looking more and more like the grooms had switched.

A fleeting relief loosened my lungs. But until Renz was out of this hellhole and in a hospital, I couldn't think of a future past that.

I lowered my eyes at the bouquet. Three sunflowers stared up at me, their merry faces giving me a tiny lift.

"Am I marrying you?" I asked, without looking at him.

"Yes."

Tommy took his place at Sandro's side as his best man. I was still reeling from the turn of events when the priest started, "We are gathered here today…

"Do you Bianca De Lucci take Alessandro Rossi as your lawfully wedded husband?"

The tears came. The irony of that statement just hit me where everything inside me revolted. Those were the words I dreamed of hearing ever since I turned twelve. That one day I was going to marry this man beside me.

I raised my eyes to Sandro.

He was staring grimly into my eyes. He didn't want this, but he was doing this to save me. This was not the fairy tale I imagined, but the choice was out of my hands. I did this, Renz could go home.

"I do."

The priest asked the same of Sandro, and he answered, "I do."

"By the power vested in me, I now pronounce you man and wife."

I stared down at the bouquet and realized I'd mangled one sunflower and its petals lay torn at my feet.

"You may now kiss the bride."

My head remained bowed.

His finger came under my chin and lifted it so I could look directly into his eyes. There was a trace of apology there.

And when his hard mouth touched mine, it was the briefest kiss in history.

It was worse than the time I kissed him by surprise.

He'd responded then, before pushing me away.

Now all I got was a pity kiss.

CHAPTER Five

Sandro

I stood beside Bianca as they loaded the sedated Renz into the back of a van. He tore up his stitches when he refused to leave without her. But Bianca was a Rossi now.

My wife.

Fucking hell. I didn't know whether I was pissed or pleased about it.

I wanted better for her. A better man. A better life. Anything other than being surrounded by my family. My senses were heightened and on full alert. I needed to get her out of here.

"Renz…" Bianca choked, and if I didn't have my arms around her, she would have climbed into the van with her brother.

Tommy came up beside us. "Once the driver drops him off at the Mount Sinai emergency, he's gonna let me know and I'll give the De Luccis a call."

"Plates of the van?"

"Taken care of."

When the vehicle's door slammed shut, Bianca sagged against me. My arms tightened around her, but she didn't turn to me. I wasn't a source of her comfort, but a convenient choice to lean on. I had no illusions about what was going on in her mind right now. Bianca may be part of the legitimate side of the De Luccis, but she wasn't naïve.

And I was right. She pushed away from me and glared with teary eyes full of contempt and questions that were sure to come. "You're the boss now?"

My answer was a slight nod.

"How? You're not a made man."

"That's where you're wrong."

She backed up another step and, for a moment, anguish crossed her face before more contempt wiped it away. "When?"

"This morning."

"That fast? The commission…"

"Approved it," a voice said behind us.

I closed my eyes briefly in agitation. I wanted to break it gently to her. Damn it to hell. I turned to face Raffa.

Also known as the Blind Don, Raffaello Rossi was the only surviving brother of my father's four brothers. He had a shock of white hair and usually wore light-colored designer suits, but wore black for the wedding and my noon ceremony to become a made man. His blindness came from the shrapnel of a car bomb in an attempt on his life. From my sources, he wasn't totally blind but could see blurry images. He probably would have been boss if it wasn't for his disability.

"Have you been planning it for a while?" Bianca asked.

"Just made the request the other night."

At Bianca's dubious look, I added, "Luca expedited."

The commission was like the government of the American

mafia. Luca was one of its most influential members. Its role was to control the violence among its members to keep it at a level below public and law enforcement scrutiny. They also approved admission into the made-man roster.

"That son of a bitch," Bianca muttered.

"Now, now, he's part of your family, right?" Raffa clucked. "Aren't you going to give your uncle Raffa a hug? We're also family now, yes?"

Bianca's response was to wrap her arms around herself and clasp her biceps in a gesture of defiance. "No, thanks."

Fuck me.

Raffa looked in my direction. The dark glasses worked wonders to mask the intent behind his words, but I'd known him long enough to read between the lines. Or at least know what he wanted to hear.

"You have your work cut out for you, nephew?" he asked.

"Looks like it," I said under my breath.

"What work? If you think—" Bianca sputtered.

"We'll talk," I cut her off. She was digging her hole—*our* hole—deeper and deeper.

Raffa arched a brow my way. "Maybe three weeks is not enough."

Bianca unwrapped her arms and stepped toward Raffa. "Three weeks for what?"

"Three weeks for you to learn your fucking place as my wife." I grabbed her arm and dragged her back to the house. "Let's go."

"Happy wedding night," Raffa called out.

The *stronzo* was finding amusement with his machinations. He was more than an adviser; he was the puppet master who manipulated the Rossi bosses. Raffa had his own minions who carried influence with the soldiers.

I caged Bianca with my arms to prevent any attempt of hers to break away. I put myself between her and Griselda as we passed my former fiancée. I wouldn't put it past Griselda to start trouble again.

Gian was furious at my deception with Griselda because it cost him an alliance with the Philly mob.

She was still insisting she was pregnant but wouldn't confess who the father was because it certainly wasn't me, and I made that clear to Gian and Raffa when I insisted on marrying Bianca.

What a perfect storm of a clusterfuck I found myself in as the new boss of the family.

"Where are we going?" Bianca demanded. "And what is that three weeks about?"

"I'll explain once we're clear from here."

I hurried her through the house before someone else insulted her. I was a hair trigger away from massacring the entire Rossi family. My friendship with her wasn't a secret. And it was obvious I became boss and married her for her protection. My plan of getting us out of this mess was a work in progress and I didn't want Bianca running her mouth and complicating things.

Tommy caught up with us. "Which phone are you using?"

"Three."

"Okay. I'll let you know as soon as Renz is delivered."

Bianca drew in a ragged breath but didn't say anything. We moved through the kitchen and exited the back door.

A Rossi soldier tossed me the keys to a blacked-out Expedition. "Boss."

"Thanks," I muttered. I rounded the vehicle with Bianca. She was still in her wedding gown. "Do you want to sit in the back? Would it make you more comfortable?"

She glared at me.

"Or maybe it's not a good idea," I said. "You might strangle me with your garter."

"Don't give me ideas."

"Wow, wife, that's kinda vicious."

"You suggested it."

I opened the door. "Up you go, Sunlight."

"Don't call me that," she retorted. "You don't get to call me that ever again."

Her barb wasn't enough to erase the relief that swept through me now that I'd gotten her out of the family's scrutinizing eyes.

But I had to face the next problem.

Bianca was my wife, and I didn't know what to do with her. When we said our vows, guilt was my constant companion. Bianca deserved a fairy-tale wedding, and I'd given her a nightmare instead. Still, I derived a bit of satisfaction that I'd chipped away at her picture-perfect life and had given her a dose of reality in mine.

Forget a dose. It was a baptism by fire.

I slid into the driver's seat and started the engine, not wasting time leaving everyone behind.

"Where are we going?"

"Another house. The one here won't escape the De Luccis for long." I glanced at her. "Your dad called Raffa."

"Dad hasn't had communications with the Rossis in a long time."

"They haven't talked in over fifteen years."

"Since that time Frankie tossed me into the pool?"

I smiled grimly. How interesting her perspective of that day had changed. "What happened to *since I rescued you from drowning*?"

She scrunched her nose. "Dad would have fished me out."

"But he didn't. I did. I punched Frankie for doing that to you."

"What's the point in this, Sandro? You're still one of them. Back there, I didn't recognize you as the boy who was always nice to me."

"And only you," I murmured.

For the first time since the whole ordeal started, Bianca snorted a brief laugh. The mood shifted in the vehicle. Or maybe it only felt that way to me. Since I met her when she was a child, she'd always been the sunlight in my darkness.

At first, it wasn't even Bianca. It was Ava De Lucci who I wished was my mother. She doted on her sons, and I envied the De Lucci boys. And then their younger sister came along and they all doted on the hellion that was Bianca. She gave me something to look forward to in those mafia gatherings where I was largely ignored in favor of Frankie.

I pretended she was my younger sister.

But that all changed the night I stormed the fraternity house and yanked her off a college kid in a jealous rage.

"My family never understood that."

Her statement jerked me back from my thoughts and it took me a few seconds to rewind to what was last said.

"I felt contempt for everyone except you?"

"Yes."

"I liked Ava," I answered. "And you were a good kid."

She harrumphed. She got annoyed when I referred to her as a kid, because when she was five, I'd been fourteen and considered a kid myself.

"Before that pool thing, you found me hiding in a closet with a busted lip and—" I started.

"I'm not doing this," she mumbled and look out the window.

"Doing what?"

She cast me a scathing glare. "This! Strolling down memory lane. Reminding me when I believed in you."

"Surely you didn't go from believing in me to hating me overnight," I drawled. More like a few days.

I could feel her irritation at how lightly I was treating the situation. However, I didn't want to delve deep into our shared history. Not right now. I glanced in the rearview mirror to make sure my men were following me. Owning a dance club, I didn't depend on Rossi soldiers in matters of security. I didn't trust all of them and had my own men.

"You know how they say there's a thin line between love and hate?" she asked.

"Fair enough. So that means there's a chance you'll fall in love with me again."

Silence. She realized she admitted she loved me. She'd never spelled it out that what she felt was love. I felt the affection in her hugs and when she told me to take care. Again, this was before the fraternity house incident. That marked the beginning of Bianca driving me crazy with wanting something I shouldn't have.

"That's a lot to expect."

"You're my wife."

"I was forced to be your wife," she shot back. "You know my family is against the made-man culture."

"There's Dom."

"My cousin is a confirmed bachelor. If he ever takes a wife, it would be for an alliance, not love."

"You don't have a good outlook on made men."

"They should take a wife who knows what to expect," Bianca's voice rose. "Tell me, Sandro, about that oath you took today before you said your vows to me."

She got me there, so I didn't answer but kept my eyes on the road. At my continued silence, she gave a snort.

"Exactly. You became a made man who swore loyalty to the Rossi crime family. That they will come first before your wife and children. And then when you said your vows to me, you promised I came first. You will be with me in sickness and in health, but we know that won't be true when mafia business comes calling."

"Bianca."

"Just look what happened to Luca!" she said. "Natalya was giving birth and he couldn't be bothered."

I pinched my brows because there was no defense. Bianca was right.

"What would you do, Sandro? Would I come first?"

"You'll always come first, but while I try to figure this shit out, you'll have to trust me and not defy me at every turn."

"You mean show them I'm your meek mafia wife?" Contempt laced her tone like arsenic.

"In case you haven't noticed, Raffa has expectations." I shot her a brief glance. She was still looking out the window as if she was going to find salvation or answers outside the confined space of the vehicle.

We arrived at a red light. I picked up her hand in a way that felt like the past few days hadn't happened. Before I crashed Nico's wedding. Before I collaborated with Luca to bring down my own brother. "If you ever cared for me at all, you'll be patient a little longer. You, of all people, know I never wanted to be boss."

She glanced at our joined hands. I could make out her sad smile in the dimly lit interior. She lifted her gaze to mine. "Most of this is my fault. And what the hell was that with Griselda? Are you her baby daddy or not?"

Of all the… I was so pissed that she would believe I would marry her while another woman was pregnant with my child, I refused to answer.

At my continued silence, Bianca said, "There's something else going on there, and now that I'm your wife, I deserve to know."

"O-ho, now you're playing the wife card?"

"Is this how it's going to be? Us at each other's throat? Why not give me a straight answer?"

I gave a humorless laugh. "You've grown up around the mafia enough to know that no one gives straight answers."

I could feel her eye roll.

The whole Griselda shit show still left a nasty taste in my mouth and I didn't feel like explaining it.

The safe house was another ten minutes away. We stewed in silence while I recalled the ceremony. Despite her defiance in her makeup choice, she could never hide the beauty of her heart-shaped face and the stubborn chin she inherited from Ava. She might not have her mother's red hair, but Bianca's rich dark brown glinted red under most lighting, and in that ceremony room, it magnified her rebellion. And what a hauntingly beautiful rebel she was as she marched down the aisle toward me.

I chanced a glance at Bianca. Her forehead was plastered to the window and she had fallen asleep.

An ache tugged at my chest.

My bride.

Warmth grew in the ache. She trusted me enough to fall asleep.

CHAPTER
Six

BIANCA

I startled awake to see the SUV driving down a narrow road…no, a driveway surrounded by trees. An involuntary yawn escaped while I straightened in my seat, casting Sandro a glance. "How long was I asleep?"

"Fifteen minutes."

I couldn't believe I fell asleep like that. But for two days I'd been keeping vigil over Renz. Afraid he'd take a turn for the worst. Afraid that they would separate us. It was the kind of sleep where I wasn't sure if I was unconscious or awake, like I'd been hopped up on caffeine, where my mind was awake and my body was jittery. At the wedding ceremony, adrenaline fueled my every move, and now I wanted to crash and sleep for a year.

"You were out of it," Sandro added.

"Where are we?"

"One of my properties."

That wasn't the answer I was hoping for, but I was too exhausted to argue. I needed my wits about me when I was sparring with Sandro. I took in the area. We were outside the city for sure.

Before Sandro pulled into the garage, I made out a modest colonial-style house with shutters and siding. Gray metal cabinets lined the garage and there was a covered vehicle in the corner. It was too wide to be a motorcycle, too small to be another car. Maybe an ATV.

"I'll come get you."

Before I could say anything, Sandro had already exited the SUV. Stubbornly, I shoved my door open. He caught it before it hit his face and glared at me like I'd done the most childish thing.

"You're not carrying me over the threshold." I slid down from my seat and planted my feet on the ground. "Let's not take this farce too far. Lead the way."

"Smart-ass."

"You love my smart mouth."

All I heard was an exasperated sigh, but he just had to have the last word by putting his hand on my lower back. He pushed open the door leading into the house, but before I went through, he held me back and whispered in my ear, "And the things I can do to it."

Shocked because that was the first time he'd reciprocated any of my baits with sexual innuendo, I refused to budge another step.

I turned to him at the same time he crowded me into the house. "What game are you playing at?" The question came out in a croaked whisper, but I was blaming it on my lack of sleep.

He clasped my shoulders so we were face to face. "You're my wife now."

The way he said *my wife* was like a switch and the expression I saw on his face was nothing like the gentle possessiveness I'd daydreamed about. No, this was fierce in its intensity, like a brand of total ownership.

"I thought…"

"You have no idea."

He guided me further into the house as if hurrying us along. "Aren't you going to show me around?" I asked sarcastically.

"Later. There's shit I have to do."

"Really?" We were going up the staircase when I said, "On our wedding night? Oh, I forgot, the family comes first, not your wife."

When we arrived at the top, Sandro caged me against the wall.

A startled yelp escaped me, and I glared at him. "Sandro, what the hell?"

He pressed his body against mine, surprising me, my eyes going wide. Initially, I ignored how our bodies had smashed up in the kitchen, but there was no way to ignore this now. Tension and heat rolled off him. His fingers dug into my shoulders, but I was too caught up staring at the raw feralness etched on his features.

"Are you saying you want me to fuck you?"

My mouth fell open. Sandro was a series of out-of-character shocks this evening. Forget sexual innuendos, the crudeness with how he said those words unsettled me. Who was this man? This stranger? But what he said pissed me off. "Why are you doing this?"

"There's no halfway, little girl. I'm trying to give you space. To get used to the idea of being my wife, but if you insist on running that mouth and taunting me… Like I said earlier, I can think of a better use for it."

"Are you saying this is going to be real?"

His face inched closer, his mouth a millimeter from mine. "Let's find out."

"I…" My gaze swept downwards. Once upon a time I would have seized his jaw and kissed him. But my fury from the last few days, this forced marriage that obliterated my childhood dreams, and, most of all, the image of Renz's bloodied chest, sent a repulsive wave of nausea up my throat.

"No, thanks."

Sandro reeled back, and a wariness stole the determination from his face.

That's right, Sandro Rossi. I'm forever over you.

"What? Am I supposed to be grateful you married me?"

"I saved you from marrying Gian."

My hatred slightly abated. "I'm thankful for that. But let's not make this marriage sound like it's what either of us wanted. Or even pretend it's normal."

He studied my face, but I refused to look away. His jaw hardened, and finally, he stepped back and I lost the heat of his body. He walked down the hallway. "I'll show you to your room."

My room. Not ours. Was it too soon to feel relief?

We stopped in front of a door. "This is yours." He pointed to the room on the left.

He regarded me thoughtfully. "We've known each other a long time, and it's not the first time we've slept together but—"

"That's different!" I snapped. "And it wasn't on a bed." It was usually on his sleeper sofa when we were doing movie marathons.

"But," he repeated. "We're both going to get a good night's sleep." He raked a hand down his face, frustration evident in his expression. Well, I was only getting started. I would make him so frustrated he would beg my family to take me back.

"I'm sure we both need it and then we're going to discuss what the fuck we're doing," he said.

"Sounds good to me."

He checked his phone. "That's Tommy. Your dad and Nico are at the hospital and are with Renz."

I didn't realize how bogged down I was with Renz's condition. It was as if it had entombed my entire being in a quicksand of anxiety and I had finally taken my first step out. I exhumed that anxiety with a ragged exhale, but fresh worries soon crept into its place. "When can I talk to my family?"

"It'll be a while."

"Is this the three weeks your uncle is talking about?"

He gave a brief nod.

"Some kind of indoctrination into the Rossi crime family?"

"No," Sandro said. "He wants to see Cesar De Lucci squirm."

I couldn't even understand his vendetta against Dad. "He's sick."

Sandro shrugged. "It's the sadistic disease in the Rossi blood."

I thought about his brother and the rumors about Frankie's cruelty to his wife and the prostitutes he used. Despite my current situation, I felt the need to say, "You're not like that, Sandro."

He smiled faintly. "Hold that thought."

I never feared Sandro when it was just the two of us, but those two days when he was surrounded by Rossis? It was as if he was a different person and that they controlled him.

We continued staring at each other. Finally, he cleared his throat, thumbed his nose, and walked to the closet. "There are clothes here you can use. We'll get you some more. Can you eat? I can send the guys to get something."

My mind was in priority mode, and my whole body was trying to survive. Sleep. Then food. I should've been starving because I'd barely eaten anything, but even the thought of chewing felt like a chore. I guzzled a can of Coke on our way here and I needed to pee.

I shook my head and checked the closet, too tired to ask if Griselda picked the clothes for me or even drill Sandro about our unfinished conversation in the car about her. But when I peered inside, the contents of the closet surprised me.

These clothes were in my style.

My eyes fell on the carved box on a skinny accessory tower inside the closet. "What's this doing here? I don't want it."

His mouth tightened. "I wanted something familiar in this room for you."

"You think it's going to comfort me?" I picked up the box to hand it back, but Sandro's hands wrapped around mine.

"Keep it for now." His voice was gruff. "Please."

A pleading I hadn't seen in his eyes before made me reconsider. Its rawness cut a slit through the wall of my anger.

"Fine."

"We'll talk about the situation tomorrow."

"Oh, you bet we will," I retorted, setting the box down. "We'll have some ground rules too if we're going to be stuck in this house together."

"You're not a prisoner here, Bianca."

"I don't have a phone. I can't talk to my family. I can't leave."

"Consider me your family now."

Bitterness wrapped itself around my heart at how twisted and wrong those words sounded to me when I'd wanted to hear them for so long.

The irony didn't escape me, and my lack of response only led to an uncomfortable silence between us. The silence stung with palpable hurt. Mine was mixed with anger. Sandro's… I tried not to read too much into the flash of regret that broke his mask. He'd schooled his features again. But Sandro had been rejected all his life and I was doing it to him now.

He raked his bottom lips and broke our stalemate. "Do you need help getting out of that wedding dress?"

Heat flushed my cheeks. I hadn't thought about taking this monstrosity off me. "There are faux buttons in the back, but it's really a zipper. Er, you can help me with the top zip."

I turned my back to him, and I felt him come up behind me.

"Who helped you with this?" he whispered near my ear.

"No one. I was quite the contortionist."

The sound of the zipper lowering sent an awkward chill through my veins. I stepped away. "Thank you."

"No problem. I'm briefing the guys on the security around the property. It'll take me fifteen minutes at most. I'll be in the room across from you if you need anything. There's no lock outside this door. And there's bottled water right there."

Sandro retreated and closed the door. He used to send goose bumps of exhilaration through my veins whenever he was close, but I wondered if this last act of fuckery had finally broken my obsession with him.

Or maybe I was just overwhelmed from the past three days.

I picked a sleep shirt from the top shelf of the closet and headed to the bathroom. I looked a fright. My makeup had run through and mascara lines tracked down my cheeks, reminding me of a corpse bride. I felt like a corpse. A drug store cleanser sat by the sink. I had sensitive skin, but vanity was the last thing on my mind. I scrubbed my face until it was makeup-free. I didn't look any better. My eyes were puffy and bloodshot and the dark circles under them looked like I hadn't gotten rid of the smeared mascara.

My head needed to find a pillow, so I stepped out of my wedding gown and donned the sleep shirt. I eyed the box sitting on the accessory tower and, as if hypnotized, lifted the lid. I picked up the silver cuff and stared at it. It was probably the wrong thing to do if my objective was to excise Sandro from my heart. But I was desperate to cling to something that made me happy long before things became complicated between Sandro and me. When I was simply a girl with a harmless childhood crush.

I got on the bed and crawled under the covers, holding up the cuff against the moonlight streaming through the window.

I remembered that day Sandro had given it to me.

He's not here.

I had been looking out the window of my parents' row house overlooking Tenth Street. It was my twelfth birthday and Mom assured me she invited Sandro.

"Bianca," Mom called from behind me. Her hand clasped my shoulder. "It's rude to ignore your guests."

"I'm waiting for Sandro."

Mom gave me a sympathetic smile. "I know, sweetie, but you also know his time is not his own." Ever since he turned eighteen, their crime family kept him occupied. I hardly saw him anymore.

She coaxed me away from the window and back to the festivities.

The first person who noticed us come into the dining room was Matteo. "Smurfette, where were you?"

"Stop calling me that, especially in front of my classmates. I'm twelve."

He shot me an irritating grin.

"Matteo," Mom admonished.

"Okay, baby sister." He hugged my shoulder, but then whispered in my ear, "But just for today."

I punched his side.

"Ouch," he said dramatically.

"Stop being a wimp," I returned. "Your fan club is here."

Almost every single girl in my all-girl class was here because half of them had a crush on Matteo. The other half had a crush on either Nico or Renz. It was irritating as hell.

It was another thirty minutes of me socializing and craning my neck to the entrance of the dining room before I saw him.

Sandro walked in, looking hot and handsome in black. Beside him was his current girlfriend, a blonde named Holly. She was better than Griselda, who was always dismissive of me. I was glad Griselda dumped him. Holly was nice to me. I rushed to greet them. On my way, Nico rolled his eyes, but I ignored him.

"Happy birthday, Sunlight," Sandro said. I noticed the bruising under his right eye and a cut lip. It wasn't there when I saw him two weeks ago. It reminded me of the first time I found him hiding behind the stairs at one of the family parties. But I knew he didn't want me pointing it out, especially not in front of Holly and my family.

He was here. That was all that mattered. Even if he brought Holly.

He handed me a gift. A small box wrapped in craft paper and baker's twine. I hurriedly unwrapped it and gave a delighted squeal when I saw the gorgeous silver cuff I'd been eyeing at a Brooklyn store. "How did you know?"

He glanced briefly over my shoulder and I followed his gaze to Mom. "I had help."

I stared at the silver cuff again and then at the smiling Sandro. Frankly, his barely there smiles were the ones that set my heart racing the most.

The rest of the room diminished to Sandro and me.

I was marrying him one day.

CHAPTER
Seven

Bianca

The first thing I noticed when I woke up was the sound of rustling paper. I pried open my eyes. Pistachio-colored walls discombobulated me a bit until I remembered where I was and how I got here. I jumped out of the bed and padded to the windows. Barred windows. A tree reached that second level of the house, and a squirrel perched on a branch, holding a nut, stared at me.

"Are you making a ruckus or what?" I mumbled. "What time is it?"

The squirrel seemed to get out of his frozen state and scampered away. Fine. I was not Snow White who had a talent for charming woodland animals. I turned around and eyed the closed door. Sandro said it wasn't locked from the outside, but I didn't feel like confronting him at the moment.

I looked around the room for something that could tell me the time. Nothing.

My brain needed more sleep, but my stomach was now making it known that it was hungry.

I spied the silver cuff peeking out from under the pillow. At one point in the night, my memories slipped straight into a dream. I pushed it under the pillow, and climbed on top of the covers and stared at the ceiling.

Where did my dream cut off before the squirrel woke me up?

Oh, my mother. When Sandro asked her what I might want for my birthday, she told him about the silver cuff at the Brooklyn shop Mom patronized. I inherited her love for costume jewelry. Mom never frowned at my friendship with Sandro, unlike the men in the family. Maybe because when I found Sandro hiding behind a staircase, bleeding from his mouth and nose because his father hit him, I went to Mom and she patched him up.

Sandro had begrudgingly accepted help, but he called me an interfering little shit.

I scoffed. *Well, this little shit grew up and you're married to me, asshole.* I glanced at the door again, wracking my brain on whether he informed me I was supposed to stay put until he came and got me.

My stomach gurgled again.

A hangry De Lucci waited for no one.

After a long hot shower where I swore I'd scalded every inch of skin, I cleared the fogged-up mirror and checked my reflection again. The bags under my eyes were still there, but my eyes weren't red anymore. I put on sweats and slip-on shoes.

I gripped the door handle and tested it. The lock on my side disengaged, and it opened. Huh, Sandro wasn't lying. He wasn't too worried about me climbing out the window because of the bars.

My first step out of the room made a loud creaking noise. Fucker. Obviously, he'd hear me if I left this way. I stared at the door opposite my room and listened. I didn't hear any movement. What the hell time was it?

Was this some kind of test? Some kind of sensory deprivation? The rest of the floor wasn't as creaky, and I wondered if the floorboard outside my room was the only one deliberately set that way. I continued down the hallway toward the stairs. Stairs that led straight to the foyer and outside. To freedom. But really, I remembered the long-ass driveway from last night and I was sure we weren't in Manhattan. I had no money. No phone.

And… I sniffed the air. Bacon. My stomach grumbled some more, but my feet were following the lead of my nose and skipped down the steps. I cast one last longing look at the entrance and then followed the direction of the aroma into the kitchen.

A woman stood with her back to me and was clearly responsible for the delicious smell. She had dark hair cut in a bob and was wearing a peach-colored shell dress. Strings of an apron were tied behind her neck and its ruffled edges appeared at her sides. The first thought that came to my mind was *thank God she has an apron* because that wasn't a dress meant for cooking in.

A heap of grocery bags was strewn over the counters and floor. How long were we staying here?

"Good morning."

She whipped around, spatula raised. "Oh, you're awake." She was at the ceremony yesterday—I refused to call it a wedding. She appeared older than me. But it was really hard to tell with her flawless skin. Her smile, at least, looked genuine. Still, I considered her part of the family who condoned this forced marriage and held me and Renz hostage.

I gave her a tight smile, letting her know what I thought about the situation hadn't changed.

Her eyes lowered briefly. "Let me get this bacon out of the pan before we have a grease fire."

"Where's Sandro?"

While she expertly transferred the sizzling bacon to a paper-lined plate, she said, "He's in the study with Tommy." She lowered everything on the counter beside the stove and approached me. "Where are my manners? I'm Divina, Tommy's wife."

She stopped a foot from me. Her smile froze at my refusal to act like what was happening here was normal. She turned away. "Well, as I was saying, Sandro is with Tommy." She smiled again as if recovering from my earlier rudeness. "I see the clothes fit you?"

"You picked them out?"

"Yes, I did. And the groceries. Sandro gave me a list, but I added my own."

I slid my butt onto the barstool. This was interesting. "And you do everything the family tells you?"

Divina pushed the platter of bacon toward me but kept her eyes on the plate. "Yes."

"Don't you have kids to mind?"

I didn't miss the sadness that flashed through her face. "Maybe next year."

"Do you want kids?" I shook my head. "I'm sorry. It's none of my business." I picked up a slice of bacon and started munching.

"Actually it is," she said.

Wait? What? I furrowed my brows at her. "Explain."

"Sandro is now the don, and you're his wife."

"Yes, but that doesn't give us the right to tell you when to start a family of your own."

She laughed a bit nervously. "No. No. Not at all. Tommy needs my support to settle in the next don and his wife. It was never the right time to have kids." She huffed heavily. "There was so much turmoil in the organization to find a stable leader."

"You lost two in the last two years."

"But Tommy feels now that Gian is not going to be boss." She gave me a hopeful look. "I'll have a little bambino of my own soon."

Ah, hell no. "Divina …" I didn't know what to tell her. I had no plans to stay married to Sandro. I didn't know how to get out of it yet. But he represented everything my father was against. "You know the circumstances about how Sandro and I got married."

"I know. He was your childhood friend."

Jeez. That was how she was looking at it? The disconnect was disconcerting. It was like I was trapped in a dark comedy. "They threatened my brother's life."

"Yes, but Sandro saved you from marrying Gian."

"I can't even speak to my family." Then something occurred to me. "Wait a second. Are you saying this is a normal thing that happens in this family?"

She gave me a smile that confirmed it, but also a smile that said I was making a big fuss over nothing. Were all the Rossi women brainwashed to do their men's bidding? I thought about Griselda. She stood by and watched Sandro marry me. She skewered me with a stare that, if it had real venom, would've killed me. I said my vows but she didn't object at all when the padre asked if anyone was against the marriage. Come to think of it, I didn't remember the priest asking if anyone objected.

The ceremony was a complete haze.

"I just warmed this up." She nudged a basket in front of me. "There are bagels, croissants, and muffins in there." Thinking of croissants reminded me of Renz.

"Have the guys eaten?" I asked, falling back into polite courtesy.

"No. Actually, I was supposed to let Sandro know when you're awake."

"No need," a voice spoke from the opening of the kitchen.

I turned in my seat to see Sandro and Tommy striding in. But my attention was solely on my new husband. He had such a commanding presence, impossible to miss, yet he could choose to be invisible if he wanted to be.

He prowled to my side and kissed the top of my head. "Did you sleep okay?"

"Yes."

"Good. We have things to discuss." He plopped a jewelry box in front of me.

I didn't even need to ask him what it was. Still, when I flipped open the lid on the box, I was shocked at the size of the diamond. "We don't have to do this."

Irritation flashed across his face. He took the ring and jammed it on my finger, joining it to my wedding band. "Yes, we do. Get used to wearing it so you can prove to your family that I didn't skimp on the ring."

It was the most unromantic thing a man could do and yet I found it hot. For the first time since this ordeal started, his actions warmed my cheeks. But I was determined not to fall into Stockholm syndrome. I had standards, dammit. A big-ass ring wasn't going to make this fucked-up situation okay.

"I can barely lift my hand." I made a production of doing exactly that and letting it drop on the counter.

"Smart-ass," he muttered.

"How can they see it when I can't even see them?" I pointed out.

"Three weeks. We satisfy the Blind Don's request and you can see them."

"Do we always have to do what he says? I thought you were the boss."

Sandro looked over to Tommy and Divina and that was when I noticed her face had taken on a comical expression of worry as if no one ever questioned Sandro.

"Tommy, I'll talk to you tomorrow," he said in a measured tone that sounded a lot like he was praying for patience. "Seems like I have to spend some time with my *new bride* and acquaint her with how things work." He gave a brief nod to Divina. "Thank you for helping with the clothes and the groceries."

Divina looked like she had won the lottery. She smiled, and the smile differed from the one glued to her face earlier. This one seemed more genuine. It reached her eyes.

"Thanks, Divina," I clipped.

"Anytime. Just call when you need anything," she gushed and tucked her arm into Tommy's.

I held my tongue on another smart-ass reply, but exchanged a look with Sandro. I didn't have a phone, ergo I couldn't call her.

So I simply extended the smile on my face in acknowledgment.

When the couple left, Sandro turned to me and tipped his chin at the food on the counter. "Eat."

He walked over to the coffee machine. "Coffee?"

"Yes, please."

When he returned with two mugs, he set one in front of me and leaned a hip on the edge. He was staring at the top of my head and I didn't want to look at him because he was doing that leaning thing that made him hot again. I should picture him a foot shorter with a wart on his nose and buck teeth.

I glanced up at him.

Nope. Not working.

Let's face it. I was once obsessed with this man. I couldn't simply stop finding him attractive. The parts I hated about him always lurked beneath the surface.

The Rossis' attack dog.

I thought he'd retired and was on the outs with the crime family after Frankie's death. But apparently not. You never left the family. That had always been the mafia way.

"There might be hope for us after all," he rumbled.

I couldn't decipher his expression. Fond or amused. The corners of his mouth were twitching and there was a gleam in his eyes that made me shiver, not with dread like in the past few days, but with an anticipation because we were alone. Was he imagining what to do with my mouth like he threatened or was he contemplating what to do with me in my captivity. "What do you mean?"

"You pick up things fast."

"I'm not following."

"You didn't push your questions about Raffa, knowing it would put me in a difficult position. I'd have to tell you off in front of them. And you weren't sarcastic about the phone thing."

"It's not about picking up fast," I said. "We're husband and wife in front of Tommy and Divina. Mom always told me not to fight in front of other people, especially arguments that would put your partner in a difficult position."

Sandro grinned. "I always liked Ava."

I rolled my eyes. "I know."

He continued to stare at me like I was a specimen under the microscope while taking a sip of his coffee.

"Are you going to tell me your grand plan of getting us out of this mess, or are you just going to stare at me?"

"I see you're getting your spunk back."

"Is that good or bad?"

"I'm not sure yet."

"Can you sit down? I'm having a hard time craning my neck." I tore a piece of croissant and stuffed it into my mouth. "These are good but not as good as the way Renz makes them." I paused. "Before you tell me anything else, do you have news on Renz?"

Sandro sat on the barstool next to me and angled my way. There was a gentling in his eyes. "He's staying in the hospital for another day or two. None of my men can get close enough to find out, but we managed to get to a nurse who knows the nurse taking care of him. Security is tight, Bianca. But word is your dad and brothers are on a warpath, and Dom is trying to calm them down."

A rippling of goose bumps dotted my arms. "What did you expect?" It made me pissed at Sandro all over again and I had a feeling this would be a familiar refrain. Alternating between being mad about our current situation and bittersweet about our shared history. "So what do we do in the meantime? Cards on the table. Being married to a made man and being the wife of the boss is a far cry from what I want in life. It's eating me inside how I've let down my dad, my family…so you better come up with a plan."

"I won't be boss for long."

Wait. What?

CHAPTER
Eight

Sandro

Was I fucked in the head? I derived immense satisfaction from seeing the shock on her face. But I wasn't sure whether it pissed me off, or it was self-directed anger. Relief. I should be feeling relief that I was finally rid of her obsession. But last night, I saw the disgust on her face when I was about to kiss her. Her rejection was an unexpected kick in the gut and I felt hollowed out. It fucked with my head. I couldn't sleep. I wanted to barge into her room for a do-over.

Fuck me.

"What?" she rasped, eyes widening. "What do you mean? You went through all that trouble."

"Smoke and mirrors," I told her. "Tommy is taking over, but neither Raffa nor Gian knows that's my plan. They have to believe that I'm serious about being the boss."

She looked at me doubtfully. "But how will Tommy take over? You're simply stepping down?"

I stared at her, not answering. She caught on. One simply didn't stop being the boss. He either died or got injured enough from fulfilling his duties. Bianca's eyes glistened with what suspiciously looked like tears and they unraveled my insides. Fuck stopping myself from touching her. I cupped the side of her face. "I'll have to disappear, baby. Fake my death. That way they won't come after you."

Fury flushed her face red. She shoved my hand from her cheek and stood. "That's crazy talk. Surely there's another way."

I shrugged. "Maybe. But right now, that's how we're playing it."

Her shoulders sagged, and she sat on the barstool again as if the revelation weighed her down. A slew of emotions crossed her face. Sorrow, as if she'd already lost me. She would never lose me. I would always watch over her as long as I lived. I watched her sleep last night. There was a camera installed in her room. I wasn't a total pervert. I shut off the feed when she undressed. Something rolled through my chest when she picked up the silver bracelet I'd given her for her twelfth birthday. She fell asleep holding it and I hoped it gave her comfort.

When she left her room this morning, the sensor under the floorboard alerted me she was awake and on the move. It was time to tell her my plans, if only to gain her cooperation.

But there was one secret I had to keep from her because I didn't know how to move forward with it. To take over from Gian as boss, I had to consummate the marriage with Bianca and produce an heir. That was one of Raffa's conditions. His three weeks was a minimum time frame for getting Bianca pregnant. He pointed out that Cesar would do everything in his power to file for a divorce, but the existence of a child with De Lucci and Rossi bloodlines would complicate things.

"If there was any other way, I wouldn't have forced you to marry me," I told her.

Anguish etched her features. "But what about the dance club? The life you built in Harlem. What will happen to that?"

"I'll sign it over to Tommy. Don't worry. I survived a Russian prison, I can survive this."

"And I'm supposed to be okay with your plan?"

"You'll get to return to your family. Have a life. Marry someone else."

"Fuck you, Alessandro Rossi."

"Do you want to?" I returned evenly.

Her mouth fell open.

And fuuuuck. I fixated on her mouth so I wouldn't fixate on what her pussy would taste like. Goddammit. As much blood I had on my hands, it felt dirty to think of her in terms of sex or blow jobs because, for the longest time, she was like a little sister to me. Then she lost her virginity to that fucker and it made me realize she wasn't a child anymore. Still, it would be another two years before I realized Bianca had grown hips and tits and mastered the way to drive a man crazy with a flick of her hair. That was when things started changing—fast. And once they did, there was no turning back. The first time she got me hard, I was so horrified, I got drunk, puked my guts, and stood under a scalding hot shower as though it would burn off my guilt for lusting over her.

Even now, the flames of hell licked at my heels as I challenged her with my eyes.

When she was a child, her face reminded me of those mischievous angels. Chubby cheeks and bouncy dark brown curls, which glinted red in the sun. Bianca's face had lost the baby fat of youth and had morphed into an exquisite, heart-shaped face with defined cheekbones and a stubborn chin. But her power was in her eyes. Deep-set, thick lashed. When the lighting was just right, each dark iris was surrounded by a burst of yellow gold that flared like the petals of a sunflower into an outer ring of dark brown. Other times, like when she wanted something they darkened into a soul-gripping shade of brown.

Her family called that look her puppy-dog eyes. And I agreed with them until, in the last four years, puppy-dog eyes slowly transformed into the call of a siren. Now I wanted to drown in them before I devoured her lips and sank into her heat.

Our conversation had shifted, including our silent one.

Her mouth slammed shut and her eyes dropped to her plate. Her cheeks were still pink, but I knew it wasn't anger anymore but an awareness of me as a man.

My cock hardened behind the zipper of my jeans. I shifted in my chair and adjusted myself.

She caught my movement, and I didn't know whether to laugh or groan. I opted to take a sip of coffee.

"Are we consummating the marriage? Because…it's not like I'm a virgin."

"Don't remind me."

Her gaze snapped to mine. "Why? Because you're the reason I lost it?"

I raised a brow. "Are we talking about this now?"

She stood, picked up her plate, and rounded the counter to head to the sink, turning on the faucet. "I was stupid."

I barely heard her above the rush of running water.

Getting up from the barstool, I strode to her, turned off the faucet, clasped her shoulders, and turned her around. "Maybe. But you were only seventeen and you let Griselda goad you."

Her eyes flashed. "And how does Griselda fit into our drama? I'm going on a hunch—she's not really pregnant, is she?"

"I never asked for confirmation."

"Then what's the deal about being engaged to her?"

"We were never going through with marriage, but simply discouraging Gian from forcing her to marry into the Philly mob and forming an alliance from hell. Gian called our bluff by throwing us an engagement party." That was another level of fuckery. I agreed to help Griselda because we'd been engaged before. Even when she broke things off with me first, I had already tainted her chances of a lucrative marriage match. *No one wants Sandro Rossi's leftovers*, Griselda screamed at me more than once. Guilt about that festered after Griselda remained unmarried year after year. That was why I practically handed over control of the club to her and why I didn't want the same thing to happen to Bianca, but too late for that now. A widow had a more respectable status than a former fiancée. That was why faking my death was one avenue I was considering so Bianca could escape my family. The De Luccis would never abandon her.

"The three of us have formed a weirdly toxic relationship." She meant me, her, and Griselda. "I want to leave the past in the past. I've yet again screwed with your life and hers. Maybe I deserved this, but not Renz. He got caught up in my preoccupation with you."

"Preoccupation?"

She glared at me. "Obsession, all right? But I'm over it."

I crowded her against the sink and caged her in, lowering my head, and said, "Oh, no, baby. We're going to show how obsessed we are with each other. We're married, remember? We're crazy about each other."

She narrowed her eyes, but I could almost imagine the pounding of her heart. Her chest rose and fell with her rapid breaths. "We don't have to pretend if it's just the two of us." She pushed at my chest.

When I refused to budge, she hissed, "Sandro."

I let her scoot out from under my arm and put distance between us. She shifted her attention to the bags on the counter. "We need to put these away." She glanced around the kitchen. "I don't know where you want these."

I sauntered lazily over to her. I never thought I'd like playing house with a woman, but with Bianca, I was looking forward to it, however temporarily.

"I hardly use this property. The pantry is empty. Do as you please."

"There's enough food for six months in here." She was exaggerating, but she still wouldn't look at me. I followed her around the counter where she found a large cooler. She flipped the lid open. "Okay, there's enough meat in here to feed an army." She let the lid fall and looked at me. "Are we entertaining while we're holed up in here?"

"I don't know." I lowered my head. "You're changing the subject."

She averted her gaze, but not before I saw the irritation in them. She was still a far cry from being on board with being married. It had only been a day, so why was I so impatient? She had years of patience waiting for me to react to her as a woman I could fuck, and when I was finally coming around to the idea of it, she was icing me out.

The irony.

The future remained murky, but I would worry about that later and it seemed she was still digesting the news I gave her about faking my death.

"We need to put this away." She opened the freezer. "The meat will not fit in here."

She was determined not to discuss learning to be man and wife.

"There's a chest freezer in the garage." I lifted the cooler. "I'll put it there."

"Good." She stared at me as if seeing me in a different light. "It's strange."

“What? Like we’re living in domesticated bliss,” I teased.

She narrowed her eyes. “Go.”

“Yes, wife.”

She held open the door for me as I hauled the cooler into the garage. As I unloaded the meat into the freezer, I thought back to the different points of the conversation we never finished. Bianca felt guilty about the second time Griselda and I broke up. That was the time I just returned from Russia. The time after my father’s funeral and I was reeling from sordid revelations about my parentage. The time Griselda became a bad habit, a familiar body, and a reliable hookup. I spoke nothing about love or a relationship and made it clear our connection was simply sex. But after the damage she’d inflicted on Bianca because of me, I was done with her. It wasn’t only Griselda’s scathing words, but I found out she set a sociopath in Bianca’s path. And I confirmed the boy was indeed a sociopath five years later when he came into my club, roofied coeds, and raped them. But I had always kept an eye on Warren Winslow ever since that time Bianca called me the night that fucker took her virginity.

I almost didn’t answer my phone.

CHAPTER *Nine*

Six Years Ago

Sandro 26, Bianca 17

Sandro

"Sandro."

"Bee, it's midnight." I woke up annoyed because I hadn't slept in three days staking out a mark. I was not in the mood for idle chatter.

"Can you come get me?"

That was when I came fully awake, my heart slamming against my rib cage. "Where are you?"

"I didn't want to call Matteo or Nico or Dad." She stumbled over her brothers' names and her voice sounded like she was on the verge of tears. Meanwhile, I was about to have a panic attack.

"Where. Are. You?"

"Ninety-First near Jamaica Avenue."

"You're in Queens?" I knew where that was. It was close to her friend's house and a popular nightclub. I put her on speaker and threw on clothes. I kept her on the line and hustled out of my condo and got into my GT4. She'd been dating, but I didn't know which boy it was this time. I didn't think it was anything serious. I'd been busy keeping up with the jobs the Rossis threw my way rather than keeping tabs on Bianca. The jobs kept my mind off what Raffa had told me about my father.

The thirty minutes it took me to get to Queens felt like an eternity, and after blowing past the speed limit and cutting through cars, it was a wonder I didn't get pulled over. When I arrived at the location she'd given me, I immediately spotted her. My vehicle slowed, and she recognized the Porsche. Red hazed my vision when I noticed the way she was walking. Gingerly. As if she was in pain.

I squeezed the GT4 between two vehicles, jumped out of the car, and rushed to her side.

"Sandro," she cried and limped toward me.

"Whoever hurt you is dead," I growled, wrapping her protectively in my arms. I was having trouble regulating my breathing. "Who do I kill?"

"No one. I wanted it to happen, but…"

It. What *it*? But I knew even if my mind rejected *it*. I struggled for composure. A volcanic rage misfired inside me. A faulty trigger. I inhaled sharply, exhaled, and then put my hands on her shoulders in a painstakingly measured effort to draw her away and look her in the eye. "Was it consensual or not?"

"Can we go, please?"

She was evading, but I had my answer. That sorry-ass was never gonna stick his dick into another woman again.

"Where is he?" I demanded.

"Sandro!" she shrieked, almost hysterical. "Can we leave?"

Every cord of muscle running through me wanted to hunt that fucker down. I would go house to house if only Bianca gave me a name, but she was clinging to me like I was a lifeline and she was drowning. I had to take care of her first.

"All right, all right." I was gonna figure this shit out later.

I scooped her up and carried her to the vehicle. When I set her down to open the door, I noticed a dark streak on my right forearm.

Blood from the back of her thighs.

I couldn't breathe and the words came out flat. "You're bleeding."

"Virgin," she mumbled.

My chest cracked wide open when it really hit me. Bianca was no longer a girl, but a young woman. How did this happen? There was anger at myself for not watching over her and being more present in her life. I knew she went out on group dates. Her older brothers were overprotective, but what the fuck happened?

I asked her if she wanted to go to the hospital and she said no and said if I asked her again, I could drop her off at the corner.

As if I would.

I didn't know how we got back to the condo. I'd been on autopilot. I asked her once more if the fucker forced her, but she insisted it was consensual. That was when I called Griselda because I knew jack shit about how to console a girl who'd just lost her virginity, and from the looks of it, it was an unpleasant experience.

My mental state was far from pleasant. I was murderous. Delirious with rage that I feared I might frighten Bianca with the look on my face. I couldn't hide it. Someone hurt my Sunlight. I thirsted for their blood, but I didn't have a fucking name.

"Really, Sandro?" Griselda accused the second I opened the door. "You avoid my calls and you expect me to come running *for her*?" She was not my girlfriend and she should have known better than to complain. And I would have set her straight, shut down her delusions, but I needed her help with Bianca.

"Lower your voice," I hissed. "Whoever the fucker is that did this to her is going to pay!"

"She was raped?" She turned rigid.

"She denies that's what happened."

Griselda relaxed. "It's unpleasant the first time. That's normal."

"Can you check on her? She's in my room. In the bathroom right now."

"She has a mom and older brothers." She pushed past me. "Why did she have to call you?"

"I don't know." But I was glad as fuck she did.

We both approached my room, and I rapped on the door. "Are you decent, Bianca?"

"Yes."

When I opened the door, Bianca stood there wearing the T-shirt I'd given her. She looked so frail and lost right now, I wanted to hug her. But when she saw Griselda, a weird, almost angry expression crossed her face. "What is she doing here?"

"Apparently, Sandro thinks we need some girl talk."

The mocking in Griselda's tone made me second-guess bringing her here. Among all my girlfriends, Griselda was the only one Bianca seemed to despise, but short of calling Ava, which Bianca adamantly didn't want, I was out of options.

"Do you want anything, Bee?" I asked.

"Blueberry soda." It was her comfort drink.

"I'm out of it in the fridge, but I'll get it at the bodega."

I might have exited the room too quickly. Talk about comfort zones. I hated getting in between women's drama, but I had a nagging feeling about leaving Bianca with Griselda. I was almost at the elevators when I remembered I didn't have my wallet. I already racked up a bill with the bodega owner since I'd been busy. Might as well settle it.

When I returned to the condo, I heard raised voices.

Shit.

"Why won't you just die or disappear!" Griselda screamed.

What the fuck?

I slowly closed the door and stealthily moved to the bedroom.

"Oh, believe me, losing my virginity was like dying," Bianca shouted back.

Griselda scoffed. "Oh, spare me. It always hurts the first time."

"I know."

"But what do you do? You call Sandro to pick you up the second you lose your virginity. Just because I told you he likes experienced women and not virgins, you think simply losing it will make him finally notice you as a woman? It takes more than that, little girl."

Bianca didn't answer, but I'd heard enough.

I stepped into the room, clenching my fists to keep from throttling Griselda. Women and children were a no go for me, but I had the oddest desire to make an exception. "Get out of here, Griselda."

She whipped around. "Sandro…"

"Get out! Before I toss you out the window."

She gasped and quickly left the condo. I slammed the door and returned to the room. Bianca was sitting on my bed and seemed to have shrunk into the smallest version of herself.

But it wasn't that she was afraid of me. I think it was more from the humiliation that I'd heard.

"Oh, baby." I was torn between my fury at Griselda and my heart breaking at the price of what my friendship with Bianca had caused her. Of course I recognized hero worship. I couldn't say I didn't like it. I enjoyed doting on her, but I was ashamed that it was when it suited me and I missed the memo that Bianca was now a young woman. Her crush on me was no longer innocent and had repercussions.

"I want to go home," she mumbled.

"No."

"Sandro." She averted her gaze to stare at the headboard. "I don't want to talk about it."

Funny, I didn't want to talk about it either when it came to feelings, but I was all over it when seeking retribution. "I want a name."

"No."

"Fine. I'll find another way." And I would have it before noon.

"Don't hurt him," she said, still talking to the headboard. "It was consensual. I was just too embarrassed to stop him. I wanted to get it over with."

I didn't know how to talk her through the horrible experience, but she needed to know one thing. "Sunlight, look at me."

She huffed and met my eyes. They were big and luminous, and I'd never seen them more steeped in despair. She lost something tonight. Something precious that she should have given to a man who cherished her.

"I don't know much about these things," I admitted. "About a girl's first time, but this much I know…don't ever be afraid to say no. No means no. Got me? Anything else is rape."

She didn't say a word, but nodded.

I clasped the back of her head and brought her close.

I kissed her forehead, and when I drew back, I asked, "I'm going to go get that blueberry soda. Want anything else?"

"Can we watch a movie when you get back?"

"You got it."

CHAPTER
Ten

BIANCA

I found Sandro staring at the freezer in the garage, lost in thought. He said he remembered something, and when he saw me holding the six-pack of blueberry soda, a smile crossed his face. Divina must have cleaned out the stores for my favorite drink, but Sandro's thoughtfulness did something to my hardened heart. It cracked a little and let some of my fondness for him sneak through. How something as ordinary as blueberry soda could bring back the good times. It wasn't easy to find and only a few Manhattan bodegas carried it, but he made an effort to stock it in his fridge.

Plus, his revelation about being the interim boss ate at me. He was going to disappear, fake his death, so I would be free? As much as my feelings toward Sandro were in limbo, I would never be okay with that, especially since this whole predicament started because of my obsession with him. There had to be another way. One that we could both live with.

Sandro had been right all along when he said we didn't work. Now that I'd seen the world he'd been trying to hide from me, I agreed.

But I intended to make the best of my situation. I had the tenacity from both sides of the family. I was a De Lucci and a McGrath. We didn't wallow. We made shit happen. Well, right now, that was getting dinner ready.

Sandro had been called away and I was left alone to do as I pleased. I glanced around the kitchen. Groceries were still scattered about. I had only put away the perishables. A layer of dust covered the shelves and I cleaned what I could so I could get started on the sauce for the baked rigatoni. If I was going to survive my captivity, which, if I were honest, was better than being locked in a room, I should make my stay bearable. Be useful and keep my mind busy as I counted my days to freedom. Growing up, the kitchen was a sanctuary. I was determined to make this kitchen mine.

"Damn, it smells good in here," a voice called from the mouth of the kitchen. I turned and a smile spread across my face when I recognized the big, burly man in fatigue-colored cargo pants and a gray shirt striding into the kitchen.

"Sticks!" He was the head of security at Sandro's dance club. While he engulfed me in a bear hug, another man behind him who I didn't recognize, walked straight to the counter and set down shopping bags imprinted with the label of a kitchen equipment store I'd given Sandro. Sticks was the only one who'd been with Sandro for years. He used to be a member of a motorcycle club before he joined Sandro's team at Club Aristos.

"So, who's watching the club when everyone is here?"

"Club's indefinitely closed, sweetheart." He ran his hand over his bald head. He was the epitome of club bouncer, his physique so at odds with his name.

"What? Why?" This was news to me.

"Kinda hot right now." He winked at me. "Now that the boss has kidnapped his bride."

My smile fell. "My family is looking for me." It was more a statement than a question.

"Harlem is crawling with De Lucci soldiers and those military types who hang around The Grindhouse."

I crossed my arms. "And you're okay with Sandro kidnapping me."

Sticks mimicked the gesture of my arms, the warmth on his face cooling. "You and your brother put him in a difficult situation."

"They should have dropped us off at the hospital."

Sticks laughed. "You're not that naïve."

"Renz is the last person who would threaten the Rossis. He's a business owner, not mafia."

"You really think your pop is gonna let this simply slide?"

"How is forcing me to marry a Rossi the best idea?"

"Uh, guys," the man who came in with Sticks interrupted. "Should I head back outside?"

Sticks exhaled deeply. "Bianca, this is Miller. Do you need his help around the kitchen?"

Miller had already slunk toward the exit of the kitchen and a pettiness in me kicked in. "As a matter of fact, I need some shelves cleaned."

I could hear the other man groan, but Sticks chuckled. "Consider him your slave for the rest of the day."

"Where are you going?" Miller muttered to Sticks.

"Got admin stuff to do, or do you want to handle it?"

"If you mean deal with Griselda, no, thanks."

I forgot Griselda was the club's manager.

"That's what I thought." Sticks looked at me. "He's all yours."

. . .

Somehow, Miller and I worked around each other. I found out he was a former army veteran. He was thirty-two and grew up in Memphis. Single. Unlike Sticks, who was brawny, Miller should have been the one to be called Sticks. He had taken off his worn-out tee and had on a stringer tank top. And the only reason I knew what those skinny-strap tanks were called was because I'd heard Nico, my gym-rat brother, mention them often. Still, it looked out of place on Miller's runner's build.

He hopped off the countertop where he used it to clean the top shelves.

"All done," he announced. He looked longingly at the pot of minestrone I was stirring. "You preparing a feast?"

"Since I found out there are six guys in the bunkhouse, I'm making sure I have enough." Sandro and I hadn't discussed what he expected from me yet, but I fully intended to cook for everyone on this property. Baked chicken and potatoes were in one oven, and rigatoni was in the other one. I was also making garlic bread.

"Do you want a bowl of this?" I asked. "It's ready."

"I could use a bowl." His smile was almost shy and he couldn't meet my eyes. A flush crawled up his neck. Maybe I could gain his sympathy. Sticks more or less pledged his loyalty to Sandro. But Mom always said the way to a man's heart was through his stomach. If I were nice to Miller, maybe in a few days I could convince him to let me use his phone. But…ugh. I didn't want to get him in trouble. So I nixed that devious idea.

There was no harm in gaining allies, though. Soup bowls sat stacked beside the stove, so I opened the lid of the pot, and stuck a tasting spoon in it.

"Since you're the only one here, see what else it needs?"

I blew on the spoon and held it out.

"I'm not…uh…an expert…uh…in this." His face was flaming

by now. How could Miller work as a club bouncer if he got tongue-tied around me?

"Tell me if it needs salt."

"What's going on here?" a voice boomed.

The hand holding the spoon rattled and spilled the soup.

Annoyed, I turned to see Sandro striding into the kitchen. My tongue went dry at the leashed power I imagined straining under his well-tailored black suit. Raw aggression saturated the room. Sandro's dark brown eyes were almost black. His wavy black hair was messier than usual, and an errant curl fell across his forehead adding to the wildness in his expression.

When I found my words, I said, "What does it look like I'm doing? I'm giving Miller a taste of my minestrone. I'm feeding your men."

"I didn't tell you to."

I closed the lid, tossed the spoon in a dirty cup, and turned to my husband, hands flying to my hips. "Well, I'm going to do it whether you like it or not."

My peripheral vision caught Miller slinking away, and that was when I saw Sticks, who was trying not to laugh.

Sandro's glare narrowed at Miller's retreating form. "Where are you going?"

"Outside," Miller said.

"Not so fast. Let's get one thing clear."

Sandro started after Miller. I grabbed his arm. "Don't you dare—"

He switched his glare to me. "I'll deal with you later." Then he looked at Sticks. "Keep her here."

Sandro shook my hand off him and went after Miller.

I started to follow, but Sticks blocked me. "Please don't get me into trouble, too."

"That's blackmail," I exclaimed.

"I'll have to put my hands on you, and I don't think boss is gonna like that either."

I tried to get around him, but for a man of his bulk, Sticks was annoyingly agile.

"Look, let Sandro make things clear with Miller. Boss knows he hasn't explained to the rest of the crew just how close they're supposed to get to you."

"This is ridiculous. Then why isn't he the same with you?"

"For one thing, he knows I'm crazy about my wife and he's known me for years."

"Miller's been with you for two."

Sticks raised a brow. "Just how chatty did Miller get? The man's private."

I shrugged. "I didn't give him a choice."

~

Sandro

I stormed ahead of Miller and into the outside patio, away from the bunkhouse where the other guys could see and hear.

Miller was a good bouncer. He ignored the girls who flirted with him to gain entrance to the club and single-handedly took care of belligerent or drunk patrons twice his size. So it was a shock to see him all flustered and staring at *my* wife like he'd fallen in love with her.

I spun on him. "What the fuck?"

"Boss?" His brows furrowed.

"What was that in there?"

"Your wife was offering me a taste of her minestrone."

I clenched my fists, trying to fight back the red clouding my vision. What I was hearing was, *Your wife was offering me a taste of her lips*. As I blinked, cruder words formed and red turned to murderous.

I sucked in a giant, ragged breath. "That's the last time you're going to be around Bianca alone."

"Boss, it was all innocent, I swear." He swallowed. "I just have never seen…ah fuck…"

"Never seen…" I gritted. A muscle in my eye started jumping. "Finish it."

He backed up a couple of steps. "I don't think it's a good idea."

"Finish what you were gonna say," I growled, deleting the distance between us until our faces were a breath apart.

"She's gorgeous and…she just has this energy around her. I mean…it's hard not to get drawn in. I was doing my job…but she's so nice to me. No girl has ever been that nice to me unless they wanted access to the club."

Ah, fuck. His words punched holes into my jealous rage and it leaked out. Miller was one of Sticks's pet projects. Three of the bouncers at the club were military veterans who'd come home from their deployment with PTSD and were abandoned by their families. I financed their recovery and offered them jobs as long as they stayed clean and regularly attended their veterans' group meetings. Miller joined us two years ago, and from the looks of it, he was able to take back his life and find a purpose.

As long as his purpose wasn't drooling over my wife.

I wasn't immune to Bianca's charms and guileless gaze. She had enough practice on the men in her family who had spoiled her rotten. Another thought occurred to me. "Has she asked to use your phone?"

"No, boss." Miller scratched the back of his head. "Sticks made that clear. Total isolation." There was an accusing tone lacing those last two words. Dammit. This was dangerous. I'd briefed my men on dealing with crime family business: *Always look the other way and do not get involved. If something bothers you enough, come to me first.* That was before I became boss. An oncoming headache pressed against my skull.

"Come on," I grumbled. "Let's make sure my wife knows she can't use any of my men to defy me, either."

When we returned to the kitchen, Bianca had a glower on her face. She and Sticks were in a stare-off. Palpable relief crossed her face when she saw Miller was unscathed.

"What the hell was that, Sandro?"

"Hello to you too, wife." I didn't pause and walked straight to her. I grabbed her by the elbows, hauled her against me, and slammed my mouth on hers in a quick but devouring kiss. Quick enough so she wouldn't be able to bite off my tongue, but fierce enough to brand her as mine. I set her aside, and she speared me with a lethal glare and wiped her mouth with the back of her hand.

Her defiance was making me hard, but I was supposed to gain her cooperation, not further alienate her.

"I needed to make a few things clear with Miller."

"Oh, that I'm your willing wife and not a captive?"

I prayed for patience. "No. That I'm a jealous son of a bitch and I will cut out his eyes if I catch him staring at you like a lovesick puppy."

Sticks coughed a laugh, while Miller gave a strangled sound.

"That wasn't how he was looking at me," Bianca whispered.

"You have no idea about your effect on men, Sunlight." Men like Miller, like me, had lurked in the dark for so long, we starved for the sun. Bianca's light was forged in a morally gray world and still had the resilience to remain pure. "So Miller gets a pass. But I want to make it clear to Sticks." I gave my head of security a look. "None of the men are to be in a room with you without him."

"Because I'm immune to your charms," Sticks deadpanned.

"Get out, both of you. I want to have dinner with my wife."

"Oh, but I made enough for an army," Bianca protested.

"Is the food ready?"

"Almost."

"Then they can come back when it is."

I stared pointedly at Sticks again and he took the hint and left the house with Miller.

I nodded to the minestrone soup. "Your husband is here. Aren't you going to offer me a taste?"

Bianca huffed and spun away from me. "You are such a Neanderthal. I don't understand what you want from me."

She uncovered the pot and took a spoon to dip in the soup. She blew on it a bit before offering it up for a taste.

Her cheeks were flushed, probably from laboring over the hot stove, but I couldn't help noticing her hitched breathing. Our eyes met, and as I lowered my head, her eyes dropped to where the spoon disappeared into my mouth. When she withdrew it, I licked one corner of my lips. "It's as tasty as I remembered."

The whole scenario was familiar but also different.

As if knowing where my thoughts went, she asked, "When was the last time you came to our house?"

"The one on Tenth Street or the De Lucci mansion?"

"Either, the last time."

"Before Russia, Tenth Street."

"My fifteenth birthday?"

"Yeah."

CHAPTER Eleven

BIANCA

We stared at each other as if both of us remembered that time. Two months before my fifteenth birthday, Dad had grounded me because he found out I'd been skipping classes to spend time with Sandro. No matter how innocent the circumstances were, it had been an ugly confrontation. With no phone, and under Dad's scrutiny of my every movement, Mom intervened. Sandro had reached out to her, knowing my birthday was coming up and he had to leave the country for a while. Dad had relented, but the men in my family had been downright hostile during my birthday party. Sandro didn't seem to care. A few weeks after he left, I received a package. In it was a Russian nesting doll. And then, months after, he seemed to have fallen off the grid. At first, I thought Dad found a way to get rid of him until I heard Dom telling Dad that Sandro was in a Russian prison. I was distraught. My grades plummeted.

Sandro returned for his father's funeral after being gone for a year. The way it was told, the Rossis negotiated his release.

Post-Russian-prison Sandro was different from the man I knew. Much darker. More tattoos. Much, much more. He ignored my calls and didn't even talk to me for another six months.

The timer on the rigatoni interrupted my excursion into my memories.

"I'll get that," Sandro said.

The oven was a side by side instead of the stacked configuration. He grabbed a dishtowel, and I moved aside to give him room to maneuver the hot Pyrex out of the oven.

"Smells good, baby." He set it on the counter.

Like my siblings, Sandro wasn't helpless in the kitchen. When he was sixteen, he asked Mom if he could work at Eamonn's for the summer as a prep cook. But his parents shut that down. Distaste saturated my tongue. Carmelo and Wilma Rossi were the biggest asshole parents I'd ever met. They always favored Frankie over Sandro in mafia gatherings, it was a wonder why Sandro accompanied them at all. Mom once told me it was all for show. Carmelo died from a heart attack, and from what I'd last heard about Wilma, she was in a psychiatric hospital. Rumor was that Frankie's mental issues came from his mother's side of the family.

After Sandro grabbed the second Pyrex and laid it to cool beside the first one, he grabbed my hand and led me to a barstool. Maybe he wanted to chat some more, but we didn't have to act like a couple when people weren't around.

He sat on the barstool and pulled me on top of his lap.

"Sandro!"

"You're saying no to a shoulder massage?" And as if to show me exactly what I would be missing, his fingers kneaded the tight muscles below my neck.

"Oh, God," I moaned at the unexpected and sheer relief that overwhelmed me. "Don't stop."

He mumbled a soft *fuck* and then hissed in my ear. "Keep making those sounds, Bianca, and I'll make you see God for sure."

The pressure of his fingers made me want to purr, but the threat in his voice sent a pulse of wetness between my thighs. I thought of sliding off his lap, but I wasn't willing to forsake a massage for propriety. Throwing all caution to the wind, I shimmied my ass up his muscular thighs and landed on his erection.

He groaned, "Bianca."

I bit my lower lip. Flames licked between my legs and tingled up my entire body. Playing with fire was an understatement, but I was tired of Sandro's sexual innuendos. It was time to see if he was all bark and this was another game to him. I twisted around on his lap. Now I was straddling him. His hard and big cock nestled against my pussy.

We were face to face.

His eyes glittered with unmasked heat. I shivered with excitement. *He isn't yanking me back into an obsession with him, I told myself*, but can't I be a little curious? I struggled to keep my arousal under control. Mind over body.

"Bianca, what?" I challenged him.

The words barely crossed my lips when I lost his eyes and he was kissing me. His tongue forced my mouth wide open and…

Holy hell!

Unlike earlier, where it felt like a shut-up kiss—which pissed me off—this one was unrestrained need.

My mind barely registered this because I was so busy feeling him everywhere. I was rubbing myself on his erection while he devoured my lips. His hands were under my ass, squeezing the flesh there, and helping me along. Pressure building. Core swollen. Wet. Slippery. I tore my lips from Sandro and concentrated on my pleasure. My fingers dug into his shoulders as I used them for leverage to rub myself to an orgasm.

"That's it, baby," he growled hoarsely. "Take what you need."

"God, Sandro, I'm close!"

I continued rocking against him until a wave of exquisite pleasure fractured me in the middle. My pussy pulsed and pulsed, and the more I clenched my thighs around his, the more intense the throbbing became. *So good. So good.* I buried my face in the crook of his neck while my release came over me in a rush. Sandro simply hugged me. Murmuring in my ear how glorious I looked when I came.

My clit was still sensitive. The slightest pressure against his erection sent shock waves of sensations that were addictive as hell.

"It won't stop," I whispered in his ear.

Sandro gave a choked chuckle. "Mind giving my poor cock some mercy before I blow behind my pants?"

That woke me up from the sexual fog. I was feeling too hot and bothered, and I wanted to wipe that smirk off his face.

"You shouldn't have done that!" I yelled.

He started laughing, an incredulous look on his face. "Baby, I was just giving you a massage."

"You knew that would happen," I panted.

"Does that mean you can't resist me?"

"What the hell do you want from me, Sandro?" Suddenly I was feeling ashamed. Mad at myself, mad at him. "Do you want me to become obsessed with you again? Because remember what happened the last time? My brother got shot!"

The humor fled from his face. "You need to stop blaming yourself for that."

"So, should I blame you?"

He opened his mouth to say something, but the timer on the

baked chicken cut him off. He started to rise, but I growled, "I've got this."

I couldn't believe what had just happened. How could I be so weak and pathetic? Didn't Renz almost dying teach me enough? Self-recrimination ate at me. As I lifted the sizzling chicken from the depths of the hot oven, I mentally reinforced my barriers.

I refused to be a part of this crime family.

I was too disgusted with myself to have an appetite. I dropped the tray on the counter. Sandro's gaze scorched my face, and when I turned to look at him, there was a question reflected in his eyes.

"I'm going to do what is required of me to meet Raffa's demands. My goal is to get back to *my* family. Do what you must and make Tommy the boss." I buried every part of me that had loved this man since I was five and pushed words out of my mouth I thought I could never say to Sandro. "If you have to fake your death so I can be free of you, of this marriage, then do it."

I stared at the food I had prepared all day. "I'm not hungry. Feed your men."

~

Sandro

"If you have to fake your death so I can be free of you, of this marriage, then do it."

I had taken shrapnel to the chest, but it didn't compare to the stinging pain of Bianca's words. My mixed signals had pushed her too far. I wanted to keep her, but I didn't know how without forcing her into a life she never wanted.

Marriage to a made man.

Still, we were running out of time, and I needed us to be on the same page. Bianca was adaptable. My fear of losing her had me playing with her heart. It was unfair to her.

I couldn't leave our conversation where we left it, so I brought her a tray of food. Food she prepared for me and my men. I also included a blueberry soda.

I stopped in front of her door and knocked. "Baby?"

"I'm not hungry."

"I'm coming in," I said in a firm voice.

"Fine. It's unlocked anyway."

When I opened the door, she was already sitting up in bed with arms crossed over her chest. Defiance was evident in every line of her body, even her eyes. "I'm not apologizing for what I said."

I laid the tray beside her. She went for the soda and sipped with a straw.

"I wasn't expecting you to."

"This situation is fucked up."

"I know."

"I'm just…for a moment, being so close to you, I was curious about what we could have been," she rushed out.

"Me too. For a moment, I wished I could shut off my brain and convince myself that I am worthy of you." There were things about my past I hadn't told her. My gaze intensified on her face as if I wanted to memorize every line, every curve, and every feature. From the arch of her brows that could communicate so much sass to the sparkle in her eyes that could bring a hardened assassin like me to his knees. I didn't want to think about her mouth, her lips, which were right now sucking on…fuck. I swallowed. "That I'm not the bastard son of the Rossis. That I don't kill people for a living, and I didn't force you to marry me. That I don't have to leave this fucking life and you after I set up Tommy to be the next boss."

"Despite what I said, there has to be another way. Fake your death? You think I'll find happiness knowing that?"

I reached out and, with the back of my hand, caressed her cheek. "You have to, Sunlight." I swallowed through the tacks in my throat. "After all this, just focus on all the shit I brought down on you and your family."

"That's crazy talk and you know it," she snapped. She pushed me away, but not before I saw the glistening of tears. "Well, what else should we make for dinner? Maybe we could start a countdown to your last supper."

Her voice cracked with those last two words. I couldn't stand it anymore. This distance between us wasn't…us. I walked around the bed to her side and sat beside her, drawing her into my arms.

She turned into me and buried her nose at the center of my chest.

"I still hate you," she breathed against me. "But I don't want you to die, Sandro."

"I'm not dying." I chuckled.

She gazed up at me, cheeks stained with her anguish. "At the beginning of all this, I didn't care if you burned in hell with all the Rossis."

"I know. I saw that hatred." I never wanted to see it directed at me again. I couldn't get the image out of my head, and it gutted me each time I remembered it.

"But now, that's not what I want."

"Are you sure?" I teased.

"It's not funny." She tried to shove away, but I wouldn't let her. "I would have married Gian…"

"Over my dead body," I snarled. "And I mean it. I don't know what I would have done and how it would have ended, but it would have never ended with you married to him. I might have risked Renz and you might've hated me for the rest of your life, but if it came down to you or your brother, I would always choose you."

"Don't ever make that choice."

"What? You'll sacrifice yourself."

"We'll all be alive. And if my brother died because of me, then you'd be consigning me to a life where I wished I was dead."

And that was the only reason I didn't risk Renz's life. "I get that. But this is for you, Bianca. I had no business being your friend." But she was the sun in my darkness. She was addictive. "I need your cooperation so I can get you out."

It looked like she was going to argue, but it was as if a resolve crossed her face and I wasn't sure I trusted it. "I could act like a dutiful mafia wife."

My mouth twitched.

"Support my husband. Not complain about the time he spends away from me. And help settle problems with the WAGs."

"I'm all for the first, but I'm not sure whether the second is in your nature, and I know the third comes naturally to you."

Her brows furrowed. "How do you know?"

"It's just in you to be empathetic, Bianca."

"Not to everyone."

I sighed. "Hold your temper with Raffa and Gian. And also Griselda."

"Griselda? You think I'm going to fight with her over *my husband*?"

"It's not that," I stressed. "She's used to handling the Rossi women since Frankie became a widower. Joe's wife left the family and disappeared. Technically, it should have fallen to Divina, but between you and me…she's too nice. Griselda is more assertive."

"Why do you need me if Griselda is handling things? Especially if our marriage is temporary?"

I was starting to hate the word *temporary*, but until I could figure out a way out of this mess, then I couldn't give Bianca any hope that I was going to come out of this unscathed and alive. I'd made too many enemies as an assassin. Even if they couldn't connect me to any of the kills, the fact remained I had a reputation.

My phone went off, and I sighed.

"Duty calls?"

"Yeah." I unwrapped my arms from around her and stood, but I had to stress the importance of our goal. "Tommy is going to be boss. I need you to help Divina come to terms with our endgame."

CHAPTER *Twelve*

BIANCA

"I called my friend," Divina said.

She came by this morning to help me do a walkthrough of the house and start my duties as Sandro's wife. However temporary that was going to be.

A sitting room on the second floor made me sneeze the second we walked in.

"I only cleaned your room and Sandro's when he informed me where he planned to stay," she said.

"I'm sorry he made you do that."

"He was making his moves without Gian noticing."

"So only you and Tommy knew?"

"Pretty much, and Sticks. And of course, Raffa."

We walked to the next room. It didn't have any furniture, but could be used as another spare bedroom. There were six bedrooms on the second floor that were separated by the sitting room. It opened straight to a central staircase. The first floor was mostly functional rooms. Besides the kitchen, a study, game room, living room, formal dining room, and home theater completed the layout.

I approached the dusty windows. Grit and time weathered the glass opaque. A rustic ranch house stood diagonally across. "Is that where Sticks and the other guys are staying?"

"Yes. This used to be a horse farm, and that was a bunkhouse."

"How big is the property?"

"Ten acres."

Probably a horse hobbyist used to own this. "So, what are we supposed to do?" I asked Divina. "Sandro didn't leave any instructions." I didn't want to waste energy prettying up this space if we weren't staying long, but I certainly wouldn't want to live in a place that made my skin itch with dust flying everywhere. "Where are we anyway?"

Divina didn't answer. I turned to look at her and she dropped her eyes. "I'm not supposed to tell you."

"So, I'm still a prisoner."

"Bianca…"

"That's fine." I figured after I woke up with Sandro gone this morning that nothing had changed. I still wasn't allowed a phone or any access to the outside world. "You're aware Sandro is grooming Tommy to become the boss?"

"Yes." Her gaze was still looking everywhere except me. Dammit, she wasn't ready, and I had a sinking suspicion she never would be.

I walked to her side and gave her arm a quick squeeze. "What do you need from me, Divina?"

Her mouth trembled. "I wish I was less timid."

I could see that as a problem. I wasn't familiar with the Rossi culture, but I didn't like that it appeared she didn't have a life of her own. "In what way?"

"I don't know how to contribute unless I am told what to do."

"Is that what you think you should do? Contribute to the Rossi crime family? How about what you want?"

Divina burst out laughing, although it bore a vitriolic tinge to it. "That's not how it works."

"Each crime family is unique. Do you want to manage charities? Sometimes, wives stay out of the husband's business and remain oblivious to it."

"Rossi wives used to be that way, but after what happened to Joe's wife, remaining ignorant about her husband's mistress and his side dealings, I told Tommy I don't want that for us."

We walked out of the sitting room and returned to the first floor. "I need more coffee for this." I'd had breakfast and a mug of coffee. But I was still feeling the exhaustion from the collective events of the past few days.

I got the second pot of coffee going and turned back to Divina. "I didn't ask. Did you grow up in the mafia?"

"No." She gave a tight smile. "My family owns a restaurant in Brooklyn and that's where I met Tommy."

"Were you forced to marry him?"

Again, an evasive look. "Not really. I liked him. But my father owed the Rossis money. Tommy paid it off to the family."

"Did you marry him because you felt indebted?"

"I love Tommy," she whispered.

Maybe I needed a double shot of espresso for this talk. "I'm not seeing the problem, Divina."

Her jaw tightened, and for a split second I saw rebellion flash in her eyes. "I don't want him to become the boss, but he wants it. And I love him. It's important to him."

Ah…hell. I wasn't equipped to handle this. I didn't say anything for a while, but grabbed our used mugs and rinsed them to warm them up again, contemplating what to say.

"Does Tommy know you don't want him to be boss?" I asked finally.

She shook her head. "But I have to be supportive."

"Are you resenting him for wanting to be boss?" How I felt about Sandro being boss didn't factor here.

"No. I knew that was a possibility when I married him. I don't want to feel like a failure. He's done so much for me and my family."

I didn't have any answers for her. Sandro thought all she needed was to become more assertive. *Men.* Assertiveness was a personality. It was something that couldn't be taught overnight. Growing up with three older brothers with dominant personalities shaped me into who I was today. Mix the De Lucci bossiness with McGrath stubbornness, and I was the result. And it depended on what I felt strongly about.

That was why my brothers called me sweet, but a psycho. I could be sweet about one thing and psychotic about other stuff.

But I had also known Divina for less than a day. What did I know about all her hopes and dreams?

We both turned toward the kitchen entrance when we heard the front door open followed by voices. Sticks appeared with a big smile on his face. A lanky boy in a fisherman's cap and dark coveralls stood beside him.

"Look who's here!" he said.

"Sloane!" Divina exclaimed. The two rushed toward each other as if they were long-lost friends. "I haven't seen you in forever."

"Busy with jobs." The melodious voice was unmistakably feminine.

I raised a brow. Sloane was a girl.

"I'll leave you girls to it," Sticks said. "Boss just called."

Before I could ask him where Sandro was, he retreated. I focused on the newcomer. She was slightly taller than me and I couldn't discern her build from the oversized clothes. Reddish hair peeked underneath her cap. I wasn't sure if it was short or she had it bunched under it.

"This is Bianca."

Sloane raised her hand, and I couldn't help raising mine to shake it. "Nice to meet you, Sloane."

The lip of the cap partially shadowed her eyes. Freckles smattered her nose and cheeks. Her skin was creamy and pale, like she hardly saw the sun. Her pinkish lips were generous and defined.

"Divina said you were aloof. You seem normal to me."

"Sloane!" Divina reprimanded her before turning her flushed face to me. "I'm sorry, but…"

I laughed. "No. Don't be. I wasn't welcoming yesterday." I turned to Sloane. "And it's not nice embarrassing your friend that way."

"It broke the ice, didn't it?" Sloane retorted.

"Do you know my situation here?"

"Yes. Forced to marry Sandro. I was expecting a hysterical bride, so I'm glad you're quite the opposite. Okay, what job do you girls have for me?"

My mind was spinning. I loved no-nonsense people who got to the point, but Sloane broke all the sound barriers.

"Slow down," I enunciated. "We're still having coffee."

Sloane made a point of checking her watch.

"We'll pay you for the entire day or week since it seems you'll have to do the entire house."

That got her interest, and she looked at Divina, who appeared surprised at my offer. "Uh, Bianca…"

"Does she know my rate?" Sloane deadpanned.

Uh-oh.

"Tommy said as long as Bianca needs you. Sandro will pay."

"Just out of curiosity, what is your rate?" I asked.

"A thousand an hour."

That jolted me. I wasn't sure if I was outraged or impressed. "That's highway robbery. Even lawyers don't charge that much."

"Sloane, stop messing with her."

"I'll give you a fifty percent discount." She winked. "Okay, coffee sounds good. But the clock is ticking."

I didn't balk at her abrasiveness. It was probably because of her hypnotic voice. I'd never heard anything like it. It was just the right amount of huskiness and almost had a musical quality to it. "Do you sing?" I blurted out while sliding her a mug of coffee.

Her mouth tipped up at the corners. "If I had a dollar for every time I hear that…no. I have a terrible singing voice, but before you ask, I have also gotten offers to do those sexy hotlines."

"I never thought about that. So you prefer cleaning?"

"It's a family business."

"Sloane wanted to be a nurse," Divina said.

"What happened?" I asked.

"Debts to be paid." Sloane raised the mug to take a sip. "Huge debts." I saw regret and sadness in her eyes, but her mouth quickly corrected to a smile as she said, "This seems like a big enough house. Might make a dent in that debt. I don't normally do residential cleaning, but Divina is a friend."

"Thank you." Divina gave Sloane a hug.

After the coffee break, we worked through lunch, then stopped in the afternoon for pizza because the men were hungry and wondered where lunch was. I told Sticks to tell one of the guys to get pizza because Sandro forbade delivery.

We continued to clean until late afternoon. Sloane was a workhorse. She had shed the top of her coveralls to reveal a tank and firm arms and curves underneath. She took off her fisherman's cap and replaced it with a bandana. Her hair was up in a messy bun.

We'd cleaned three bedrooms and most of the first floor. We

were in the home theater now and she insisted on waxing the leather chairs. The home theater was an exact replica of what we had at the De Lucci mansion. Sandro had seen it. I wondered if he had it copied. And if he did, I didn't know how to process my emotions about that.

"I could see a girls' night here with all the wives and girlfriends," I told Divina, but I was thinking more about my family. Cleaning the house kept my mind off them, but coming into this theater reminded me of Mom and Dad, my brothers. Renz.

"Hey, include me too," Sloane said.

"Of course, you're the one who is doing the hard work." By this time, Divina and I were sitting on the couches, exhausted, while Sloane showed no signs of flagging. She said she'd been doing this since she was old enough to hold a mop. It used to be her mom and older brother. Her dad abandoned them. But when her mom died, her brother ended up in a gang. That was when she found cleaning for the mob paid much higher. She had to drop out of nursing school to either keep her brother in rehab or out of jail.

"I'm thirsty," Divina announced. "Want anything?"

"Blueberry soda."

"I've never had one of those," Sloane said. "Get me one too."

Divina made a humming sound and left us alone.

Sloane gave the entrance to the theater another look before she said, "Thanks for looking out for my friend."

"I don't know what you mean."

"It means…I worry about her. The men in the Rossi crime family are a bunch of misogynistic assholes stuck in the eighties. Tommy is the exception, but he can't be everywhere."

"Divina should talk to him."

"She doesn't want to because Tommy has enough problems with Gian. They're vying for underboss position since Sandro took the top spot and the men are confused about who's in charge."

"It's only been a few days."

Sloane shrugged and continued polishing the leather. My thoughts went back to my conversation with Sandro. How he was positioning Tommy for boss. Could Divina rise to the task? I'd hate for Tommy to be pushed out because Divina couldn't handle the pressure and waste Sandro's sacrifices.

Fake his death?

Despite what I told him, I would never enjoy my freedom if that was the price.

I cleared my throat, still parched, and that was when I noticed Divina had been taking too long.

I went looking for her and ran into her in the foyer, exchanging harsh whispers with Miller.

When Miller saw me, he paled. Poor guy. Sandro must have scared the shit out of him.

"Don't worry, I won't tell," I teased.

Divina spun around and gasped, "Oh, no."

"What? Weren't you going to get us snacks and soda?"

"Well…well…well…the little girl is playing house."

My spine stiffened in recognition of the voice. I turned to see Griselda descending the stairs.

Indignation surged. "What are you doing here?"

She didn't seem in the least bit ruffled and continued her lazy descent. "I came to get my earrings. I left them in Sandro's bedroom the last time I was here."

"She's lying," Divina said. "Sandro hasn't been in this house for over a year."

Griselda glided up to us, her mouth twisting in derision. "Look at you. Where are your loyalties, Divina? Some kind of sister-in-law you are. You're kissing ass to Bianca now?" She skewered me a head-to-toe appraisal. "She's not going to last."

"Sandro wouldn't leave his bedroom unlocked," I said.

She dangled a set of keys in her hand as she walked up to us. "I have the keys to everything that belongs to him."

"Don't listen to her, Bianca."

Griselda's nose flared as an irritated expression flashed through her face. "You better bet on the winning horse, dear sister-in-law, because their marriage"—she stabbed a finger in my direction—"is a sham."

"Let's talk about a sham," I shot back. "You tried to pawn off a pregnancy on Sandro, and guess what, he doesn't give a fuck if you're pregnant or not because he told me the baby is not his." He didn't deny not sleeping with Griselda, but it was going to be at the top of my list of questions to ask him.

"And your marriage, Bianca?" Griselda sneered. "You don't even sleep in the same room."

"Did you go into my bedroom?"

"I don't have to. Sandro's room is still all Sandro without a trace of you." She laughed in a way that brought back all her jeering from my teenage years.

"Get out," I said.

"Oh, I will." She swept past me and opened the door, but she wasn't done. She turned around again. "Sandro will never touch you. He'll always think of you like a little sister."

My mouth wanted to sneer and tell her I just had an orgasm grinding on Sandro's big, hard cock. But I was selfish about sharing that, even if it might give me pleasure to wipe the mockery off her face.

At my silence, she snorted another laugh. "Just you wait until I tell Uncle Raffa."

"Maybe you should admit to him first that you're not pregnant."

"Oh, he already knows I'm not," she snapped.

Then it dawned on me. "They're pissed at you for faking your pregnancy, aren't they? That's why you're trying to redirect their anger toward me and Sandro. To distract them from your lying."

"Just like Sandro is lying to Uncle Raffa about making this marriage real? You really think I buy that Sandro wants to be the boss for long?" She studied my face, trying to discern the truth, but when I showed her nothing, she gave the whole grand foyer an assessing gaze full of contempt. "Don't get too comfortable in this house."

She didn't bother closing the door, probably so I could hear her triumphant laughter as she walked away from me.

I slammed the door behind her and pivoted to Divina. "Did you know she was here, and that's why you made the excuse to get us drinks?"

"I was trying to avoid a confrontation."

"And if I hadn't come out, would you have kept it from me?"

"I don't know," Divina whispered.

"Hey, what's taking the refreshments…?" Sloane came up and broke off. "What happened?"

"Griselda happened." I speared Miller with a look. "Where's Sticks?"

"He went to town to get something," Miller replied. "Look, I can't say no to Griselda unless Sandro says so. She's the club's manager, so technically, she's our boss."

"What a clusterfuck," Sloane muttered.

"You think?" I retorted. "I'll talk to Sandro and clear it up." But nothing was more disheartening than my disappointment with Divina. Was it her fault, though? I'd had enough dealings with Griselda to know her expertise was in stirring trouble. Even fabricating it. Were there really earrings? If she indeed had keys to this house, I was going to demand she give them up. But that was not my immediate concern.

"Sloane, Miller, can you give Divina and me a minute?"

When the two left us, I told her, “Sloane is right. This situation is a mess, and you’re being put in the middle, but you have to choose, Divina. If Sandro fails, Gian will be boss. And you know who he’s in league with.”

She nodded.

“The Philly mob. I’m trying to help. The consequences of Sandro failing are unacceptable to me. He’s been my friend since childhood. If you’re torn about what to do, then you need to have an honest conversation with Tommy. Sandro needs people he can trust, especially with the power struggle going on. Do you understand?”

“I do.”

“Text Sloane and tell her to meet us in the kitchen.” This encounter with Griselda had left me thirstier and surprisingly hungry. Damn, if I ate my weight in stress, my family would have to roll me out of here in three weeks.

When Sloane met us in the kitchen, I had a pitcher of margaritas ready.

I’d emptied a bag of chips on a platter and microwaved a bowl of queso.

“What are the guys doing for dinner?” Divina asked.

“They can fend for themselves,” I said. “I think they’ve ordered enough pizza to last us a few days.”

Divina gave a light laugh. Kind of a forced one, but it left no question she was still feeling guilty about what happened. “They sure did.” Then, as if she knew we couldn’t sweep this under the rug, she said, “It isn’t Miller’s fault.”

“Did I say it was?” I poured the margarita mixture into glasses and slid them to the women. “I think the problem here is the new chain of command. Dance club business…it’s Griselda, but here in this house, I have the say.”

Sloane laughed while taking a sip of her margarita. “Hate to tell you, Bianca, but it's kind of hard for you to assert your position if you're not even allowed a phone."

"Sloane," Divina snapped.

"What?" Her friend went wide-eyed with mock innocence. "I'm just stating the obvious. How will people listen to her if her position is clearly as a captive?"

"Let's put it this way, assume this is my kingdom and I'm just denied a passport beyond it."

Sloane snorted into her drink.

"What?"

"Whatever you say, Mrs. Rossi."

I looked at Divina. "Your friend is snarky."

Sloane grinned.

"And annoying."

She grinned wider.

We continued to snack on chips and queso, and when we a ran out of queso, I opened a jar of salsa. I would worry about the empty calories later. Sloane entertained us with interesting clean-up jobs. Apparently, she didn't only work for the Rossis but a slew of criminal organizations.

The door to the house opened to a barrage of voices.

And screaming.

We all looked at each other, eyes wide, before we scrambled to our feet. "What now?" I muttered.

We rushed out of the kitchen and I was relieved to hear Sandro's voice giving orders.

But anxiety rippled in my chest when I saw the change in the foyer.

The once pristine marble flooring was now covered in a pool of blood.

CHAPTER
Thirteen

BIANCA

I saw Tommy first. "Where's Sandro? Is he hurt?"

But his eyes were on Sloane. "Good, you're here. Study. Now."

Tommy's voice was grim. "He's fine. It's Al."

He turned away from us. Sloane hurriedly buttoned up her coveralls and rushed alongside him while being briefed. Maybe margarita night hadn't been such a good idea.

More men poured into the house, all chatty and boisterous.

Well, hell, maybe it was just the right idea, especially when working for the mob.

I clasped Divina's hand and tugged her along. "Come on. Make a note that we need to stock up on medical supplies." Probably have enough to do minor surgery. I thought about Renz again.

Everyone congregated in the study and it was chaos. Probably because a man was shouting.

Some were laughing.

What the fuck?

"Ugh, that son of a bitch!" he yelled. "That double-crossing son of a bitch."

Someone chortled, "Good thing he didn't get you in the ass, Al."

"Fuck you, Arnie."

Al and Arnie? The Scavo brothers. Tommy and Griselda's uncles and the ones who had a scuffle with Ivy last year. My marriage ceremony to Sandro was still a blur, but I remembered them in the front row.

"Look who's here…baby De Lucci." Gian walked up to us, but before he got to within a foot of me, Sandro appeared and shoved at him.

"That's Mrs. Rossi to you."

I quickly scanned my husband and the relief was immediate. He didn't appear to be bleeding. He was in all black, but he wasn't tracking blood.

I steeled my spine in case Sandro asked me and Divina to leave, but his attention was on Gian.

"Look at you," Gian sneered.

"Look at me, what?" Sandro got in his face. "Your faulty intel almost got us killed."

"What's the matter, Sandro? Can't take a little heat?"

What I'd learned dealing with older brothers and the mafia was not to get in between their egos. But my role as Sandro's wife became clear. Like a beacon, it signaled me what to do. Or what I wanted to do.

I pushed through the crowd of Rossi soldiers.

Sloane was looking over Al. He was lying on his chest across the desk. He was the lankier and taller between the two brothers. But the way I identified them was through their hair. I wasn't sure who was older but Al's hair was black, while Arnie's was gray.

Papers and books were strewn over the floor like they'd been shoved off the desk to make room for Al.

"What do you need?" I asked her.

"I need my kit. It's in the van, but I might not have enough gauze."

"We have medical supplies in the bunkhouse," Sticks piped in.

Sloane handed Divina her keys. "Get the kit. You know what it looks like."

"I'll go with you," I told Divina.

Sandro gripped my arm. "I need to talk to you. Let Divina handle it. Sticks, get your stash in the bunkhouse."

"On it, boss."

Sloane walked past us. "I need to wash my hands."

"Good idea," Al called. "Don't want to die of an infection."

I lunged to yell at Al, but Sandro hauled me from the room. Hand firm on my biceps, he led me up the stairs, after which he dragged me into his bedroom and shut the door. Then he backed me against it, pressing his body to mine.

I was breathing hard, mostly from matching Sandro's strides, but my heart almost skipped out of my chest when he lowered his face close to mine.

His eyes were dark and furious.

Before he could say anything, I burst out, "I don't have control over everything, but I will not have women spoken to that way in my presence."

"Got it."

"Then why did we leave the study?"

"Al's got a smart mouth that's going to get him killed. You don't want me shooting Al for insulting you."

I stilled. I didn't want someone dying for simply insulting me. "The answer is removing me from the scene? How about talking to them about respecting women not only in the family, but in general?

Don't think just because the Scavo brothers are friends now of the De Luccis, I haven't forgotten that he almost hit Ivy. If hitting women is an accepted practice of the Rossis, that is *not* okay with me. I understand the business of protection money, but if I'm going to be identified as a Rossi whether it's temporary or not, then I'm not going to stand for that."

"Got it."

But the tension that was thick between us didn't seem to have anything to do with Al. "Anything else?" My voice had fallen into a whisper.

His eyes were no longer angry, but no less intense, with an unnamed emotion that sent my senses skittering into overdrive.

It was heat. It was yearning. A yearning similar to mine until the last few days obliterated that emotion and left me with conflicted pieces.

"Why are you looking at me like that?" I gnashed my teeth. I was determined not to fall for Sandro's magnetic pull. I refused…*refused* to drown in my obsession with him again.

I lost his eyes when he dropped his forehead to mine. I held my breath in suspense on what he was going to do next.

"This was a fucked-up day and I hated seeing you in the bloody aftermath of family business." He exhaled a ragged breath that sounded like surrender. "But a selfish part of me loved coming home to you."

Oh my God. And damn him!

"Sandro…" Why did he have to say the sweetest things at the worst time? Why? Why? Why couldn't he have said this years ago when I threw myself at him?

A groan rumbled deep in his chest before his mouth claimed mine.

Sandro

My control snapped.

I was tired of fighting it. I kissed Bianca with all the pent-up hunger I had kept in check for the past four years. My body trapped hers against the wall, and I could feel the pounding of her heart. Our tongues dueled and my fingers dug into her ass to bring her level, keeping her pinned.

When Bianca showed up in the study in the middle of blood and Rossi soldiers, I battled between my belief that she didn't belong in my world and the overwhelming urge to keep her at my side.

I wanted her to belong.

I needed her to be mine.

Mine. Only mine.

Her body stiffened and her detachment from me wasn't physical until in a split second it was. She yanked at my hair with one hand to break the kiss, while she pushed at my chest with the other.

I lost her mouth, and when I tried to capture it again, she twisted her head away.

I persisted, cupping her jaw to bring her lips back to mine, but the angry tears in her eyes stopped me from kissing her. "What?"

"You have to ask? We're temporary. You're going to disappear, remember? So why start something that will make it hard for us to leave each other?"

Leave each other? The possessive beast inside me reared its ugly head. Seeing Bianca in the midst of all the ugliness in my world sealed her fate. I was never letting her go. She'd had her chance. I kept my obsession with her at bay, but now it was too late for her. "You're mine."

She narrowed her eyes. "What are you playing at?"

Slowly, I eased my body from hers, letting her slide down the wall.

"I'm tired of fighting it, baby."

She bit her bottom lip, and I groaned. "No. Don't do that."

She released her pouty lips, but suspicion etched her entire face. Fair enough. I hadn't convinced her of my commitment, which was still new to me, anyway. If groveling was what she wanted for all the shit I put her through, I would slog through it. But at the end of it all, Bianca was mine.

"You know I don't trust those words out of your mouth, right?"

I gave her a brief nod. "I just have to prove it."

"Just yesterday, you told me you're faking your death to set me free."

"I want to find another way."

Her brows rose, but before she could say anything, yelling from downstairs broke our moment.

She let out a resigned, if not irritated, sigh. "Your timing sucks, Alessandro Rossi."

I dragged a hand down my face and emitted a pained chuckle. "Yeah, well, we better head back down there."

"We better. I don't want them thinking we went away for a quickie."

"Come on. Before I change my mind and do just that."

Blood had rushed to my groin, but I was thankful the jacket of my suit hid my erection. I clasped her hand and tugged her out the door.

We ran into Divina.

"Tommy sent me to get you." The high color of her cheeks belied the relief in her eyes. It was as if she knew what we were doing.

"Don't worry, Sandro didn't ask for a blow job."

Jesus.

Divina's gaze flew to mine, and I gave a shake of my head. "Baby, you're ruining my reputation."

"Verdict's out on that," Bianca quipped.

"Hey." I stopped walking and turned her to me. "I grit my teeth hard enough when men think of you in that way. So before I get a grip how this"—I pointed between us. And *this* meant my possessiveness—"is going to go, please have mercy on the man that would look at you the wrong way."

"You're serious?" There was an awestruck expression on her face.

I gave her a brief nod. I knew I had a big problem on my hands with the way I reacted to Miller. And tonight, when we were surrounded by the family, I had the urge to put a bullet through every single one of them who looked at Bianca in a disrespectful way. More than a few men leered at her. If they hadn't backed off when they saw me head off Gian, there would have been a bloodbath. But then Bianca left us to our bullshit and took charge. Except Al decided to run his mouth, and I'd hate to shoot the man who had my back when everyone else ostracized me once Wilma revealed I wasn't her son.

When we reached the top of the stairs, soldiers were heading for the door.

"I thought my husband was insane when he sent me to get you," Divina said.

"Does Sloane have all that she needs?" Bianca asked.

"Yes, she's working on getting the bullet out."

I barked at one of the soldiers to clean up the blood on the floors.

"Sloane's here," the soldier whined.

"Sloane is busy with Al. Clean it up," I ordered.

"They can use Sloane's stuff. Let me show them." Divina hurried down the steps ahead of us.

"And, Divina, don't do it for them. If they complain, send them to me," I said.

"No," Bianca said. "I'll talk to them."

Tommy and Gian met us at the bottom of the steps.

There was a smirk on Gian's face.

"Seems your wife is more important than debriefing your men," Gian said.

"She is," I returned evenly. I looked past him at the soldiers converging around us. "Listen up." I glanced at Tommy. "Take note."

When most of the men had gathered, I said, "This meeting with the Albanians didn't go as planned. It seems they want to get rid of us rather than find another distributor for the drugs in our possession. Gian, Tommy, and I will talk tonight. The rest of you can go home. Good?"

There were mumblings of the affirmative.

"One more thing," I said. "In this house, if my wife tells you to do something, you do it. No talking back. Got me?"

I smiled inwardly at Gian's surprised look. There was hushed laughter and a few grumblings, so I added, "Any disrespect to her is a disrespect to me. However, if she asks for a phone or a connection outside the Rossis, that's a negative."

There was a louder round of laughter this time.

"You just had to clarify that, didn't you?" Bianca griped.

I glanced over at her and grinned. She was more amused than angry. "Just fulfilling our deal with the Blind Don, baby."

"Boss, it's getting hard to give the De Luccis the runaround," Arnie Scavo said.

"You've been in this business longer than me, Arnie. You can talk outta your ass and people are gonna believe you. Three weeks. Just stay away from De Lucci territory and you'll be fine."

"How about your club in Harlem?" Gian asked. "Why is it

closed? Griselda's been bitching that you're bleeding money, paying temps and full-timers."

"That's none of your business, is it, Gian?"

I gave him a flat look. My club laundered money for the Rossis and other crime families, but it was at my discretion. I could easily shut him out, but since I was the boss, it would be more complication than it was worth just to spite him.

"Just saying," he muttered. "You may want to give Griselda a call."

Bianca muttered something I didn't catch.

As for Gian, he was purposely causing problems between me and Bianca. I glanced at her. She had gone to Divina, who was looking pale.

"You guys can go." I walked toward the study. "Gian, Tommy. Office now."

"Al's still in there with Sloane." Tommy strode alongside me.

"That's fine."

I caught Bianca in the corner of my eye, but she wasn't paying attention to me. She was talking to Divina. I tipped my chin at Sticks and he nodded in return to keep an eye on the girls.

The second Tommy, Gian, and I entered the office, I slammed the door and had Gian up against it.

"Sandro, what the f—"

His eyes bulged when I pressed my forearm against his throat. He started choking, face turning purple. Tommy lunged toward us and put a restraining hand on my arm.

"Easy, Sandro," Tommy warned.

"You try to cause trouble between me and my wife again, I'm putting you in an early grave," I told him. I stepped back and let him go.

Gian wheezed, bent over, and clutched his knees. "What the fuck is wrong with you?" He was having trouble getting the words out. "Griselda is being a pain in my ass because you ditched her to marry a De Lucci. Might want to try to calm that bitch down."

"Hey, that's my sister you're talking about," Tommy snapped.

Griselda could be a bitch, but guilt tweaked at the center of my chest. I wished she wasn't a Scavo so I could send her away.

"You shouldn't have faked being the father of her baby," Gian told me. "We had a good thing going with the Philly mob."

"We want nothing to do with the Philly mob," Tommy told him and I let him take the lead.

"No? Or should we discuss how Rossis should stop faking pregnancies?" Gian made a jab against my parents.

"Enough!" I growled.

"Guys," Sloane piped in behind us. "I'm still here. If you're going to discuss mob family secrets, I'd rather not hear it."

I walked over to the couch where they'd transferred Al. "How is he?"

"He's fine. The bullet lodged itself near the bone but I was able to extract it. No artery." She blew out a breath. "Same with the one in his arm."

"Thank you," I told her. "Send Divina the bill and she'll take care of it."

Al groaned on the couch. "I want my bed and a warm body. Take me to my *goomah*, Tommy."

"What? You don't want Griselda taking care of you?"

"She's going to drive me to an early grave with her nagging." Al opened one eye. "She's pissed at Sandro, and a pissed Griselda is not a picnic to be around."

"Neither is a grouchy Al," Tommy teased.

"Hey, show some respect, pup."

When Sloane left the room, I said, "So what are we doing about your Albanian friends, Gian?"

"Got a text from them. They said it was a misunderstanding.

They expected to see me, and not you. Thought you were there to whack a boss."

"You serious? Didn't you communicate that you're no longer in charge?"

Gian scratched his chin. "They don't like last-minute changes."

"I don't want that pallet of cocaine sitting in our warehouse. I want that out."

"This has nothing to do with the change of plans," Tommy said. "They don't want to take it back because they're going to lose money."

"We'll just have to sell them direct to dealers," Gian said.

"That's even worse than handing them off to the Albanians," I said.

"Then you'll have no choice but to eat the cost. We can dump it in the ocean, but if you ask me, that's money we'd lose and we can't afford it," Gian said smugly. My cousin was up to his passive-aggressive attitude. Outwardly, he seemed to be all about the good of the family, but inwardly he was seething. However, he was strategic. There would always be doubts about him being the next boss unless I failed spectacularly, then no one would question if Gian took over. That was why he stepped aside without so much as a glare and a grumble.

"There's always a choice," I told them. I looked at Tommy. He wasn't sure what I meant either, because we were out of options. I hated keeping my backup plan from him because I was going outside our crime family.

CHAPTER
Fourteen

BIANCA

“I don’t think I can do this.” Divina raised the teacup with shaky hands.

We were in the kitchen. I made tea for her because she’d suddenly felt cold and couldn’t warm up. Sloane was sitting beside Divina but was drinking a Red Bull. She looked exhausted and was silently listening to Divina and her misgivings about what happened tonight.

When Divina and a soldier had gone to pick up cleaning supplies, he told her that Al was standing beside Tommy. And if their uncle hadn’t pushed him away, Tommy would be the one bleeding out in the office.

“Surely this is not a one-off.” I poured more tea into her cup and also mine.

“It’s never hit me this way.” She swallowed. “I was never there.”

"Mafia wives are never as involved," Sloane said. "They stay in the kitchen to prepare food for the men after all the business is done."

I stilled. "Am I supposed to be cooking?" That was why I wanted to talk to Sandro this morning. I didn't know what he expected from me. But if he was the one who was hurt, no one would keep me from his side. It reminded me again of Griselda slamming the door on me after Sandro was shot. It reminded me of Griselda showing up this afternoon. I was Sandro's wife now. He made it clear that in this house I was in charge, but I wanted it clarified to Griselda, too.

"Nah," Sloane laughed. "There's still leftover pizza."

"What?"

Sloane laughed harder. "Where were you? I lost you there for a moment."

"I remembered something." I stared at Divina. "Let's hope this is not a common occurrence."

"Let's," Sloane agreed and took another sip of her Red Bull. "But you have to be prepared given the change of leadership."

Sandro entered the kitchen and informed Divina, "Tommy, Al, and Arnie are waiting for you."

"I should get going too," Sloane said, rising.

"You don't have another job to do, do you?" I asked.

"Just a small one. You need me tomorrow?"

"God, no," I said. "Only when you have time. Get some sleep. You worked so hard today."

She shot me an appreciative smile.

Divina couldn't muster a change of expression. She was still trapped in the what-ifs of her thoughts. She got off the barstool and followed Sloane like an automaton.

"Divina," I called and sprinted to her. Before she could fully turn, I wrapped her in a tight hug and whispered in her ear. "Rest tonight, Tommy is fine. We'll figure it out tomorrow."

At her surprised look, I had to stop and think of my impulsiveness. My reaction was a one-eighty from the standoffishness with her yesterday.

"Hey, do I get a hug too?" Sloane piped in.

"Yes, you do." With my other arm, I dragged her into my embrace with Divina. In a way, we had found a common ground. We were in this family, not by choice, but by coercion. Admittedly, Divina was in love with Tommy, but their marriage was turning out more overwhelming than what she signed up for. I gave the girls another squeeze before letting go.

"Thank you." There was a catch in Divina's voice.

When they left the kitchen, Sandro was looking at me with his arms crossed. "What was that all about?" His tone was casual but his gaze was piercing.

"Just girl bonding."

"Is that right?" He opened the fridge, surveying the contents, and grabbed a beer.

"Do you want me to make you something?"

He looked over his shoulder and lifted the pizza box out, letting the door of the fridge swing shut. "You think I'd rather have you laboring over a stove than hearing about your day?"

"Here, let me heat that up."

"I'll eat it cold." And he proceeded to do so. "So, how was your day?"

I watched him as he took a swig of beer. He'd unbuttoned more buttons of his dress shirt and exposed that strong, tanned column of his throat.

I got distracted for a moment. "We cleaned the rooms. That Sloane is an interesting character."

He sat back against the barstool. "You seem to get along."

"That's a good thing, right?"

"You're settling in, then?"

"I don't know." I schooled my features and looked directly at him. "Griselda showed up and thinks she has a run of the place."

Every line in Sandro's body stiffened and his face grew scary. He dropped his half-eaten pizza back in the box. "Why didn't you tell me this earlier?"

"Are you serious? You had a man bleeding in your study. I don't know what happened, but you clearly had bigger problems. That said, since we're talking about our day…"

I did my best to shrug it off, but I couldn't. Remembering Griselda was here made me want to foam at the mouth all over again. I didn't know if it was being possessive of Sandro or just this place and the people around me.

He considered this briefly. A muscle twitched in his jaw before he asked, "What did Griselda want?"

"She needed to pick up her earrings from your room."

He muttered an expletive that sounded like *bitch*. "She uses this place sometimes, but I'm telling you now, I haven't fucked Griselda since that time I threw her out the night you called me from Queens."

"Six years ago?"

He nodded. "I owe Al and Arnie a lot and you know I grew up with Tommy. She's a good club manager, and it's impossible to avoid her. But make no mistake, I'm making it clear where she stands when it comes to you."

"She said she has the keys to your kingdom."

"It makes it easy to move things in and out of the club. But I was going to get my keys back from her anyway." His voice lowered. "I want you to have them."

Or change the locks on every property that Sandro owned. I

hated that Griselda stirred a pettiness inside me. "Miller and the guys didn't know how to handle her."

"Where was Sticks? He wouldn't have let Griselda pass."

"He was on an errand."

"Dammit, all right." He resumed eating his pizza, but it seemed like he was running through different checklists in his head. I didn't want to add more to his problems. I could handle Griselda now that I knew Sandro had my back, and that I wasn't stepping on any organizational hierarchy. And he hadn't slept with her in years. I brought his attention back to business. "So what happened tonight?"

"We're trying to get clear of the drugs," he said without hesitation.

This was good news. And that he was open about what he was doing might make living with Sandro easier to swallow. I was figuring out my objection to the made-men culture was keeping the women in the dark about mafia business. "This is good."

"Yeah. Tommy and I are checking over the financials with the accountant tomorrow. Make sure there are no hidden streams coming from human trafficking too."

"You could talk to Dom if you want other options for revenue." The De Lucci crime family steered clear of two things: drugs and human trafficking. Other businesses were fair game.

Sandro drained his beer before answering. "Right now, I'm on the De Lucci shit list."

"Any news you can tell me?"

"Renz is scheduled to be discharged tomorrow. Your dad is blowing up Luca's phone."

"Why?"

"He found out that Luca was my sponsor to fast-track the made-man ceremony with the commission so I could marry you."

"And Dom?"

"Dom is sending every De Lucci soldier into our territory."

"He's not supposed to do that."

"He's straddling the line for sure. Intimidation without confrontation."

"And?"

He hitched his shoulders as though saying it was as he expected. "Tensions are high."

One wrong trigger and there would be an all-out war. But both families wouldn't want that. The commission would come down on their heads if it caught the attention of the public.

I walked to the fridge to get water. "Want another beer?"

"Sure."

"Is there any other way I can see my family sooner? I mean, even talk to them. See them over FaceTime. They just need to know I'm okay."

I popped the cap off his beer and handed it to him. Sandro was already shaking his head before I finished my sentence.

"I saw Raffa briefly today," he said. "He's enjoying Cesar's suffering."

Too late, Sandro realized he said the wrong thing because he must have seen the expression change on my face before I realized my whole body had locked up in fury. Any effort to be on the same page, same line, same word disintegrated.

He quickly blanked his expression.

That pissed me off further.

"Bastard," I managed to get out.

"You need to hold your temper around him, Bianca."

"Why?"

"What did I tell you earlier?"

"You have no choice but to kill a man if he insults me."

"Exactly that."

At first, I thought it was endearing how Sandro was so protective of me, but an uglier conclusion was taking form, especially in light of Dad's suffering. My dad, who'd done nothing but want what was best for me, was suffering at the hands of the Blind Don, who was using me to fuel his revenge. "Is that your way of keeping me in line?"

"If you think I'd manipulate you that way, then I'm disappointed with you."

His words sliced into my already ragged heart. My mouth curled in anger. There was no remorse on his face to soften the blow. He'd become a stranger once again. He was always going to be one of them.

"Well, fuck you, Alessandro Rossi, and fuck this marriage. Imagine how disappointed I am in you!"

His face hardened even more. A muscle in his jaw jumped before he took a swig of beer.

I couldn't stand to be around him. Fuck him. Fuck the Rossi crime family. Fuck them all to hell.

"I'm going to my room. I can't stand your company."

And for the second night in a row, I stormed out of the kitchen. But instead of the silence that followed me yesterday, the sound of something crashing, probably an overturned chair, reached my ears.

"Bianca!" Sandro growled my name. Each syllable was punctuated with exasperation. Even if I couldn't hear his footsteps because of his specialized stealth footwear, I quickened mine.

Before I reached the bottom of the staircase, fingers grabbed my waist and he lifted and tossed me over his shoulder.

"Put me down!" I pounded his back.

"No."

He was starting up the stairs when I spotted the front door opening and in my upside-down state, I saw Raffa and Griselda walk in flanked by men in suits I figured were like his Secret Service security. If there was any doubt of Raffa's importance in the family, the fact that he had an entourage of men protecting him erased my questions.

I would have panicked thinking that they were coming for Sandro, but Sticks and Miller were with them.

Sandro angled their way, and I could feel his whole body freeze. He backed down the steps to face them.

"Put me down." I was glad I was wearing joggers and not a skirt or my ass would be on display. Speaking of which, Sandro hugged my legs with a hand over my ass in what felt like a brand of possession.

"Quiet," he growled to me, and then, "What's this all about, Raffa? I thought we agreed to talk about this shit tomorrow."

I stilled. I promised cooperation in front of the others, so I fumed in silence.

"Yes, but Griselda seems to think you're not keeping your end of the bargain."

"And what is that?"

"You're not staying in the same room, so I assume you haven't consummated the marriage."

That nosy bitch.

"I was giving Bianca a chance to adjust, but as you can see, you're interrupting our foreplay."

I didn't know whether to be mad or laugh. But I could definitely hear Sandro's men laugh.

"So, is that all?" Sandro continued. "Because I've got all this aggression from what happened tonight and *my wife…*" He gave my ass a swat. I inhaled sharply. "Is being a brat and I think she's had enough time to adjust."

Oh, he was going to hear it from me.

Raffa gave a pained laugh. It seemed Sandro embarrassed him. "I'm sorry for interrupting, nephew. Yes, what happened tonight can wait. Take care of your wife. Get her pregnant, even better."

"You simply believe them?" Griselda shrieked.

"Shut up, Griselda," Sandro snapped. "You're forbidden to step foot into this house without permission from Bianca or me. Do I make myself clear?"

"Fuck you, Alessandro."

"Sorry, that's my wife's job."

Again. My conflicting emotions. Pleased and annoyed.

"Let's go, before you humiliate yourself further," Raffa said. He could only be addressing Griselda.

Sandro moved toward the entrance. It was getting uncomfortable on his shoulder. He slammed the door and I heard him turn the lock.

"You can put me down."

"Hell no, I enjoy having you at my mercy."

I was too furious to be turned on. Seeing Raffa only brought back the image of Dad's worried face. All my life, my father's main objective was to keep our family mafia adjacent and not actually in it. I was going to be his biggest disappointment.

When we got to the top of the staircase, I renewed my struggle, pounding on his back because he had the presence of mind to lock down my legs.

"Stop fighting," he growled.

"You're a bastard just like all of them."

"Yes, but this bastard is your husband."

"I'm sure Dad has drawn up the divorce papers."

He pivoted into his room and dumped me on the bed. I lost my breath momentarily and found myself staring at the ceiling. When I heard the door slam, my gaze switched to the looming outline of Sandro stalking toward the bed. He was on me before I succeeded in scrambling off. His weight bore down and I hated how my body came alive.

I pushed against his shoulders. My hips squirmed against his, but I was feeling something very hard rubbing against my thigh.

I ignored the pulse of my arousal between my legs. I wasn't giving in.

The sounds in the room were my grunts and his.

He grabbed my wrists and slammed them on either side of me. Somehow, he had wedged his hips between my legs, and when he adjusted, his erection rubbed right along the seam of my pussy.

My moan was loud in the room.

He froze. "Did you just come?"

I glared at him, indignation resonating loudly in my vehemence. "No!"

A corner of his mouth tipped up and he repeated the motion.

"Sandro, stop it!"

He raised a brow. "You're saying no?"

I was too mad to have this go further and have me regret it later, so I gritted, "I'm saying no. Let me go."

He immediately released my wrists. I expected him to be pissed, but there was a warm glint in his eyes and a proud look on his face. I remembered our conversation years ago about "no means no." And with that memory, it reminded me there was still something I wanted to ask him.

"You got it." He pressed a kiss to my forehead. "But you'll have to sleep in my room."

I exhaled a heavy breath. Of relief, a bit of disappointment. Gah! My feelings for Sandro were all over the place and he made it so hard to stay mad at him. "Fine. I don't want Griselda having more ammunition to use against us."

His face turned serious. "I don't like that she's still between us, baby. If anything about her bothers you, let me know immediately. I'll take care of it."

"No," I said firmly. "I'll take care of it. As long as you'll have my back."

"Always."

CHAPTER *Fifteen*

Sandro

Bianca emerged from the bathroom dressed in sleep shorts and my old tee. I could see the shadows of her nipples and I wondered what torture I'd consigned myself to for the night. I smelled her arousal earlier and I ached to bury my tongue between her legs.

But having her share my bed was enough. For now.

Bianca is mine. Those words snarled in my head over and over ever since I saw her in the study tonight, surrounded by Rossi soldiers and the blood of my family.

"Your turn." She smiled shyly.

I jumped up from the bed before I grabbed her and tossed her on top of the sheets again. My control was on a razor-thin line. The vanilla, citrus scent that clung to her skin made me salivate.

I was hard before I even stepped into the shower. I was used to getting shot at and being neck-deep in dicey situations, but Bianca in my bed as my wife? It pushed everything aside.

I grabbed my cock and squeezed. I imagined her in the kitchen rubbing herself to completion. I imagined setting her on the kitchen counter and eating her out. I imagined her on my bed, naked and begging me to fuck her.

My hand slapped against the tile as a few strokes up and down my length had me spurting cum all over my hand. The cold water sluicing over my body did nothing to quell the raging inferno racing through my veins. Bianca and I had passed the point of no return. The image of her face in the throes of coming while rubbing herself all over my cock was forever seared into my brain.

I panted, leaning both hands on the tiles while I waited for the fever to leave my body. A part of me still didn't want to touch her, but I was lying to myself if I thought Bianca would remain untainted by my touch for long, especially if she slept beside me.

I shut off the water and toweled dry. Then I threw on a shirt and athletic shorts as a barrier from the temptation lying in my bed. I exited the bathroom to the sight of her all curled up like a kitten and I had to stifle a groan. Dammit. A hellish night was in my immediate future. She said no earlier and I respected that. I wasn't about to be a hypocrite. But one thing was for certain, I was determined for Bianca De Lucci…no…Bianca *Rossi*…to beg me to fuck her. I had a feeling that once I was buried deep inside her, there was no version of our story where I was letting her go.

Not to another man.

Not to her overprotective family. Admittedly, I went crazy when she said her dad probably had divorce papers drawn up. I threw her on the bed, intending to edge her with my mouth until I extracted a promise from her that divorce was out of the question.

"I think I fell asleep." Bianca stirred.

"That's good." That was good she probably didn't hear me groaning her name while I jacked off to X-rated images of her.

Her eyes had a hard time staying open. She reached out her hand. I didn't think she was even aware she did that. But I didn't waste time as I slipped into bed, thirsty for a connection. She snuggled closer to me and grabbed that hand, cradling it against her cheek.

"We need to talk," she whispered. "There was something else I wanted to ask you, but I forgot."

"We can talk later."

She didn't respond. Her breathing evened out and I knew she was asleep again. My right hand was still trapped under her cheek. I didn't want to move and wake her. I enjoyed watching her sleep. A smile touched the corners of my mouth. I was whipped for this girl. Always had been.

These past few days had changed the trajectory of our relationship, but I remembered the exact moment when I realized my affection for Bianca had morphed from fondness and protectiveness into something else.

~

Four Years Ago

Sandro, 28, Bianca, 19.

Sandro

I got into my car on a Boston side street. Housekeeping wouldn't find the Russian arms dealer until morning. It was a straightforward kill: *Inject him with a paralytic drug undetectable by tox screens, and let him drown in a bathtub.* I'd studied his movements for days. I didn't have to go through any bodyguards. He was on the run anyway because he'd pissed off the Moscow mob and ended up in a fleabag motel.

I sent an image of a very dead Russian to the one who hired me to confirm the kill.

A text immediately came back. "Confirmed."

The family should get the 600K in their offshore account. Done with my part, I took out the sim card and smashed it along with the phone. I scattered the pieces for several blocks. The people willing to pay those contract prices wanted clean jobs. The work of professionals and not hooligans wanting to play at hit man. Under the radar of law enforcement like the feds, and definitely no publicity. We had a network of local cops in our pockets to bury these incidents in paperwork and solved cases filed under suicide.

I slipped out my other phone to text Tommy, but that was when I saw messages from Bianca.

BIANCA

Can't wait to see you toborow.

Want ice cram afterrrr!

My mouth twitched and I texted back.

You'd think Harvard would teach you how to spell.

I put the phone on the dash and started driving toward my hotel. Since the job was in Boston, I told Bianca I could meet her for lunch tomorrow. I missed that brat. Away from the watchful eyes of her dad and brothers, she was likely having the time of her life, probably breaking hearts left and right. Five minutes later, her reply came.

Shhorrry. I think I'm tipsy.

That was followed by a string of nonsensical emojis.

My heart rate spiked. I was still in the middle of the Boston grid and found parking. I had a feeling I was going to Cambridge or wherever the fuck Bianca was.

I grabbed the phone and texted.

Are you drunk?

The bubbles went on for a while and then disappeared. I waited. Five seconds passed. Nothing.

BIANCA! ARE YOU DRUNK?

No need for shitty capitals.

Shouty!

More nonsensical emojis.

Where are you?

Don't know...

🤪

I'm fiiinee! See you tomorrow. See, I can spell.

I ignored her next notifications and checked her location.

It was at a frat house.

Fuck. *Fuck.*

She was drunk and some horny frat boy probably had his hands all over her—I shook off that thought as a murderous rage was taking over. I was still in bloodlust, but I'd settle for blistering her reckless ass. I wasn't a stickler for twenty-one being the drinking age. I was more concerned about how she'd be taken advantage of in her inebriated state. And judging from her text, she was way over her limit of good judgment. It took me fifteen minutes to get to her location. I passed the frat house. The party had already rolled into the streets. A car left a parking spot, and I immediately slid the Taurus into it. I was thankful I brought my work vehicle just in case Bianca had to throw up.

I got out of the vehicle and slammed the door. My head was on a swivel, keeping an eye out for Bianca. I checked my phone. I was right on top of her. I entered the frat house, narrowly missing a guy throwing up on the floor. Despite owning a dance club, the pounding music fueled my agitation. I was getting pissier and pissier.

Christ. Beer pong in one corner. Sleazy dancing in another. People making out in the middle of the floor and on the couches. It was useless to call out Bianca's name. The more I moved through the house, the more crowded it became. Scenes like these made me thankful I didn't go to college.

Stale beer and cheap wine assailed my nostrils and there might be the smell of puke and piss in there too.

I ignored the coeds trying to rub against me. My singular goal was to find Bianca.

My gaze drifted to the stairs. She'd obviously gotten over her experience with Warren Winslow, but I had not. What if she was in one of those upstairs bedrooms? What if I found a boy fucking her while she was drunk, or worse, passed out? Fury took the form of red mist in my head. I was halfway up the staircase when I turned my head and saw a couple making out on the couch.

The pink checkered short skirt was a dead giveaway. And I recognized the back of her head. She was in a full-blown make-out session with some punk in a varsity jacket and he had a hand up her skirt. I rushed down the steps and leaped down the last three, and then shouldered my way through the crowd.

I may have shoved people aside.

"Hey, man, watch it."

More than a few guys tried to get in my way.

But a stare from me had them backing off. I just killed a man tonight, and these guys were lucky I gave them latitude for the stupidity of youth.

I got to the boy who had his hand up Bianca's skirt. I hauled him off her and threw him aside.

Bianca's mouth gaped. Her lipstick was smeared and her hair. Fuck. She had fuck-me hair.

The stirring in my groin horrified me.

This was fucked up. This was simply adrenaline.

My reaction to her stunned me speechless.

"Alessandro? What the hell are you doing here?"

She surged up and shoved at me and would have fallen sideways if I hadn't caught her elbow.

"That's why," I gritted, finding my words. "You're done. And going home."

"You fucker!" someone shouted behind me.

I shoved Bianca away and spun in time to see the varsity-jacket guy's fist flying at me. It was no contest. He was drunk and missed me by a mile. I even waited for him to straighten up before jabbing him in the face, breaking his nose, and sending him to the floor.

"Chris!" Bianca shrieked, trying to go to him, but I'd hooked her around the waist and set her behind me again.

"It's Joey." The boy glared at her while swiping his bloody nose.

Joey's friends gathered around him and helped him up.

"Anyone else?" I asked them. "Need I remind you she's not twenty-one and you're giving her alcohol?"

"Fuck, man, she doesn't even know your name. Is she worth it?" one of them asked.

Not waiting for them to come into committee with their next move, I grabbed Bianca's hand and dragged her out of there before I changed my mind about not killing anyone else tonight. She didn't have a choice because I was plowing through drunken college kids, deaf to her rants and her attempts to free her wrist from my hold.

"You have no right!"

"That was embarrassing, Sandro."

"I don't want to leave!"

Once we were outside, I backed her against the wall and caged her in. "This is what's gonna happen. I'm taking you back to your apartment. And you're sleeping off your bad decisions."

"You're not the boss of me!"

Images of what I came upon flashed through my head, sending my temper soaring. "You don't even know the name of the boy who had his hand up your skirt!"

"I was having fun," she retorted. "Do you know the name of every one-night stand you've had?"

"You're only nineteen, Bianca. Don't—"

"Don't spout your holier-than-thou attitude at me. You think I don't know why you're in Boston? It certainly wasn't to meet me for lunch." Despite the slurring in her words, the condemnation of the hypocrisy of my actions was crystal clear. I had no problem taking a life, but I was bent out of shape with her having sex. But my soul was a black hole. In an eclipse, she was the ring of light around my darkness, and with my selfish reasoning, I wanted her to stay that way.

Innocence and light.

Not innocent anymore, a voice in my head taunted.

"I'm not discussing this." I grabbed her hand again. "You're going home. End of. You're staying in your apartment if I have to park in front of it to make sure you don't leave."

We resumed walking.

"You're a lunatic." She tried to pull away, but my grip was firm. I unlocked my car and stuffed her into the vehicle.

"I came with a friend," she yelled when I slammed the door on her.

I slid into the driver's seat. "Text her."

"How do you know it's a her and not a him?"

I didn't answer her. We were going to devolve into a sniping war and it wasn't gonna make sense in the end.

The center of my chest heaved like I was going to have the motherfucking end all of heartburns, or quite possibly, I was on the brink of a coronary. The Taurus screeched out of the parking space, narrowly missing another car that had the unfortunate timing of backing into my lane on this narrow street.

I rode my horn and skidded around it.

"I hope no one recognized me as one of your passengers," Bianca muttered. "I don't want to be an outcast."

Welcome to my world, baby.

"Are you going to say something?" she demanded.

I continued to stew. But I was also trying to avoid making sense of how she looked so fuckable. I wanted to be the one with my hand up her skirt. Was she wearing panties? Fuck.

"Sandro, watch out!"

The light had turned red at the intersection.

I hit the brakes. Goddammit! My arm shot out as the momentum threw us forward. A silver Ferrari narrowly missed the front of the Taurus.

"Are you trying to fucking kill us?" Bianca shouted.

"Sorry," I muttered. I put the car in reverse and patiently waited at the stoplight. I glanced at her. "You okay?"

Her lips trembled. She crossed her arms, hugging her biceps.

"Fuck, I'm sorry, Sunlight."

"Just drive," she whispered.

When the light turned green, I focused on getting us back to her apartment without wrecking the Taurus. That was unacceptable with Bianca in the car with me. I could be reckless with my life, never with hers. *Absolutely* never with hers.

Twenty minutes later, we arrived in an upscale apartment building with top-notch security. I knew this because I'd checked it out before she moved in. I shouldn't have worried because I was sure Cesar wouldn't have slacked in Bianca's living arrangements, but I couldn't help following up with my inspection.

"I'll walk you to the door," I said.

I unbuckled my seat belt, and she did the same with hers. But when I opened my door, she hadn't budged.

"Bianca?"

"Are we not talking about this?"

"We're not ready. You're tipsy."

"Oh, believe me, all tipsiness disappeared when I saw my life flash in front of me," she retorted. "What the hell, Sandro?"

She had to remind me again of that scene in the frat house. And I was pissed at myself all over again at my reaction. Her proximity wasn't helping either. Neither was the darkness in the vehicle.

"You can't just pull me away from my friends."

"Friends?" I sneered, getting worked up. "Do you remember his name?"

She hesitated two seconds too long. "Joey."

I made a derisive sound.

"You have no say in who I kiss, much less who I have sex with. I get you think I'm still a child. You'll always see me as a child, but I'm a grown woman."

"You have no idea," I growled under my breath.

"No idea of what?"

"Never mind," I said. "Get out."

I wasn't expecting what happened next. And in retrospect, I could have put an end to it quickly.

Bianca climbed over to my side and sat on my lap, right over my growing boner.

She gasped. "You're hard."

"Get. Off," I snarled, gripping her shoulders, but I didn't find it within myself to move her. She felt too good. I could feel the heat of her pussy. Hell, I bet her panties were soaked. I wondered if it was for me. My fingers tightened. I was jealous. Jealous of whatever fucker made her wet.

We stared at each other for a second, maybe two, and then she pressed her lips to mine. I didn't react, but when she pushed her tongue between my mouth, it was game over. Soft lips seduced me and turned my brain to mush. Lust overpowered logic and razed all restraint to ashes.

I grabbed the back of her head, angled mine and kissed her deeper. She tasted of strawberries and I had the murderous compulsion to erase that boy's kisses. Bianca whimpered in response and ground down on my cock, making me harder. She continued to rock and I continued to kiss her. One of my hands traveled down her body with the intent to drive my fingers into her soaking cunt. But the flash of headlights from an oncoming vehicle snapped me back to my senses.

Of where we were.

Of what we were doing.

I tore away from the kiss, hoisted her off my lap, and deposited her back into her seat. She'd landed in a tangle of limbs while I shoved out of the vehicle, dragged in air, and pressed my heated body against the car, waiting for the blood to return to my head.

"Get out." I shut the driver's door, giving her a few moments to untangle herself. I didn't need to ask her again. Her door opened and she got out.

She didn't look at me. She ran toward her apartment building. I didn't call out her name. I didn't follow her.

Bianca and I had crossed a line tonight, and we could never go back to what we once were.

Because I wanted nothing more than to fuck Bianca De Lucci and the guilt of it made me sick to my stomach.

When she was safely in her building, I brought up our text thread.

I can't make lunch tomorrow. I'm heading back to Manhattan tonight.

BIANCA

Figures.

I fucked up. I'm sorry, baby.

She didn't respond.

I drove back to my hotel, cleared out my things, and returned to New York. When I arrived, I took a long hot shower as if I could scald my skin and sins enough to absolve me of what I'd done. Not for killing a man, but for wanting to fuck the girl who'd always been like a sister to me.

Bianca was right: I had a fucked-up sense of morality. I should stay away from her.

I got drunk for three days straight. Thankfully, with Bianca in Cambridge, there weren't many chances of us seeing each other. She started spending her summers abroad with her parents.

Calls and texting between us stopped.

That was when I resorted to stalking.

CHAPTER Sixteen

BIANCA

It had been two days since the Rossis brought home a bloodied Al Scavo. Two days since the Blind Don checked up on us to make sure we were upholding our end of the bargain consummating the marriage—which was creepy as hell. Two days before I finally had a decent night of sleep in Sandro's bed. And the reason I slept peacefully was because my husband didn't come home last night.

The glaring light of the morning jolted me awake. My arm shot across the bed to Sandro's unslept side and I sat up quickly in a slight panic. Did something happen? Sticks would have awakened me, right?

I jumped out of bed, threw water on my face, and gargled mouthwash. I didn't even bother with my hair. There was a chill in the air, but it might have been the goose bumps of alarm climbing up my spine. I was in flannel pajamas and the print made it difficult to discern my nipples, but I threw on a thick terry robe, anyway. I exited Sandro's room and made my way to the stairs.

The smell of coffee hit my nose first, and I listened briefly for voices. When I heard none, I slowly descended the steps. This whole scenario reminded me of my first morning here.

An arrangement of sunflowers in a rectangular vase sat on a console table in the big foyer. Their merry faces chased away a quarter of the anxiety inside me. Gaze transfixed, I cleared the bottom steps and walked toward them. A bubble of joy suffused my chest.

"Do you like them?"

I spun around to see Sandro leaning against the wall, arms crossed. As usual, he was in black. Exhaustion lined his features, but his eyes were as penetrating as ever. It looked like he hadn't slept.

"Did you just get in?" I asked.

He gave a brief nod, eyes unwavering. "Did you sleep well?"

I bit my lower lip, walking toward him. "I did. What time is it?"

"Eight."

I slept ten hours straight. "Looks like you need sleep yourself."

"I have to head out again, but I just wanted to check up on you."

"Sandro, you need sleep," I insisted.

"I'll be fine, baby." His voice was soft and warm. It made my stomach do acrobatic flips. I couldn't hold his eyes and walked into the kitchen. That was when the aroma of freshly baked bread hit my nose.

Beside another vase of sunflowers on the counter sat a bag with the label of Jabbin' Java.

"Ohhh…" Tears stung my eyes, and like the sunflowers, it became my sole focus.

"It wasn't Renz who made them, for obvious reasons," he said.

I peered into the depths of the brown bag and picked up a croissant and inhaled its familiar buttery notes. I pulled one apart. My mouth watered as the flaky layers revealed themselves. "These look so fresh…When…?"

"They open at six thirty. I had Sloane pick up a selection while I waited in Harlem."

"Sandro…?" What was he playing at?

"Come on, let's have breakfast."

"I thought you needed to leave."

"Are you saying you don't want my company?"

Not waiting for me to respond, he put his hands on my shoulders and guided me to the breakfast table by the window. I was still under the influence of sleep inertia, or maybe I was mesmerized by this little touch of home, of my husband, who was clearly sleep-deprived, yet felt the compulsion to cater to my needs.

He set a mug of coffee in front of me. "This is the Jabbin' Java house blend. I made sure Sloane included a couple of pounds of beans too."

Sandro brought the paper bag to the table, along with two plates. I sipped the coffee and closed my eyes. The familiar brew brought me comfort. Then I opened my eyes to see Sandro watching me with a hint of satisfaction on his face.

He nodded to the paper bag. "Eat."

I picked through the bag and put the croissant I had split on my plate and put a whole one on his.

"I really appreciate this." I took a bite of mine and resisted the moan that wanted to escape my mouth. "You really didn't have to do all this. I mean, you could have come home earlier and slept instead of waiting for Jabbin' Java to open."

"I came home at three this morning," he admitted. "When I entered the bedroom, you were dead to the world. I didn't wanna risk interrupting your sleep." He gave a derisive chuckle. "It had been a hellish past two nights for both of us."

"Sleeping together used to be easier."

A warm glint entered his eyes. "Whenever you played hooky from school?"

"That wasn't hooky. I was feeling unwell."

He cast me a dubious look, letting me know I was full of shit. I'd totally been playing hooky.

"Tommy called me an enabler." A small laugh gusted past his mouth.

Sandro never cared for school. He didn't go to college, and he didn't finish high school senior year because it was around that time he found out Wilma wasn't his mother. He had "bad-boy rebelling against authority" down pat and it only fueled my obsession with him.

I didn't get a phone until I turned fourteen, so texting each other didn't start until then. Sandro usually slept during the day and I feigned illnesses to get out of school early to hang out with him. I had a suspicion he'd bribed the school nurse. He usually picked me up on a street corner to take me back to his apartment. Sometimes Tommy would be there with his then girlfriend and we'd watch a movie, sometimes, it was just Sandro and me.

In my mind, I pretended to be Sandro's girlfriend. Sigh, even when he was with me, there were times he was on the phone with some girl. When girls my age had delusions of their teen idols or rock stars, mine had always been Sandro. But despite my obsession with him, I never made a move to kiss him. I knew I was too young. Sandro wouldn't cross that line. And I wouldn't risk making a move of my own until I was of legal age because I didn't want to risk ruining our friendship before there was a real chance between us.

See? Delusional. But I told myself I was playing the long game.

My escapades lasted for an entire school year. Not that I cut classes all the time, maybe once a month, and not even for an entire day. Except that one time when Sandro and I had planned to watch a special edition trilogy. I skipped classes at noon. I had just set a bowl of popcorn on the coffee table when the buzzer to his apartment went off and we thought it was the pizza we ordered.

It was, but beside the pizza delivery guy, was Dad. When he saw me standing behind Sandro, wearing my school uniform, I wanted to sink into the floor.

I'd never seen Dad so angry.

He didn't say anything; he just punched Sandro across the face. Then all hell broke loose.

"You're remembering that day?" Sandro broke through my thoughts.

I nodded, my cheeks heating as if experiencing the humiliation all over again. "I was so embarrassed."

"If Cesar hadn't known the man I am, he would have killed me."

"I think Dad was pissed because you were a bad influence regarding school, not that he thought you were a sexual predator."

Sandro nodded briefly, thoughtfully. He took a bite of the croissant, chewed, and chased it with coffee. "It was more than that. He said our friendship was getting inappropriate. He convinced me about it then."

Prior to that scene, Mom had found out I was skipping classes. Either a nurse had come clean or Renz ratted me out. She had warned me it had to stop, but she kept it from Dad until he found out. He and Mom had a big fight that lasted for days. Again, my suspicion was Renz, because Nico and Matteo were away at college. Dad confiscated my phone and grounded me for the summer. I was so mad at everyone; I told them I wanted to die.

Yes, I was that dramatic.

"The next time I saw you was on my fifteenth birthday, but you disappeared to Russia afterward."

"You thought your old man finally got rid of me."

"Yes. I hounded Dad and made him swear on his life that he had nothing to do with it."

"Poor Cesar." He reached across the table and laced our fingers. "Now he might be planning my funeral for real."

"Don't say that." I let out an exhale that reached the bottom of my feet. "Despite what happened these past few days, I still want to believe we're going to get out of this unscathed."

"We will," he said. "I told you, baby, I want our marriage to work. I'm not letting you go."

This whole scenario was making much more sense. "So this whole croissant-and-sunflower thing…"

"You might not see your family for a while, but the least I can do is ease the wait for you. Give you a reminder that there's something good waiting at the end of this."

"Are you going to be a part of what's waiting for me at the end?"

This time he clasped my other hand, holding them in his, and despite the tiredness around his eyes, the fierceness in them glittered. "Yes," he said succinctly. "I meant what I said, Bianca. I love coming home to you."

"Flowers. Food." I gave an impish grin. "Sounds a lot like courtship."

At first, I didn't understand the frown that appeared between his brows, but then he let go of my hands and reached inside his pocket to slide out his phone.

I tried not to let his work deflate me. "Family business?"

"Yeah." He put down the phone and grabbed my hands again, bringing them to his mouth to kiss my knuckles. "It's going to be a busy next few days."

“I’ll be right here.”

He stood. I could see his entire body hesitate. Sandro really didn’t want to leave me, but he had his job, and I had mine.

I got out of my seat and hugged him. “Please take care.”

He didn’t utter a word. But the kiss on the top of my head and the extra tight squeeze he gave me communicated everything.

CHAPTER Seventeen

Bianca

Another five days went by and Sandro and I had fallen into a routine. I continued to sleep in his bedroom and finally got used to sleeping beside him. Sometimes, I would even roll into him, and he'd let me. I usually woke up before he did at six, so I could give him extra time to sleep. If I were honest with myself, it was because I was too conscious of his morning wood. Many times, I found myself with my leg thrown over him and he would be stiff as a board. I knew he couldn't sleep. And he'd already been coming home early in the morning. Sandro needed his rest so he could be clear-headed as boss.

He didn't wait for Jabbin' Java to open anymore, not if he wanted to catch a few hours of sleep and sit down to have breakfast with me, but food from my brother's café seemed to magically appear every morning. These little gestures were melting the last residual anger I felt for Sandro. I was still pissed at the situation, at Raffa's edict. But I recognized the effort he was making to keep the balance. Besides, it almost felt like a courtship. Aside from the food, my full set of skin care products appeared in the bathroom one morning, including a basket of luxurious bath bombs and my favorite scented candles. I remembered Divina and me talking about the brand I used a few days ago.

Sandro and I didn't have enough time for any meaningful conversations about the future, but we spent our few stolen moments reminiscing about the past. Unearthing our bond helped ease my acceptance of the situation and reminded me of who Sandro was to me. Our marriage was real to him but questions remained. I wasn't sure how it was going to work. Would he stay as boss? Did he expect me to go on the run with him when he faked his death?

That evening, Miller arrived with a whole feast of fish and chips from Eamonn's, my family's Irish pub. After dinner with the guys, I retired to the theater to watch a series. There was no internet. No connection to the outside world. I tried my best to ignore the fact that I was still a prisoner in this house.

By this time, there were seven sunflower arrangements scattered in different rooms and they provided much needed shots of joy to lift my spirits.

Something woke me. I had fallen asleep across the love seat in the theater room. The projector was off. I didn't even recall what I was watching.

There it was again. Voices.

My heart jackknifed in my chest. Friend or foe? Then I heard Sandro's low baritone and my nerves calmed down.

I stuffed my feet in fluffy slippers and made my way to the front of the house, relieved that there was no blood on the floor. I wondered if I'd developed some sort of PTSD. It was quite an introduction to the Rossi crime family on my second night here.

The voices were Sticks, Sandro, and Tommy.

It was three a.m.

"Why are you still awake?" Sandro walked to me and gave me a brief kiss.

"I hoped to wait up for you. I fell asleep in the theater." The acrid smell of smoke was all over him. He was wearing black as usual, but there were smudges above his stubble line.

"Why do you smell like a chimney?"

"Go to sleep, baby." He gave me a nudge toward the stairs.

"No," I said firmly. "What happened?"

Sticks and Tommy looked at each other. Sandro continued staring at me. Almost pleading with me to let it go.

"What. Happened?" I blew out a breath. "What burned down?"

Why even mince words?

"There was a fire at the club."

Blood drained from my face. I swayed and clutched Sandro's arm. "How bad?"

"Not bad."

"It's going to be closed for months," Tommy informed me in a way that didn't hide that he was shooting the blame my way.

"Tommy…" Sandro growled.

"What? She needs to know. First Gian's poker game and now this." I heard from Divina the cops raided their poker game yesterday. Gian was pissed. One of his soldiers was in jail, and it looked like the racketeering charges were going to stick.

"You think my family did this?" I challenged.

"Who else?" Tommy replied.

I looked at Sandro. "Do you believe it?"

"What I believe doesn't matter. The De Luccis are within their right to retaliate," Sandro said.

"Exactly. But they wouldn't do this. Blatant destruction of property…" I paused. "Was anyone hurt?"

"A couple of guards," Sticks said.

"I'm sorry." At least Sticks didn't look as condemning as Tommy.

The front door opened. Gian and Griselda walked in with Raffa.

I was immediately on guard with the wave of hostility entering the house.

"Oh good, she's awake," Griselda sneered.

A threatening sound rumbled in Sandro's chest as he pulled me close.

"Look what your family did!" Her eyes flashed viciously.

"Enough, Griselda!" Sandro snapped.

"Enough? Enough?" she shrieked. "It was our sweat and blood that built that club. And now, because of your stupidity over this girl, everything is up in flames."

"Sandro's the stupid one?" I shot back. "Why don't you ask Raffa here how his ridiculous conditions keep me from my family? Was that your intent, huh?" I shot Raffa a glare when he couldn't see me. I ignored Sandro's warning squeeze on my shoulders. "You were setting us up to fail. But regardless, you know what? My family wouldn't do this. This isn't their MO."

Gian advanced on me, but Sandro must have had enough. He didn't even warn his cousin. He simply shoved him.

"Don't even breathe her air," Sandro warned.

Tommy grappled with Gian to hold him back.

"My wife…" Sandro stressed those words. "Is right. The De Luccis won't try anything destructive while they're not sure of Bianca's situation."

"Surely you're not suggesting we just tuck our tail between our legs," Gian sneered. He looked at the Blind Don. "Raffa, do you see now who you backed as boss? He's pussy-whipped. He's more concerned with his wife's feelings than the Rossis' interests and will never put us first."

"I am putting the Rossis first," Sandro spat. "Do you really want this to become a bloody street war with the De Luccis? Tit for tat. When will this end?"

Raffa, who'd been quiet through all this exchange, finally said, "Are you absolutely certain that the De Luccis aren't behind the club fire?"

Sandro was silent.

"They aren't," I answered.

"I wasn't asking you, little girl," the old man said. A smirk curved his mouth. "Do your job, Sandro. Figure out this shit. In the meantime, try to curb your wife's tongue. She should know her place in the family and give us that Rossi heir."

As they turned to leave, Sandro went for his gun. I grabbed his arm.

Griselda saw what was about to happen and gasped. That was when Gian started to turn, but I'd already stepped in front of Sandro.

Gian smirked. "Oh, look at that, your little wife trying to protect you."

"Come on, Gian." Griselda grabbed his arm. "Let's take Uncle home."

As the three left, we heard Raffa mumbling about being too old for this shit.

Tommy slammed the door before turning back to Sandro. "What the fuck, man?"

Sandro gave me a flat stare. "Go to bed, Bianca." He turned to Tommy. "Office."

Sticks and I were left in the foyer.

"You don't believe my family would burn down the club, right?" I asked.

Sticks sighed. "Not a hundred percent, no. And Sandro feels the same. But like he said, it would be a fair retaliation."

"This is so fucked up. We need to do something. Get word—"

"Oh, hell no." Sticks gave an incredulous laugh. "Don't turn those big doe eyes on me. I like my head where it is."

"But if we don't—"

He yanked open the door. "I'm heading back to the bunkhouse. I need some sleep. I suggest you do the same."

Sandro

When we entered the study, I headed straight for the scotch. I took two glasses. Poured one for Tommy and another one for me. Then I threw myself behind the desk. Tommy stood in front of me, tossing back his scotch. He grabbed the bottle in front of me and poured himself another one.

"Easy on that."

"Easy on—" he sputtered. "Tell that to yourself, Sandro. What the fuck was that out there? Were you really going to shoot Uncle Raffa?"

"I'd probably nick his ear." Though putting a bullet through his head would take care of most of our problems.

"Look, I get that you're protective of Bianca, but do you think shooting an old man, a blind one at that, is going to endear you to her? You're only putting a target on her back, showing everyone how little it'd take to push you over the edge."

"What's the matter, Tommy? Afraid you would have to step up as boss sooner?"

"Fuck you, Sandro. Is that what you're doing? Forcing Raffa's hand to replace you as boss? It wouldn't be me at this point, you know. It'd be Gian."

"I don't think you deserve the position as much as Gian," I replied.

"What? Because I think the De Luccis set fire to the club? It's a logical explanation."

"You're letting your emotions rule your judgment."

"And you're not?"

"Mine will not start a bloody war. And as much as the thought of killing a blind old man sounds unsavory, let's not forget this is the same man who has slaughtered men and their families. Who doesn't care about collateral damage. His blindness came at that price, but it still doesn't absolve him of the many innocent lives he's taken."

"And you, Sandro?"

"I have a code. I only take jobs to kill men with criminally black hearts." Or rapists.

"So how are we going to launder the money coming in without a club?" Tommy instantly changed the subject because we'd had this discussion before. My assassin's code. It helped that my first kill was a big one. I'd been able to dictate my limits. No women or children, even as collateral damage. All because I wanted to look Bianca in the eye and not flinch.

Losing the club would make it a challenge to achieve our six-month plan to position him as boss. But I was wavering about what to do next because I was determined to keep Bianca.

A significant part of me still maintained this: The De Luccis wouldn't risk Bianca with a big move like this. That they trusted me enough to keep her safe even when I cut off all communication. But

I couldn't be everywhere while I ran the family, and that was why I had Sticks on this property. Someone who was loyal only to me and who couldn't be corrupted by money and influenced by mafia politics.

"This is a mere setback. We should get rid of our toxic assets first and rebuild from there." I leaned back in my chair. "Now, where are we with the cocaine?"

Tommy's mouth flattened, and he regarded me as if he wanted to talk about the fire some more, but thought better of it. His shoulders sagged in resignation. "The Toronto Albanians contacted me. They're willing to take it off our hands for what we paid."

I tried not to smile. Luca came through, after all. According to Luca, the relationship between the Toronto Albanians and their New York counterpart was on shaky ground and it was the perfect opportunity for a power play. New York didn't want our cocaine? Then fuck them.

It was four thirty when I snuck into the bathroom of our bedroom. I'd been sitting in soot and the smell of smoke for half the night; washing all the grit away lifted some of the weight off my shoulders. I decided to just wear shorts when I slipped into bed with Bianca.

She immediately rolled into my arms. "All done?"

"Yeah."

"You smell good." She rubbed her nose against my chest.

"You should have joined me in the shower." So much for sleep, I was getting hard. I purposely stayed out late to reduce our time in bed. And I refused to sleep elsewhere. Taking care of Rossi business was a perfect excuse. But each night, she seemed to trust me more and started rolling into me when I slipped in beside her. I had brushed her full tits, gripped her tiny waist, and had my hands all over her generous hips and ass. Fuck. Forget getting hard. I was fully erect.

She gave a small laugh. "We haven't even had sex yet."

"Oh, is that the order of things?"

"Hmmm."

"Why aren't you asleep?"

"I'm sorry about the club."

"I don't want you thinking it's your fault."

She didn't answer for a while and I thought she had fallen asleep. Then her fingers drew circles over my chest. "I don't want you to go shooting people simply because they insulted me or looked at me wrong."

"I wasn't going to shoot Raffa," I admitted.

"Then—"

"I was going to give him a warning. You probably shouldn't have challenged him earlier."

Her fingers stopped circling. "I'm sorry."

She was silent for a few beats before saying, "What is this about producing a Rossi heir?"

I stiffened. At the beginning of all this, the thought of consummating the marriage was not even part of my plan. That changed rapidly the second I made Bianca my wife, and I wanted a taste. But I was also a coward, because I knew once I had a taste, I would never let her go. Boy, was I wrong. I didn't even have a taste, and I decided to keep her. I was jealous as fuck of Miller, and I wanted to rip off the head of any man who even looked at her with lust or stars in their eyes. It reminded me of the time after I watched Bianca in that fashion show. I returned to Club Aristos and destroyed my office.

But I would never, ever become my father. I would never force myself on a woman. I would never force a woman to have my child. Bianca only knew that my father had an affair with my biological mother and she died during childbirth. Raffa and Wilma were the only ones alive who knew the whole sordid truth of how I came into existence.

A product of an atrocity.

Raffa wanted to prove I was my father's son.

"Sandro?" Bianca's voice was tentative. "What's wrong?"

I blinked back my dark thoughts. I couldn't bring myself to tell her about that part of my life yet. She would recoil. Be disgusted. "The reason Raffa wanted me to keep you from your family for three weeks was because he thought I could get you pregnant by then."

"What?" She pushed up on an elbow. "Why didn't you tell me this?"

I raised a brow. "Are you going to have sex with me to fulfill that request?"

"No, because that's a crazy request."

"Exactly."

She got off the bed and stood in front of it, glaring at me. "Then why did you agree to it?"

"That's the only way to get Raffa to agree to me becoming boss. I was going to worry about it later. Also…" I swallowed the tacks in my throat. "I would get to keep you longer."

She just stared at me. But her features went through several emotions. Surprisingly, none of them were anger. She pursed her mouth and her eyes gleamed with tears.

"Sunlight…" I whispered.

"Damn you, Sandro," she exhaled raggedly. "Why can't I stay mad at you?"

"That's a good thing, right?" I patted the space beside me. "Come to bed, baby."

Even taking sex out of the equation, I enjoyed behaving like a married couple.

She sniffled, and walked around the bed and got in beside me. "You should have told me sooner."

I dragged her into my arms. Fuck, she felt so good. *She* made me feel good. Whenever I was in Bianca's presence, I didn't feel filthy or disgusted with who I was.

"What if I'm ready?" she ventured.

This time, I was the one who untangled myself from her. I sat at the edge of the mattress and couldn't help the derisive laugh that escaped my lips. "Don't say that. You're not."

"How do you know?"

I stared her in the eye and pointed between us. "I need you to be okay with this. Are you?"

"In what way? We're married."

"Do you feel married to me?"

She had to go chew on her bottom lip. *Jesus Christ.*

"It's a weird state," she answered.

"Because you were forced into this."

"So were you."

"That's what you think. I simply found an opportunity and did not feel guilty about it."

"Because you saved me from Gian?"

"Yes, but I also got what I wanted. But did you get what you want, Bianca?"

"I'm not a white-picket-fence kind of girl."

I stood up. "No, you're not. But are you finally okay being married to a made man?"

She averted her eyes.

"That's what I thought. Until you're okay being married to every aspect of who I am, then, no, I'm not gonna fuck you."

I leaned over and brushed the back of my fingers along her face. "There's too much beauty in our history. Despite the times when we're mad at each other, I don't what to ruin it. But make no mistake, I already consider you mine. I'm not letting you go ever."

Her eyes met mine in surprise.

"I'm going to earn that right to fuck you…and be your husband in every way." I walked back into the bathroom and shut the door, locking it because my self-control was fraying and it wouldn't take much from Bianca to make it snap.

Time for a cold shower.

CHAPTER Eighteen

BIANCA

Two days passed after the club fire. Everyone was on edge. I saw Sandro for a few hours yesterday and he hadn't come home overnight. I hadn't seen Divina since then either. If Tommy turned on Sandro, Divina would, too. If that happened, Gian would become boss.

There was nothing else for me to do. I could only organize the kitchen so much. We had enough groceries. The house was clean. I didn't feel like walking the property. I could feel Sandro's men were split about blaming me for the club fire. At least Sticks kept them in check, and Miller still smiled at me.

It was midmorning, and I was moping over coffee. What freaking timing. Everyone was turning against him just when I was coming around to being married to him. And if staying married to him meant he had to remain boss, then I wanted him to succeed. He didn't spell it out to me, but it was the only way.

The pressure would be off Tommy. That would make Divina happy, but would Tommy be fine with it?

The sound of car doors slamming reached my ears. It was faint, but I also heard voices. Sandro? My heart raced and I rushed to the foyer. It rattled against my rib cage when Raffa and Griselda walked in.

Again?

The same men in suits who were with him the other evening flanked Raffa's sides. An older gentleman in spectacles, wearing a button-down shirt and khakis, was with them. The fact that he looked nervous fueled my swelling anxiety. I recognized him as the mob doctor who tended to Renz.

But what worried me was the absence of Sticks and Miller.

With difficulty, I pushed the words out of my mouth. "Is Sandro okay?" Was he hurt and they were bringing him here to be treated? My secondary concern was if they were coming to pick me up because *he* was dead. *Please, oh please, let Sandro be all right.*

"Sandro is fine," Raffa said.

I glared at Griselda. "You can't be here without my invitation, remember?"

Her malicious smile made my throat tighten. "Where's Sticks?"

One of Raffa's guards grinned, revealing a gold tooth. He also had a scar across his right eye. "He's takin' a nap."

"What did you do to him?" I shrieked. Fear compounded with anger propelled me forward. "What is this all about?"

"I think I'm getting the wrong end of the bargain. Sandro's not close to fulfilling the requirements of your marriage."

"Is this about consummating the marriage again?" I snapped, but I was glaring at Griselda because, for whatever reason, she appointed herself as my tormentor. She was the instigator who started this whole drama. "Well, I'm sorry to inform you I'm not a virgin and we don't have a bloody sheet to prove it to you!"

Raffa sneered. "Such a shame, really. I didn't think about that when I agreed to Sandro's terms."

"He's trying hard to help this family survive. And if you're going to blame him for the club fire, then blame Gian for starting this clusterfuck."

"You were the one who gatecrashed the Rossi gathering," Griselda snapped.

I glared at the gold-toothed soldier who prevented me from shoving Griselda out the door. "Get out of my way. I don't know what you did—"

I never finished my sentence. Gold Tooth and another soldier grabbed hold of my arms and started hauling me farther into the house.

"Are you nuts?" I struggled, stumbled, and slammed into the console table. The vase of sunflowers crashed onto the marble floor. This time, their merry faces did nothing to quell the insidious dread inside me.

And as my feet dragged across the floor, I watched Griselda crush their beautiful blooms under her heels.

"Get your hands off me!" I screamed again. The desire to claw at Griselda's smug face warred with my worry about Sandro and his men.

Gold Tooth stopped and whispered in my ear, "It gives me great pleasure to have my hands on you. I want to do more, just like what your husband did to my eye."

"I don't know what the hell is going on?!" I punctuated my yelling with profanities. I fought them even when my arms felt like they were getting yanked out of their sockets. "Sandro won't stand for this!"

They wrestled me into the study where Gold Tooth shoved me into a chair, took out his gun, and pointed it at me.

"What's going on, Raffa?" I hated how my voice sounded thin and thready.

"You think I don't know that Sandro was going to shoot me the other day?"

I narrowed my eyes at Griselda. I fucking hated her. She didn't say a word, but the gloating on her face told me everything. I had to do damage control.

"Listen to me, Raffa. Whatever Griselda saw, it wasn't Sandro's intent. He admitted this to me after I questioned him about why he drew his gun. You know him better than this. Otherwise, the Rossis wouldn't trust him with important jobs."

"And has he told you of these important jobs?"

"No. But he has a reputation," I retorted, trying to regain bravado. "So, what's this visit about? Are you all afraid to ask Sandro about his intentions that night?"

"This here is our mob doctor." Raffa made a vague wave and the man in spectacles stepped forward. In his hand was a briefcase.

Confused, but with a sense of growing terror, I said, "I'm not sick."

"No, you're not, but he's going to check if you've had sexual intercourse in the past few days."

"What? And how? Sandro and I used a condom."

Then I realized my mistake when a cruel smile slashed across Raffa's face. "Then Sandro is in violation of our agreement because the agreement is to make you pregnant. To breed an heir and join our families. And if there's no effort toward that goal, then your marriage will be annulled. You will marry Gian and you can forget when you'll see your family."

"It may take more than three weeks to get pregnant!" I was on the pill and obviously I hadn't taken it since captivity.

"But it's not helping if you use a condom, right?" Griselda put in, while checking her nails. While pretending that what they were doing was not beyond unhinged. She turned to Raffa. "I told you Sandro won't touch her. He thinks of her like a sister. And that's why he's protective of her."

"Sandro wasn't honest about our deal, was he?" Raffa asked.

"The three weeks? He was. Including the agreement to make me pregnant."

"Three weeks was what he told you, but I can extend it depending on my satisfaction at seeing your father suffer."

"You sick son of a bitch."

He leaned in the direction of the mob doc who seemed uncomfortable with the situation. "Maybe you should wash her mouth after this."

"You know who my father is?" I yelled at the doc. "You touch me against my will, not only will you lose your license, but he will destroy you."

"Don't listen to her," Gold Tooth said, pointing the gun at the doc. "Get it done."

"You guys are beyond barbaric!" I was still yelling and trying to get out of the chair, but more men were holding me down. There were three of them now. "I already told you we used a condom."

"I'll give you a taste of what to expect until you give me proof Sandro is breeding you," Raffa said.

"You're insane!" I screamed, and I continued screaming like a wild animal in the fight of its life.

"Remove her pants," Gold Tooth told one of his soldiers, then leered at me. "Maybe I can have a taste, eh?"

Angry tears finally spilled down my cheeks. This was a nightmare. I flashed backed to when I lost my virginity to Warren. It was nothing compared to this. That time I wanted to lose it and backtracked, but this time I was being touched without consent. Bile rose in my throat.

Hands grabbed at my sweatpants.

"Noooo!" I kicked Gold Tooth and almost got him in the groin. Angered, he drew back to pistol-whip me.

Until half of his head exploded.

~

Sandro

I moved through a mist of red and systematically dispatched the three soldiers holding my men at gunpoint. Sticks was lying on the ground, but he was slowly regaining consciousness. Raffa's men should have kept a checkpoint at the entrance of the driveway.

They watched our Expedition approach complacently because I had Gian drive with Arnie beside him.

Arnie got out first to obscure my movements. I exited the SUV, gripping two silenced nine-millimeters with a semi-auto shotgun slung across my chest. I quickly got off three rounds and dispatched those motherfuckers.

I rushed into the house, shooting the guard in the foyer and the one standing right in front of the study. I tried not to read too much into the forbidding omen of the ruined sunflowers. That I wasn't too late.

What greeted me when I stepped into the room turned the red haze into a bloodbath.

I ejected the magazines from my nine-millimeters and shot two soldiers with the chambered rounds. Then I tossed those guns and went for my Benelli M4 shotgun.

The people in the room were only noticing my entrance. The asshole in front of Bianca was about to strike her with his gun, not realizing he had lost his men. That was the advantage of suppressed gunfire.

But I needed this finale to quench my thirst for blood.

The shotgun boomed, and his head exploded like a watermelon.

I stepped into the room, pointing the barrel at the doctor. I spared him. For now.

I spared Raffa and Griselda. For now. Training in military-type kill houses honed my skill to identify and separate immediate threats from civilians.

I had half a mind to shoot Raffa and end his miserable existence, but my wife was in shock.

Blood and brain matter had splattered over Bianca.

"Did he touch you?" I nodded to the doctor.

"I didn't. I didn't," the doctor cried.

Bianca sprung out from the chair and dove into me with a choked sob. With my arm around her, I aimed my gun at the doctor's head. "Did. He. Touch. You?"

"No," she mumbled.

"Get out of here." I motioned to the doctor with my shotgun. He didn't waste time scrambling out of the room.

I turned my gun on Raffa. "All your men are dead."

That was when I noticed Arnie. He stepped forward, "Boss…"

I ignored him, my finger tightening on the trigger. "Tell me why I should let you live."

"Go ahead," Raffa sneered. "You were going to shoot me, anyway."

"I wasn't going to kill you. So you throw a tantrum? Well, that tantrum has cost you all the men you brought with you."

"Sandro!" Griselda gasped. "They are our family!"

"And Bianca," I enunciated, "is my wife. Two of them were here when I gave the warning that no one disrespects her. It's an insult to me. This goes beyond disrespect."

"So, what are you waiting for? Shoot me," Raffa said. "Then you can do whatever you please."

Bianca touched my side. "Don't give Raffa further ammunition to mess with our lives."

"He'll be in his grave."

"And he'll have the last laugh and mock you from his grave." Goddammit. Why did she have to make sense?

"You already took out eight of our soldiers," Arnie tried to be the voice of reason. "You take out the Blind Don too and the Rossis won't come back from this. The commission will get involved and morale will sink further."

"I'm within my rights—"

"As I was within mine!" Raffa shouted. "You threatened me. You coward. You threatened a blind man."

"Then come after me and not my wife!"

"Then you're even, Sandro," Arnie said. "Bianca's not hurt. They didn't touch her."

"She has bruises on her," I roared. Red welts in the form of fingers circled her wrists. Bloodlust was still a riptide inside me. Killing eight men wasn't enough. "She's covered in blood!"

"I'm fine." Bianca's soothing voice washed over me and she tightened her hold around my torso. "Help me get rid of it." She paused. "You all better leave."

Griselda, who wouldn't look at me until then, glared at Bianca. "You ruin everything!" she screamed. "You're like a cat who always lands on her feet!"

"Griselda…" I warned. I was at the root end of my patience. If I were inclined to kill women, she would be at the top of my list.

I heard a growl of fury, before I realized Bianca had shoved away from me.

"You fucking bitch," my wife snarled before launching herself at Griselda.

CHAPTER Nineteen

Bianca

"You've messed with me for the last time!" I raged, tackling Griselda to the floor, straddling her body, and smacked her across the face. She covered her head with her forearms, and I was frustrated I couldn't scratch her eyes out.

Everyone had their breaking point. Griselda had flicked my crazy switch.

"Someone get this bitch off me!" Griselda screamed.

"Not so tough now, huh?" I clawed at her arms. There was no excusing her harmful manipulations. "You let other people do your dirty work. Well, I'm not afraid to do mine." Bits of Gold Tooth's blood and brain rained on her.

Fingers gripped my shoulders to pull me away. "Bianca…"

It sounded like Sticks, but I was still caught up in the maelstrom of my fury. I felt violated when Gold Tooth grabbed my arm and hauled me away. When unwanted fingers tried to undress me, expose me. If Sandro hadn't arrived in time, I would be scarred for life and there would be three more bodies in the study because that would have been Sandro's breaking point. The doc, Raffa, and Griselda would be dead. She should've been thankful she was alive.

"Get your fucking hands off her," Sandro boomed. "This is long overdue."

"Sandro," Griselda cried. "How could you…"

"He could because I'm his wife," I snarled. "And his loyalty is to me." I got off her and yanked her up by her hair. "Get that through your damned head, Griselda!" With a fistful of her hair, I dragged her out of the study the way Raffa's men had dragged me earlier. She tried to fight me, but my fury was greater than her spite and I was livid beyond rational thought.

I stalked across the foyer with her shrieking behind me. Most of Sandro's men stood by as we passed them.

"Help me!" Griselda scraped my arm with her nails to dislodge my grip, but she knew if she fought too hard, she'd end up with a bald spot. We reached the open door and I jerked her through. That was when I released her. I was panting hard. All the heat seemed to have gone to my head. She swiped at her face and stumbled down the steps.

"You're a lunatic," she croaked out. She was sobbing, her face blotchy and mascara smudged around her eyes.

"Bitch," I shot back. "You haven't seen lunatic yet. They don't call me sweet but a psycho for nothing, and you've triggered my psycho."

Arnie hurried Raffa past the threshold, not even stopping to say goodbye. I realized what a fright I looked. Like Carrie on prom night covered with pig's blood. I remembered my words on my wedding day to Griselda. It might have been a prophecy.

Arms hugged me from behind. "You okay?" Sandro's voice rumbled in my ear.

I turned in his arms and gazed up at him. His eyes were fierce and wary at the same time.

"I'm a mess."

"A little blood doesn't bother me." But I had a feeling it wasn't a little blood. He gave me a light shake again. "Are you okay?"

"I'm thinking…" And that was the truth. The carnage and dealing with Griselda were too much to process right now. I held up my hands that were shaking. "Sandro…"

"That's adrenaline, baby," he said.

Oh, that was probably why I felt invincible when I handled Griselda.

Sticks approached us with a wry grin on his face. "Queen," he called me and then turned to Sandro. "I'm sorry they got the jump on me. Miller is watching Gian." He glowered at the body in the foyer. "I wasn't expecting them to go on immediate offensive when they arrived. How did you know?"

"Gian was acting weird and Tommy was not answering my calls. I couldn't get a hold of you guys. What happened?"

"One of our men is working with Raffa. He put in a jammer."

"You know who it is?"

"Miller took care of him."

"Gian told you about Raffa's plans?" I asked.

"He had no choice. I played Russian roulette with his head."

. . .

One hour earlier

Sandro

Tommy wasn't answering his phone. My calls kept going to voicemail.

Meanwhile, Gian was pacing at the rear end of a commercial truck that held our pallet of cocaine. He took a drag of his cigarette. He rarely smoked, and it was usually when shit was so dicey, it was about to hit the fan.

Something was up, and he and Tommy were keeping it from me. Maybe they were colluding to get rid of me.

Two other SUVs loaded with soldiers were parked beside us. We were all waiting for Tommy.

Arnie was leaning against the back of the truck but he was looking at me and then looking at Gian. The older Scavo had always been a soldier. He'd never wanted to be in charge of decisions, saying he liked the street work better. Earlier, I told Arnie to call Tommy just in case it was me he had an issue with. After all, Tommy was still pissed about the club. But he'd been sending Arnie's calls to voicemail, too.

I wasn't gonna drive three hours to Birmingham to meet the Toronto Albanians if my instincts were clawing at me to stay. So I called our contact and cancelled the drop-off, saying things were too hot right now.

Gian's eyes narrowed at me when he heard me change the plans. "Are you insane? Tommy worked so hard to get that meeting."

"Yeah, yet he's not here. So where is he, Gian?"

"I don't know. He must still be in a snit about the club."

I walked to the back of the truck where Arnie was standing. "You have your revolver on you, Arnie? Can I have it?"

Brows furrowing, he didn't question me but tossed me the gun. I checked the weapon. Tipped out the rounds and put one back in and spun the cylinder.

I walked back to Gian. With astonishment etched on his face, he foolishly squared off against me, his eyes darting between the gun in my hand and my face.

When I pressed the muzzle to his forehead, he dropped the cigarette and froze.

"How about you?" I asked softly. "Are you having a snit over something?"

"Boss…" Arnie stepped forward.

"Don't interfere, Arnie."

"What's the meaning of this?" Gian roared, his hands stiff at his sides, but he immediately shut his mouth when I cocked the gun.

"Are we heading into a trap?"

"This shit again."

I pulled the trigger.

Click.

Gian ducked and screamed.

"Oops," I said.

When he realized he was still alive, he yelled, "Are you crazy? Raffa will hear of this!"

"Wrong chamber," I told him. I pushed the cylinder out and dropped the cartridge in my palm to show Gian it was loaded. His eyes widened in disbelief. I chambered the round and spun the cylinder again. I pointed the gun at him.

"I repeat. Are we walking into a trap?"

He hesitated one second too long. I pulled the trigger again, and he jumped.

Empty.

"Boss," Arnie called my attention again. "Maybe we could do this another way."

"Yes. Yes. Listen to Arnie. Goddammit. You're insane!"

"I wouldn't be who I am if I wasn't." I spun the cylinder again. There was a trick to Russian roulette, but it was still a game of deadly chance. Gian was too flustered to spot the rim of the round, but I could. I'd played this game too many times. But this turn of the cylinder, Gian was out of luck and I still wanted my answers.

I pressed the muzzle to his forehead. "So, what has you on edge?"

Gian was trying not to cry. He flattened his mouth to keep his lips together. Not so tough now, eh, motherfucker? My fingers tightened on the trigger.

"It's Raffa," he rushed out. "He found out you drew your gun to shoot him."

"I wasn't gonna shoot him," I said, keeping my voice and hand steady, but a chill raced down my spine. "Who told him? Griselda?"

"Raffa and I walked in on Griselda and Tommy arguing about it."

Fuck!

"Is that why Tommy's not here?"

"I don't know. He probably doesn't know how to face you…"

I spun away from him and returned the revolver and bullets to Arnie. "Watch him." All other thoughts deserted me except for the need to get to Bianca. Raffa was a vindictive son of a bitch and God only knew how he would retaliate. As I headed to the rear of my SUV, I called Sticks. His phone had a strange message about being out of range before going to voicemail. It was the same for all the guys at the bunkhouse.

Fuck! *Fuck!*

I lifted the back gate of the SUV and the lid of the trunk

covering my arsenal. I armed up with two nine-millimeters and a shotgun, screwing suppressors on the pistols because I liked my silent kills.

"What are you doing?" Gian shouted. Arnie was still pointing a gun at him.

"What do you think?"

"You think I'm going to let you get away with putting a gun to my head?"

I deleted the space between us, my voice low and lethal. "If Bianca's harmed and I find out I could have prevented it if you'd come clean sooner, I'm gonna make you wish you were in hell. Now…" I tossed him the keys. "You're driving." I turned to Arnie. "Sit beside him." I gave instructions to the rest of the crew before I slid in behind Gian. "I don't like shooting men in the back, but I'll make you an exception. One wrong move and you'll be shitting in a bag for the rest of your life. Are we clear?"

CHAPTER *Twenty*

Sandro

I studied Bianca carefully as I recounted the events that led up to her being covered in blood.

Her adrenaline withdrawal was brutal. Her hand tremors had progressed to full-body shudders. I needed to get the blood and brains off her.

"What will you do with Gian?" she asked unexpectedly. The fire in her eyes that sparked when she went after Griselda morphed into blank slates.

My jaw hardened. "If he knows what's best for him, he'll stay away until I'm ready to deal with him."

She gave a series of nods and transfixed her attention on the body in the foyer as if seeing it for the first time. Then she untangled herself from me. I fought against yanking her back. She was processing the massacre. Witnessing the brutal killer that was her husband.

"Baby, let's get you cleaned up."

It was as if she didn't hear me. She wandered to where the broken sunflowers lay on the floor and knelt beside them. Her fingers feathered the mangled petals.

Then she rose and stared at the mirror above the console and gasped.

That's it.

I stalked to where she was, swept her into my arms, and headed up the stairs. She didn't fight me. Seeing her reflection in the mirror had drained her of remaining strength.

"Take care of this mess," I threw behind my shoulder. "I need to see to my wife."

"I can shower myself," Bianca whispered.

"Let me do this for you, baby."

I carried her into the hallway bathroom. No way was she going to remember this day each time she entered my room.

I started the shower and stripped her clothes as fast as possible. I discarded mine in a heap beside hers but kept on my boxer briefs. I put her into the shower and got in behind her. Blood turned the water into a swirl of crimson. Her body was cold. So, so cold.

"Bianca." I cupped her face. Her beautiful brown eyes were flat. I combed my fingers through her hair, thankful she didn't seem aware of the gruesome bits falling off her head. "You're all right, baby. I got you."

"I know you do," she answered, and a weak smile tried to form.

I pressed a brief kiss to her mouth.

When the water ran clear, I grabbed the shampoo and lathered her hair. While I let that soak, I picked up the soap and did the same to her skin.

"I really can do this, Sandro," she protested. "I'm okay."

No, she wasn't. She was in delayed shock. I doubted she'd ever seen a man's head explode in her life, and if she continued to be in my life, I doubted that would be the last time, either. Despite the warmth of the water, goose bumps rose on her flesh and that was when I noticed more bruises on her arms. The marks of rough fingers.

I was torn between taking care of Bianca and wanting to resurrect Raffa's men and run them through a wood chipper, alive and screaming. I blinked away my murderous thoughts before Bianca sensed my roiling rage.

How could I let this happen?

"I'm so sorry, baby. I'm so sorry." I pressed my lips against hers again. Her cold, pale lips. The anguish of my failures overwhelmed me and sent me to my knees. Resting my head on her womb, I begged for forgiveness.

"I'm so sorry. I'm so sorry. I'm so sorry."

"Sandro." Her voice washed over me. Still soft, but there was a resoluteness threading her tone. "It's not your fault." She ran her fingers through my hair as if she was the one comforting me. "We'll be okay."

The logical thing to do was return her to the De Luccis and not give a shit what happened to me. Let the Rossi crime family self-destruct. But the truth was, I was so tired of holding back. I'd been holding back for four fucking years, trying to let her go. Hiding the crazy inside me. Hiding the blood of the monster that ran through my veins. The violence I was capable of.

I rose to my feet and continued cleansing her of the aftermath of Raffa's machinations, both of us lost in our own thoughts.

Bianca surrounded by danger freed the monster I was hiding from her. The monster that had always been lurking beneath the surface.

There were many things to discuss. I killed eight men for her. She wondered if I was all talk as a form of manipulation to keep her in line, but now she knew. I let her see the killer inside me. To see the man who wouldn't hesitate to kill for her.

After she was clean and Bianca's body had warmed enough, we got out of the shower. I dried her hair and dressed her in my shirt and her pajama bottoms. She was still listless, but she kept repeating that it was not my fault.

I settled her on the bed and it was not long after that she fell into a deep, exhausted sleep. She didn't stir when a knock sounded on the door.

"Boss." It was Sticks. "Tommy is downstairs."

I looked down at a sleeping Bianca. I didn't want to leave her, but I needed answers.

The bodies had been removed from the house, but the tracks of blood were everywhere.

Tommy was in the kitchen, helping himself to a beer.

Like it was just another day for the Rossi crime family, except today, I killed our own.

When he saw me, he immediately lowered the bottle and pointed in the direction of the driveway. "Rossi soldiers are camped at the mouth of the driveway. Sticks wouldn't let them through."

"My orders. Only those who came with me earlier are permitted."

"They want to show support for you, Sandro," Tommy said. "I briefed them on what happened. Raffa had no excuse going after Bianca the way he did." He cast me a furtive gaze. "I heard Bianca tossed Griselda out on her ass."

"She deserved it."

"Divina and the other women concurred."

I wouldn't be surprised if Griselda tried to make it sound like she was the victim.

"In case Griselda didn't get the memo, let me make it clear: I don't want her anywhere near my wife. All club business will now go through you or Divina. I don't even want her shadow within my sights."

Tommy was about to say something, but thought better of it when he saw whatever he saw on my face. Yes, I was still furious.

"Now, I want to get back to Bianca, so let's get to the point," I said. "Where were you?"

"I couldn't face you." He dropped his gaze to the tiles before returning it to mine. "I confronted Griselda to make sure she kept her mouth shut about you drawing a gun on Raffa. I shouldn't have brought it up at Raffa's house."

He waited for me to say something, but I continued glaring at him. "Look, I know if I went along to the meeting, I couldn't keep it from you and I knew how much you wanted the deal with the Toronto Albanians."

My mouth curled mockingly. "Well, guess what? That deal didn't happen and thank fuck because I got back here in time before those assholes violated my wife."

He scrubbed a hand over his face. "If I had known Raffa was gonna do that…I swear, Sandro…I had no idea."

I believed him, but I was too pissed to let it go. "We've been friends a long time, Tommy. We've had each other's back. You should have given me a heads-up the second that happened."

"I know." He dropped his gaze. "Raffa went ballistic. I should have known he would retaliate."

"You should have called me immediately when it happened. Showed up at the meet at least and come clean."

He exhaled heavily. "Gian was there, I heard."

"Well, Gian had more guts to show up."

"You're all about Gian now?"

I stalked toward him and he backed away until he realized how stupid it was. If I really wanted to put the hurt on him, there was nowhere for him to hide.

"Don't you dare"—I jabbed his chest with a finger—"give me that. You can't be boss this way. You show up no matter what."

"So you're saying Gian deserves to be boss more than me?"

"No. I'm not stepping down. Not while Bianca might face retaliation. Because it wouldn't take long for our enemies to know I would kill anyone who touched her. They will go after her to get to me. I need all the power of this position. There's no stepping down after this."

"I understand."

"You should." If I knew Bianca would leave with me, get a new identity far away from Manhattan, maybe on the other side of the world, I'd fake our deaths. However, she wouldn't want to be cut off from her family. But killing the men who threatened her had forever sealed her fate to mine.

I went to the fridge to get a beer. Uncapping it, I drained half of it. "I already postponed the meeting with the Toronto Albanians to two days from now."

"How's Bianca?"

"She's sleeping." My shoulders drooped. "I need to figure out a way for her to see her family."

"Raffa…"

A derisive laugh escaped me. "Fuck Raffa. After what he did, he's lost his credibility as an elder. I decimated his minions, including those two loyalist fuckers as unhinged as he is. He made a big mistake coming for Bianca."

"Well, our capos and soldiers are waiting in the wings to declare their loyalty to you," Tommy said.

"Good." I pointed my beer toward the foyer. "Supervise the disposal of the bodies. They're already outside. Contact Sloane for a more thorough cleanup. Can you do that for me? I need Sticks on top of other things." Mainly finding out if we had more leaks in our security.

"Of course."

"I don't want to leave Bianca's side so soon after shit like this happened. You're my underboss. Let our men know I appreciate their support."

"You don't want to do the whole *Godfather* kiss-the-ring thing?"

"Fuck no. I don't want this place crawling with mafia soldiers while my queen is vulnerable. Got it?"

Tommy moved to leave. "Don't worry. I got this."

"And, Tommy." He turned to look at me. "Don't screw up again."

CHAPTER
Twenty-One

Sandro

Bianca wanted to stay in bed the next morning and I indulged my girl. I reviewed the security footage. She gave quite a fight. I was damned proud of her. She told me that Raffa wanted the mob doc to gather evidence that she and I were having sex. I couldn't even wrap my mind around how unhinged that sounded. But we were the mafia. If we had a middle name, "unhinged" would be it.

However, this should not have surprised me. The Rossis had historically manipulated the pregnancies of their women. Bianca's uncle, Charles McGrath, had an affair with Sofia, Raffa's sister, and gotten her pregnant. My grandmother took her to Italy to hide her pregnancy, and when they returned, they gave the child to the McGraths to raise. Charles, at that time, was in prison.

And then there was my own screwed-up parentage.

I was eighteen when Wilma dropped the bombshell to the entire Rossi crime family that I wasn't her son. Carmelo had pissed her off for the last time, and she revealed the whole sordid truth.

He forced her to fake her pregnancy because she couldn't have more children.

There were actually companies that provided you with fake baby bumps and sonograms. I had to wrap my mind around that, too. I guess if you could fake death, you could fake anything. It made sense why Wilma showered affection on Frankie and appeared to hate my very existence despite how I tried to make her love me. I had crafted handmade cards and gifts that were discarded in the trash. At around eight years old, I took the hint and became the withdrawn, antisocial son of the Rossis. A beginning of a fresh hell because Carmelo became frustrated with me and started using his fists to make a point. Come to think of it, that was probably why I never understood the concept of love because I'd never received it. I built walls around myself to hide the fact that I was unlovable.

When the truth came out, I hated Wilma less and despised Carmelo more. In a way it was her absolution for why she wasn't able to love me the way she loved Frankie.

I stopped calling her Ma and she'd been fine with it.

Wilma told me my biological mother died at childbirth, but Raffa revealed the truth after Carmelo's funeral when I was twenty-four, recently released from a Russian prison.

Bianca shifted on the bed, calling my thoughts back from my fucked-up past. She didn't know the complete story. She deserved to know, especially after Raffa's deranged actions yesterday.

Spending the day with her reminded me of her truancy in high school and how I enjoyed corrupting her perfect life a little. This morning, I read while she slept. We watched TV together in her waking moments. She'd become clingy. Always wanting to keep a part of us connected. Holding my hand, touching my arm. She was so soft and warm and sexily cuddly. Her smell was intoxicating.

The swell of her tits through the worn-out tee was driving me nuts. Whereas I didn't feel any lust in the shower yesterday, today was different. The desire to bury myself in her lush heat was overwhelming.

She sighed for what seemed like the hundredth time and I asked for what seemed like the millionth time, "How are you feeling, baby?"

"Fine."

"Do you want to talk about it?" The *it* was my murderous actions yesterday. She hadn't even mentioned Griselda again.

"Not yet."

Around nine p.m. Bianca got up and went to the bathroom. I heard the shower start and waited patiently for her to come out, reining in the urge to barge in there. The water stopped after exactly eight minutes twenty-five seconds. The sink faucet turned on, then the blow-dryer. Another seven minutes and fifteen seconds went by before she came out of the bathroom. Her hair was up in a ponytail.

She'd thrown on a robe and, without another look my way, left the bedroom. I swallowed a curse and went after her.

"Bianca…" I mumbled softly.

She ignored me.

Fine. If she hadn't been clingy earlier, I would be bald by now with the way I wanted to pull out my hair.

She descended the steps and I held back from sweeping her in my arms and carrying her back to the bedroom. The men had mopped the floor, leaving no traces of blood. If there were, it wasn't immediately evident. The stench of death and bleach still hung in the air. Sloane hadn't come by yet.

Bianca entered the kitchen and started taking eggs, bacon, sausages, and vegetables out of the fridge. She went to the pantry and grabbed onions.

She hadn't eaten since this morning.

Bianca brought out the chopping board. Then she grabbed a big fucking knife from the wooden block.

I stiffened, remembering her words to Griselda. Did any of her introspection today trigger the psycho?

"Baby…" I walked toward her.

"Turn the oven to three twenty-five," she said, not looking at me.

I scrambled to turn on the oven to her required setting.

The blade of the knife reflected in the lighting. It winked at me before she positioned an onion underneath and cut it in half with a decisive stroke. I was glad it wasn't a cucumber.

I brought out my phone and tapped over to the surveillance app. I switched off the cameras in the kitchen, then texted Sticks.

FYI, I turned off the security cams in the kitchen.

STICKS

Boss?

Don't turn it back on

I didn't want footage of her in a robe, looking sexy as fuck. That'd plant ideas in my men's heads, then I'd be forced to shoot them too. But also, in case she stabbed me, I didn't want there to be any evidence.

As expected, Sticks wasn't gonna be on board without further clarification, especially given the events of the past few days. I heard the front door open and close, but I intercepted him at the mouth of the kitchen.

"What?" I asked.

He looked past my shoulder, but I pushed him to the side where he couldn't see Bianca, while I could still monitor her.

"She has a knife." Sticks pointed out the obvious. Which was made more obvious when the *chop-chop-chop* sound of the knife furiously hitting the cutting board reached our ears.

"She's cooking."

"Obviously."

Sticks raised a brow.

"I consider that a win. Get out of here."

He still didn't budge. "When do I check back on you?"

"You don't."

"Boss, give me something here."

"If you find me bled out in the middle of the kitchen, I deserved it," I gritted. "Protect Bianca at all costs. Get rid of my body if you must."

"Christ…"

The *chop-chop-chop* of the knife continued and was the only noise that punctuated our staredown.

"Fine."

"Don't you dare turn on the surveillance."

"I'll text you every half hour."

I wanted to snarl, but every second arguing with Sticks was every second not keeping my full attention on Bianca. "Fine."

His gaze flitted behind me again.

"What?" I snapped.

"I've seen this behavior."

"This?"

"Back in Afghanistan. Our convoy got hit by an IED. It was blood and gore before the quick reaction team repelled the attack," Sticks said, but his eyes had taken on a thousand-yard stare as if he was reliving that day again. "LT…our lieutenant… let's just say he tried to save the leg of one of our boys, but he bled out and died. A lot of us were just shell-shocked, you know… The aftermath of an explosion is just surreal…unreal…" He paused. "Chaos… Even after we'd been evacuated from the scene, it was as if we're still there." He tapped the side of his head. "In here."

I stayed silent, letting Sticks go through whatever mind space he'd drifted to. He'd seen the worst of war and somehow juxtaposed it with what Bianca experienced, so my panic abated. I should trust in her resilience.

"What happened?" I prodded.

"LT left the barracks. He went to the cook and next we knew we were chowing down under a tent and LT was the one serving us. It was his way of coping." Sticks nodded to where my wife continued slicing and dicing vegetables. "From the first day, that's how Bianca had coped with the situation of her captivity. In the kitchen."

"Well, I'll be damned." I glanced back at my wife and I was already feeling more settled with her behavior. "Then I'm going to let her cope."

"I'm still checking on you every fifteen minutes."

"You said half an hour."

Sticks grinned and flicked me a mock salute before heading out.

I returned to Bianca and sat mesmerized as she methodically prepped whatever she was cooking. After another ten minutes, she set a baking pan across two burners. "Smells good, baby. What are you making with all these ingredients?"

"Dad's frittata."

Slight panic arrested my heart. There was one man I could never see myself replacing as Bianca's number one—at least not yet. So she was thinking about her dad. It didn't mean she was wishing I'd never been a part of her life.

"I've never tasted your dad's frittata."

"It's breakfast food, but I'm feeling like breakfast for dinner," she said.

"Same, baby. Need any help?"

No answer.

Okay. That was all right. Maybe I was interrupting her Zen moment thinking about her dad. Her overprotective and doting dad. Her cocoon-her-in-bubble-wrap-before-letting-someone's-brain-matter-splatter-over-her dad.

I sat and marinated in a sludge of resurgent unworthiness, desperate to know what was running through her head. Was she going to demand I let her go? Did she realize I wasn't worth the trouble?

I was tempted to reach for a beer but decided to get drunk on her movements. The knife rested beside the cutting board. A bowl containing diced onions sat beside it. Neatly arranged on a chopping board were rows of diced peppers and mushrooms, zucchini and broccoli.

Bianca deftly drained the bacon fat, then removed it to set it upon paper towels. Then she began sautéing the Italian sausage. When that was done, she began cooking the vegetables. It slowly registered in my brain. A delicious aroma soon wrapped around us replacing the stench of bleach and death. Bianca was turning the house back into a home. That was why she didn't even turn on the vents immediately and only did so later.

She stirred eggs into the mix of vegetables, scattered the cooked Italian sausage and crumbled the bacon into the pan. She was making enough for an army again. Bianca was going to feed me. Feed my men. She was about to put the pan in the oven, when I interjected. "Aren't you forgetting the cheese?"

She set the pan down, closed the oven, and turned to me.

A trace of a smile touched her lips. They twitched. "It's a sin not to have cheese in the frittata. What was I thinking?"

"What are you thinking, Bianca?" I asked softly.

Finally, finally, her eyes met mine.

She cocked her head in a familiar thinking gesture. She grabbed the bags of shredded cheese and emptied them into the pan. Then, with a wooden spoon, she stirred the contents carefully. "Next time, no prepackaged shredded cheese. I like to grate mine into the food."

"That'll be a lot of grating."

"Well, you're here."

"Yes, I'm here." I moved closer.

When she raised the pan with both hands, I opened the oven door for her. She positioned it in its depths, straightened, and set the timer.

I closed the door and leaned against the counter. She moved to the opposite side, so we were face to face. We locked eyes again. Then she dropped hers and studied the tile floors.

"What's on your mind, baby?" I rephrased the question I asked earlier. She didn't reply immediately, but somehow, deep inside, I knew she was done working things out in her head.

Still not looking at me, she said, "I don't know how I was okay with you killing eight men. Was it just yesterday?" she mused. "It seems like it was a long time ago."

Relief buoyed my chest that she wasn't feeling sorry for those motherfuckers. "They deserved it."

This time, her eyes met mine. "Why didn't I want you killing Raffa, then? He was the one who gave the order."

"Baby, one thing you need to understand about Raffa. His blindness came at the price of his past atrocities. And he uses his blindness as an excuse to get a pass."

"But he asked you to kill him."

"He has nothing to lose. I killed two of his henchmen who had a lotta influence with the soldiers, basically cutting him off at the knees. He can't get traction anymore. Tommy told me there's a big shift in loyalties."

"Is Tommy right?"

"Too soon to say," I admitted. "Raffa's considered the old guard. He's slowly losing influence, and after what he did to you, it's an atrocity no one in the modern mafia wants to be associated with. One reason the Rossis are failing is because they failed to evolve."

She gave a hum of assent.

"Wanna sit?" I glanced at the timer. "Looks like we have another hour or so."

She shrugged and moved to the breakfast table near the window.

"You want anything from here, baby? Blueberry soda?"

She gave me a small nod. When I got her settled with her favorite drink and I had taken a much-needed swig of beer to lubricate my parched throat, I asked, "Anything else bothering you?"

"I went after Griselda," she said. "Did I cause a problem between you and Tommy?"

"Nope."

She cocked a brow before narrowing her eyes in the first signs that her sass had returned."Really?"

"Really," I replied.

"She had it coming." She took a long sip of her soda. "Griselda has had it coming for a long time." A smile twitched the corners of her mouth. "I didn't register it much then, but I remembered you telling Sticks not to interfere."

"I did."

"Thanks for that because I'm not regretting showing Griselda the door."

"You shouldn't."

"There's a difference between being a doormat and picking your battles. Showing empathy or being a sucker."

"As I said before, baby, I have your back."

She raked her teeth over her bottom lip.

"Out with it. You have more to say."

Her eyes lost focus for a moment, much like how Sticks had grown distant earlier. "Seeing all that blood…it's like a horror movie." She paused, as if choosing what to say, how to say it. "But

I'm fine. More than fine. You were right. I went through the shock. And I tried to reconcile my gut and logic that you've done the right thing.

"Then I remembered the time a rival family kidnapped Liz. We were all on lockdown at the De Lucci mansion. When the guys returned, Matteo and Nico tracked blood all over the floors. There was this manic look in their eyes…much like yours were yesterday."

I understood that look. Bloodlust.

Bianca took a couple of chugs from her drink. "I'd never seen my brothers that way. I was unnerved. It was as if they'd become strangers. Dad had come in with them and he saw the expression on my face."

"Did Cesar go with them too?"

"Of course. Matteo was only twenty-three then. Nico, twenty-two. Dad had more experience. I think that was the first time…"

Bianca didn't finish, but I got it. It was probably the first time the brothers had shot and killed men. "What did your dad do when he saw your face?"

"Nothing at that moment because Mom and I were rushing out the door on the way to the hospital to be with Renz and Liz while the guys cleaned up. The hospital discharged her the same day, and when we brought her home, that was when Dad pulled me into the kitchen and told me to help him prepare something for everyone to eat. Which I thought was weird because we could have just told someone to bring us food. Mom was with Renz, helping him take care of Liz.

"They made Renz stay in the car. He hadn't kept up with defensive training, but after that, Dad made sure we both practiced shooting and self-defense skills."

"I don't blame him." Cesar had many enemies. Raffa being one of them.

"But yeah." Her exhalation was rough and long. "While Dad made frittata, he explained that Matteo and Nico insisted on being part of the rescue and there are things that needed to be done. I mean, Dad already knew I wouldn't look at my brothers with any less love for killing those assholes who thought it was okay to kidnap a pregnant woman. But I clung to that time with my dad. In our world, there were things we needed to take into our own hands because our enemies would never play fair."

"And I was the fucker who kept interrupting you sorting shit out in your head."

Bianca gave a tiny laugh. It lit up her face.

Thank fucking Christ.

"It also reminded me of a question I wanted to ask you."

"I'm an open book." I was thrilled to have my Sunlight back. I failed to detect the wary hesitation on her face and her next words dropped an anchor in my gut.

"I don't know why Warren Winslow popped into my head."

God fucking dammit. Fuck. I hated that name.

"Raffa's men dragged me into the office," she continued. "I had a flash of him. You remember him, right?"

How could I forget? "What about him?"

"He drowned in their family home. The police said he had drugs in his system."

"Looks like an open and shut case," I said shortly.

Bianca put the bottle down, crossed arms over the table, and leaned forward. "Now's the time to tell me the truth, Sandro."

We stared at each other and I let her see the truth.

She winced. "I just want to know why."

"You want to know if I killed that fucker for taking your virginity?"

"Yes."

"He's a rapist."

"I guess… The night was fuzzy."

"Bianca." I reached across the table, uncrossed her arms, and grabbed her hands, holding our linked fingers on the table. I was afraid she'd bolt. This was a momentous confession, and I wanted to look her in the eye when I told her.

"Did you or did you not tell him to stop?" I asked.

"It was dubious consent," she whispered. "I was drunk. He was drunk, but in the end, what he did was wrong."

"I will not argue the point and force you to accept that you were raped. It's hard enough that you struggle with it. But *do not* for one second think Warren didn't deserve to die."

She gave a tiny gasp at the venom in my tone. Her eyes widened, but she didn't flinch from my hardened gaze.

"Yes, I killed him," I stated fiercely. "Yes, I pumped him full of drugs before I threw him into the pool to drown. I wish I made him suffer more. I wish I tortured him. Since the time I picked you up with blood running down the back of your thighs, I watched him." I rattled that off quickly. It was like a poison I'd kept inside me and I couldn't wait to expunge it. "But he was eighteen at that time. I wanted to erase his pathetic life, but I couldn't kill him. Yet." Me and my fucking code. I grappled with myself. He wasn't a child, but he was still too young.

"You put him on your hit list."

"And he was forever on it. I waited five years. And when he graduated from getting women drunk to roofieing them, I was done waiting. The fucker needed to die." I repeated my earlier statement. It was my mantra for five years when it came to Warren Winslow. Bianca was silent as if absorbing what I was telling her.

"I don't regret it. You'll just have to live with what I've done. Can you?"

When she was still silent, I said, "If you need proof, I have copies of police reports and video footage from my club."

"Should you be keeping those?" she asked.

"Does that mean you're okay with what I did?"

"I don't know what I'm becoming," she whispered. "I guess since Warren's family is rich and influential, nothing came from the complaints?"

"Nothing. Nada. They were paid off or threatened."

"Threatened?"

"Yes. The Winslows actually have a relationship with the Rossis. They approached us to intimidate their workers during labor disputes. That was how Warren came on Griselda's radar. She was adamant she didn't mean for you to get hurt. She thought Warren was like any entitled teenager and his arrogance and good looks would be a distraction for you."

"You know what? I'll just add this to my list to chew on…"

Her gaze dropped to our joined hands. Could she handle more?

My phone's walkie-talkie went off. *"Boss,"* Sticks said. *"Gian is here."*

What did he want? He had a lot of balls showing up here.

"Send him away," I told Sticks.

"I think you really need to hear this."

There was an ominous tinge to his tone that gave us pause.

"What's going on?" Bianca asked.

Gian had been blowing up my phone the whole day. Probably anxious about my decision regarding him. Probably wanting to get in on the meet with the Toronto Albanians tomorrow. Well, he was out of luck. I officially announced Tommy as underboss. "I hope it's to tell us Raffa finally did the right thing and—" I was going to say "ate his gun" but it was too soon to put that image back in Bianca's mind. "Fled to Siberia."

"Boss?" Sticks asked again.

"Let him through," I responded.

"Sorry, baby," I sighed. "I'll get rid of him."

Gian had terrible timing, showing up when I was having breakthrough conversations with Bianca. I wanted to tell her about my mother. After everything we'd been through, I was confident we would be okay. That she wouldn't care about the depravity that birthed my existence.

When I opened the front door of the house, Sticks was on the walkie-talkie talking to the guard at the front of the property. "Is Tommy with him?"

Sticks asked on the walkie-talkie. "Tommy Scavo with them?"

"Negative."

Come to think of it, I hadn't heard from Tommy since I texted him this afternoon confirming our meet-up tomorrow.

Gian's Escalade rolled down the driveway, and I patiently waited for him to park and get out of the SUV. He was not welcome inside the house.

When he exited the driver's side, I called out, "That's as far as you go."

"For God's sake, Sandro. We have bigger problems."

"If Raffa is dead, then good riddance."

"No, dammit." He walked around the front of the SUV. "Someone shot up Jabbin' Java."

CHAPTER Twenty-Two

Sandro

"No!" A scream ripped out from behind me. Bianca. Shit. I was still absorbing Gian's news when she flew past me, but I hooked her around the waist and held her back.

"It's you!" she cried. "How dare you hurt my family again!"

"I didn't do this!" Gian shouted. "Can we please go inside?"

"Baby, please. Let me sort this out."

She struggled in my arms for a few seconds before my pleas registered with her. My mind went a little crazy that she was wearing a robe in front of my men and Gian. But it rapidly became a secondary concern. She'd just come to grips with yesterday's events. And now this? I swallowed the roar of frustration. The hits just kept coming. How soon before she realized I was more trouble than I was worth and forced me to return her to the De Luccis?

Darker, malignant thoughts lurked on the fringes of my mind.

Of chaining Bianca to the bed. Of making sure she would never leave me. It was the depravity in my blood. I was becoming *him*.

Bianca was mine.

"I need to talk to Renz. I need to talk to my family, Sandro." She glared at me, but I continued to battle with myself. "You said it. Raffa has lost the loyalty of the Rossis. You're in charge now."

"Let's talk in the study without her," Gian told me.

We moved just inside the entrance. That was as far as I was willing to let my cousin into the house.

"Whatever you have to say, you can say it right here. And the study is still bloody in case you've forgotten." It wasn't, but it still reeked of the consequences of my murderous rage. "I need to call Dom and tell him it wasn't us."

"What? Do we know that, though?" Gian said. "Tommy seemed hell-bent on retaliation against the De Luccis about the club."

"He's not that reckless," I told him. "I don't know where Tommy is, but maybe you do, Gian?"

"How dare you insinuate I'd harm one of our own," Gian snapped. "You'll do anything to protect your wife. Are you forgetting the oath you took, Sandro?"

"I took many oaths that day, including my wedding vows, which, if you remember, I said after the made-man ceremony."

Gian's mouth curled into a derisive snarl.

"Call Dom." Bianca's tremulous voice broke our staredown. There was a pleading in every single line of her face, not to mention her eyes that would make me do anything she asked at this instant.

I gave a brief nod. "Wait here. Sticks." I exchanged a look with him that said "guard my wife." I walked into the study. Sloane was coming tomorrow to do a thorough scrubbing. But I wondered if this house had served its purpose. No way did I want Bianca to remember what happened in this room each time she had to cross its threshold. I headed to the wall safe and opened it, reaching for a phone I hadn't used since I married Bianca.

The call was going to be brief.

I powered up the device and swiped Dom's number.

"Rossi," he growled.

"It wasn't us."

"That speculation has come up."

"Mutual enemies?"

"Or just yours."

"Fuck you, Dom."

The derisive chuckle grated, but I detected exhaustion and frustration in it too.

I asked, "Anyone hurt?"

"No." He gave me a gist of the damage before he said, "We have Tommy Scavo. Straightforward exchange.Tommy for Bianca."

"And if I say no?"

"That's the price. Otherwise, I have nothing else to say to you." He ended the call.

He didn't even ask to talk to Bianca. Negotiations were over.

I wanted to smash the phone, but I powered it off and secured it back in the safe.

I wasn't giving her back. They could see her, but only when I was at her side and they accepted me as her fucking husband. I felt cornered. I needed time to weigh my options, but the searing possessiveness for my wife was blinding me to every option except one.

Keep her.

"Did you get a hold of Dom?" Bianca asked when I returned to the foyer.

"I did."

At the disbelieving look on her face, I ground my molars together and debated what to tell her.

"And?" she clipped.

"No one was hurt. It happened right after the closing time. It's just property damage, but just like the club, it might take weeks of repair." I spoke in an even calm tone like it was just another day in Rossi land. "They do have Tommy."

"Why didn't you let me speak to Dom!" Bianca cried at the same time Gian asked, "And?"

"I kept it short," I said. "All that matters is that no one was hurt. And Dom confirmed they have Tommy. He didn't ask to talk to you."

Bianca was having a hard time regulating her breathing. A flush pinkened her cheeks in a sure sign of her temper.

"I didn't ask for details." I kept Dom's exchange condition to myself for now. "They considered a third-party was involved."

"We were thinking the same thing," Bianca said.

"You guys had a productive conversation while I was gone?" My mouth hitched at a corner.

"Are you finding this funny?" Bianca snapped.

"No, but it sure beats freaking out over it. The De Luccis are not going to harm Tommy beyond what's accepted interrogation. Leaving a trail of bodies isn't their MO."

Mine wasn't either. Yesterday was an exception.

"Well, maybe you could ask them about my poker game and our soldier in jail," Gian asked.

I shot him an irritated glance. "We take care of our business with Toronto first."

"And Tommy?" Bianca asked.

"He can hang on a bit."

"But why?" The tone in her voice suggested she was fast losing patience, and it scored another welt on my conscience that I was keeping Dom's bargaining chip from her.

But I didn't have to worry because Gian answered for me. "Tommy was careless. Let him learn his lesson."

Bianca glared at Gian and then at me. "I'm going to check on the frittata."

"Looks like I'll be accompanying you to see the Toronto Albanians, after all," Gian said smugly.

~

I barely set foot in the kitchen when Bianca attacked me with, "Is he gone?"

"Gian? Yeah."

"This fighting in front of other people is harder than I thought," she fumed. "I don't know how Mom put up with Dad when all I want to do is punch that smirk off your face."

I snagged her around the waist and dragged her against me. "Thank you, baby. But you don't have to hold back every single time." I cocked a grin. "If you think I deserve it." I looked past her. "That frittata looks good. Sure smells good."

"Ugh." She put her arms between us and squirmed out of my embrace. Her tits brushed against my abs and the softness made my dick jump.

I was fired up.

She was fired up.

Which reminded me about her attire, and I injected all seriousness on my face. "I don't want you showing up in a robe in front of my men with barely anything underneath it. I would have stabbed Gian in the eye if he so much as leered at you." He would have too, if we didn't have this huge problem of Tommy missing, the Jabbin' Java incident, and the Albanians. Not to mention my rift with Raffa.

"Are we seriously talking about your jealousy right now?" As if to stress how ridiculous she thought I was, she threw her hands on her hips.

I was secretly delighted she didn't flinch when I mentioned stabbing Gian in the eye.

"Yes." I crowded her against the counter. She didn't back down. I yanked her forward with one hand so she was plastered against me again, and with the other, stroked between her legs. I could feel her heat through her shorts. She wasn't wearing panties.

Fucking fuck.

She closed her eyes and gave an involuntary moan.

"That's it, baby," I grunted.

Her eyes popped open, outraged, but I also discerned need. "No!"

I raised a brow. "Are you saying no to an orgasm?"

She was breathing hard, her lips pressed into a thin line. "I'm mad at you."

"Because I won't let you see your family?"

"Yes!"

"Soon."

"Why not now? As in…tonight!"

I let her go and stood back. "No. I'm not giving you back."

She looked outraged. "I'm not a thing to give back!"

"That's not…" I scraped a hand over my face. How could I tell her I didn't trust she would return to me? That when she saw her family, she would be relieved to be shielded from the violence in my world. How I was terrified once she returned to the De Luccis, they would make her disappear again. Just the thought of that made me feral. I glared at her and grabbed the top of her shoulders where she wasn't bruised. "You're mine, Bianca."

Her mouth parted and her eyes flashed. "Really? You wouldn't even fuck me. Oh, wait. You want me to accept every part of you first. Guess what? I already do."

"You don't know everything," I said quietly. My hands fell from her shoulders and I twisted around, grappling for words to explain the past only a few people knew.

"What?"

I rubbed a finger across the top of my mouth. "I'm not only a bastard son, Bianca."

I felt her step closer. "Never call yourself that. You're a Rossi."

"And I wish I wasn't."

I faced her and gritted out my confession, "My mother didn't die in childbirth."

Her eyes widened. "What? She's alive?"

Oh, baby, my life was more fucked up than that. "Carmelo took a fancy to a beautiful exchange student from Turkey. Kidnapped her. Kept her hostage in the basement of the Rossi mansion."

Bianca's face grew stricken and her eyes filled with tears.

"Are you revolted yet?" I asked, the ugliness in my blood seeping through my words. "Do you see where this is going?"

"I'm disgusted at your father, not you," she whispered.

"You're not?" A derisive smile curved my mouth. "When Gian told us the news about Jabbin' Java, the logical thing to do was make plans to return you to your family, but everything inside me rejected that idea. You know what went through my mind?" I loomed over her, tapped my temple, jabbing it repeatedly the way psychos do when the voices in their head drove them off a cliff. "I wanted to chain you to my bed. I don't want to let you go. How am I different from Carmelo?"

Bianca met my gaze straight on. "Sandro, you are *not* your father."

I closed my eyes briefly, drilling the heel of my right hand against an eye socket. *Am I not?*

Soft hands picked mine up and held them against her beloved face. I would know its shape anywhere, even with my eyes closed.

"Look at me, please," Bianca whispered.

I opened my eyes and she repeated, "You are not your father."

All restraint shattered.

Our mouths crashed against each other. My tongue dove between her lips and it was as if I depended on her for oxygen. As if she was my salvation from the unraveling storm I had unleashed with my confession. Teeth scraped, tongues tangled, and I explored deeper and deeper. She tasted of mint and carnal promise. I backed her against the breakfast table and lifted her on top of it.

Her robe fell open and her nipples' outline against a thin tank top drove me wild. I latched on to her neck. Unlike in the shower, where seeing her naked didn't spark an ounce of lust, this time, feeling her nipple against my palm drew a groan as if I were in pain.

"I can't be gentle," I snarled.

"Don't be," she panted. "Show me who you are."

I ripped her tank top, exposing her breasts, and I bowed down to take a mouthful while I squeezed the other one. But the lure of her cunt drew me lower. I grazed my teeth over her belly, straight to the scent I couldn't resist. I leaned back and looked at her pussy. Her pink pretty pussy that was all mine.

All fucking mine.

I dove straight in. She cried out, her knees caging my head, her hands in my hair yanking me closer while she pushed her hips up to meet me. So fucking responsive.

I ate and feasted, ravaging her tender flesh, licking, nipping. I tongued her clit. Lapped around it and sucked. She moaned and sobbed, and I continued drawing her cries. Felt her swell on my tongue. I could never get enough. I inserted a finger, and then two. Fuck, she was too tight. I would hurt her if I simply shoved inside her, which was what my body was gearing to do. My hand went to my shorts. I palmed my erection.

Throughout this delirium of need and want, I paused. I stared at my fingers inside her pussy and tried to add a third. She squirmed and her breathing hitched. I withdrew them all. She was too small. I was going to hurt her, especially with how rabid I was feeling.

"Sandro?" She propped up on her elbows, brows furrowing.

My eyes scorched over her. All laid out and open. It was so easy. Make her mine. But this place. It was wrong. I exhaled a breath and scooped her from the breakfast table and left the kitchen.

"What happened?" she asked as I went up the stairs.

"I'm not about to fuck you on that table."

"Why?"

"I can't be gentle."

"Well, I was enjoying feral Sandro."

I groaned against the top of her head, "Don't, baby. It's not gonna happen, all right? Not like this."

I entered our bedroom, still carrying her, and gently laid her on the bed. She sat up and swung her legs around to sit back on her heels, eyeing me as I stared at her. She was specifically eyeing my erection, which was hidden beneath my T-shirt.

"Don't look at me like that," I snapped.

"Sandro, I'm not a virgin. You're not going to hurt me," she mumbled.

"You sure about that?" I lifted my shirt and exposed my cock. She gaped, eyes wide, hand slapping over her mouth. I wanted to laugh, but I was also worried.

"I'm going to rip you apart." I dropped my shirt.

"Uhm…maybe go slow?" she squeaked and then had to bite her lower lip.

I made a guttural sound before shooting her a pained smile and climbing into bed beside her. "Come here. Ain't happening."

"Sandro."

"Quiet, baby." I gathered her in my arms.

"Are you doing this because you don't want to be like…"

I stiffened.

"…him," she finished.

There was no other way to describe what was rampaging inside me. All sorts of fucked up for sure. I was exhausted yet charged and liberated because I finally confessed the darkest secrets of my family.

"I'm only going to talk about this once. But in putting you first and not hurting you, I can unequivocally say I'm not him." I breathed through my nose and pushed through before I changed my mind about telling her about the vile acts of the man who raised me. "He's a monster who repeatedly raped my mother to give him a child. The only thing I'm thankful for is my existence ended her tortured one."

"Sandro…" Tears spilled from her eyes and she reached for me and cupped my jaw. "I'm sorry about your mother. What—"

"She tried to escape with me. One of the soldiers felt sorry for her and helped her, but they were caught. Carmelo had them both executed."

She sobbed silently. I hugged her close. "Finally telling you is a relief. Don't feel sorry for me. I went after the men who killed my mother. They died painful deaths. Pity I couldn't do the same to Carmelo."

"Your poor mother." I made out her garbled words against my chest. The wetness of her tears soaked through my T-shirt. I hadn't thought about my mother in a long while. I'd never known about her real fate until I was twenty-four. That was when I included rapists on my hit list. That was why what happened to Bianca when she lost her virginity added to that purpose. That was why I murdered Warren Winslow.

"When did you find out the truth?" she asked more clearly.

"After Russia. At Carmelo's funeral. Raffa had known all along."

"Did you find out more about your mother? Her family?"

"They got scared and somehow they went into hiding, left Turkey and moved to an oblast in Russia. I went looking for them there and I fucking guarantee you Carmelo had me thrown in prison because I was snooping. Raffa admitted as much because he negotiated my release. He told me the truth about my mother and said I would only cause other people to get killed if I didn't leave it alone."

I lost one year of my life in Russia.

Her sobs subsided into occasional hiccups. "I shouldn't be able to wrap my mind around it, but I can. After Raffa's insane actions yesterday, nothing surprises me anymore." She pulled away slightly so she could look me in the eye. "You are not them, Sandro." Her conviction was fierce.

She had no idea how her belief in me was everything.

"I will never hold the circumstances of your birth against you," she added softly.

"I know you won't." I pulled her close again and kissed the top of her head. "That's all that matters to me. But understand, I'm never letting you go."

"I still want to see my family."

Dom's words came back to haunt me. *Tommy for Bianca.*

One problem at a time. "Let me get tomorrow sorted out first, then we'll talk."

CHAPTER Twenty-Three

BIANCA

Sandro left with Gian around six this morning. I packed them frittata to go. I'd been reeling from the revelations of the past few days, especially the bombshell Sandro had dropped last night. It made me reevaluate all our interactions. His reluctance to be with me. He felt unworthy because the blood of a rapist ran in his veins. The story that circulated was that Sandro's mom was Carmelo's mistress, who became pregnant.

The tenderness between my thighs reminded me of the ferocity with which Sandro devoured me. And, oh God, his monstrous cock. He was long and girthy… Was I frightened? Maybe. Was I turned on? Hell yes.

I'd moved on from being the sheltered daughter of Ava and Cesar De Lucci into being the wife of Alessandro Rossi, mafia don and former assassin. Extreme circumstances forced us into our roles, but after struggling with how to survive this, our paths became clear.

Sandro needed to step up permanently as the boss. I needed to step up as his wife.

If Gian was telling the truth, then someone was capitalizing on Raffa's revenge against Dad, hoping for an all-out war between the De Luccis and the Rossis. That it involved both sides of my family made me even more determined to find out who was behind these malicious hits.

The lack of news about Jabbin' Java was making me antsy. I was consoling myself that no one was hurt and I could be patient a while longer. But Divina was driving me crazy.

She arrived around six thirty this morning. It was as if she was waiting for the men to leave. There was pumped-up security and new faces. No Rossi soldiers. I wasn't sure whether Sandro still mistrusted them or it was because the family was stretched too thin. After all, Sandro took out eight of them.

Sloane arrived at nine but was in the study removing the last traces of that bloody day. Divina and I hung out in the living room with a regular TV for company and we were on our second pot of coffee. She kept scrolling on her phone, and I kept side-eyeing her. It would be so simple to find out what was going on with Tommy.

"Do you want me to call Dom and ask about Tommy?" I asked casually. When Sandro came back from his business with the Toronto Albanians, we were going to have a serious chat about seeing my family. I had an odd feeling that he was still keeping something from me, but my husband had so much on his mind, I didn't want him distracted.

She glanced up from her phone and I saw the war in her eyes. "What are the consequences, though?"

"To me? To us? To Tommy?"

"Everything."

"From what I can tell, the Rossi crime family is experiencing a monumental shift. Even if Sandro says Raffa has lost his influence, it's still too soon to tell if it will last. And without Tommy, he's short an underboss."

I hated that Gian was the one accompanying him to see the Albanians.

I flipped through the channels, trying to find more news about the café, but with the limited access, all I got were cooking shows. "Is there any news on the *Manhattan Tattler*? Can you at least give me that?"

"Yes, that's the only one reporting," Divina said. "Nothing new."

"Have they made connections between the Rossis and De Luccis?"

"There are some comments, but I think one of the popular discussion boards is talking about the coincidence of the club fire and the Jabbin' Java incident. They haven't mentioned you."

"Because I'm low-key. Except that time of the fashion show." But most of social media had their eyes on Nico and Ivy then. "How about Ivy's socials?"

"She hasn't mentioned it, but she has been asked in one of her posts."

I had a feeling they were up to something. The last thing I wanted was a retaliation. I was sure grabbing Tommy was part of the plan to find out about me.

Divina surged up from the couch. "I can't take this waiting around."

"Calm down."

She burst into tears. "It's easy for you to say. It's not your husband who's being held hostage."

The irony.

"Imagine how my parents and family feel."

Her breath caught and she had the grace to look ashamed. "I'm sorry." She looked around her. "There must be something we can do."

Desperate times, desperate measures. And I wasn't above using Divina to end this bullshit. I checked the clock. The meeting with the Albanians was around nine or ten. Sandro should already be there and there was no distracting him now.

"There is, but I need you to fully be on board with this."

She stopped crying long enough to ask, "What?"

"This is an abomination." Sloane cringed. "Do you know how much this cost?"

The four of us—Sticks, Sloane, Divina, and I—were staring at the coffee stain on what I realized later was an authentic Persian rug. "I didn't think Sandro was into collecting these."

"He got that as payment from someone who owed him money," Sticks said. "A boatload of money."

"How much?" I asked, not with a little dread.

"Two hundred Gs."

"What?" Divina and I exchanged looks. Maybe we should have picked a cheaper rug to ruin. But the living room was the quickest route to the side exit of the house away from the bunkhouse.

"Sloane is here, so it's not a problem," I quipped instead.

"I don't know, Bianca." Sloane squatted and studied the roughly two-foot-diameter stain. "I don't want to make it worse." She picked up the edge of the carpet and ran her fingers several times over the back. "This is an antique."

"I won't hold you liable," I said. "I'll sign anything."

"If you all don't need me," Sticks said, backing out of the room. "I'll go back outside."

Despite my costly actions, I laughed. "Don't worry, I don't think Sandro intended for you to be responsible for my housebreaking."

He waved me off.

When we heard the front door close, Sloane stood. "This is a nutty plan." I'd already briefed her on my scheme so she wouldn't contradict me on anything in front of Sticks. "But I love it."

"Is it really hard to remove the stain?" I asked.

"I can remove it. The question is the damage it will leave on the carpet." Then she winked. "Just kidding. But the cleaning foam, brush, and a lot of patience should do the job. But I'm more interested in the other plan."

The other plan meaning escaping the house that had been my prison for over two weeks. Why not just wait it out?

Because another day of Divina's anxiety might drive me over the edge.

And I wasn't waiting around for Dad or Dom to execute a retaliation. Desperate times and all that. What if they acted out of character and only escalated the problem?

Forgive me, Sandro.

Forty-five minutes later, I was climbing into the back of Sloane's van. She parked it in a blind spot to the surveillance cameras. Divina was keeping watch from the foyer and told me Sticks was in the bunkhouse.

Sloane joked she could roll me in a carpet and load me into the van using a hand truck. I didn't tell her I wouldn't oppose such an idea as a last resort.

"Now is the time to say no," she said with her hand on the door.

"What the fuck!" Sticks's voice boomed from behind us.

"Shit," Sloane muttered and moved aside, leaving me in full view of Sticks with a worried Divina scampering after him.

His face was etched in disbelief, and I could say he was angry. I'd seen his resting dick face at the club when he intimidated entitled patrons, and right now, his scary-bouncer mode had been activated.

Sloane stepped in front of him. There was something in her hand.

"Move aside," Sticks growled.

"Sorry, Sticks," Sloane said and zapped him with a stun gun.

My mouth dropped open when Sticks went down like a pile of bricks.

I jumped out of the van, worried. "He might have a concussion."

"Oh my God, Sloane," Divina shrieked. "What did you do?"

Without answering her friend, Sloane went to the van and grabbed two rolls of duct tape, tossing one to me. "Bind his legs."

I didn't hesitate. She tipped Sticks on his chest and stood-straddled over his body to bind his wrists behind his back.

When Sticks was coming around, Sloane tore off a piece of tape and plastered it on his mouth.

"This is not your first rodeo, is it?" I asked.

I finished rolling the duct tape around Sticks's ankles.

Sloane shrugged.

"Why are you helping us?" I should be suspicious. What if Sloane was working for whoever was causing trouble between the two families?

"Look, you can either trust me or stay here. In either case, I'm screwed because I went along with your plans for escape."

"I'm in your debt and you know I'll feel guilty if they take it out on you."

"I'm helping Divina. And maybe you could put in a good word for me with the De Luccis."

Sticks started writhing on the ground and mumbling, probably cursing, behind the tape. If his eyes were lasers, Sloane would be incinerated.

"Decide. Because when I leave, your best chance of seeing your family"—Sloane looked at Divina—"goes with me."

"You're crazy," Divina said, climbing into the van. "But I love you."

"Love you too, girlie."

"Well, hell, this is it for sure," I grumbled. "Sorry, Sticks, I'll be sure you get freed when we're clear."

Sloane didn't dramatically screech out of here, but went the regular normal speed.

"Good. No one seems to be around. And there are only guards at the entrance to the driveway during the evening. I didn't see any today."

"They have perimeter sensors," I told her. "Once you leave the driveway, they'll be alerted."

"Yes. But they won't see anything, so keep your heads down."

"Unless someone tries to contact Sticks."

The van started rocking. I knew we'd reached the long unpaved driveway. Sloane sped up. "It's a bouncy ride back there."

"So where is this property, exactly?"

Sloane told me the area was around an hour from Manhattan.

Wow, okay. I could just imagine all the round trips Sandro took if his business was in Manhattan or New Jersey.

"The Rossi mansion in Scarsdale is being watched, according to Tommy. That is why it's abandoned for now. Sandro is proposing to put it up for sale," Divina said.

"But it's been in the Rossi family for decades," I replied.

"Yes, but the family needs more liquidity."

"How bad are the finances?"

"Tommy is tight-lipped," Divina said. "Sandro is in way better shape. He minded his business in Harlem and didn't do crazy shit like Frankie and Joe. So it's a good thing he has separate accounting from the family. Speaking of which, Tommy also said the Rossi accountant might be embezzling."

I heard Tommy and Sandro talking about it, too.

"You're handling Sandro's books. Why don't you handle the family's?"

Divina shrugged. "No one suggested it, except you."

"I like you," Sloane told me. "You get shit done."

"Or have shit blow up in our faces." The two of us laughed. Divina looked ready to throw up. Maybe it was the rocking in the van, but I was sure it was because for the first time since marrying into the Rossis, she was going against a boss's wishes.

I grabbed her hand. "Don't worry. This won't blow back on you. You'll be an unwilling accomplice. After all, it was Sloane who stunned Sticks. You didn't even take part in tying him up."

"We can say we kidnapped you at stun-gun point—"

"Stop it," Divina cut her off. "I'm sick and tired of being the follower and playing it safe." She glanced at me and Sloane. "Both of you are rubbing off on me."

Sloane and I laughed again.

"Not sure the guys will be pleased with that," I said. "Are one of you being tracked on the phone?"

Sloane tossed her phone to the back of the van. "Turn it off and take out the sim."

And keep our fingers crossed.

The drive to Manhattan was smooth, but rife with trepidation. I noticed Sloane kept checking the side mirrors. Both of us continued to keep Divina entertained and unworried about the consequences of our actions. It was obvious that she had done nothing this wild in her life. With the few days I'd spent with her, she was the quiet and bookish one in her family. The obedient daughter.

Sloane was the opposite, but maybe that was why they were best friends. They tried to look at what was missing in the life of the other.

Although I didn't think Sloane was wild by choice. She was opportunistic, and sharp, and maybe it was because she was dealt the bad cards in her life, shouldering the debts of her family. With a brother constantly getting in trouble with gangs, she was constantly bailing him out. Plus, she'd mentioned a relative needing senior care. At least that was what I'd gleaned from the snippets of our conversations and why she was doing this.

When the familiar Manhattan skyline came into view, tears sprung to my eyes, and a pressure sat in my chest, making it hard to breathe. The agony of how much I missed my family came roaring back along with my hatred for the Rossis. For two weeks, they held me prisoner, cut off from the people I loved. I'd never been more impatient with New York traffic, but there was something comforting about being stuck in the hustle and bustle after being trapped in a quiet country house.

I needed the city.

Finally, the van coasted onto Twelfth Avenue and we were ten minutes away. I glanced at Divina. Her head was down, staring at her turned-off phone as if willing it to come to life.

"We're almost there," I said.

She glanced up with unmistakable fear in her eyes. "You think Tommy will be okay? They never sent proof of life."

I tried to find the words to tell her. It could go either way. My family was ruthless, but calculating. Killing Tommy Scavo made little sense. "They have the underboss of the Rossi crime family. They wouldn't damage him too much without getting the information they needed."

She dropped her head again, but a suppressed sob escaped her.

"Cut it out, Divina," Sloane snapped. "You're being unfair to Bianca. You're mafia for Chrissakes."

I really, really liked Sloane, but a crack began to appear in my excitement to see my family. The price that would come with it. Would Sandro think I betrayed him? Would that show him where my loyalty was?

I shoved him out of my mind. I would not let my guilt taint my reunion with family.

Heavy traffic met us again on the turn into Forty-Ninth Street.

"I walked by the café yesterday after it was sprayed with bullets," Sloane said.

"You didn't tell me that."

"Duh, because you would've asked endless questions. It was crawling with hot dudes in suits and in cool military gear. Surprisingly, the cops didn't stay very long."

When she didn't add more, I pressed. "And?"

"There was a gal I recognized from the *Manhattan Tattler* that was being a nuisance."

A sour taste coated my tongue. "Romero."

"Yes, that one."

"She has a hard-on for the New York Five Families."

"I hate her," Divina muttered.

"Same here." She ambushed Sera and Matteo on their date. She left Nico and Ivy alone, probably because Ivy wasn't mafia.

The vehicle finally made the turn onto the street where The Grindhouse building was located. I could barely keep myself from getting out of the van because running toward the café would be faster than the crawl of vehicles. We were hitting Hell's Kitchen at high noon and were running into the lunchtime crowd.

We were a block away when I spotted Nico. He wasn't in a suit, but was in fatigue-colored cargo pants and a black tee. Standing beside him was Trevor, who was similarly attired. There was no question they were assessing building security. Their heads were huddled together and they were staring at the café, which I didn't have a clear view of yet.

"I'll drop you girls here and find parking," Sloane said. "A van stopping right in front of the building isn't a good idea right now."

I dragged in a deep breath before I passed out.

"Ready?" I asked Divina.

I shoved open the door and the early October air filled my lungs with the freedom that had eluded me.

I jumped out of the van and resisted the urge to run. Divina was behind me, but at that moment, my focus zeroed in on the dearly familiar form of my brother.

"*Dearthháir*." Emotions clogged my throat, and the endearment came out as a ragged whisper. We were at the street corner and too far for them to hear me anyway.

Trevor saw me first. I could almost see his mouth form, "Holy fuck."

Nico's body whipped around, stiffening and alert like he was about to be ambushed, and then he was moving.

Toward me.

I ran.

Toward him.

I was bawling and mumbling *sorry* over and over again.

"Bianca." His voice cracked hoarsely, just as I hit his body at full tilt.

His arms surrounded me. He lifted me and buried his face in my hair.

I was home.

CHAPTER Twenty-Four

Sandro

"Kaz Doku? He still has loyalists?" I asked.

The man in front of me was only known as the Toronto fixer. He was the go-between for the Albanian mob based in Toronto and the Rossi crime family.

"It didn't come from us," the fixer said. "But yes, your problems…the burning of the club and the attempt to put you on a collision course with the De Luccis is coming from the New York Albanians."

"That's why they didn't want to take our coke?"

"Yes."

"So why help us if we're not gonna help you move product any longer?"

The man smiled. "You got Moretti to thank for that, but we're thinking of switching into something more legit. So this goodwill…" He tipped his chin to Gian who was overseeing the transfer of coke from our truck to theirs. "Hopefully we can do business in the future."

"Won't your guys in Manhattan have a problem with that?"

"Let's just say Toronto and New York haven't been on the same page for a long time. We need new blood. Excise the Doku loyalists." He shot me a smile that told me he wasn't entirely on my side and I had something to prove. We didn't shake hands, but exchanged chin lifts before he walked away.

With the fixer some distance away, Gian came to my side. "That was easy enough."

I turned toward our truck and started walking. "All done?"

"Yeah, let's get out of here."

"Tommy did all the negotiating."

"I'm surprised they didn't complain when it wasn't Tommy they were meeting."

No one from my side knew Luca was involved. That was why the fixer and I had a chat out of earshot of the other men.

"What can I say, Gian? You just have to trust me." I walked to my SUV and nodded to Arnie. He was the one driving the commercial truck back to Manhattan.

I addressed another Rossi soldier who called out my name. "What is it?"

I was only half listening to the soldier as my past came roaring back. Kaz Doku was the Butcher of Toronto and had been an archenemy of the Rossis. Both Carmelo and Raffa held him responsible for the death of their brother in the same car bombing that blinded Raffa. He was my first kill. The job no one thought I could pull off. Carmelo thought he was sending me to my death. Outside of Raffa, Carmelo, and Frankie, no one knew for sure if the Turk was the one who assassinated Kaz Doku. The Rossis systematically got rid of Doku supporters and a new leadership emerged. So why was this happening now?

The words of the soldier finally registered in my head.

Bianca. Escaped.

"What do you mean Bianca escaped?" I snarled.

"Sticks was trying to call you but you weren't answering."

"You know our phones are off. Why is yours on?"

"The Albanians left and—"

Never mind. I slid out my phone and powered it up.

Gian and Arnie gathered around me.

The second Sticks answered the phone, I clipped, "What happened?"

"Sloane helped Bianca escape."

"Sloane?"

"Yes. Bianca had some bullshit excuse about a coffee stain on the Persian rug."

"The one in the living room."

"Uh, yes."

I closed my eyes. Dammit, Bianca. "Then? You left them alone?"

"What was I supposed to do, boss? It's Sloane. But I caught them sneaking into the van and that bitch Sloane fried me with a stun gun."

I knew that girl was a maverick. "Do you know where they are now?"

"Divina's phone is back online. You're not going to like it."

"They're at The Grindhouse."

"Yep."

"Gather everyone and head to Manhattan. I'm still at Binghamton, so it's going to take me three hours to get there."

Three fucking hours I didn't really have. God fucking dammit, Bianca.

I ended the call and dragged a hand down my face. "Fuck."

There were not enough cuss words in the world to describe what I was feeling.

"Wife flew the coop, boss?" Arnie asked.

"Yeah. With Divina and Sloane." I stalked toward the Expedition that followed the commercial truck. I asked Arnie for the keys.

"Arnie, come with me." I handed the keys to Gian. "Drive the truck back to the warehouse. Await orders."

Gian asked, "What are you going to do?"

"Get my wife back," I said. And I might have to beg.

Bianca

We were gathered in the back of the coffee shop, away from the debris and destruction of the front. Heavy commercial tarps covered the shattered windows and the bullet-riddled walls of the café. A few booths were already dismantled. The bar needed repairs and Renz lost one of his espresso machines.

Nico ordered the construction crew off the premises.

"Nice place…well, except for that." Sloane nodded to the wreckage and slid into a booth. Divina took the seat in front of her while I sat along the edge beside her.

Nico approached us. "Dad and Mom are on their way. So are Matteo and Sera. I couldn't get ahold of Renz. They went in for a checkup."

"How is he?"

"He's going to be better now," Nico said.

Before I could ask him further, Dad and Mom rushed through the side door.

The look on my parents' faces…it was heartbreaking. I hadn't seen Dad and Mom so haggard. It was as if they'd aged ten years since the last time I saw them. There were bags under their eyes and creases on their faces that weren't there before. A sign of lack of sleep and weight loss.

The tears came before I could stop them.

"Dad, Mom."

I stepped into Dad first because he seemed to be the one who needed the hug the most. When it came to emotional turmoil and Dad's hands were tied, as was in my case, Mom had always been the strongest.

I was crushed in his familiar strength and the consoling scent of Dad's cologne assailed my nostrils, transporting me back to being his little girl, where my palm always found comfort in his warmth and heartbeat. In true Mom fashion, she hugged us both, sliding into the role of the glue that held the family together.

No words were spoken, but when I shifted, my heart splintered seeing the tears that fell from my parents' eyes. Dad was ashen beneath his tan and Mom was paler than pale, given the contrast with her red hair.

Dad cupped my face and gave me a kiss on both cheeks while Mom squeezed my hand. "You're really here." His ragged whisper cracked my heart further. I had never, ever heard such torment in Dad's voice. It was as if he'd gone through the nine circles of hell. "I failed you, *piccola mia*."

My little one. Dad hadn't called me that in a long time.

"You did not fail me. It was my fault."

"I won't hear of it." Murderous revenge chased away the shadowed despair in his eyes. "Now that I have you back safely, I'm going to send those Rossis to hell where they belong..."

Alarm dampened the elation of seeing my family. I did not consider this. I was thinking there would be a sit-down between the

De Luccis and the Rossis. I was Sandro's wife and that made me a Rossi too.

"No," I said firmly.

"No?" Dad's voice pitched dangerously soft. "Because of the Rossis, your brother was shot. Because of the Rossis," he enunciated, "my children were kept from me and you were forced to marry one of them."

"Did Renz explain what happened?"

"They should have returned both of you after the incident. Not hold you prisoners. Your brother could have died of complications because they withheld proper medical care!"

"No argument there. That was Gian Rossi's play, but Sandro is the boss now."

"Maybe we should discuss this later," Mom put in.

I glanced at her thankfully.

He was about to object, but she gave him a look. Dad clenched his jaw.

I exhaled a deep breath, but dragged in another one when his eyes narrowed over my shoulder. "Who do we have here?"

He walked past me to stand beside Nico, looking at Sloane and Divina like specimens under a microscope.

Mom held me to her side and wiped a strand from my face. "I missed you, Peanut."

"Missed you too, Mom." I gave her a reassuring smile, but I couldn't abandon the two women who helped me escape.

"You're Tommy's wife?" Dad asked Divina.

I walked past Nico and Dad and stood in front of the women. "She is. Where's Dom?"

"Where's my husband?" Divina asked in a voice that trembled.

"Yeah, where's Tommy?" Sloane asked in a firmer tone.

"And who exactly are you?" Nico asked her.

"I'm the one who got your sister out," she replied.

"Are you waiting for a reward?" Dad asked.

"Dad!" I was appalled.

"I'm not saying no," Sloane responded without missing a beat.

I rolled my eyes and gave her a dry look. "What? It wasn't out of the goodness of your heart."

The side door opened again and in walked Dom, Matteo, Sera, and Ivy.

More emotional reunions ensued. Ivy and Sera got to me first.

"Renz is on his way back," Matteo said. "Damn, sis, we were so worried about you."

"I'm fine. But it looks like you guys are worse for wear." Their faces were too grim. The guilt mounted. "Did you guys even think Sandro wouldn't look after me?"

"I knew he would," Mom said. "That's what I was telling the boys."

Matteo's jaw hardened, but it was Dad who answered, "He's got things to answer for. We welcomed him into our home and he wouldn't answer our calls."

All the men in my immediate family were understandably pissed. Dom stepped forward.

"Cuz, glad to see you're okay." I couldn't read his face. My dad's side of the family was the legitimate side. Nowhere did they expect that Dominic "Dom" De Lucci would step up to be the boss of the De Lucci crime family. He'd been boss in the five years since our great-uncle became too sick to continue. It didn't sit well at first with Uncle Paulie who was in the same mind as Dad to keep their children from being made men. Aunt Carlotta and Luca were more encouraging for obvious reasons and Emilio Moretti, of course, was ecstatic and died happy when his grandson became the youngest boss ever to take over a powerful New York family.

I gave him a tight smile before saying, "We have to talk."

"Bianca," Dad started. "You don't have to…Dom and I—"

"Dad," I said firmly. "I'm married to a boss now—"

Everyone started talking, cutting me off, the arguing giving me a headache.

"Not if I can help it," Dad spat with so much menace, and even if I knew it wasn't directed at me, it momentarily made me quail and reconsider whether I was in over my head, but when he added, "I can have the divorce papers drawn up and served—"

That was when I snapped, "Fuck no!"

"Bianca," he ground out. "This is not a phase."

Blood rushed to my face, both from embarrassment and hurt. Was there a reason for Dad to think otherwise? No. Because I'd been fickle with what I wanted in life. First, I wanted to become a PI like my McGrath cousins before I finally settled on an economics degree from Harvard. Then there was that fashion show and all my hero worship of being like Ivy. Uncertainty weighed me down for a second, but I had to be honest.

"Dad. Let's not talk about this here before we"—*you*—"say something we regret."

Mom put a hand on Dad's shoulder, but even before she did, the fury on his face had softened and I witnessed a father's pride and pain on his features. This was the conflict inside me. There was no question Dad only wanted what was best for me. If he could shelter me from all this, he would. But I was twenty-three years old. It was time for me to chart my path.

He sighed. "I didn't mean you're flighty."

"I never gave you reason to think otherwise," I said. "But it's time for me to make my own mistakes and not have you as a safety net."

"My daughter was forced to marry," he gritted. "It was hardly your mistake. You were coerced. To have you blackmailed…"

"I am not considering divorce. This is not a phase, Dad. Thinking of divorce at this point is like quitting before giving the marriage a chance." I took a step toward Dad and I hated that I saw betrayal on his face. "This is Sandro we're talking about—"

"He's a Rossi."

"So?"

"Over my dead body will you be married to a Rossi."

Standing behind Dad, Mom rolled her eyes and I tried not to smile because he became visibly peeved whenever anyone made a comment about me getting betrothed to Sandro.

"You think this is funny? All my life I made sure my children wouldn't become made men."

"Yet you have no problem enjoying the benefits of being connected to one." I nodded to Dom.

"Damn, cuz," Dom said. "Shots fired. Who is this girl?"

"Don't encourage her," Matteo snapped.

"I'm not your baby sister anymore," I snapped back at my brother. "I'm a grown woman married to a made man. Now." I switched my gaze to Dom. "Where is Tommy?" I tried to ignore the hostility emanating from the other guys, but I wanted the assurance, especially for Divina.

"Are you negotiating his release?" Dom asked. "Because that was the condition I gave Sandro."

"What?"

"You for Tommy."

I blinked. I had a terrible poker face and my sly cousin caught on.

"Well, I'll be damned," Dom muttered. "He never told you."

"Never told her what?" Nico asked.

I had no room for annoyance, outrage, or indignation concerning my husband keeping this secret from me. What I was feeling was less guilt about taking action against his knowledge.

"It doesn't matter now." I leaned forward. "Just know I'm not simply playing mafia wife. I have a duty to the women of the Rossi crime family. And apparently there's nothing more to negotiate if your condition was me for Tommy."

"Is Raffa Rossi holding something over Sandro's head?" Nico asked. "Because it's common knowledge that in spite of who's boss, he always has a say with how Rossis do business."

Again, I wish I played poker.

"What if he's blackmailing Sandro?" he continued. "We obviously know how you feel about him."

"You better release Tommy. And soon," Sloane spoke behind me. "I didn't risk my neck for nothing."

"Excuse me, who are you?" Dom demanded.

"She got me out," I said. "Be nice."

Trevor entered the café and handed Dom a printout. Matteo and Nico read over his shoulder.

"She's going to be paid handsomely for it," Dad said.

"Money is nice," Sloane said. "But it's not everything. I'm doing this for Divina. Since the Rossis came into her life, they've done nothing but push her around."

"And you're her champion, I presume," Dom mocked. "Sloane Scott? Of Scotty's Cleaning Service. Looks like here, you're in need of cash."

"You have no right!" Sloane shrieked when she realized what my cousin had in his hand. She made to grab the piece of paper from Dom. Of course, my cousin, who could be annoying as fuck, held the damning information out of reach.

"Dom, seriously?" I scolded.

All levity disappeared from his face enough to make Sloane back down. "You bring an unknown into De Lucci territory." He didn't need to stress that this building was the heart of the De Lucci crime family operations. That was why we were in the café despite the construction. It was the only public place. He wouldn't let a rival crime family into The Underground—the basement—

nor the residential spaces above us. "I make it my business to know."

"Sloane is just helping," I told him. "But let's not get side-tracked. Tommy?"

He sighed and slipped out his phone.

"Your cousin is a giant asshole," Sloane said in my ear.

"I thought you wanted me to introduce your business."

"I'm having second thoughts."

"My men are bringing him over," Dom said. "Sandro is blowing up my phone."

Matteo and Nico mentioned the same thing.

"Well, answer it," I said. They'd confiscated Divina's and Sloane's phones so no one could call them either.

The men looked at each other and I wanted to knock their heads together with their identical smug faces.

"Payback is a bitch," Nico said.

The café door opened again, and Renz appeared.

"Bianca?"

I burst into tears.

CHAPTER
Twenty-Five

Bianca

I thought I'd run out of tears, but seeing Renz on his feet instead of lying down in pain or heavily sedated did a number on my heart. It also gave added perspective to Dad's and my brothers' anger and their burning desire to sever my connections to the Rossis.

I was in a turmoil between guilt, duty, and my love for Sandro.

Love? I'd always loved him. But there were different types of love and at this moment, I couldn't analyze which spectrum it fell on.

Because right here, right now, I was overwhelmed with love for my De Lucci family.

"I'm so sorry," I cried as Renz one-armed me to his uninjured side. I didn't know how many times I'd repeated the apology. But I would repeat it until they told me to shut up or gag me. But it was as if a balloon of warmth expanded in my chest. I'd been on a roller coaster of my feelings for Sandro, and I wondered if I was reluctant to find happiness with him, to fully commit to him until I'd seen with my own eyes that Renz was okay. That my obsession with Sandro didn't cost my brother permanent damage.

"Not your fault," he said fiercely. "How many times have I told you this?"

I raised my eyes to his and tears were streaming down his face. "It doesn't matter how many times you tell me, I would never forgive myself if the unspeakable happened to you."

If Renz died.

I would have made Liz a widow.

Sam wouldn't have a father.

Oh, God.

The horror of it consumed me again, competing with the fullness in my heart. But crying was cathartic.

I didn't know how long Renz hugged me while I drenched his chest with my tears. My brothers and Dad continued to protect me and they were putting all the blame on Sandro. This would have to change. But baby steps. I wasn't their innocent sister who got into scrapes and came up smelling like roses. It was because it was always Sandro who found me in my less angelic moments.

"Just know we don't blame you," a feminine voice said beside me.

I turned my attention to Liz. My dear sister-in-law, who had more patience and kindness than anyone I knew. I let go of Renz and hugged her so I could whisper in her ear, "We're sorry to put you and Sam through this." And the *we* included Renz. I imagined Liz had been through hell when Renz and I went missing. When I pulled away, I swiped the tears from my eyes and said, "I hope Renz wasn't a terrible patient."

She gave a brief laugh. "He's been stubborn about his pain meds, and he's still on a round of antibiotics. But one of The Grindhouse gym members is a TCM practitioner. He took one look at

Renz and said his Qi was misaligned. Also, Ivy figured it was his guilt and anger that's preventing him from healing. That was where we were earlier for a consultation."

Nico was the TCM believer because he was the health nut, more so with Ivy's influence. I was more a pop-a-pain-med kind of gal, but I could have an open mind.

"Bianca is back, so I'm sure I'll get better," Renz grumbled.

Liz and I glanced at each other and grinned. "Where's Sam?"

"She's in the apartment with the nanny," Liz said. "Figured we'd get the grown-ups settled first."

"Good idea."

"I'm hungry," Renz said. "Anyone want food?"

"See? He's already better." Liz grinned. "It's the first time he wants to cook."

"Or we could just order from Eamonn's," Mom said dryly.

"Good idea." My brother was already heading into the kitchen. "But let me get some appetizers started."

"I'll help!" Liz called after him.

"Me too," Sera and Ivy said in unison.

Mom got on the phone with Eamonn's.

The guys had settled around the twenty-seat communal table. Divina and Sloane were still in the booth in front of it.

It was like a demarcation line, and I was in the middle. "When is Tommy getting here?"

"Maybe ten minutes with traffic," Dom answered.

"We should call Sandro and tell him everything is fine."

Dom looked at Dad and my brothers.

"No," Dad said. "He let us suffer for over two weeks. He can last another few hours."

"This is not a tit for tat!" I fumed.

"Isn't it?" Matteo nodded to the damage of the café.

"It wasn't us," I said.

"Wow," Dom said. "Are you considering yourself one of them now?"

"Dom," Dad warned. "Let's not make this worse."

Mom returned, and her eyes made the rounds at everyone at the table. "Food is on the way. From the looks of it, everyone will feel better once their blood sugar isn't crashing, hmm?"

"Food isn't going to fix this." My stomach grumbled loudly and made me a liar.

Sandro

"I want to talk to Bianca," I growled into my phone.

"Looks like they want you to suffer a little," Luca said dryly.

My convoy was still an hour from Manhattan. At a rest stop, I switched driving with Arnie. Cops were all over the interstate and I couldn't drive without my lead foot weighing down on the gas pedal. The last thing we wanted was to get pulled over and have a cop discover a trunk full of illegal weapons. I had two sub-machine guns hidden in the spare tire compartment. It didn't help that the De Luccis were declining my calls.

It was payback.

"Can't you do something?"

"Hey, they're my family too. But Dom released Tommy. He's in the café. I hear they're enjoying an Irish feast."

"What the fuck?"

Luca chuckled. "This is good. Now don't screw this up."

He ended the call.

I hated when he did this, but he was Luca Moretti. He suffered no fools gladly. At least this drama between the Rossis and the De Luccis was keeping his mind off his missing wife.

I slipped the phone back into my pocket. It was pushing three in the afternoon.

"No luck?" Arnie asked.

"None." I'd probably pissed off the De Luccis enough by hitting redial over and over. We were grown men behaving childishly.

Motherfucker.

I tapped the corner of the window and willed the Expedition to travel faster.

Bianca

"It wasn't us who did this!" Tommy repeated.

We were still gathered around the communal table. When Tommy arrived, I was outraged to see the bruises on his face. He couldn't open one eye. Divina gasped a sob when she saw him, and I glared at Dom.

But would I expect anything less? We were the mafia. Someone had tipped off Dom where Tommy was the same night somebody shot up Jabbin' Java and Tommy wasn't too far from here. But my cousin was smart enough not to jump to conclusions.

"I believe the Rossis didn't do this," I told them. Mom was right. Everyone was calmer after eating or maybe it was the carbs from the mashed potatoes, but at least the smirks from my family didn't aggravate me like earlier. "Just as we believe it wasn't the De Luccis who set fire to the club. Not your MO."

Dom was about to say something, but I cut him off. "Now Gian's poker game, though, I wonder."

"No idea what you're talking about." Dom's face remained neutral because he was being watched, but I didn't miss the look Matteo and Nico exchanged. Meanwhile, Trevor's mouth twitched, and he disguised his smile by taking a sip from his super-sized soda.

Matteo and Nico may be mafia adjacent, but the secret organization my father started, The Archer Syndicate, kept the underworld in check. They were more organized and technologically advanced than the average mafia, moved easily from corporate boardrooms into the underworld, and with Dad's financial resources, was virtually unstoppable in getting things done. Heads of the Syndicate were called Archers. Their soldiers were called Arrows. The organization didn't have the bullshit recruiting requirements of other crime families based on race or gender. They didn't care whether you're white, Asian, or Arab. Italian or Russian. Male or female. It was based on skills and alignment of beliefs. Most of its members were ex-military, like Trevor and my cousin Ronan, or financial powerhouses like Matteo and Ivy's brother, Daniel.

A popular move of the Syndicate was to leak information to law enforcement and let them do the cleanup, especially when it came to human trafficking. I had no love lost for Gian, but illegal gambling was a revenue source Sandro was keeping. I needed to have a chat with Matteo, who was the current head Archer, but this conversation had to happen without Divina and Tommy present.

A commotion outside captured our attention.

"That's as far as you go, Rossi!" someone shouted.

My heart leapt to my throat. *Sandro is here.*

I got out of the booth, but Nico stood in my way.

"What the hell?" My blood boiled. "Move!"

"He'll need to face us first," Matteo said.

I tried to sidestep my brother, but he stepped in sync with me. Exasperated, I glanced at my mother. "Mom."

She looked resigned. For a moment, I forgot that this was not a sibling squabble where she had the power to settle our arguments. For a moment, I felt powerless. That I was out of my depth dealing with a situation like this.

"Bianca," Tommy called my name.

I glanced at him. There was encouragement on his bruised face. He still believed in me.

"You've come this far, girl," Sloane whispered.

Divina pursed her lips and nodded.

Dad and Matteo had already exited the premises.

"You can't keep me from my husband!" I gritted into Nico's face.

His expression remained unbending. "Watch us."

Trevor took his place to keep me contained as Nico followed Matteo and Dad. Tommy tried to get up, but one of the soldiers who brought him in pointed a gun at him.

"Is that necessary?" I hissed at Dom.

He nodded for his soldier to lower his weapon. "Then stay in here and let *your* family do what they gotta do."

"Fine," I growled. "It's probably a good idea that those stubborn asses are distracted." I mentally asked God's forgiveness for calling Dad a stubborn ass.

Dom looked amused. "What's on your mind, cuz?"

I crossed my arms. "Reopen negotiations."

CHAPTER
Twenty-Six

Sandro

The De Luccis were ready for us.

I told Arnie to stop at a street corner and I hoofed it to the café. The place was crawling with De Lucci soldiers as well as their paramilitary security, but I had Sticks and the club bouncers flanking me.

"Don't interfere," I told them. "Let's not escalate tensions."

"They're going to beat the shit out of you if they don't shoot you first."

I clenched my jaw in determination. Bianca was worth it. "I deserve it." But each step closer to the café was like marching to the gallows. The De Luccis wouldn't let me talk to Bianca and had quit responding after they confirmed she was with them. Luca had served as the middleman, cautioning both sides to keep their temper.

But if they kept my wife from me, there was no telling what I would do. Bianca was coming home today. She was sleeping in my bed tonight.

"That's as far as you go, Rossi," one of the De Lucci soldiers ordered. He was dressed like a mall cop, uniform and all, but I knew it was just to keep everything looking legit. His hand was on his weapon.

"You're gonna cause a scene in the streets?" I taunted. I slowed my strides, but I refused to raise my arms in surrender.

I took another step. "If you know who I am, then you should know you shouldn't make an enemy of me."

"You've got some nerve showing up here." Matteo appeared with Cesar backing him up. Their hardened jaws and their clenched fists dictated how this was going down.

Fine.

"You of all people should understand this," I said.

"I did not force Sera to marry me."

"You married her under false pretenses."

And that was the last word exchanged between us. Matteo's fist flew and I braced for it. It cracked against my jaw and I tasted blood. He planted another one in my solar plexus. But I caught his wrist and, using that as leverage, flipped him over my hip and sent him crashing to the concrete flooring.

Cesar's punch connected with my cheekbone, but I blocked a blow meant for my torso. I had no desire to hurt Bianca's father, just like the time he beat me up when he found her in my apartment.

Another one landed in my gut.

Fuck, I felt the rage in that one and it emptied my lungs of air. I folded over, but before he could use his knee to my chin, I twisted and landed a hit to his middle.

"Don't hold back," Cesar snarled.

"I'm showing respect, old man." I grinned. "Feels like old times, eh?"

"Fuck you."

I left myself open for another jab and I felt my brow split. I spotted Nico stalking toward us.

Oh, for fuck's sake. Where was Bianca? Did she abandon me to the men of her family?

I wasn't making progress into the building, and before my frustration could bleed into my fists and actually put the hurt on someone, I caught Cesar's arm and swung him toward Matteo, who was about to rejoin the fight.

I met Nico head-on. "Cesar and Matteo already took jabs at me. I want to see my—"

I didn't know what happened. One second I was going full force into Nico, prepared for him to hit me and I was gonna block, and the next I was on the ground on my chest. My right arm locked behind me with his knee on my back.

The fuck?

"You underestimate how pissed we are, Rossi," Nico growled.

"Are you taking lessons from your wife?"

"We spar a few times a week," the smug fuck returned.

"Don't you dare kick him!" Bianca screamed at someone.

"I wasn't," Matteo said.

Wife, it's about time.

The truth was, I had to pull punches because it was her family and I was telling myself that was the only reason Nico had me on the ground. Being on good terms with the De Luccis may come with perks. Sparring with Ivy Wu. That woman could kick ass and become a valuable associate.

"Good! Let him go, Nico!" she demanded. And then she was kneeling in front of me. "Are you all right?"

The moment I got to my feet, I snatched her in my arms. I was dizzy with relief, which didn't bode well for my reputation, but all I cared about was she didn't hide behind her family.

"You're bleeding." She tentatively touched my brow.

"Don't get it on you."

Her eyes narrowed indignantly. "Why not? Are you still treating me like breakable glass?"

I couldn't help it, so I ignored the question and muttered, "I'm damn happy you finally showed up."

She glared at me before turning her displeasure on her family, reminding me we had an audience. "I'm very disappointed in all of you! Ganging up on my husband like that."

My husband. Despite my throbbing face and the pain in my torso, the organ in my chest expanded with smug satisfaction.

"It's our fucking right," Matteo grunted, but a wariness tempered his declaration as if he was reassessing the situation. All the men in Bianca's family had narrowed gazes, observing how she was interacting with me. I hoped it was clear as fuck that I didn't mistreat her. I couldn't say the same about the rest of my family. It probably explained why Bianca was wearing a sweater to hide the marks on her arms and wrists. Otherwise, the De Luccis would have had a kill-on-sight order on me.

"What? To defend my honor?"

Nobody answered.

"It's okay," I muttered. "I expected it."

"Shut up, Sandro," she snapped before staring up at me in irritation. "And what the hell was that? You think you can just waltz in here?"

"You left. You think I won't come after you? I always will."

"It's my fault," Divina announced. She approached with Tommy at her side.

"That's not what I heard." I squinted at Sloane, who appeared to be hiding behind them.

But my secondary concern was Tommy. "You okay, man?"

He nodded and gave a thumbs-up. His face was battered, but the fact that he was upright and walking, I couldn't say that wasn't a justified response, especially since we returned Renz drugged, with a bullet through him, and flat on his back. And that didn't even cover Bianca's kidnapping and forced marriage.

"You're not leaving with her." Cesar stepped forward, menace etched on his face. There were rumors about Bianca's father's brutality beneath his expensive suits. That he'd been responsible for many disappearances of Rossi capos, including Raffa's best friend.

"And you're in no position to start a war with me." It was one thing to show respect, and another to show I was intimidated. A new tightrope crystallized as I balanced my duties as boss and my commitment to a woman with an overprotective and powerful family.

"But I am." Dom stood beside Cesar.

My arms tightened around Bianca. "You really wanna do this?"

"No," Dom said. "I'm giving Tommy back in light of good faith to have Bianca spend time with her family."

"The Rossis are her family too," Tommy interjected.

"Seriously? You're going to renege on negotiations?" Dom asked.

"What negotiations?" I roared and took a giant step back with Bianca, ready to get her out of here.

"I don't like your phrasing," Tommy told Dom. "Bianca considers herself a Rossi, too. She told you clearly and concisely."

"She told him what?" Cesar turned on Dom.

Apparently, I wasn't the only one left out of said negotiations.

"Guys…" Bianca attempted to pull away from me, but I wouldn't let her.

"Dad," she started. "Dom, Tommy, and I agreed. I can stay overnight—"

"There's no such agreement," I gritted. "We're leaving."

But when I spun around with her, it was to see we were surrounded by De Lucci crew. Trevor being one of them and there was a challenge on his face, daring me to make another move.

Sticks was with me. Gian and the Rossi soldiers were around the perimeter but there was no way I was going to start a gunfight in broad daylight because I hadn't given clear instructions to Gian and he might find the perfect opportunity to eliminate me and Tommy.

No way was I risking my wife in the line of fire.

"It's just for a night," Bianca whispered.

"Sandro," a female voice said behind us.

We turned around. It was Ava. It was obvious she wanted to come forward, but Cesar had his arms around her the same way I had mine around Bianca.

"Just for tonight, *son*," she said.

Son.

Ava accepted me. For the first time since I found out my wife escaped the house, a semblance of calm placated my aggression. I loosened my hold around Bianca. She didn't abandon me. She stood up for me. There was no reason not to trust she would return to me.

Sensing that I was about to relent, Ava freed herself from Cesar—albeit, he grudgingly let go—and moved in front of us. She touched my jaw. "Welcome to the family, Sandro."

"Mom." Bianca hiccuped a sob. Her emotions came through in a body shudder that cracked through my resolve to bring her home with me.

"Can I get a hug?" Ava asked.

Dammit. That resolve crumbled. I released Bianca and gave Ava a tight squeeze. I breathed in her ear, "Thank you." I was reduced back to the boy who had wished Ava was his mother. And now she really was. I wasn't fucking this up. Bianca was worth it to put up with the insufferable men in her family.

"I would invite you over for our impromptu gathering tonight," Ava continued. "But I fear you've got your hands full." She nodded to Tommy.

If I stayed over at the De Lucci camp right now, the upheaval in the Rossis would be catastrophic. Especially after what happened with Raffa. All the progress I'd achieve in getting rid of the toxic assets would be for nothing. My brain processed the next moves. Given what happened with Tommy and Bianca's escape, I needed the De Luccis to protect my wife while I got my house in order.

"Are you going to be okay?" Bianca asked. "Tommy and Dom assured me you would be."

"Everything will be fine." If I couldn't lead the Rossi crime family without putting Bianca first, then I didn't want the position as boss.

My thumb brushed over her naked ring finger. "But we'll have words about you not wearing your rings."

She grinned sheepishly. "I helped Sloane clean the rug and didn't want to ruin them."

I tamped down the feral possessiveness rampaging inside me. But Ava extended an olive branch. It would give me great pleasure to show her I was more evolved than her sons and husband.

"Tommy, Divina, and Sloane are allowed to leave," I told Dom.

"No one is stopping them," he replied.

I glanced at Cesar. "I'm coming for Bianca tomorrow. I'm gonna find a place in Manhattan so she will be more accessible to all of you—"

Bianca tugged my arm and I gave her a questioning look.

"Don't do any house hunting without me."

I controlled the grin that wanted to form. Her statement filled me with an anticipation I had no business feeling. It was hope. So much fucking hope that despite our uncertain road ahead, a future with her was possible. "Sure, Sunlight, whatever you say."

"This is weird as fuck," Nico interjected and I could commiserate with what he was feeling. Being with Bianca as her husband and around the De Luccis seemed like an alternate universe. I was determined to make it a reality.

"Hey, stop that," Bianca retorted. "Or I'm leaving with Sandro."

The De Lucci men clenched their jaws, and it was hilarious as fuck how identical they looked to each other when they glowered at me.

"It's hard to leave without you," I confessed.

"But he has to." Tommy grabbed my arm. "Let's go before they change their minds."

I hauled Bianca into my arms once more and gave her a quick, devouring kiss. Still, after I let her go, I couldn't help touching her. I'd be lucky to make it through the night. Her luminous eyes stared up at me with adoration. It was the mature version of the look she'd given me when she was younger. I convinced myself I didn't know what love was, but these past two weeks, I finally assigned that word to what I'd felt for Bianca all along. It was an unspoken emotion between us. A love that had taken many forms over the years.

I loved her when she was my friend, but now, as my wife, I was *in love* with her.

Tenderly, I ran two fingers down her cheek before nodding to her brothers, Cesar, and Dom, and pivoted away to head back into the streets of Manhattan.

The Grindhouse building had a throughway that separated Jabbin' Java from the boxing gym. Two other businesses were on the ground floor, both owned by the McGrath side of Bianca's family. A private investigations firm and a law office. I also knew for a fact they had a basement, which was ground zero for De Lucci operations.

With Bianca as my wife, I wondered how to navigate the complexities that came with her family.

When I emerged from the throughway, a small crowd had formed. It wasn't regular Hell's Kitchen pedestrian traffic. I spotted the *Manhattan Tattler* reporter Romero among them. These were mafia groupies.

Fucking hell.

"Alessandro Rossi!" The wide smile on her face almost had me retreating into The Grindhouse. "Is it true you married Bianca De Lucci?"

"No comment."

Arnie was waving his arm at me from a street corner where the Expedition was double-parked to make a quick escape. Good, reliable Arnie.

"Are you the boss now?"

I quickened my strides. When they weren't getting answers from me, they turned to Tommy. "Were you being held captive? Was this in retaliation for the hit on the café?"

"No comment," Tommy replied. "I'm not about to admit I got my ass kicked at the boxing gym."

I swallowed a smile. Sticks and the other Rossi soldiers swarmed around us and kept Romero away.

Jesus Christ. The contract killer in me sweated with this attention. I worked in the shadows, but I better get on board quickly with my new position as the don of the Rossi crime family and what it meant to be married to Bianca.

Sticks opened the center row of the Expedition. I was in this role now. I wasn't gonna ride shotgun or be the driver.

I slid into the seat.

"Raffa wants to see you," Arnie said.

"I'm not leaving Manhattan," I told him.

"Well, you don't have a club either."

Dammit, he was right. "Head to the Wisteria." If the *John Wick* movies had the Continental, our underworld had the Wisteria. Neutral ground for everyone including warring or unstable crime families. "I'll make the call."

CHAPTER Twenty-Seven

Sandro

"So where do we stand, nephew?"

It was just me and Raffa in a meeting room at the Wisteria. Gian and Tommy were outside. This was so Raffa and I could speak freely.

With Bianca safe with her family, I was done humoring his long-running grudge against the De Luccis. I had a feeling he was waiting for either me or Bianca to call his bluff.

"You're going to accept that I don't answer to you anymore," I told him. "You have disrespected my wife for the last time. I should kill you, but I won't. The morale of the Rossi crime family has been in the trenches since Frankie took over."

Raffa removed his glasses as if he wanted to see me clearly without them. His eyes had taken on a grayish hue and, it used to be when he did this, it was to intimidate. To let the person know he could see right through them despite his blindness. But I stared right into his soulless eyes. Finally, he put his glasses back on and said, "What do you need from me?"

"You're going to back me up when I announce to the other crime families that I'm the new don."

After we got rid of the cocaine, the weight on my shoulders eased. I was a quick fixer. I got rid of threats. Negotiations weren't my thing, but I could learn it. I could learn it as long as Bianca was at my side and that was the only way to keep her.

"Really?" His brow hiked up. "You're not planning to hand it off to Tommy?"

"No. I'm the only one who deserves that position. Not even Gian."

"Gian said you played Russian roulette with his head."

His tone sounded serious, but I detected a hint of amusement, even pride. It'd been years since Raffa had been my ally. He'd been one of my staunchest supporters after I got rid of Kaz Doku. I fell out of favor when it was clear I had no plans to be more involved in the family business. Sometimes I wondered if his ridiculous impositions on my marriage to Bianca were not only to get back at Cesar, but also at me for resisting his attempts to mold me into the next boss. Vindictive bastard.

"It was an expedient way to get my answers," I told him.

"He's my son."

"Your adopted son. I'm more your blood than he is." I didn't have to point out that if his men had inflicted lasting trauma on Bianca, I would have razed the entire family to the ground.

He leaned back in his seat and steepled his fingers over his protruding belly. "So tell me. Where do you expect to take the family? You have no club to launder the money coming from drugs. Oh wait, you don't even have the drugs. Protection rackets are not making enough money. You have the smuggling of goods, but you're in competition with everyone else."

"Put the Rossi mansion up for sale. It's our biggest asset."

Naked anger contorted Raffa's features. He leaned forward in his seat. "Are you out of your goddamned mind? You grew up there. I grew up there."

"Doesn't hold fond memories for me. It's where Frankie was gunned down." Where I chose Bianca over my half brother. "I'm sure there's going to be some rich schmuck who's gonna drop a obscene hunk of cash for the notoriety." Maybe even make it into a museum, but that wasn't my scene. "We're gonna get around a hundred fifty mil easy for those structures and the property. The basement vault contains artwork that would fetch another two hundred million at an auction."

"You've given this a lot of thought. What about your legacy?"

"What legacy? My mother—real mother, was kept captive in that mansion," I gritted. "Repeatedly raped by Carmelo until she gave birth to me. Then he had her killed. You think I wanna stay there? You think I wanna raise a family haunted by the memories of his despicable acts?"

I couldn't even call Carmelo Rossi Pop anymore. He was nothing but a sperm donor.

Raffa averted his face as if he couldn't stand the anger I was radiating. It took me years to come to terms with my origins. I was a product of a heinous crime kept in secret by the Rossi leadership. But I didn't want to dwell on the past because I saw a future with Bianca.

"We will use the money and build new infrastructure," I said. "Gambling and gaming. Real estate."

Raffa faced me again. "Who put these ideas in your head? Luca?"

"You never liked him, did you? But he's at the top of the food chain now, even when people try to tear him down," I said. "My club remains mine. I don't intend to use Rossi money to rebuild it.

It has insurance." And I had my own money. I wanted full autonomy in the running of it. "It should be ready in two months. Leave Manhattan, Raffa. Spend your miserable last days in Italy. Be a gangster there if you want to. But in my organization, you will cease to have a say."

"Not everyone is going to be happy with this."

"The only one left with discontent is Gian. And I think I made it clear what will happen to anyone who defies me by going after Bianca."

A slight sneer curved his mouth. "You're going to become a puppet of the De Luccis."

"I didn't become your puppet, Raffa." I smiled grimly. "Are you saying they're more ruthless than you?"

I stood, leaving him fuming in silence. "This meeting is over. Have a comfortable retirement." It was more than he goddamned deserved.

~

Bianca

"They'll come around." Aunt Lottie glanced over at where Uncle Paulie was saying goodbye to Dad and my brothers.

Mom threw an impromptu dinner and I considered it a success. Most of my immediate family opposed to my marriage didn't make any derogatory comments about my husband or try to talk me into a divorce.

Aunt Lottie was the only one who was giddy with the situation. "Paulie was the same when Dom announced he wanted to go into *the family* business, but see, they come around." I remembered the agreement was that Dom had to finish college first.

She cupped my cheek. "Now, my niece is married to a boss."

"Why didn't you?"

She glanced over my shoulder and beamed. "Paulie was too charming."

My uncle walked to our side and gave my aunt a fond kiss. "You were my perfect fit, *cara*." During her heyday, Carlotta Moretti was *the* sought-after mafia princess. She was the gorgeous, spoiled daughter of Emilio Moretti from his first wife. Paulie wasn't even a consideration because he wasn't in the mafia or a made man. Offers came from top crime families all over the world, but she fell in love with my uncle and fell out of favor with Emilio because she followed her heart.

Before his death, Emilio got his wish, though. Dom became a made man and the chill from the Moretti side thawed, especially since Dom and Luca dealt with a lot of inter-organization business.

Speaking of Dom, he joined us by the door.

"You're leaving, too?" I asked.

"Duty calls. Sandro wants a word. Apparently, he had a meeting at the Wisteria with the Blind Don."

Anxiety bloomed at the pit of my stomach. "It all went well?"

He glanced at his parents and winked. "We'll discuss later."

Paulie rolled his eyes. "Stop rubbing it in. You're making Cesar and his boys nervous."

And as if not listening to his dad, Dom hugged me and said loudly, "Welcome to the dark side, cuz."

"Fuck you, Dom." That came from Nico.

He and Ivy were behind me. Matteo and Sera, Renz and Liz with Sam were behind them.

"What is this? A mass exodus?" I asked.

"I think you and Dad have plenty to talk about," Nico replied.

"Not sure I'm ready for it," I spoke through the corner of my mouth.

Sera pulled me into a tight hug. "You got this." Besides Lottie and Dom, Sera was the most pleased with my marriage to Sandro. She teased Matteo that she was living vicariously through me.

"Congrats again on the pregnancy." Sera was three months pregnant with the baby due in April.

Her face glowed. "Thank you."

"I'm sure you're going to spoil her," I told Matteo. He scratched a brow and breathed out a rough laugh that held a tinge of anxiety but I had no doubt he would make a great father. He was known as the Raptor of Wall Street after all. Laser-focused on a goal. And right now, that was creating his own family with Sera.

Before my thoughts could veer into the direction of Sandro and me starting our own family, Renz and Liz were next to say goodbye. I became teary-eyed all over again. Those two days Renz and I had spent in captivity forged a different bond. Hard to define, it stretched between us whenever our eyes locked.

"Hey, no more tears," Renz said in a tone that steadied my unraveling emotions. It was as if he wanted to put the whole experience behind us so I could stop blaming myself. "I'm stronger. And I always had faith in Sandro."

"Is that why you didn't add your two cents and kick his ass?"

"Oh, I intend to challenge him in the boxing ring when I get back into fighting form." He glanced at his brothers. "Like grown-ups would do."

Matteo coughed into his fist. "Like Dad?"

Sam tugged on my arm. I glanced down at her. "Yes, sweetie?"

"Can I be your flower girl?"

"Well…"

"You know you're going to have another wedding, right?" Ivy's eyes danced with laughter.

No question about it, and Carlotta confirmed, "We won't accept anything less."

"All right, guys, we better go," Liz announced.

My heart was brimming with happiness after they left. I missed them more than when I was on my three-month sabbatical. I guess because I could talk to them at any time and return when I was ready. Another reminder not to take them for granted. I thought I needed to find myself outside of family. I didn't need to go far away to do that.

My new phone was in my pocket. I didn't know what happened to my old one. Sandro probably had it. Or it had been destroyed. But Trevor had deactivated that one and cloned me another one with the same settings and contacts.

I turned to face my parents. Mom was in the kitchen, finishing cleanup. I headed in her direction to help her when she glanced up. She smiled at me briefly while tilting her head toward the living room where Dad was pouring himself a drink.

There was no avoiding this talk. Dad hadn't been chatty at dinner, letting Aunt Carlotta and Mom carry the conversation. My brothers were careful with what they said. I think because their wives were there to keep them in check. But Dad let the bantering slide off him. Gave one-word answers. Brooded and stared at me when he thought I wasn't looking. I could hear the gears turning in his head. He'd probably already mapped out the steps to sever my ties with Sandro. Draw up divorce papers. Pack me into a plane with a new identity. He'd probably already chosen a destination.

It was up to me to convince him that Sandro wasn't a phase. The sooner he understood this, the better.

I stopped at the mouth of the living room and leaned against the arch. "So…"

He turned around, and without Mom and my brothers, I'd never been more awkward with Dad in my life. More than the time he glared at my prom date the whole time the poor guy was here. Well, maybe less than the time he caught me at Sandro's apartment and dragged me home. Dad had always been the number one man in my life. Sandro and my brothers came in second and that depended on who pissed me off the most. But Dad? No matter how many times his protective actions irked me, he was forever on that pedestal.

"I know you feel I let you down." Might as well rip off the Band-Aid. "And at first I thought I'd be disappointing you."

"Disappointment was never a feeling I associated with you, Bianca," he said, dropping his gaze to the amber liquid he was twirling in the glass.

I entered the room cautiously. "There's a *but* there…"

He exhaled a heavy sigh. "It's not disappointment, but failure." He glanced up. "My failure."

"Dad…"

He gestured to the minibar. "Do you want anything to drink?"

When I shook my head, he walked to the brown leather couch and sat. I sat beside him, rigid and unsure of what to say next. I linked my hands together on my lap. I used to lean against him and he would have an arm around me. But the wall of words we couldn't say to one another kept us a foot apart.

Dad broke the silence first. "All my life I wanted to see the Rossis rot in hell. It had been my mission." He took a sip of his drink. "Now I have to give that up."

He said it in such a petulant, grudging way, a small laugh escaped me. "I'm sorry I ruined your plans."

He glared at his drink before glancing my way with a rueful smile, briefly disrupting the taut lines of his countenance. "They're not in the best financial situation."

"Sandro is looking into it. There seems to be a problem with the accountant."

Dad scoffed. "Their accountant is a weasel. Carmelo, Frankie, and Joe weren't the brightest bulbs when it came to fiscal responsibility. I don't want to see my daughter want for anything."

"And any help you give me would be helping the Rossis," I said. I put my hand over his. "I'll be fine. You can only offer guidance. I'm not expecting you to bail the Rossis out simply because I'm a part of their family now."

We fell into silence again. But the silence was rife with Dad's simmering thoughts and his misgivings about my husband, but specifically, who he represented.

He drained his glass and blew out a breath. "Are you sure this is what you want, *carina*? Just say the word and I'll have you out of the country. I can make this whole thing disappear."

"Sandro isn't backing down."

"He couldn't find you those three months you were in California," he pointed out.

"Things have changed between us, Dad. I'm his wife now. And you saw him. He finally claimed me in front of everyone."

He didn't answer.

"I've loved Sandro Rossi all my life. I've loved him since I was five years old."

"That was hero worship."

"Agreed." I pursed my lips. "Let me put it this way: I've had affection for him all my life. There was a time, I admit, I was obsessed with him." I grinned at Dad. "It's not only the men in our family who get hit with obsession."

"That was my worry. I was afraid Sandro would take advantage."

"He never did." I raked my bottom lip, not sure if Dad wanted to hear about my less than stellar behavior, but he needed assurance that Sandro did all he could to respect me. "Even when I threw myself at him."

Dad gave a pained chuckle and scratched his brow the same way Matteo did when he was unsure or embarrassed. It was a rare occasion when the men in my family found themselves in situations where they didn't know what to do. "That's…good," he said gruffly.

I rolled my eyes. "What? No reprimands? You think your little princess can do no wrong?"

"You're always going to be my little princess," he said sharply. "He's not taking that away from me."

"Oh, Dad." This time I scooted closer and picked up his hand. "You're not losing a daughter. Can't you see you're gaining a son in Sandro?"

He stared at our joined hands. "I took advantage of him having affection for you. It was like having another son to look out for my youngest child."

My mouth twitched. "So you did see him as a son."

"It didn't worry me at first until you were old enough to date."

"Let's not talk about my dating life." All the men I dated paled in comparison to Sandro, especially now that I'd experienced the intensity of what it meant to belong to him.

"I should've sent you to a convent."

I laughed. "I heard Sera had also been threatened by her *nonno* and Luca." I gave Dad a reassuring smile. "Sandro is not a phase. Yes, I was forced to marry him and he did so to protect me. But it gave us a chance to explore the feelings that were there all along. Sandro has always felt unworthy."

"No man is worthy of you."

"Says every dad about his daughter."

"I just worry, *carina*."

"I can't stop you from worrying, but I hope you'll let me make my own mistakes."

Dad didn't answer except to harden his jaw. I was afraid by the time this was over he would need to see a dentist to check the condition of his molars from all that grinding. I didn't know how else to soothe him. I myself didn't know what the future held. But I admit it was a mixture of excitement and anxiety. I needed Sandro right now, but the Rossis needed him more. It wasn't an overnight fix anyway. To convince Dad I was going to be okay was to show him proof. In time, I could give him that proof.

I was committed to this marriage. It had been my dream. A dream that had taken a detour into a nightmare, but its challenges were exactly what I needed. I didn't need a change of place to find myself. I needed to get thrown into the deep end and claw my way out of it on my own. Because to exist in the darkness of Sandro's world, I needed a little darkness in myself. To survive, I needed the grit. Not to be sheltered from it.

Mom walked in with a tray of milk and cookies. "How are you two getting along?"

"We'll get there. Right, Dad?"

After my epiphany, the pull of leaning into my old man was automatic. His arm came around me and he kissed the top of my head. I spread my palm over his chest, feeling his heartbeat. The heart that was full of love for his children. It was soothing to know in all this turmoil I would always have my parents' love.

"You never thought that I would become your most problematic child, did you?" I teased.

Mom laughed, handing me a glass of milk. "I think he's always known you'd be his biggest headache."

I straightened on the couch and protested, "Hey, I'm not bad."

"I thought three older brothers would be enough to keep you out of trouble, but I forgot you have McGrath blood in you," Dad teased back. The grimness in his features was gone. Without a doubt, it was largely due to Mom's presence.

"Hey, is that a jab at me?" Mom mock-glared.

"Do I need to give you two a moment?" I asked dryly.

"No, *carina*," Dad said. "Just sit between us, would ya?"

I resumed leaning against him. "Let's watch a movie."

And with my parents on either side of me, that was what we did.

We were back to a semblance of what was familiar, and I should've been content, but deep down was a gnawing ache of something missing.

Or someone.

CHAPTER Twenty-Eight

BIANCA

It was three a.m. and I couldn't sleep. I looked around the bedroom I had grown up in. Boxes remained unopened. Mom hadn't touched anything. My vanity, the bed, what I'd left on them. All untouched. It was as if she was saying that I would always have a place to come home to.

I reached for my new phone and texted Sandro.

I can't sleep.

His reply was almost instantaneous.

SANDRO

Me neither.

How are you?

Fine.

I miss you.

There was no response.

I shifted on the bed and texted again.

I wish you were here.

Again, no response.

He must be busy. Disappointed, I put the phone down. Then it lit up.

SANDRO

I'm outside.

What?

Street corner of your house.

I'll let you in.

You better.

I jumped off the bed. My feet must have sprouted wings at how quickly I exited the bedroom. I had the sense to open and close the door quietly. My bedroom was on the fifth floor of my parents' row house and it was a wonder I didn't trip down the stairs in my race to the bottom…

Where I ran into Mom.

She had a glass of water in her hand and her hair was disheveled.

Hmm…

I did not want to imagine my parents' nocturnal activities.

"What are you doing awake?" I asked.

She raised a brow. "What are you doing awake?"

"Sandro is outside." I grinned sheepishly. "Is it okay if I let him in and stay here?"

Mom gave a short laugh. "Oh my God…this reminds me of…" She broke off and gave a shake of her head. "Of course. He's your husband."

"Same alarm code, right?" I didn't want to wake up Dad. It was embarrassing enough that I ran into Mom and it felt like I was in high school sneaking in a boyfriend.

"Yes, it is."

"Okay, then."

I shuffled past the kitchen toward the entrance. I cleared the alarm, opened the door, and stuck my head out. The chilly night air pebbled goose bumps on my skin, but I wondered if it was from the weather or the anticipation of seeing Sandro. A shadowed shape headed my way and Sandro's form became apparent after it cleared the canopy of trees. He strode to me in an easy gait. He had changed his suit, but it was still black.

If the weather was colder, I bet he would be in an overcoat to conceal more weapons. I knew he had a gun under his suit. A knife and another backup gun strapped to his ankle. Seeing him in this urban setting, it occurred to me no matter where we were, I was married to a lethal man.

It made me shiver.

He hastened up the steps, and his hands hit my hips, backing me into the house.

"You have to be—"

His mouth slammed down on mine, and I was up against the wall beside the entrance. His hands skated over my sides, rough and desperate, while his kisses consumed me.

When he let me come up for air, I breathed, "Wow."

His eyes gleamed, and he flashed me a grin.

Door I mouthed.

He stepped back. His movements were still relaxed while he closed it without a sound. Then he caged me against the wall again.

"What were you doing standing outside?" I asked.

"I was debating whether I should climb up the building."

I snickered. "You'd be hitting Dad and Mom's balcony first if not getting reported by a neighbor."

"Yeah, that wouldn't make a good impression."

"Or you could have texted me first."

"What's the fun in that?"

"Well, we couldn't have fun if you were injured or in jail."

His hands went to my butt and lifted me up. My legs wrapped around his torso.

"Your confidence in my abilities needs work." His mouth hit mine, ghosting over it. "I'm going to hammer it into you."

The threat pulsed between my legs. I squirmed against him, gratified to hear him groan.

He walked us to the stairs. "You'll have to make sure I'm heading in the right direction to your bedroom."

He'd never been to my bedroom, but he knew it was not street-facing like my parents' room was. Plus, it had been a while since Sandro had been inside our home. Certainly not after he came back from Russia.

"Fifth floor."

"That much I know."

"Make sure to turn right."

He was wearing his stealthy dress shoes and I could barely hear a sound. Scorching heat emanated from him and I couldn't help playing with him. I licked the shell of his ear.

"Behave."

"You really want me to?"

"We have to talk first."

"Ugh, Sandro, I swear, if you're not inside me tonight, I'm going to put a chastity belt over my vagina for real."

His rough laugh was a half groan, half growl. "You're making it hard."

I stifled my amusement against his shoulder. "I don't know how to interpret that."

He grunted. But when he adjusted his hold on me, my pussy brushed his erection.

And he. Was. Hard.

Oh, my. Sex to me had never been mind-blowing. That time I lost my virginity was traumatizing; it turned me off trying for a while. After that, my boyfriends weren't that experienced and couldn't find my clit to save their lives.

Then, after my first year in college, Sandro started sabotaging my relationships. I was pleased at first, thinking he was going to finally make a move. I had no doubt it was jealousy that had him dragging me from the frat house. But he disappeared after that. And when he resurfaced to stalk me, that was when our mutual stalking dance started, but it'd become too painful after he had Griselda send me away that fateful night he got shot rescuing Sera.

Seeing my brothers get their happily ever after ignited my determination to find mine, and since Sandro made it clear it wasn't going to be with him, I decided to move on.

But he wouldn't go away.

Until I did.

"Which one?" he muttered.

"The last door on the right."

The bedrooms remained empty after my brothers moved out. My heart clenched. Beautiful memories echoed in the corners of this house. And if tonight went the way I wanted, another momentous one was about to be made.

Sandro stopped in front of my door. He opened it and proceeded inside. After he closed it, he lowered me and braced me against the door.

"Now we talk," he murmured.

"About what?"

"Tell me I'm not reading it wrong."

"You're not reading it wrong, Sandro." My words cracked because they were full of a certainty I hadn't felt in a long time. My years of not knowing what I wanted to be, who I wanted to be, was because the man who was the epitome of everything I craved didn't want to be with me. But here and now, my dream was within reach. The man I'd loved for most of my life was going to be mine in every way.

"I already told you, I accept every aspect of who you are and I can't wait to be by your side to lead the family." I understood Sandro more now. His need for my absolute consent. His mother never had a choice, and I believe what happened to me and Warren Winslow also made it necessary for him to be cautious with me. My heart clenched with the overwhelming emotions for this beautiful, broken man whose priority was always to protect me.

He dropped his forehead to mine. "Good. Because I don't think I can do this without you."

"What?"

"All the goodness that remains inside me is because of you. Every line I didn't cross was because I didn't want to obliterate a future with you."

"Sandro…"

"Deep inside, even though I knew I didn't deserve you, I was too selfish to let you belong to another." His voice turned guttural as he pressed into me. Sandro was all hardness and caged aggression. My husband was on the edge.

"So what do we do?"

"Bianca," he growled. "Even before I fuck you, you need to

know, there has never been a version of our story in which I let you go."

"I don't want you to let me go," I whispered.

A weighted silence descended that suppressed even the sound of our breathing. Then my whole body was moving, or rather Sandro was moving me.

We went flying into the air, or it felt like flying. We crashed on top of my bed, and his weight descended on me. And we went feral.

Lips and limbs tangled all with frenzied longing. One second he was devouring me with a kiss and making me pant for air, and the next my sleep shorts disappeared and he'd spread my legs and his mouth was on me.

Tasting, seeking, licking. I gripped the bedsheets. Sandro was keeping me on the edge.

Seriously? I moaned my frustration.

He gripped the outside of my thighs, keeping me open.

My hips squirmed.

He paused and growled, "Stop moving."

"Stop teasing," I retorted.

His answer was to make a broad swipe across my sensitive flesh.

"I'm not teasing, baby," he mumbled, or at least I thought that was what I heard. "I'm savoring." His tongue speared inside me, and he used his nose to rub against my clit. He was good at this. Just keeping the slightest pressure to drive me crazy without getting me off.

"Sandro!"

He stopped. "Shh…you don't want to wake up the house."

He replaced his mouth with his finger. Inserting one and following with another. He pumped while he continued to kiss around where I needed him the most.

Somehow, the thought of being caught only fueled the frenetic energy thrumming through my body. My lower body was all boneless and weak, the core of me crying for release. My skin was one blazing inferno. His hand reached out and squeezed my right breast, flicking a thumb over a nipple.

Finally, Sandro went full assault on my pussy. He applied the perfect pressure with his tongue and I exploded on his mouth. I swore I heard a slushy sound, just as an exquisite throbbing held me captive. I pulsed and pulsed. I moaned some more, but this time in throbbing ecstasy. I remembered belatedly to muffle my moan and gripped one end of the pillow and screamed into it. Judging from how slippery I was becoming against his mouth, I was drenched and ready.

Sandro planted kisses on my skin on the way up my body. He settled on his knees and removed my shirt.

"Skin to skin." He started removing his clothes. Tossed his suit jacket on the floor. I sat up and unbuckled his belt while he unbuckled his shoulder holster, dropping it with his gun to join his suit. Shirt, pants, gone. I traced the outline of his abs down to his erect cock. Like last night, his cock gave me pause. Especially his girth. *Hung like a horse* came to mind.

I felt his stare drill into the top of my head.

I glanced up at him. His eyes were smoldering, jaw tight.

He wasn't asking me again. This was happening.

I swallowed and exhaled deeply. Never letting go of my eyes, he pushed me back against the pillows and settled between my legs.

Still watching me, I felt the head of his cock crowning my entrance, inching in. He closed his eyes briefly and gritted his teeth. "I'm not gonna last."

I tightened my thighs around him.

"You're so beautiful, baby." He continued to push in.

I was so wet, but the girth of him was stretching me to an uncomfortable degree.

Sweat beaded on his forehead. His jaw was clenched and his gaze was a mixture of agony and possessiveness.

"It's been a while," I whispered.

"Don't say another word," he growled. "I don't wanna know."

"But—" My breath hitched. "Are you in?"

"Not even halfway."

Oh my God.

He edged in slowly. Was he thicker in the middle?

His words came back to me. *I'm going to rip you apart.*

He was not joking!

Hysteria bubbled up my throat. "Sandro…"

"Don't tense." His eyes were going feral. "Please don't fucking tense." It was like he'd become the devil and I was at his mercy.

He spoke through clenched teeth, "Does it hurt?"

"No. It's uncomfortable."

"I'll go slower." His voice was strained. He withdrew slightly to push in again.

I hadn't had sex in a year. That was what I was going to tell him. But I got it. I didn't want to know who was his last or when, either.

He lowered his head and kissed me while he paused his entry into my body. I tasted me. I moaned into his mouth and he resumed his inward glide. And just when I thought I couldn't take any more, he rasped, "I'm all in."

"Thank God," I breathed and I meant it.

"I'll let you get used to me," he murmured. He planted kisses all over my face, stroking my forehead, all the while saying, "You're such a good girl." He moved slightly, as if peering down at where we were joined. "Look at you taking all of me."

"I was worried there for a while," I admitted.

He chuckled briefly with a hint of self-deprecation. "Me too."

After a few seconds, he said, "I'm going to move now."

I gulped, giving a brief nod. The anxiety of not being able to take all of him was fading.

He started to pump. I was full of him, tight around him, but after the third stroke, my body slowly molded around him and the pleasure returned.

"You're mine now, Bianca," he growled with fierce possessiveness.

The enormity of this moment hit me.

"I've always been yours."

CHAPTER
Twenty-Nine

SANDRO

Being inside Bianca was heaven and hell.

Her pussy gripped me like the tightest fist and had me almost coming before I even thrust. And when I pulled out to drive back in, all that suction made my eyes roll back, my body shudder. I knew sex with her would blow my mind. But I never imagined it to be like this. Delicious torture. Like I'd given her my goddamned soul, and I had no desire to get it back.

"Mine now." I kept repeating those words as I drove inside her over and over. First slowly, and when she adjusted and put her heels over my ass, I sped up.

I entwined our fingers and slammed them on either side of her head and continued thrusting. Seeing her beneath me, her mouth open, eyes luminous with arousal, so reminiscent of all my tortured dreams about fucking Bianca, I needed to go deeper. So deep I'd rather drown in her beautiful eyes than wake up to any reality where she wasn't mine.

"Mine now," I repeated savagely. I shifted to my knees, surprising her when I tugged her whole body up with me while still embedded. Fingers gripping her sides, I lifted her and slammed her down on my cock. "No one else. No one else gets to be inside you like this."

Her eyes flashed and her nails dug into my shoulders. She did a swivel with her hips, and I gritted my teeth against the pleasure, not wanting to come.

"You too," she breathed. "You're not going to be with anyone else but me."

"I haven't for years, Bianca." Her eyes widened in surprise, but I was so stripped raw by that admission, I buried my nose in her throat and inhaled. Each time our bodies moved against each other, my cock swelled harder and harder.

Finally, I raised my gaze to her. She was looking at me like I could move mountains for her.

My wife.

"Fall back," I whispered.

She shot me a sultry smile and leaned away. The shadows and light of the bedroom only emphasized the work of art that was Bianca's body. I traced the curve of her torso with the tips of my fingers and outlined the full swell of a breast.

I yanked her back upright. "You're so fucking beautiful, you have no idea."

Then she did that thing with her hips again. I latched on to a nipple and she moaned so loud, I sucked harder while impaling her repeatedly on my cock. The temptation to flip her over and take her from behind was strong, but I fought against it. The first time I came inside her, I wanted to watch her face. I wanted to watch her fall apart.

But I was on the edge of exploding. I tipped us over so she was on her back again. And with the back of her knees under my elbows with my hands on either side of her, I powered inside her. Fast. Hard. Over and over. Bianca was sobbing and begging me not to stop. So I didn't. Tenderness forgotten, I unleashed the wildness that had been fighting to break free. And the second she cried out and I felt her tight cunt ripple around my cock, I let myself go and emptied inside her.

I shuddered and groaned. I captured her lips for a brief kiss, but I was panting in such a way that I couldn't catch my breath. I collapsed on top of her, but quickly rolled to her side. We were a tangle of limbs and bedsheets. Bianca burrowed into me and my arms came around her.

We stayed silent for a while.

"That was…" she breathed.

A side of my mouth curled up. "Yeah."

"Oh my God, we finally did it."

I let out a rough chuckle. "And we're going to do it many more times."

Bianca went up on an elbow and stared at me. "No regrets, right?"

"That's my line," I said. "No more pushing away. And no more running away either."

"I wasn't running away. I just wanted to see my family and help Divina."

I pulled her into the circle of my arms with her head resting on my chest. "I meant when you disappeared for three months. Don't ever do that again. Don't ever hide from me."

"I was tired of your hot-and-cold treatment. I wanted to move on."

Long ago, the thought of Bianca moving on was a bitter resignation, but now it was like icy claws of fear digging into my chest. I circled the skin on her bicep. "I just…never thought I'd feel worthy of you."

"Yet you couldn't stand me with another man," she finished. And as if that fired her up, she gave me a hard shove. "I'm getting pissed about that again..."

I grinned. "Angry sex is fantastic."

"Don't deflect. What do you mean you haven't in years?"

My smile disappeared. "I don't wanna talk about it."

"Oh, no you don't." She extricated herself from my embrace and straddled my hips. I had to groan as my fucking cock jumped in response. She grabbed my jaw. "Tell me what you mean. You haven't slept with anyone in years?"

I locked my jaw and tried to out-stare her, remaining silent, but her tits were distracting and it was only setting my blood on fire again. It was like once I yielded to the temptation of Bianca, my coping mechanisms crumbled.

"Well?"

"Yes."

"I find that hard to believe. Your office at the club is a revolving door of women."

"That's not true."

"You always had a woman in there."

"I was trying to discourage you from showing up at the club," I growled. "But yeah, I told them I was trying to turn you off because you were wasting time on me, but they knew better. That's the easiest two hundred bucks for fifteen minutes those women ever made. They didn't have to do anything except keep their mouths shut about what was going on in that room."

"What was going on in that room?"

"Nothing. They sat there and drank my whiskey. Some of them even tried to give me relationship advice."

Her mouth twitched. "How long?"

I couldn't stand the sweetness in her voice and eyes. "Since the day of the frat house."

I could see her do a mental computation. "Four years? You were celibate for four years?"

"I," I growled. "Couldn't touch another woman when all I could see was your tight little body in your short skirt, your hot cunt grinding on my cock and those sinful lips on mine."

"Our encounter in the car."

"Yes," I snapped. "I felt like I was cheating on you when I thought of having sex with another woman to rid myself of whatever witchcraft-hold you had on me."

"You avoided me," she whispered. "I thought I ruined us by coming on to you. Then all these mixed signals of one second being cold and then stalking me—"

Her eyes flashed with fury before she scrambled off the bed.

"Where are you going?" I stared at my erect cock, ready to go another round.

"Cleaning you off me," she retorted.

Oh, hell no.

I sprang off the bed and stalked after her. She was running a towel under the faucet.

"Let me do that."

She handed me the warm towel and I wrung out the remaining water. I crouched in front of her and wiped my cum off her.

"Why are you smiling?" she asked.

"Because cleaning you up is useless. I'm just going to dirty you up again."

She gave a huff that was a mix of annoyance and mirth. "Caveman."

I rose to my feet, tossed the towel in the sink, and trapped her against the counter. "Don't hear that as real complaining, baby."

"I just…" she whispered. "We wasted so much time."

I sobered a bit because it was a time I didn't want to revisit, but I felt this discussion was long overdue. "I don't think so."

"Easy for you to say. You're not the one who kept on making a fool of herself."

"Don't say that." I lowered my head and inched my face closer. "I didn't want to destroy our history."

She glanced away and fixed her stare on the right. "I don't understand how you could stand me going out with other guys if you've felt that way since the frat party." Her head dropped.

"Bianca, look at me," I demanded.

When she finally gave me her eyes, I said, "It wasn't easy. For the first six months, I was disgusted with myself for reacting to you that way. I struggled to wrap my mind around the idea that you were someone I could fuck and do all sorts of filthy fucked-up things with, because, baby, that night, I imagined you riding my cock. I tried to scald the image from my mind with the hottest shower of my life, but flashes of your panties and what it was covering just wouldn't leave me at peace. I even imagined you bent over the car and fucking your c-...pussy and—"

Her brow rose. "Cunt, you can say it. You already did earlier."

"Sunlight." I gripped her jaw. "That's exactly the war I've been waging inside me."

Her lips rolled in an attempt to hide a smile. "Like you can't decide whether to respect me or degrade me?"

"Yeah."

"You know we girls discuss this." She cupped my hand at her jaw. "Treat me like a whore in bed and treat me like a wife outside of it."

"Never call yourself a whore," I muttered.

"Sandro, you're still not separating the young girl you cared about and the woman who's your wife," I chided. "You just railed me against the headboard, and I swear I could feel your cock in my throat." She smirked while my dick jumped happily, eager for another round. "Now you're backtracking again."

I was. I released her jaw and held up my hands. "I'm still getting used to it, all right? These hands of mine—"

"Are steeped in blood." She grabbed my hands and held them against her heart. "You've told me that so many times. I have always accepted that part of your life, and every time you bring it up, it sounds like an excuse. A broken record. And this made-guy stuff? I'm all in. And what you told me about Carmelo? I don't care. It doesn't factor in how I feel about you. What remains and what I can't understand is how you can be so stalkerish and possessive and let me sleep with someone else?"

Rage shot up my head so fast, I twisted away from her and slammed my left fist into the tiles.

The tiles cracked.

"Sandro!"

"Ian Peterson. Dustin Lawrence," I rasped. "Those are the men you slept with."

I turned to face her.

She tried to grab my left hand, but I held it away. "Leave it." It didn't throb as much as the ugly jealousy pounding in my head and chest. The eye twitch that always accompanied the raging thoughts of another man fucking Bianca. "Even when you were away at Harvard, I knew. You dated them long enough for a semester but then broke up with them afterward. And the ones you fooled around with when you were in Manhattan like that Ethan guy…"

"You stalked and confronted us," she said dryly.

"I tried to keep away. I told myself I deserved to suffer for the years you were jealous too." I let out a derisive laugh. "But it was useless. You can ask Sticks how many times they had to replace or repair the drywall in the office at the club. I couldn't help scaring your boyfriends away, even when I knew that was wrong and selfish. I kept telling myself they can't protect you the way your family can."

"Why did you fight it so much?" she said in a low raspy whisper I almost couldn't hear.

"I'm nine years older than you, Bianca. And you know about my fucked-up origins. You deserved to experience college and the love you'll never get from me."

"And what kind of love is that?"

"The one that doesn't live in shadows and death." I swallowed. Because I was the grim reaper to some and Carmelo's blood flowed inside me, but I've come to terms with these things now. "I wanted to wait until you were old enough to make up your mind. That being with me wasn't a leftover adolescent crush or obsession. I feel ancient compared to you." All the evil I'd seen. All the times I'd numb myself to feel mercy and sunk into a black, black hole. Bianca always brought me back to the light. I wondered if that was why I nurtured our friendship. She was that one pure thing. I finally tainted her, but I no longer felt guilt.

I was smug as fuck.

"And now?"

I gave her a feral smile. "And now I'm going to erase every man who came before me."

I scooped her up and fucked her against the wall.

CHAPTER *Thirty*

BIANCA

"What are you doing here?" I opened my bedroom door to Nico. My *broodiest of the brood* brother had an amused gleam in his eyes.

"Delivering clothes as ordered," he said.

"I told Ivy."

"It's *my* clothes." Nico had more or less the same build as Sandro, but my husband probably had an inch or two on my brother, so the request was for a T-shirt and athletic shorts. There was nothing we could do about shoes, and Sandro had no problem walking barefoot until his men could bring him clothes.

Right now, we'd been summoned to breakfast.

"Is everyone here?" I asked.

"Matteo and Sera are on their way. The rest are here," Nico said. "No Aunt Carlotta, so don't worry. Just us."

"Whew, okay. Now scoot."

"Where's the husband?"

"In the shower. And wipe that smirk off your face."

"Why? It's funny." He breathed a small laugh. "You should have him do the walk of shame at breakfast."

"I'm trying not to be obvious, okay?" I tried to close the door on my brother again, but he stuck his foot in between the door and the jamb.

"What's the matter, Smurfette? I'm sure Dad can be civil."

My stomach twisted in knots. "When Matteo arrives, don't gang up on my husband."

Nico's eyes softened. "Don't worry, you're worth it, and I believe Sandro knows that goddamned well. He'll put up with your annoying family."

"Aw, that's the sweetest thing you've said about Sandro. Now go." I gave him a gentle shove and shut the door. Still, that didn't dispel my trepidation. Sandro wasn't used to this much family in his business. He'd always been a loner, even before Wilma spilled the secret. He was never the favored son. I didn't want Dad to make him feel like he was still undeserving of me.

The shower stopped. After Sandro fucked me against the wall last night, I told him I didn't want to do all the things in one night and that included shower sex, although he tried to entice me into joining him this morning. But I had plans for us. I wanted us to check into the grandest hotel where no one would bother us, order room service, and just get lost in each other. But it was still my girlish dream, and I had to accept that it might not happen for some time.

I just had to be patient.

The bathroom door was ajar, so I pushed it open to see Sandro in all his naked glory, wet from his shower, with drops still glistening on his tanned skin. The tattoos on his back covered some scars. I felt them underneath my hands last night.

He grinned at me as he dried himself with a towel. "Stop looking at me like that or we'll never make it to breakfast."

I tried my best sultry siren look, and gave my hair a flip and bit my bottom lip, lowering my eyes to his relaxed cock. "Well…"

"No."

"You're saying no to a blow job? You were the one who wanted to have sex in the shower."

"Baby," he groaned. "Have mercy on me." He was right in front of me. "There's nothing I want more than to have that sweet mouth wrapped around my cock, but not right now." He noted the clothes under my arm. "Especially if I'm wearing athletic shorts."

"True. I don't want you to meet my family with a boner."

"Dammit, maybe I should just wear my suit."

Nico's remark came to mind. "Nope. We're not meeting the family in your clothes from last night."

"What? Are you ashamed of me?"

"No." I grappled for an excuse that wouldn't make Sandro wary of Dad. "Sam is here and she's sharp that one. She will ask why you're dressed to go out at night when it's bright as day."

He patted my cheek. "Nice save. But I have something better to distract everyone and maybe win your dad's approval."

"You don't have to prove anything."

He walked into the bedroom and picked up his suit jacket from the floor. His hand went into his inner pockets and extracted my rings. "I sent Sticks back to get these."

He slid them on my finger like he did the first time.

The giant diamond blinked at me. It was a gorgeous ring, but I hadn't determined if I wanted to change it.

As if reading my mind, he said, "We can pick another one if you want." He dragged me into his arms. "In case it hasn't sunk in yet, I'm not intimidated by your family. And they sure as hell are not going to scare me off. The second day after we said our vows, I realized I couldn't let you go." He cupped me between my legs, and I gave a tiny gasp that sounded like a moan. "And in case *this* hasn't sunk in yet, I'm going to kill any man who thinks he can get in here."

I pushed his hand away because I didn't want to be squirming with how much I wanted to jump Sandro's bones in front of my family. "Behave. Let's get through breakfast first. And remind me we need to talk about your penchant for wanting to kill someone for simply looking at me wrong."

He sighed. "I know."

But I realized his sigh was because he'd gotten hard. I gave him another seductive come-on.

"No," he groaned, then he walked away from me and returned to the bathroom.

"Such a waste of a hard-on though," I called after him.

Sandro

Great. I was sitting with Bianca's family, in the middle of breakfast, having the hard-on from hell. I probably should have beaten one out in the shower. But Bianca's teasing about sucking me off had fired up my all-consuming need to have her in every way, every hole, and every position.

I paused.

No lightning strike of guilt split me in half at my crass thoughts about her. Good. My conscience and carnal urges were finally in sync. I'd held back long enough.

I glanced at her. Bianca looked away from her conversation with

Sera and Ivy and awarded me a quick smile. Then she found my hand under the table and gave it a squeeze.

"I hear you're going house hunting," Cesar asked casually from the head of the table.

There was less hostility coming from Bianca's family, and even if I would say the reception was barely lukewarm from the men, we were halfway done with breakfast without overturned tables and chairs.

"We are," Bianca chirped. "But we're not sure what part of Manhattan yet." She gave our linked hands another tug.

"We're checking into a hotel so I can take care of business and she can be close to you."

"And is this business going to be dangerous?" Cesar asked.

He didn't mince words, but I expected nothing less. "There's always danger, but I have people to watch her."

"Are the De Luccis caught in the middle of a war between you and the Albanians?" Matteo asked in a tone as casual as his dad's.

"I'm looking into it," I replied. "So far, the public thinks it's between the De Luccis and the Rossis." I'd seen the breaking news on the *Manhattan Tattler*. "Let the public believe that while I figure out for sure if it's the Manhattan Albanians." I wasn't about to share the information about Kaz Doku. Not until I had evidence his loyalists were involved. "But since the news of my marriage to Bianca is headlining, it might be a good idea to present a united front. That way, the people who started the fire and shot up Jabbin' Java know they can't play us against each other."

Sera gave a small laugh. "Luca texted me last night and said we East Coast mafia have so much drama."

Laughter went around the table, and I bit back my own smile. That livened up the atmosphere in the room. I got the De Luccis' worry. I was in charge of a struggling crime family. But I had to be smarter than my predecessors or suffer a short reign like they did.

At the top of my agenda was building bridges with organizations who shared the same vision.

With all the secrets I shared with the De Luccis and Chicago, strengthening our alliance made sense. Luca and I were linked from knowing the secret behind Frankie's death. Nico, Ivy, and I were connected by Joe Rossi's assassination. The inner circle would tighten. The core family.

"Now regarding the hit on Jabbin' Java." I glanced at Renz on my left. Among Bianca's brothers, he seemed to be less uptight and more accepting of me. I'd always liked Renz. Hard not to when he was prepared to turn his back on the De Lucci legacy to pursue the woman he loved and open a coffee shop. Although, according to Bianca, the coffee shop was Liz's dream, and Renz wanted to fulfill it for her until it became his passion.

"Let's not get off track," Cesar said. "I want you all to stay in Hell's Kitchen. Clearly, there's still an unknown enemy."

Nico and Matteo appeared surprised at their dad's declaration.

"Dad!" Bianca snapped.

"No, it's okay." I squeezed her hand. "I understand your concerns and I appreciate the offer, but hiding behind the De Luccis is not what Bianca and I need right now."

Cesar and Ava exchanged a glance. There was a reproving expression on Ava's face and I could just imagine her squeezing Cesar's hand the way Bianca reassured me earlier. Our women had more sense than their men, for sure.

"I'm sorry. You're right," Cesar grumbled. "I should trust you."

After that, breakfast went smoother, courtesy of Samantha dominating the conversation at the table, obviously tiring of the grown-up bullshit. Everyone was also thrilled about Sera's pregnancy and that took the heat off Bianca and me.

An hour later, Sticks showed up with my clothes.

"Should I wait for you?" Sticks asked.

"Yeah, we're wrapping up breakfast with the in-laws," I replied.

He chuckled. "I'm surprised you're still standing."

"I'm growing on them." Like mold maybe.

When I closed the door, I turned around to see Cesar leaning against the wall.

I waited for him to say something.

"I want to apologize for being a dick."

I raised a brow. "Which time?"

He huffed out a rough laugh. "Suggesting you and Bianca stay in Hell's Kitchen. My default mode is always to protect my daughter, but I have to accept that she's not exactly my responsibility anymore."

"You're right. She's mine."

He shoved his hands into his pockets. "I've only ever wanted what's best for her and letting her go…I was caught off guard. I wasn't ready. I'm still not ready."

I moved closer to him. "I've loved Bianca for a long time. That love has taken many forms, but there was a time I had to love her less, and that's so I could do what's best for her."

He blew out a breath. "I'm getting that."

I tapped his shoulder. "Come on, you can tell the women you've apologized."

He coughed a laugh. "You know it."

"I'm under no illusions that you came to me willingly."

He gave me a look.

"We're both men of action. You're protective of Bianca, and I still have a lot to prove."

That was the right thing to say because Cesar's shoulders relaxed and his chin dipped in a small nod. I wasn't taking my chance with Bianca for granted. Despite the lack of bloodshed at the breakfast table and a shaky truce forged with the men in Bianca's family, I still had to show them I deserved to be her husband, and I was going to cherish her with all my heart.

CHAPTER
Thirty-One

Bianca

I wasn't as cut out for house hunting as I thought I would be. It had been three weeks since Sandro and I had returned to Manhattan.

We moved into his condo in Lenox Hill after he had the security upgraded.

"A brownstone in Brooklyn," Sera suggested. We were having drinks at their penthouse on Fifth Avenue before heading out for a night on the town. Well, Sera wasn't drinking alcohol because of her pregnancy.

"It's too far from Harlem. Sandro still wants to be near the club. I really want something like this." I waved my hand around the beautiful space. Somehow, I couldn't picture bringing bloody soldiers through the lobby or loading them on the elevators, although Sandro assured me our life wouldn't be like that. Now that they weren't lying low from the De Luccis, the Rossis returned to a property in Harlem that they used for meetings and the aftermaths of a job.

I'd gone through several fantasies of my ideal home over the years. When I was a child, I thought I'd be a princess and live in a sprawling house like the De Lucci mansion on Staten Island. When I was twelve and decided I would marry Sandro one day, I wanted a row house like the one I grew up in. That had been my dream until I graduated from prep. In college, I was looking forward to getting one of those restored lofts like Ivy's. A side of maturity resulted from my shaky friendship with Sandro. I hooked my habitat aspirations less on my dream man and more on my independence.

When I graduated from Harvard, Nico offered me his Upper East Side apartment since he'd moved in with Ivy. That was before I decided to travel incognito across the U.S. Now, I had to consider a house with my role as Sandro's wife and all the responsibilities that came with it.

"Are you guys really selling the Rossi mansion?" Ivy asked.

"Yes." I nodded at Divina, who was nursing a cosmopolitan. "We've been assessing how to get it ready to put on the market." We raised our glasses in a toast. Divina and I had been working closely for the past few weeks. She'd taken over the files from the accountant who'd been stealing from the Rossis. I didn't know what happened to him, although Arnie let slip he was on the run and the Rossis had put a contract on his head. For a time there, the Rossi crime family was considered free game by the vultures, but now that Sandro was firmly in place, everyone was trying to kiss his ass.

It had been a relatively calm three weeks. No fire. No shooting. Just negotiations. A couple of dinners here and there with family and associates. Sandro didn't come home too late, but there were nights where I wouldn't see him until the next morning. Most of the focus was on getting the club up and running. But I couldn't complain. We even spent last weekend house hunting and catching up on a TV series.

"Is Sloane joining us?" Ivy asked.

"Yes. She'll meet us at Cardo." Cardo was a De Lucci-owned dance club and bar. "She's been busy with the smoke and water damage at the club." Sloane teased she was going to make enough money to get clear of the Rossi debt, and, from the looks of the account, she wasn't far off. After the job, Divina and I intended to leave her a hefty tip so she'd have enough to return to nursing school.

Footsteps echoed in the foyer. Trevor, Miller, and Al walked in. Al was still hobbling, not fully recovered from the gunshot wound, but he was on light bodyguard duty. He and Ivy exchanged a look. Once upon a time, they had a confrontation over protection money. Sandro had given a directive to Tommy to review all collections from that business and make sure none of the mom-and-pop shops were being targeted needlessly. Bigger businesses like warehouses in the area used the Rossi mob to ward off the smaller gangs from theft and intimidation.

I was thankful for growing up mafia adjacent and I could look at revenue streams like these objectively.

"You ladies ready?" Trevor asked.

"Are we ever!" I quipped, and just to show how ready I was, I enthusiastically jumped to my feet. Divina and I needed this break.

When we arrived at Cardo, I thought of Griselda. Since she was the club manager of Aristos, she could get ideas from Cardo to include in the rebuild and renovation. She was the one working with the contractor and architect to make the changes. I'd only seen her once since I threw her out of the house. Last week at the Rossi mansion when she needed Divina to sign off on something, we had a little staredown, but she apparently pulled up her big-girl panties and managed to apologize.

"I'm sorry."

Two words, but they were enough for now. I merely nodded my response. I considered it the start of our unspoken truce. We would never be buddies and have a girls' night out like this. I could never forgive her for what she had done. She was the only one who knew the club business inside out, and at this time when Sandro was trying to get it up and running, it was one less headache for him if Griselda took charge. As far as I knew, they hardly communicated, and it was usually through Tommy, or in the case of the finances, Divina.

"We need to plan your wedding, girl," Ivy said, breaking into my thoughts of Griselda. Apparently, everyone else remembered Sera's bachelorette party that was held here.

An ache squeezed my heart as I remembered the horror of the forced marriage. How all my girlish dreams burned to the ground.

Sera noticed my face. She grabbed my hand. "But let's enjoy the night first!"

"Amen, sister." I followed her into the club. We went directly to the dance floor instead of simply hanging out on the third level where private rooms existed for exclusive club patrons. In my desire to become Sandro's partner in every way, watching everything I said or did, I missed being carefree. *Do I have that right anymore?* I pushed away the negative thoughts. This was just growing pains. Sandro was doing a damned fine job, and I needed to suck it up. I knew even then he would never be the nine-to-five husband.

We were thrown into this situation just five weeks ago. I married the man of my adolescent dreams. Our reality is different from my fantasies…well…except the bedroom activities. My cheeks heated. Sandro was insatiable. And I craved him constantly.

I should be deliriously happy.

So why wasn't I?

"Bizarre Love Triangle" came on and it reminded me that tonight was "retro music" dance night.

"I love this song!" Ivy yelled. "Come on!" She handed both her and Sera's bedazzled purses to Trevor before dragging her off to the dance floor.

Trevor's chest rose and fell in what I could only imagine was a resigned sigh.

"What?" I asked.

"I was under strict orders not to let any guy hit on Sera and Ivy," he said.

I raised a brow at Miller and Al. They shrugged.

"No reporting to Sandro and Tommy," I told them. "What happens in Cardo, stays in Cardo."

Al grinned and did a zipped-lips gesture.

I narrowed my eyes at Miller, who groaned, "Don't put me on the spot. You know how psychotic Sandro gets when it comes to you."

"But he trusted you with me."

"After the chewing out he gave me last time, I might as well be a eunuch."

I laughed and grabbed Divina's hand. "Let's dance." Poor Miller, I still felt bad about the way Sandro went off on him that first day I met him.

The classic eighties disco music had a rhythm that had us shaking our booties. Divina and I were dressed in little black numbers. My dress hit mid-thigh, and I was in heels. Ivy was wearing a light pink satin sleeveless dress from their summer collection, while Sera was wearing a black baby doll that was both sexy and cute.

The four of us formed a circle. "We should invite Liz next time. Renz is feeling better after all."

"They're busy getting the café ready to reopen," Ivy said. "We're planning a social media blast for that."

"You're a godsend. Maybe we can do one for Club Aristos." I winked at Divina.

I had teased Sandro about it, but he said the success of Club Aristos depended on its mystique and lack of information.

A woman in a short skintight silver dress joined our circle. And although the neckline was high, it only accentuated her perfect proportions. She was taller than me, but maybe it was because of her pointy heels. She was facing Sera and Ivy, who were gawking at her.

Then Divina exclaimed, "Oh my God, you're gorgeous!"

The woman, with an enviable blowout, turned to face us.

It was Sloane.

My mouth dropped open. "Woman, you've been hiding this rocking body and gorgeous face?"

"She wants to be appreciated for her other assets," Divina yelled a little too loudly and caused heads to turn our way.

I could understand that, especially given the people she worked for. Instead of cleaning, they might force her to do something else.

"Thank you for inviting me," she told Sera.

Sera flashed her a smile. Sloane didn't accept money for her role in helping me escape, but the De Luccis extended her goodwill and other jobs. She was one of us now.

And just like the DJ had read my mind, the beats of "We Are Family" pitched in. We all laughed. We put our arms around each other and kicked toward the center. After that song, Sera and Ivy returned to the booth while Sloane, Divina, and I continued dancing.

The floor became more crowded and we started getting jostled. But when a woman stepped on my foot, that was when I knew I was done. "Ouch, watch it."

The offending patron gave me a look and didn't bother apologizing.

"Rude," I mumbled. "I'm going back to the booth. You two okay?"

Both ladies gave a thumbs-up, so the next challenge was weaving through the crush of bodies while nursing my throbbing toe. I didn't have the same longevity as I did in high school and college. Real responsibilities would do that. We should have stayed at home and played board games with my family. Thoughts spiraled in my head with what Dad had implied about being in a phase. I vehemently denied that. I was in this for the long haul.

So consumed was I with the conflict inside me, it took me a second to notice the man in a dark green rock-band tee was preventing my progress through the crowd.

He was dancing in front of me and sidestepping with me when I tried to move around him.

He clutched my elbows. "Dance with me, sweetheart."

I was *not* in the mood. I raised my hand to show him my ring. "Married."

"I don't see the husband and you seem to be having a ladies' night."

"Are you stalking me?" I demanded.

"Stalk?" he laughed. I could smell the beer on his breath, but he didn't appear to be slurring his words to be drunk enough for bad judgment. No, he was just drunk on his ego. "Just having fun."

"I'm tired and I want to go back to the booth."

I moved past him, but then he grabbed my arm and yanked me. I stumbled into him and the foot that was throbbing twisted.

"Don't be a bitch," he hissed. "I just want a dance."

Oh, hell no. I lifted my knee and nailed him in the groin.

By the time the man dropped, both Miller and Al were already beside me. "Are you okay?"

"Yes. Just twisted my ankle a bit."

"Take her to the booth," Al told Miller.

I didn't want Al to get in trouble. Not in full view of the public.

"No. You're going to sit your ass in that booth with me and the girls and do nothing."

Al's mouth tightened, but he nodded.

"You fucking bitch!" Apparently rock-band-tee guy hadn't caught on that I had bodyguards and rose to his feet.

Miller blocked him, putting on a fierce face I'd never seen on him before. "Back off. You don't know who you're fucking with."

My wannabe dance companion finally caught on that Al and Miller were with me and sneered. "You're not worth it anyway." He turned around and limped into the crush of dancing bodies.

I grabbed Miller's arm. "Let's go."

When we cleared the dance floor, the pumped-in oxygen expanded my lungs. I was still hobbling, making progress with Miller's help. Sera and Ivy shot up from the booth and met us.

"What happened?" Ivy asked and looked like she was ready to go beat someone up.

"Someone stepped on my foot and then another asshole wanted me to dance and yanked me forward. I twisted my ankle."

"You shoulda let me deal with him," Al muttered.

"Let's not ruin the night," I said. "And under no circumstances can anyone tell Sandro what happened."

CHAPTER
Thirty-Two

SANDRO

It's official. I hate girls' night out.

Contrary to what Bianca thought, I didn't have a meeting in Atlantic City. I was about to suggest a dinner date when she informed me that Sera had organized a night on the town. I wanted to tell her to decline the invitation, but she and Divina had worked so hard on the Rossi mansion and getting the accounts back into shape, we were finally getting a bead on the family's finances.

So here I was in one of the exclusive sections of Cardo, sitting at one of the high-tops, watching the dance floor on the first floor. I hated I couldn't see Bianca clearly, but at least I could make her out in the crowd.

I brought the drink to my lips and took a sip of whiskey. I'd been busy growing the construction stream of business and paying the New York Albanians a visit. Once word had gotten out that the Rossis and De Luccis were in a truce, they scattered. The ones we caught denied being involved in the club fire and shooting up Jabbin' Java. I executed the man who instigated the ambush the night Al got shot. I also let Al take care of the man who shot him.

I was so consumed with getting the organization's interests in order, it took me a few days to notice the change in Bianca. She always had a ready smile for me and was the perfect wife who I loved coming home to. Or if we had dinner with an associate, she was the perfect partner. At the end of the night, we had sex. Several rounds. I loved being buried inside her, and my addiction for her had only grown stronger. But something was nagging at me, especially in the last week. Her smiles didn't reach her eyes anymore. Frozen fake smiles.

Peripheral movement caught my attention.

Fuck.

"Look who's here." Dominic De Lucci dropped into a seat beside me and set a bottle of top-shelf whiskey on the table. "I should have made a bet with Matteo and Nico after I heard the girls were coming here."

"And why is that?"

"They can't stand it when their women are having fun without them."

"That's not the case with me," I told him confidently and finished my drink. He refilled my tumbler. "Where's Matteo and Nico anyway?"

"They're arriving soon. Just to let you know, whenever the girls are out on the town, they're lurking not too far from them."

"But Trevor is with the women."

"You have Al and Miller on Bianca, and yet you're here."

"I want her to let off some steam." I studied the amber liquid in my glass. "I grit my teeth when she has to deal with my side of the family."

"Bianca is stronger than you think. She has both the McGrath and De Lucci genes in her."

"Heard her grandpa and uncle were quite the De Lucci enforcers back in the day."

"The Fighting McGraths. Red Cillian is a legend. I have all the faith in my cousin," Dom said. "She may be the pampered daughter of Cesar De Lucci, but in time she'll adjust."

The guilt of forcing her into a marriage hadn't gone away, but I figured once I'd given her the proper wedding she deserved, it would slowly erase the nightmare of the first one.

My eyes narrowed on the dance floor. Some punk was harassing Bianca. I rose slowly from my seat to peer closer.

"Shit," Dom said, following my eyes. He got up and walked away.

I called Al.

He didn't even say hello. "Boss, we're on it." And ended the call.

I resisted the urge to call him again and texted him.

Call me when you have her.

Dom returned to me. "My security will escort the guy out."

"No," I told him. "I want a word with him."

"Dammit."

"Boss to boss, you think we'd let someone simply be escorted out after he harasses one of our women?"

He gave a measured sigh and was about to type in his phone again when he muttered, "Fuck."

"What?" Rage was an insidious feeling I kept in check, but it was a tinderbox when the safety of Bianca was in question.

"That's Trevor." He paused for a few seconds, rolling his lips. I could see him choosing his words carefully, and it only fueled my impatience.

"What?" I repeated.

"Bianca doesn't want you to know about the incident."

I checked my phone. No text from Al or Miller.

Damn you, Bianca.

Belatedly, I noted that Dom hadn't finished talking. "And…?"

"You need to calm down."

Fucker. He knew that was the last thing he should say, and he was just trying to get me worked up.

"What. Happened?"

"Bianca twisted her ankle when the asshole tried to stop her from leaving the dance floor."

I didn't wait for him to say more and strode past him. "Someone's dying tonight."

"Dammit, Rossi." Dom caught up with me and kept stride with me toward the elevators.

I stopped short of calling the cars and faced him. "Give me an alternative. But I'm getting my hands on that prick. Tell Trevor to find out everything on that guy."

"You don't give me or my men orders, Rossi," Dom warned.

I invaded his space and that was when the elevator doors slid open.

"What the fuck?" Matteo and Nico said at the same time.

"What's going on?" Nico asked.

"Someone harassed Bianca on the dance floor, and Sandro wants that someone's head to roll," Dom said.

Matteo and Nico both checked their phones.

"Is that why our wives are not responding to us?" Matteo mused.

"They're probably deciding how to keep their stories straight so

Sandro here won't have to kill someone," Dom said with amusement, as if he was used to dealing with this.

"Wrong thing to say." The restlessness in my fingers needled for action. "I want that man in a room."

"Jesus," Matteo muttered. "We're doing mob justice here?"

"What would you do if a fucker harassed Sera on the dance floor and, when she tried to leave the situation, dragged her back and she hurt her ankle?"

"I'd kill him."

I crossed my arms since I made my point.

"Wait, Smurfette wouldn't take that lying down," Nico said.

Dom was chuckling while he was typing on the phone. "Nope. She kneed him in the groin. According to my security guy, that man asked for ice after he left the dance floor."

"Let him suffer." I was losing patience. "Where to?"

"Basement," Dom said.

Zachary Hellman was an investment banker. He was twenty-eight years old, with a salary of three hundred grand a year. Not shabby for making the move from a tiny Indiana town to a midsize Manhattan investment firm. He had also developed a cocaine problem. We found a baggie on him. It was a problem typical of these high-strung financial types I'd seen at my club.

He was not high tonight. He was simply high on making loads of money for a client, which meant he was on track to make a hundred percent of his salary in bonuses this year. Unfortunately, that rush made him think he could hit on any woman.

Right now, his hands were tied behind a chair and he was mouthing off.

"I told the bouncer I was just having fun. She seemed willing."

"Willing? She kneed you in the groin."

"She was playing hard to get."

I leaned forward. "I think you're lying to me, Zachary Hellman."

His eyes widened when I said his name. Then they turned shifty. "If you want, I'll apologize to that chick. Happy now?"

"That chick…" I gritted. "Happens to be my wife."

"She didn't say she was married."

An overwhelming urge to cut off this liar's tongue had my fists clenching. I'd reviewed the footage of the dance floor. "I don't know what IQ level you have, but if a woman waves her ring finger in your face and that diamond is hard to miss, it usually means she's spoken for."

"I'm sorry. Bring her here, and I'll apologize to her on my knees," he said with all the sleaziness of a used-car salesman.

I grabbed his hair and leaned in closer. "I don't want you breathing her air."

His eyes widened as if finally realizing the gravity of his situation. "What…what do you want?"

I straightened and stepped back. "I'm giving you a choice." I took out my revolver and a knife and laid them on a table beside us. "You can play one round of Russian roulette. Or I can cut off a piece of you. A finger maybe? Or your lying tongue?" I looked over to where Dom and the De Lucci brothers were standing. "Can they reattach a tongue?"

"I think so," Nico answered as if we were having a normal conversation and not talking about dismemberment. "I know they can reattach a dick."

"Oh God, oh God. What's wrong with you people?" All the color had leeched off Zachary's face, and he started crying.

"You messed with the wrong woman, but I'll give you another choice. You fight me. No weapons, just fists."

"My wife is pregnant," he blurted out. "And I have a two-year-old son."

I sighed heavily. "I know. And that's why I'm giving you choices. I should kill you outright because you know what else I hate? Cheaters. I'd do your wife a favor and get rid of you, but I'm hoping I can teach you a lesson."

He started sobbing in earnest. "I'm sorry. I'm sorry."

I looked at Dom. "Release him."

Dom gave a shake of his head and cut his ties.

Zachary glanced warily at me and then at the door.

"Please don't do it," I muttered.

He jumped up and ran for the exit. Of course, it was locked. He pounded on it. "Help me! Help me! These men are crazy."

He was so ridiculously pathetic, I lost sight of my anger for a split second. But I remembered what this asshole did to Bianca and just the fact that he did this while he had a family waiting for him at home made me see red again.

"Zachary," I called.

He was plastered against the door, not wanting to face me.

He might get to live tonight but he'd landed a spot on my hit list. I'd be checking in on him from time to time, maybe even get him to do some laundering for the family.

I grabbed his shoulder and spun him around. Then I let my fury fly.

CHAPTER
Thirty-Three

Bianca

We were at a dessert bar at one a.m. Sera had an appetite for their chocolate cake jars and one didn't deny a pregnant woman their cravings. As for me, I had champagne and a raspberry tart. Ivy gave us a mischievous idea to take home jars to our husbands while Sloane rolled her eyes as the only single one in our group.

We were one of the few tables left and I made a mental note to leave a hefty tip.

"We'll take you home," Divina told Sloane. "I don't want you taking the subway dressed like that."

"It's a Friday night. I'm going to blend in," she told her. "You're used to getting chauffeured around and forget how it is."

I hadn't used the subway in years either. I wasn't fond of it during rush hour, but it beats New York traffic when you needed to be somewhere in time. The security around the De Luccis had tightened ever since Sera married into the family and it had never relented. I didn't see that easing soon, especially now that I was married to Sandro.

I glanced at our bodyguards seated at the corner of the bar. They seemed to have agreed with my request not to inform Sandro about the incident with the asshole on the dance floor. After what happened, we transferred to the second floor, which seemed to have a younger crowd, and we enjoyed the scene without incident.

"How's your foot?" Ivy asked.

"It'll be better by tomorrow. It just got tweaked slightly," I answered.

"I could have taught him a lesson," she replied.

"He got the message." I finished my tart. I had a pleasant buzz from the champagne.

"Something's off." Ivy leaned closer. "Did you notice how Trevor never reacted to the dance-floor incident?"

"He was letting Miller and Al handle it?" I replied, although I shot our bodyguards a longer glance. "I mean, he's got his hands full with the two of you. Besides, he didn't want to step on any toes." Then I laughed. "Pun not intended."

"Hmm…" Sera said.

"What?"

"Our husbands are surprisingly absent," Sera told Ivy. "They usually show up at the end of girls' night and they're not responding to our texts."

I slid out my phone and checked for Sandro's location. It was still grayed out, which meant he turned his phone off. This was nothing new when he was going into a meeting.

"What do you mean? Your guys show up for girls' night?" Sloane asked. "It's supposed to be a girls' night. They can't stay away from you even for one night?"

Sera and Ivy exchanged a knowing look while I snorted, "Put that way, it sounds like a red flag."

"A big red flag." Sloane nodded. "Right, Divina?"

Divina shrugged. "Oh, I don't know. I wish Tommy was more needy like that."

"Well, it appears he and Sandro aren't as clingy as my brothers," I grumbled, realizing I wanted Sandro to be like that because what the hell, he used to stalk me.

"They have a lot on their minds right now," Sera offered in an effort to make us feel better.

"You don't want Sandro to be any more intense with you." Divina shot me a pointed look reminding me about the Raffa Eight as we like to call the eight men Sandro mercilessly annihilated. A shudder rippled through me. I shut out that day, but whatever my mind went through, I coped. It was me or them. In my dreams or nightmares, it had progressed from horror to dark comedy. Gold Tooth's exploding head became a bursting watermelon, and then Sandro would appear and ask me to make frittata. I think in one of my dreams, Sandro fucked me in that room full of butchered watermelon bits with Raffa and Griselda watching. After I orgasmed, I would always end up saying, "There. Happy now? You could have spared their lives."

The dream always cut there. I didn't know what I was becoming, but my brain chemistry was altering to accept a darker side. A darkness that was needed to become my husband's queen.

"See," Ivy said. "But then, it doesn't explain why our guys are not answering our texts."

"I know," Sera said, and a yawn escaped her. "It's time for this pregnant woman to call it a night."

"Or morning," I quipped.

We said our goodbyes on the sidewalk since our vehicles were parked on opposite ends of the block.

"This was fun," I told Sera. "Thanks for organizing. We needed this." The *we* included Sloane and Divina.

"Anytime."

I shifted my hold on the bag of cake jars, praying the seams of the paper bag wouldn't give way.

"Why do you have so many cake jars?" Sera peeked into the bag. "I count eight. You know they're better when fresh, right? You don't live too far from here and could pick up more any time."

"For our guards," I replied. "Because we live in a condo and Sandro doesn't want them staying inside with me when he's not there. The poor guys are hanging outside and in the lobby."

"They'd probably appreciate a hot dog more than cake," Sera said.

"Ugh, I know, but this is still sustenance. And they have these fancy spoons."

"Oh, they'll devour anything," Divina replied.

I hugged my sisters-in-law goodbye. I couldn't have asked for better ones. This outing was exactly what I needed, and it restored a pep to my spirit.

Miller and Al were taking me home first, followed by Divina, and finally Sloane, who still insisted on taking the subway, but Divina overruled her.

"Did you guys like the desserts?" I asked Miller and Al.

"They're not bad." It was Miller who answered. "They were too light. I barely tasted anything. Now, I'm craving a donut."

I looked at my bag of cake jars again, remembering what Sera said. Whatever. The men were getting cake jars.

"Let's go pick up a box from the bodega after we drop off the ladies," Al said.

My chest shook with silent laughter, but I was looking forward to going home.

"Did you guys hear from Sandro?" I asked.

"No," Miller said. "But Sticks said he's back at the condo."

"What?" I checked my phone again. His dot was still invisible to me. And he hadn't responded to my texts.

"What's up with guys not responding to texts tonight?" I mused.

"Not my Tommy," Divina said. "He says he misses my sexy ass."

"Oooh, your hubby getting frisky?" Sloane teased, looking over to where Divina was texting.

"Hmm…maybe this night apart was good," she answered.

"It is," Al said. "You don't want your man too complacent having the little wife at home."

"Is that what your girlfriend does to you, Al?" Divina asked.

"Yeah, she drives me nuts. I have to iron my own clothes and come home to microwave dinners now because she's too busy with her different book clubs."

"Then you have to make yourself more interesting than a book club," Sloane said.

"You givin' me relationship advice, woman, when you have no man?"

"Well, you're giving them advice when your woman finds a book more pleasant company than you," she retorted.

"Shots fired," Miller crowed.

Al swatted him upside the head. "Shut up, you punk." Then he sighed. "Yeah, this book thing just started, but what I'm sayin' is, I miss her."

"Then do something, Al. Don't get complacent." I used his words against him.

We traded advice and barbs all the way to Lenox Hill and I forgot about Sandro not texting me back.

When they dropped me off in front of the condo, I spotted Rossi soldiers hovering by the entrance. One of them was on his phone, probably a handoff from Al.

I gave them a nod and handed two of the desserts to him. Then, when I entered the lobby, I handed one to another soldier and the night guard, whose face lit up with a smile.

I didn't care what Miller or Al said. Normal folks love cake. That left four for me and Sandro. I grinned secretively. I had plans.

I hopped into the elevator and punched the button for the top floor. Our condo was one of the six on that floor. Our unit was the furthest from the elevator. The hallway was narrow and it definitely wouldn't be conducive for any bodyguard to hang around and not cause suspicions with the other tenants.

My feet hastened down the corridor. I was excited to see Sandro. I realized because it was me coming home to him instead of the other way around. There was an epiphany lurking in the recesses of my mind, but I wasn't quite making the connection. I touched my keycard to the reader and opened the door.

Most of the lights were dimmed and the one in the kitchen was off.

The only ambient light came from the living room lampshade. It was a three-bedroom condo with a galley kitchen. A table that could seat six was in front of it. The kitchen area was open to the living room. And then finally, French doors led to a balcony. I could see Sandro's outline standing outside, looking at the New York skyline.

"Sandro?" I called, lowering my bag and the cake jars on the dining table. He slowly turned around and walked inside. His face was expressionless.

I stuttered a step and my tweaked ankle screamed at me.

His face grew more remote.

Why did it feel like he was a predator and I was prey? I mean, that was usually the case, but this was different. It was almost as if he was pissed at something.

"Did you have a good time?" he asked.

Why did this probing question make me feel guilty? Not

because I had a good time, but because I instructed the guys not to say anything about the dance-floor incident.

Well, duh, because it was simply guilt and I was projecting.

"Yes."

He gave a brief nod, before tipping his chin. "What's wrong with your foot?"

My face drained. *He knows.*

Still, my self-preservation was nowhere in sight. "What? I stumbled over the rug."

"Walk to me."

I didn't move. We stared at each other for long seconds. It was like a game of chicken, but I knew Sandro would win all day long.

"Who told you?"

He raised a brow. "I want to hear it from you."

"One question first."

He didn't acknowledge in movement or in words, waiting for my question.

"Is the man alive?" I asked cautiously.

That was when Sandro came unstuck and stalked toward me.

Retreat. Retreat.

I didn't budge.

My pussy clenched and warmth flooded between my thighs. I was digging this version of Sandro.

He clasped my shoulders, lowering his head, he gritted, "He. Is."

A breath of relief swooshed through me, but his nearness was too overpowering. I had to back away.

He let go of me and crossed his arms, but he was waiting for me to do the talking.

"He was a typical jerk who didn't take no for an answer."

"He shouldn't have put his hands on you."

"Agreed. But it happened. I took care of it."

"You did."

"Besides, Miller and Al were there." I exhaled an annoyed sound. "I can't believe they ratted me out after they promised they wouldn't."

Sandro uncrossed his arms and closed the distance between us. My back hit the dining table and he pressed his body against mine.

"One thing we need to get straight—you do not hide incidents like this from me. I will find out one way or another. Are we clear, baby?"

I huffed and lowered my head. He put his finger under my chin and forced me to look at him.

"Are we clear?" he repeated quietly, but the controlled feralness vibrating from his body came out loud and clear.

"You still haven't told me how you found out."

"I was there."

My jaw dropped. "What?"

With a heated look, he brushed my lower lip.

"I wasn't in Atlantic City. I was on the third floor. I saw the entire thing."

Oh my God. "But how did you get to the guy—"

"Dom was with me. There was a basement in the club, and that's where we took Zachary Hellman."

Everything was overwhelming me. I couldn't breathe. I wanted what Sera and Ivy had, didn't I? The overprotective, unhinged husband who couldn't bear to be away from me when I was having a girls' night out. Give me all the red flags, and dear heaven, it was making me want to climb his body.

"And…how did you find out this information?"

"Trevor."

I narrowed my eyes. "He played us. He knew all along what was happening." But it was Trevor. He'd worked covert ops and mastered the poker face.

I crossed my arms. "So, what happened in there? You say he's alive. Is he breathing through a tube now, or is his jaw broken?"

"I gave him a choice. One game of Russian roulette, I take his finger or another part of his body, or…my fists."

Goose bumps dotted my skin with the matter-of-fact way Sandro delivered the statement. It was his job. He'd gone through this scenario so many times and frequently it didn't end with his targets breathing. But I also recalled Sandro's words from my captivity.

My bullets, my blades, and my fists are meant for everyone else. Never you.

"Don't keep me in suspense."

"He's got a few bruised ribs, maybe broken, I don't know." His eyes gleamed. "He probably couldn't see clearly from an eye. I broke the fingers on his left hand."

"What if he goes to the cops?" I whispered. "Sandro, you can't just beat up people this way. I took care of it."

"And I take care of you," he growled. "And no, he won't go to the cops. I told him he wouldn't want to mess with us. He knows we know where he lives. He's got a pregnant wife and a two-year-old son. We have video footage of him harassing you. His father-in-law is a partner in the financial firm he's working at. Can you imagine him losing his cushy job if his sleaziness comes to light? The wife might throw him out on his ass and clean him out in the divorce."

"Oh my God." I was caught between feeling outrage for the man's family and awe at the calculating way my husband dealt with anyone who messed with me. No doubt if this Zachary guy was a mobster, he would have suffered the same fate as Gold Tooth and his cohorts.

"So don't worry about how I handle scum who try to mess with you," he said, coming closer again to me. "You should worry about yourself."

My mouth went dry. "What do you mean? You said I was safe."

His head lowered. "Not from me."

My eyes widened.

"I've got this caged aggression in me, baby," he growled.

"What aggression?" My breathing stuttered.

His mouth was millimeters from mine. The darkness in his eyes made me hot, and my nipples got sensitive under the fabric of my dress.

"Someone touched you and he's still breathing."

"That's progress."

"You're keeping incidents like this from me."

"Self-preservation."

"Whose?"

"Everyone's," I whispered. I put a hand on his chest. He was hard and warm and his heart beat under my palm. I let out a shaky breath. "Let's get rid of that aggression."

"I can't be gentle." He bit my lower lip, and I yelped. He licked it and gave me a taste of copper.

"I never want you to be."

The words scarcely left my lips when his hands went under my arms. He kicked the chairs out of the way, set my ass on the table, and moved between my legs. His erection was hard against my pussy and arousal flooded my core.

His mouth came down on mine. The desperation in his kiss spurred me to return his kisses in the same fervent way his tongue tangled with mine. The way his mouth couldn't get deep enough. His fingers bunched the neckline of my dress and he ripped it to my waist, baring my breasts.

"You're not wearing a bra underneath this?" he rasped.

"The dress has a built-in."

He didn't say anything else and dove for a nipple. I cried out at the assault, not knowing where all the sensations were coming from.

He was devouring my breasts just as he pushed aside my panties and sank two fingers inside me without preparation. The brutal invasion stung, but I was so damn wet, the pumping of his fingers brought me to the edge.

"Almost there," I moaned. I gripped his head and pushed him lower.

"I can smell your arousal," was his savage reply.

"Sandro, dammit." My heels dug into his shoulders, but as he dragged my ass closer to the edge of the table, he buried his head between my thighs.

His nose probed my pussy. He pushed the panties aside and his tongue dipped in. Up, down, nudging, biting, still keeping me from coming.

My hips squirmed. "Sandro…"

He stopped, looked up at me, and with his thumb, kept pressure on my clit. "Never keep things from me again."

"I won't. But…"

"Non-negotiable, Bianca."

I couldn't answer him, but his answer was to resume edging me. "Sandro," I whined. "Get me there."

"Do we have a deal?" His tone was guttural. It was costing him as much as me.

"Yes." I would take the orgasm for now and talk about the details later.

He ripped my panties off and ate my pussy like a starved man. I exploded right there, wetness and heat like I'd never experienced before.

Oh my God, did I pee?

But he was like a maddened animal, ravenous. All inhibitions vanished, and I was an animal like he was. I took my pleasure. I cried out again and screamed. I realized I'd been screaming for a while.

Sandro stood back. I heard the clink of his belt and the lowering of the zipper. Then he yanked me to a sitting position and impaled me on his cock. I gripped his shoulders, muffling my surprise. It was the first time he was fully seated in one stroke.

He stretched me to the limits just on the dividing line between ecstasy and pain. He lifted me by the ass and savagely slammed me down again.

I could only gasp and cling to him as he mercilessly fucked me.

No gentleness.

No asking if I was okay.

He was only after one thing.

Outright possession.

Outright domination.

And my body responded by clenching around him in another blinding orgasm.

"Fuck," he said roughly. "I can feel your cunt squeezing the life outta me."

"Don't stop," I begged. I could feel another rip-roaring release coming. It built and built. Sandro staggered to the wall and propped me against it, driving harder into me. I was going to feel this tomorrow and I couldn't care less. In all our times making love, he'd never taken me this way that was solely for his pleasure. If Sandro stripped to the core was a kink, I was all over it.

Without second-guessing, just the need to sate his basic instinct.

"More, Sandro," I begged again. My nails dug into his shoulder. He stripped me bare too and it was liberating. This was the way I pictured him taking me.

Pure passion and madness.

He hardened to steel, and possibly larger, hinting of his oncoming release. Three more hammering thrusts, and then he stilled and grunted into my shoulder. Heavy pants gusted beside my face. After a second, he started rocking into me more slowly, pressing kisses to my face, my neck, trailing up behind my ear.

He slowly let go of my legs.

My heels must have been digging into him.

We forgot everything else except becoming consumed in each other. I caressed his face while he dropped his forehead to mine.

"You okay?" he asked.

My mouth curved. "Never been more okay."

A corner of his mouth tipped up. "You liked that?"

"Very much."

He pressed his mouth to my forehead. "Got it."

Then he swept me into his arms. "Let's get you cleaned up."

CHAPTER
Thirty-Four

Sandro

I dirtied Bianca again.

"Delicious," I mumbled as I ate chocolate off Bianca's nipple, giving it an extra swirl and a suck while I moved my finger in and out of her pussy.

Her body arched off the bed and she moaned, "We're going to make a mess."

I stopped eating. "Surely you weren't thinking of covering the bed with cling wrap?"

"Ugh, you know what I mean."

"Quiet," I ordered. "Don't interrupt my dessert." I grabbed the bottle of sparkling wine and drizzled it down her body while I got more drunk on her.

"Hmm." I pressed kisses between her breasts and chased the wine to the side of her ribs. As I worshipped her body at a gentler pace, I pieced together how I had reacted throughout the evening. The way I fucked Bianca was cathartic.

I didn't become the most sought-after contract killer because I was impulsive. I did my research. If a hit didn't feel right, I aborted. Despite how I wanted to dispose of Hellman's body in a landfill, I thought about the consequences. The headache of an unplanned job. But my self-control and logic went out the window when it came to Bianca, and I was prone to strong emotions. But Bianca was like the lightning rod that absorbed the fury that coursed through my body.

And I was finding out my wife loved primal sex.

I licked her navel, which trapped the wine, and I relished the sweetest moan coming out of her yet. I could work with this. The incessant need to kill any man who looked at or touched her wrong could be channeled into something more enjoyable and fulfilling.

Was it healthy? Probably not.

I was a killer. Bianca had always accepted that part of me, but I would lose her once I started killing indiscriminately.

I needed her to be my moral compass, especially when my moral compass got fucked because of her.

I put my mouth on her cunt. Her addictive, delicious cunt that didn't need chocolate or honey. I avidly tongued her sensitive flesh. Her clit was swollen from all the orgasms I'd given her, and she'd begged me for a break. But I needed to hear her cry one more time.

I surged up her body and slammed back inside her.

"Come for me one more time."

"Sandro," she sobbed. "I can't anymore."

"I'm fucked in the head because of you," I growled. "I hate seeing you in agony, but this…" I reached between us and strummed her clit. She threw her head back and dug her nails into my back, drawing blood as she released a fractured cry. "I love seeing you cry between pleasure and pain… I hunger for this."

"You're a sadist."

Despite shoving roughly inside her, I thrusted at a slower pace. "Maybe…" Despite my words, I planted a tender kiss on her lips. "But only when you bring out my primal side."

Her eyes flared, and a satisfied smile graced her face. "Give it to me, Sandro."

And I did. I took her to the pinnacle, savoring a bond that had strengthened with a new understanding of our fucked-up union.

No. It wasn't fucked up.

It was us.

The next morning, I awoke before Bianca. We'd spent an active night together. I informed the men that I was spending the weekend with her. Tommy understood my goals. We'd talked about it. How it was important to form a strong nuclear family like the De Luccis. Unfortunately for me, my remaining Rossi cousins were scum of the earth. None of them were even capos since they kept fucking up.

We needed new blood.

I brushed the hair from Bianca's face. She was so beautiful. My Sunlight. And in sleep, she was so innocent, but I had long tainted her innocence.

New blood.

Bianca and I were going to start the new generation of Rossis. A fist of anxiety stabbed my chest at the thought. It wasn't easy wrapping my mind around it. But as the weeks went by, I'd slowly come to terms with starting a family. It wasn't unheard of for a hit man to get a vasectomy. No children. No attachments.

Bianca was on her back and my eyes tracked down her body. I put my hand on her belly, imagining my child growing inside her.

Unfamiliar wings of happiness rioted in my chest, so big that I had to exhale it to make room for more.

It was then her eyes fluttered opened, and a smile curved her beautiful lips. Made more beautiful because they bore evidence of how much I kissed the fuck out of her. Rosy. Bee-stung. Pouty.

"You're watching me sleep now?"

I didn't say anything, but a corner of my mouth hitched up.

Her eyes lowered to my hand on her belly. "What are you up to, Sandro Rossi?"

"What do you think about kids?" I murmured.

"Kids?" Her eyes widened as all traces of sleep left them. "Of course I want them…eventually."

"Eventually when?"

She laughed briefly. "I'm not having this conversation without coffee…and with morning breath."

Bianca rolled out of the bed and dashed her delectable naked body into the bathroom.

"Oh my God," she called out. "I'm still finding mousse on my body."

I glanced at the cake jars on the nightstand. We'd showered a couple of times after I ate cake off her, but Bianca somehow wanted to eat more cake in bed and dropped the mousse on herself.

I got up lazily and prowled into the bathroom. "It seems I didn't do a thorough job." I hugged her from behind and planted a kiss on her shoulder while she gargled mouthwash.

"Sandro," she hissed. "I'm all sticky."

She finished gargling and turned around. I pressed my mouth against her lips. "Good morning, baby."

"Morning. How come you smell so good already?" she mumbled.

I smiled and nuzzled her throat. "I woke up much earlier. Stop fussing. I would have woken you up with my mouth between your legs, but you needed a break."

"Then make coffee," she ordered.

I sighed and leaned back. "Are you trying to deflect the conversation?"

"From kids, no."

"It's almost noon. Do you want brunch instead?"

"Coffee first."

CHAPTER
Thirty-Five

BIANCA

When I checked my phone this morning, it was to a slew of messages from Ivy and Sera, checking if I was awake already. I responded to Ivy's last one.

IVY

OMG, the men were there last night.

What do you mean? BTW, Sandro witnessed the whole thing from the bar on the third floor.

SERA

Matteo and Nico arrived late, but just in time to help Dom calm Sandro down.

IVY

Calm?😏 Try egg Sandro on.

Ugh, my brothers.

IVY

So...Nico is tight-lipped about what happened to the guy.

SERA

Matteo is too.

The man is fine. It could have been worse.

IVY

Meet for breakfast?

Nope. I have my husband for the entire weekend and we're about to head out for brunch.

SERA

Aw, I'm happy for you, but you're a tease.

😂 Justice has been served. I do like feral Sandro afterwards. 😉Later

SERA

You can't leave us hanging!

IVY

Now who's the tease? But yay for Sandro joining the Obsessed Husbands Club.

I dressed in a dusky-rose hoodie and matching sweatpants, pairing it with platform slip-ons. My hair wasn't totally dry, but I had no patience wrangling it this morning, so I held it up with a claw clip. I didn't feel like slapping on concealer either, and used wide-frame sunglasses to disguise yesterday's excesses of alcohol, sweets, sex, plus a late night. Sans the incident on the dance floor, it was a perfect evening. An evening spent with family, friends, and ending with sizzling sex with Sandro and a few epiphanies.

A smile touched the corners of my mouth. It seemed I was

counting my blessings this morning. Was it only last night when I was wondering why I wasn't deliriously happy?

I was only twenty-three, a mafia wife, but in the De Lucci world I grew up in, women weren't second-class citizens. From the start, we were empowered, cherished, protected, and loved. Falling into Sandro's world and its misogynistic culture, I despaired at the challenges that faced me, and fear of failure was making me despondent.

But being around Sera and Ivy re-energized my resolve, and seeing how I was still the center of Sandro's universe was the refueling I needed.

Would I fall into that dark hole again? Most likely. I was thrown into a marriage before I was ready. I would not beat myself up if I was having doubts, and I would remember to reach out to the fierce women in my family. Why didn't I think to open up to Mom about my fears? After my captivity, we talked almost every day, but I maintained a façade, not wanting her to worry.

I still wanted to do this on my own. I wasn't going to run back to my parents at the first sign of trouble. I was a De Lucci and a McGrath. I needed to act like it.

I left the bedroom to find Sandro already waiting by the French doors, texting someone. His hair was still wet from the shower. He was in a gray T-shirt and black track pants.

"I'm not used to seeing you like this," I told him.

He turned and gave me a warm, assessing gaze. "Dressed for a relaxing day?"

"Yes." Although we spent a weekend together previously, that day started with him rolling in at five a.m. still wearing his standard dark suit. He didn't even sleep, insisting we have breakfast together before heading out to meet the realtors we lined up. Today, his eyes weren't bloodshot at all. Sandro thrived on very little sleep, so even a few hours could recharge him.

He said he could sleep anywhere courtesy of his training as an assassin-for-hire.

He led me out the door. "I've been planning to spend the weekend with you."

"What happened in Atlantic City?"

"There was no casino meeting," he said. We moseyed down the corridors toward the elevators. Another change of pace. Sandro was usually brusque in his strides when we had to be at a function. "You mentioned a girls' night out before I could mention my plans."

"Aw..." I was…touched. There was almost a sheepish, boyish expression on Sandro's face, and usually, *boyish* was the last word I'd use to describe him. It was the vibe of the morning. Being carefree. He was about to punch the elevator call button when I touched his arm.

"Wait, you don't usually go out…" I lowered my voice. "Unarmed."

He quirked a brow and lifted the right pant leg to reveal his piece.

"Okay, you have your backup."

"We'll have Sticks and Rossi soldiers trailing us." He pressed the button to call the elevator. "But I told them to be as discreet as possible."

"You've been relying more on the Rossis for security lately," I told him.

"When the club opens, Sticks and Miller are going to be busy. I'll be hiring people to kick our Rossi soldiers up to snuff."

The elevator came and we got in.

"Oh, you mean guys like Trevor."

"And your cousin Ronan and his men."

Ex-military. Ex-special forces.

He cleared his throat. "I know we haven't discussed your family's underground organization."

I grinned. "The Archer Syndicate. You can say it. Between us, it's not much a secret and more like going on record."

"I'll also be hiring you private security."

"Wouldn't that cause friction in the family?"

"Not if they benefit from the training," he said. "Also, I don't want anyone who can be bribed."

We discontinued our conversation when we reached the lobby. Sticks already had an Escalade brought around.

When Sandro and I got into the second-row passenger seat, he asked, "When will Jabbin' Java reopen?"

"Another two weeks," I replied. "Renz also wanted to be in better shape, especially since they're doing a social media blast."

"Go big or go home," Sandro muttered.

"You got it. Hey, I have an idea. Instead of sitting at a café, how about we picnic in Central Park?"

An incredulous expression crossed his face. "You want us to go strolling in Central Park holding a picnic basket?"

My brows furrowed. "Is that area not safe?" I was pretty sure the whole expanse of the park was covered under the protection of the De Luccis and another crime family that was our ally.

"It is," Sandro said, confirming what I already knew.

"Then…?"

Sandro cleared his throat and was staring forward. "It's more comfortable to sit in a café."

"And we can do that anywhere." My heart was sinking, but I think I knew why Sandro was acting this way. It was the macho-ness again of the Rossi crime family culture. Sandro was a boss and maybe he thought that walking through Central Park and picnicking with his wife wouldn't be a good image. Baby steps, right? But I thought back to Dad and Mom. Dad wouldn't think twice about holding hands with Mom. Matteo took Sera to see the sunrise. And Nico? Nico proposed on The High Line in front of the world.

I should let go of my adolescent dreams and think of more realistic ones to have as Sandro's wife.

I fought against exhaling a disappointed sigh so as not to make him feel guilty. "All right, we can go to a café."

Relief swept through his eyes, but an unbidden sting came to mine when I saw that. I quickly averted my gaze to the window before the tears came. It was just a picnic. Why was I being so emotional about it? I resolved to regain my composure. The morning was going well, and I didn't want to ruin it over something so small.

"Bianca." His voice was rough. "Look at me, baby."

Dammit. My tears fell, and I surreptitiously wiped at them.

But I was frozen, and I didn't want to turn my head.

"Sunlight, please look at me."

The way he said the endearment did it. And it made me more emotional. Dammit. I dropped my head to give myself time to compose myself before I glanced at him. "I'm sorry, I don't know what came over me," I whispered. "It's just, I thought when I had a crush on you, when I thought I would marry you one day, I pictured us coming to the park and having a romantic picnic."

"It was your fantasy?" His mouth curved in amusement.

I rolled my eyes. "You make it sound like a dirty fantasy."

"Then we'll picnic in the park."

"But you don't want to. I know you. Besides, I don't want you to lose your man card with the Rossis."

He gave a low laugh that was so sexy, I clenched my thighs.

"Who cares about that when I can put a smile back on your face." He tipped my chin up and gave me a long, sweet kiss. "I'm sorry I made you cry."

"I don't know why I did. It's just a picnic."

"It's not just a picnic," he told me. "The good things in our past are making the challenges of our present more worth it. It's something worth fighting for, baby."

"I don't know what to say." My words were still garbled by the emotions pushing up my throat.

"Well, for starters, you can tell Sticks where to drive."

I laughed lightly and told him.

"Baby," Sandro said softly in a voice that melted my insides. "You gotta tell me when things are important to you. We've known each other for years, but this marriage and our relationship? It's new." He gripped both my hands in his. "I'll fuck up everything else before I fuck up with you. Tell me you get that."

"I get it." My lips rolled together. There were so many things I wanted to tell him, but no other words would come except, "Thank you."

His answer was to give me another sweet kiss. When we broke apart, the look he shot me was a mixture of heat and tenderness. The tears threatened to flow again, but for different reasons. There was so much love in that look, too massive to take in. I cleared my throat and whipped out my phone so I could process another milestone in our relationship. "Let's put our order in."

We arrived at the restaurant and picked up our grab-and-go picnic basket. It contained everything we needed to enjoy a Central Park picnic, including a blanket.

Sticks dropped us off at a corner where we would be closer to the lake. Sandro helped me out of the Escalade and went to the back to grab the basket. Then we strolled hand in hand into the park.

This was surreal.

I couldn't believe one of my teenage fantasies was playing out.

He squeezed my hand, and I looked up at him, shooting him a smile that encompassed all the giddiness I was feeling inside.

Even when I noticed four soldiers trailing us, reminding me that

Sandro and I were not a normal couple, it only underlined the significance of this moment.

Sandro cared.

He was making an effort to make me happy, even with the limitations of the world we lived in.

I turned my attention back to the park. Fall colors were at their peak. The sun was low in the sky, casting a filter over the shades of orange, rust, yellow, and green.

We found an empty spot under an oak. Sandro lowered the basket, and took out the blanket and spread it on the grass.

"So, about the extra security." He picked up our conversation from the elevators. "I'm going to ask Trevor for some references. It's nothing new. The Russian Bratvas have ex-Spaetnaz soldiers guarding their family. Luca's people are getting trained by ex-military as well to keep up with the Russian mafia in Chicago. The Rossis might be the small fish and larger organizations won't cause us trouble for now, but once I make bigger moves, that will change."

He put the basket at the edge of the blanket.

I kneeled and started taking out the utensils. "Joe Rossi did work with mercenaries to get to Ivy."

He sat behind me and stretched out his long, muscular legs. "Yes. The way I see it, our family would be less on the streets dealing with gangs like Harlem. Old-school mobsters have no place in the new mafia. We don't need an army, we need skilled soldiers and deep connections in every industry.

"We'll have steadier income in a few months. Construction schemes are booming. That's why we need to get Club Aristos up and running."

I had ordered eggs, bacon, and hash browns while Sandro ordered the breakfast garbage, which was basically a glob of breakfast food, like mine, with added creamed beef and double biscuits.

We also had a baguette and butter, a box of coffee, and two to-go cups.

I poured coffee into one of the cups and handed it to him. "Divina and I are about to submit our proposal for the repairs to the Rossi estate. Whatever happened there left a lot of bullet holes in the walls."

Sandro shot me a wry smile before digging into his breakfast mess. He offered me a bite. I closed my eyes as I savored the artery-clogging goodness. "Oh my God, I should have ordered this."

"Wanna switch?"

I gave him a dubious look. "What's it going to cost me?"

His chest shook with a silent laugh. "I can think of several forms of payment."

I returned his innuendo with a bat of my lashes. "Well, we're in public, but after this, we could go back to the condo and pick up from yesterday."

"Baby, you're just going to fall asleep on our way back there."

I giggled. "True. You didn't let me sleep much last night."

"I hope you're not complaining."

I flipped open the lid of the container. "How about you give me some of yours and I'll share mine?"

He glanced at what I ordered and made a face. "I don't think I'm going to win here."

I lowered my food, went on all fours, and crawled to him. "I promise, you'll win later."

I leaned in and pressed a teasing kiss to his mouth. A suppressed groan vibrated in his chest. When I pulled back, I was struck by the intensity of his gaze.

My heart rate spiked and my lips tilted in an uncertain smile. Surely, he wasn't thinking of a full-on make-out session in the middle of the park because that was how he was looking at me.

Like he wanted to devour me.

"Sandro?"

~

Sandro

I didn't know if it was the setting, the surroundings, or simply being lost in Bianca's brown eyes. Her family always teased she'd gotten the puppy-dog eyes down pat that made them give in to her demands. But now that I was the recipient of them, I was jealous. I wanted to be the only one to fulfill her every wish.

I was so gone for this girl, it wasn't even funny.

The unsure smile on her face had me cupping her jaw tighter.

"Sandro?"

In case she didn't know how I felt because I was the dumbass who had never told her, that ended now.

"I love you." The words scraped against my throat because they were words that had never made it past my mouth in all my thirty-two years. Raw emotions churned inside me. "I'm so fucking in love with you, baby. Sitting out here, I've never felt more exposed in my life, but I hardly give a damn because I'm with you." Her eyes filled with tears and they simply slayed me. It was acceptance, love, and happiness all rolled into one. I didn't know how I knew that. I just knew. "I should have told you sooner…"

"We've always known we loved each other," she whispered. "I knew you loved me differently from how I loved you when I was twelve. But what I felt for you before pales in comparison to what I'm feeling now. It's deeper. More profound and fierce. Back then, I loved the idea of you, but now…it's everything about you. The good and the bad..."

I remembered her tears earlier, and the way they kicked me in the gut returned. "When I saw you cry because I couldn't simply give in to something as simple as a picnic, I felt ashamed. Like I didn't deserve you again."

"Oh, Sandro…don't, baby." She cupped my jaw in return.

I gave her a self-deprecating chuckle. "And I'm telling you now, if something means so much to you and I'm behaving like an oblivious dick, call me out on it."

She sat back on her heels and grinned mischievously, gathering her hands primly on her lap. "Or I can simply say *please*."

"Fuck," I groaned. "You're making me hard."

She laughed and I lunged at her. We fell back on the blanket, nearly flattening her breakfast.

"I don't know if I should give you more ammunition, but when the word *please* passes your mouth, I want to offer you my goddamned soul." I searched her eyes deeply and said, "I love you."

"I love you, too," she replied.

I gave her a quick kiss because any lingering ones involving tongue would lead to a very uncomfortable time in the park. Bianca was breathless when I yanked her back into a sitting position.

"Breakfast is getting cold," I clipped.

"Well, something else is getting hot," she replied, pretending to fan herself.

"You're such a temptress," I muttered. I didn't stand a chance. She grinned at me as she dug into her bacon and eggs.

"Want some of this creamed beef?" I asked.

Bianca shot her signature looks that drove me crazy. "Always."

It seemed every interaction with her from here on out devolved into lewd thoughts. We managed to get through breakfast. It took a while for my hard-on to go down. Afterward, we strolled through Central Park.

It wasn't an experience I would do on my own. The only time I went through this area was when I wanted to run a loop. I didn't mosey. I didn't stop to watch the mimes or listen to buskers. But doing this with Bianca by my side was everything.

Because it made her happy. It made the smile on her face reach her eyes, and it was worth every step in this park.

Just as she was supporting me in my role as the Rossi boss, carving moments out in my time to spend with her was precious and a priority.

Because Bianca is my priority.

I became boss because that was the only way I could keep her. And I would annihilate anyone who got in our way.

CHAPTER
Thirty-Six

Bianca

I grabbed my newest strappy heels before I headed out to the living room where Sandro was waiting for me. It had been two weeks since girls' night out and our weekend in Central Park. Our weekend of discovery, of talking about our hopes and dreams outside the crime family, of being honest with our emotions.

A turning point in our marriage.

When it became real.

Because we wanted it.

Not because we were forced into saying our vows.

We had discussed having kids, but agreed to wait until the organization was more stable. I had a feeling Sandro wanted to build a fortress before starting a family.

My husband turned from his spot at the French doors. He had a phone to his ear, but ended the call immediately when he spotted me.

His gaze traveled from my face down to my bare feet and then up again and then at the shoes in my hand.

"Need help?"

I grinned at him sheepishly and held out the shoes. I was wearing black satin leggings that hit mid-calf. The heels on my ivory shoes were five inches made easier by one-and-a-half-inch platform, but still.

Sandro grabbed the shoes and went down on a knee to put each one on. "Are you sure you're not gonna break your neck in these?"

I put my hand on the counter to balance myself. "They're comfy, don't worry. Besides, they're cute."

He gave a shake of his head and I caught the flash of teeth in his grin. When he got up, he didn't need to lean too far to give me a kiss.

"I thought we were just going to the Jabbin' Java family opening?"

"Well, the girls and I may want to catch up later."

"The girls, huh… How about us men?"

I fiddled with his navy-blue tie. He was wearing a white dress shirt for a change. I was slowly adding more variety to his wardrobe other than black. He didn't appear to mind. He even seemed amused at my attempts to add color to his clothes…well, white for now.

"Well, the boxing gym is just across the way. Maybe you all could work out your frustrations some more."

Sandro touched his jaw. "Nico has a mean left hook."

My brothers and Sandro had sparred a couple of times. A healthier alternative for sure than beating the hell out of each other outside the ring and without gloves. Jabbin' Java's grand reopening was tomorrow morning, but Renz was excited for us to try some of his new espresso creations.

The Italian side of our family, of course, thought anything other than straight espresso or a cappuccino was blasphemy.

As for me, I was in the mood for his bacon-and-egg brioche. It had been too long since I had a fix. I grabbed my mini bucket purse that matched my ivory heels. "Come on, let's go. I want to catch the brioche as it comes out of the oven."

I tugged Sandro's hand, but he didn't budge.

I shot him a questioning gaze. "Is there something askew with my clothes?" Aside from the leggings, I was wearing a scooped neckline. Nothing too revealing. I wanted to show off my boxy-heel platform Jimmy Choos with the flared knotted straps over the toes. It was so girly, I couldn't stand it.

He let go of my hand and dug into his suit's inner pocket. "Before you go out with the girls tonight, I have a request."

He set down a jewelry box.

I was more baffled when he slipped the diamond ring from my finger.

"Taking someone's ring off is bad luck."

Sandro's face didn't change expression, but I could just imagine his internal eye roll.

"I'm serious. It means we're going to fight."

He put the ring on the counter and picked up the box and opened it.

Nestled against creamy satin was an obnoxiously huge stone that put the word *ostentatious* to shame.

I laughed. "What is this?"

"Your new engagement ring."

"Sandro," I mumbled when he slipped it on. "This is outrageous. How much did you pay? Oh my God, it weighs a ton." I looked up disbelievingly in his eyes, but his gaze was unrelenting. "Why?"

He emitted an annoyed huff. "Apparently, your ring is not big enough."

"Are you still referring to that incident with that asshole Zachary Hellman?"

"Him and every man who looks at you and thinks they can still hit on you."

"And a flashier ring is supposed to discourage that?"

"I don't know," he answered brusquely, pocketing the other ring, linking our fingers together to signal the end of the conversation. "Just give it a spin tonight and see how you like it."

I already knew I wouldn't like it, but I had to smile at Sandro's possessiveness. Take a maybe two-hundred-thousand-dollar ring for a spin? That was insane. It made me feel guilty because the crime family was still recovering from the toxic asset removal, but Sandro had always said his money was separate, and if he wanted to spoil me with it, I shouldn't feel guilty.

That was why I didn't argue too much. It was only for the evening. Maybe I could convince him to return it.

"Get out!" Ivy exclaimed, grabbing my hand. "What happened to your other ring?"

When they heard her shriek, Sera and Mom gathered around us. We were at the entrance to the kitchen. I was about to check on Renz when Ivy emerged and her eyes went directly to my hand. I guess Sandro was right about a bigger ring being harder to miss.

I gave my most resigned look. "Sandro has it. He thinks if he gives me a gigantic ring, guys will stop hitting on me."

Ivy laughed. "It does scream taken."

"Or *married*," Mom said, giving me a kiss at the side of my head. "You're tall."

Sera dropped her eyes to my shoes. "I have the same pair, but Matteo forbade me to wear anything above a two-inch heel while I'm pregnant. Those are so comfy, though."

"That's what I told Sandro. He thought I might break my neck."

The four of us looked at Sandro, who seemed to be in a deep conversation with Dom.

Mom stroked my hair. "So, how has it been going?"

I laughed briefly. "You just checked on me this morning."

"I'm glad you're gaining more perspective on how to navigate your life in the family."

"And I'm glad you opened up to us," Sera said. She had the most experience being a mafia princess herself. "Any time you have questions about what to do, don't hesitate to call. I can meet you for lunch or dinner or whatever."

We gave each other hugs before I entered the kitchen.

Renz was laying down a tray of bacon-and-egg brioche when I walked in.

"Hey, Smurfette."

I walked over to him and wrapped my arms around his torso and rested my head on his chest. "Dearthháir."

I'd been doing this recently when I was in the feels about what happened to us. It was as if I wanted to listen to his heartbeat to make sure that he was alive and okay.

"You're feeling okay? Breathing okay?" I asked after we hugged for a while.

"Yeah. It's great not to need the sling anymore. Can't wait to meet Rossi in the ring."

I gave a mock huff. "Would you guys give my husband a break?"

"Husband, huh?" Renz teased. I stepped back so he could transfer the tray to the cooling racks.

I rested my elbows on the counter, watching him move around. His movements weren't as quick. He'd lost weight, but I heard he'd been working out again and Nico had been helping him regain muscle mass.

"Can you believe how things have turned around in less than two months?" Things were so bleak in the beginning, I never thought Sandro and I would be at this point celebrating with family. I drew the winning number in the lottery when it came to family. No one blamed me for what happened and that included Liz. I wanted Sandro to be part of my support structure because he'd had nothing like it growing up.

"It's hard to believe you're married."

I lifted my hand with the new ring. "Does this prove anything?"

"Whoa!" His brow arched. "Does this have anything to do with the girls' night a couple of weeks ago?"

"You heard about it?"

"Liz told me. Sera and Ivy spilled the beans about our brothers and Sandro being there."

I wagged my finger with the ginormous rock. "What do you think? Overkill, right?"

"You're asking me?" His gaze lowered to another tray of aromatic baked goods. My mouth watered, but I needed the answer to my question. Renz's mouth twitched. He crossed his arms and leaned against another counter. "Think about why I elected to be good at something that would allow me to be with my wife twenty-four-seven."

Why did I even bother to ask? Renz was the original obsessed De Lucci among my brothers. He embraced the whole idea from the start. "You do take *obsessed* to the next level."

He nodded to my ring. "So I understand Sandro. And I'm not surprised he's involving you in mafia business, even if it's peripheral. From what I know, most wives prefer total ignorance of what their husbands do, but not you. And Sandro wants to share his day and not have to keep it from you."

"That's how I want it."

Renz gave a brief nod. "And that's what Dad is coming to terms with."

I looked at the entrance to the kitchen. "I think he's doing better."

"And…that's why the boxing gym is a good idea." Renz circled back to how our conversation started.

Liz walked in with Sam trailing behind her. "Are you done here?" she asked Renz. "Uncle Paulie is about to say blessings." She grinned at me. "Hey, Bianca."

Sam skipped directly toward me and grabbed my hand. "Aunt Sera told us to look at your new sparkly."

I laughed and showed off my ring.

Her mouth dropped open and her eyes rounded like saucers. "It's big."

"Yep."

Sandro

The girls were talking about where to celebrate after this. They were trying to get Liz to go, but she declined and instead offered their apartment to hang out instead.

I was all for it. And so were Bianca's brothers.

"You're pregnant," Matteo told Sera. "You can't drink anyway, and you say your feet swell up when you stand for long stretches. Why not hang out on the second floor?"

"Because, Mr. Overprotective, once this baby comes, it'll be late nights and diapers."

"She has a point," Liz said.

"Let's just move to the third floor," Cesar proposed. "That way

Liz and Renz won't have to kick you guys out, since they have that opening tomorrow."

"Very sensible," Renz muttered.

I stood in a corner observing Bianca's family interacting. My family now, too. A heartburn like I'd had too much of Renz's espresso experiments burned up my diaphragm. The De Luccis had always grudgingly accepted me into the family because of my friendship with Bianca. Dom and I were good. Nico and Matteo didn't scowl as much anymore whenever they saw me. Ava had always liked me. But Cesar…Cesar was still pretty neutral. I shouldn't take it personally. It wasn't that he thought I was beneath Bianca. He'd never been a snob about money. It was always about Bianca's safety and quality of life.

Ava's eyes caught mine. She walked toward me. "We didn't have time to catch up."

"You've been busy."

"That's a beautiful ring you chose for Bianca."

"Thank you for helping me out," I said.

"Anytime." She squeezed my arm. Ava accompanied me to the Harry Winston store. I was familiar with the luxury jeweler because diamonds were a lucrative part of our smuggled goods. There was a safe at the Rossi mansion that contained a whole sleeve of the highest-quality diamonds from the Northwest Territories of Canada. A pipeline was about to be negotiated between the Rossis and the Toronto Albanians. But I wasn't about to put a smuggled diamond on Bianca's finger. She was getting the full treatment. I would have put a bigger ring on her finger sooner, but a rock that size wasn't immediately available in the store. Twelve carats. She told me it was absurd to take a two-hundred-grand ring for a spin. Little did she know the ring on her finger was over seven figures.

My gaze lifted in time to see Cesar narrow his eyes to where Ava was talking to me.

For fuck's sake. I knew he didn't like it that Ava accompanied me to the jewelry store. Jealous fucker. He retired too early and needed a different hobby other than his wife.

"I hope she'll keep it," I said. "She wasn't impressed."

Ava shot me a reassuring smile. "It's hard to impress someone who has been given everything all her life and who the men in my family can't say no to. But she's always had a special place in her heart for you, Sandro. You don't have to buy her things. Just treat her right. Treasure my daughter. I already see that you do. Cesar will come around once he's assured Bianca is in good hands."

I chuckled briefly. "I sure hope so." Ava gave my arm another squeeze and returned to the gathering. The women had reached a consensus to take the party to the third floor.

Maybe I could share a drink with Cesar and thaw the ice between us further.

My phone buzzed.

Griselda calling.

Fuck. I didn't need her nagging tonight. It was probably about the club.

I silenced her call.

Bianca bounded up to me. "Well, we're continuing this shindig on the third floor."

I wrapped my arms around her and gave her a kiss. "I know, baby."

My phone rang again.

Dammit, Griselda. With one arm still holding Bianca by my side, I dragged out my phone.

It was Tommy.

Frowning, I thumbed to answer. "Yeah."

"Uncle Raffa's house has been hit."

I wasn't sure what he meant, but dread gripped my muscles. "What?"

"They're dead, Sandro." Tommy was shouting and out of breath. I heard doors slamming and urgent voices in the background.

Sticks and Arnie came in through the side entrance.

More than a few of the De Luccis glowered at them. Arnie ignored the hostility and rushed to my side, panting. "You heard?"

"What happened?" Dom asked.

"There was a hit on Uncle Raffa."

"Is he okay?" Cesar joined in.

I was already striding toward the exit. "He's dead."

CHAPTER
Thirty-Seven

Bianca

"She can stay here," Dad told Sandro.

Sandro paused on his way to the door and stared at me, his face expressionless and his eyes flat. It was hard to read him when he consciously masked his emotions.

"It's up to you," he said.

Meanwhile, Nico and Matteo had already exited the side door with Trevor, and I was glad they weren't piling up on Sandro.

"Are you crazy? Our family needs us."

Dad was about to say something, but I glared at him. "I'm going with Sandro. Please don't interfere."

"Bianca…" Dad's eyes were tortured, but he had to let me support my husband.

"If you're coming, we have to go." Sandro pushed open the front door of the café and held it open for me. I hugged Dad and

Mom and walked through the door without looking back. I had to be decisive.

The Expedition was already waiting for us. Sticks slid into the driver's seat while Arnie rode shotgun. Sandro and I were in the back seat.

"Cops just arrived at the site," Arnie informed us with a phone to his ear.

"Who's on the phone?" I asked.

"Al. He's calling on Griselda's phone," he replied.

"Wasn't he guarding them?"

"Yes. He's also hurt, and his phone was smashed. That's why he's using Griselda's phone."

"Is Griselda okay?" I asked.

Sandro stiffened beside me. I noticed he was quiet throughout my exchange with Arnie.

"Don't know. It's chaos right now. The cops are inside." Arnie ended the call. "We need to get there."

"Griselda called me and I didn't answer," Sandro finally said, voice hoarse.

Arnie looked back. "You didn't know. It was Al who was calling you. There's a lotta confusion about what happened."

I squeezed my husband's hand. Sandro wasn't one for empty platitudes. The guilt would be there and we could talk about this later. As much as Griselda and I didn't get along, I hoped she was okay. Even if only for Sandro's sake.

Sandro's phone rang, and from what I could tell, it was Tommy.

When we arrived, the police had already yellow-taped the area around Raffa's house. Emergency vehicles crowded the streets and police herded spectators.

"Dammit," Sandro muttered.

The last thing organized crime wanted was public scrutiny and police attention, but an event of this magnitude, happening in a popular Brooklyn neighborhood, was impossible to keep on the down-low.

"Stay in the car," he told me. "Sticks, stay with her."

The Expedition parked at the edge of where the yellow tape started and Sandro stepped out.

I felt Sticks's frustration.

"Miller is guarding Griselda, right?"

"Yes," he said brusquely. "He and Al are on Griselda. She said Gian is acting unhinged around her."

"Do you know why?"

"Because Gian was expecting Sandro to fail. He was expecting to pick up the pieces, but Sandro is turning the organization around. Gian is pissed about it."

"He's mad at Griselda for thwarting his deal with the Philly mob because she faked being pregnant with Sandro's baby?" I asked.

"That's the gist of it."

He checked his phone. "Miller isn't answering."

"You think…"

"Fuck this," Sticks said. "You wanna check on them?"

"Yes."

I hated waiting around and didn't hesitate to get out. There were cops crawling around, anyway.

"Stay close," Sticks ordered and used his massive body to shield me, keeping me on the inside of the sidewalk.

Sandro spotted us briefly, but he didn't say anything. That was when I noticed Divina and Tommy. They were talking to someone on a gurney who was about to be loaded into an ambulance.

Oh my God, it was Griselda.

She was gripping Tommy's hand and her brother was bent over her. Sandro was pacing behind him.

Sticks and I came up to them. "What happened?"

"Broken jaw, probably cracked ribs." Divina sobbed. "Who would hurt a woman like this?"

"We're going to get the fuckers, okay?" Sandro stopped pacing and growled over Tommy's shoulder. The fury short-circuiting inside him was palpable.

"S..s…" Griselda chattered.

Despite our differences, I couldn't bear to see her in pain. She was covered in blood. I could only imagine the carnage in there.

"I need to stabilize her," the EMT said. "She's going into shock."

"Do we know where Miller is?" Sticks asked finally.

"Man, it's a bloodbath in there," the EMT replied and gave a shake of his head. "Jesus."

He didn't say anymore and continued working on Griselda, but he might as well have dropped another bomb of anxiety in our midst.

A man in a suit with a head of salt-and-pepper hair approached us. He had craggy features and his entire persona screamed hard-boiled detective.

"Mr. Scavo?" he addressed Tommy. "We would like to ask your sister questions."

"She's got a broken jaw, man," the EMT snapped. "We gotta get her to the hospital."

Griselda made a distressed sound and whatever energy she had, she lifted her arm and reached for Sandro. Sandro came forward and gripped her hand in his. "I can't come with you, Griselda. I need to take care of this, but I will come to you once I'm done."

An involuntary sob racked her chest, and tears spilled from her cheeks.

Tommy turned to his wife. "Divina, go with her."

She was hesitant and her eyes pleaded with Tommy, communicating that the last thing she wanted was to get in an ambulance.

Did she have a phobia of them, or maybe she didn't want to leave Tommy given her distress not too long ago when Al was shot.

The last thing the EMT needed was to worry about her, too.

"I'll go," I said.

Sandro's face was still a blank mask, but I could see the fury simmering behind his eyes. At the audacity of the people who did this. "You sure?"

I took Griselda's hand from Sandro's and told him, "Do whatever you need to do and find the fuckers who did this."

The detective shot Tommy a meaningful look. "We need to talk."

A slight relief swept through me. Of course, this was in the Brooklyn area controlled by the Rossis, which meant they controlled the cops.

"Sticks. On Bianca." Sandro turned to Arnie. "Call our men and have them guard the hospital."

"She will have two police escorts," the detective said. "I had to take Al into custody."

Tommy and the cop exchanged a look again.

The EMT and his partner loaded the gurney into the ambulance.

Before I climbed in, Sandro gripped my arm. "Thanks for doing this."

What was left unsaid was…despite my feelings about Griselda.

I had a role to fulfill as Sandro's wife.

"She's family," I told him. "Take care of the men. I'll take care of Griselda."

Sandro

I watched the ambulance drive away, along with two police escorts. I knew those cops. They were on our payroll. Sticks and Arnie followed in the Expedition.

Still, I was unsettled not having Bianca in my sights during a powder keg situation, but I was facing the biggest challenge as the Rossi boss. Our enemies wanted to expose the weakness in our ranks. At how easy it was to hit us. But how, exactly? Raffa had top-notch security around his house. He'd been living in it for decades through all the mob wars between the Five Families.

No one could get in unless someone let them in.

Did Gian cut a deal with the Manhattan Albanians and Raffa told him no? He got pissed and shot Raffa? It didn't make sense to me. Gian rarely did his own dirty work. I tried to recall the crew under him. One soldier stood out who had a trigger-happy finger.

One shot was all it would take to start a gunfight.

I recalled the time Raffa dared me to end his miserable life. Did he goad Gian or one of his men to shoot him?

The CSI and medical examiner vans arrived.

I dragged a hand down my face and exhaled a gust of frustration. A painstakingly long evening loomed before us with the number of bodies inside. When we first arrived, we were told that seven people were dead. Al had confirmed Uncle Raffa and Gian. He said he was on the second floor when he heard the one and only gunshot and Griselda started screaming. He thought for sure Gian had shot Uncle Raffa because they were in a heated argument before they locked themselves in the study. A meeting I knew about because Gian was bitching again about not being boss. Al said he was shot running down the stairs. He fell down the rest of the steps and lost consciousness. He woke up to a sobbing Griselda and a bullet-riddled house.

"You okay?" I asked Tommy after he talked to the detective. Since Tommy had been dealing with the police on behalf of the Rossis since Frankie's reign, I let him handle our connections in law enforcement.

"No, man." He dug the heel of his hand into an eye. "I can't believe this shit." We were standing side by side, but facing opposite directions. "This has to be the Albanians. We shouldn't have left any of those fuckers alive."

"And we will get them if they did this. But how did they get in?" I felt for Tommy. I really did. He must've been feeling like he let his sister down. Just when things were looking up, we were hit again. What Albanian nest did we miss? I was sure we sent all of Doku's loyalists running. "We need the surveillance in the house. Who has access to it?"

"Gian, Al, and Griselda," Tommy answered.

One of our capos approached us. "I've got my men heading to King's County hospital."

"Do Sticks and Arnie know?"

"Yes, Bianca informed them."

My wife had her shit together more than anyone here, stepping up while I made sure Tommy didn't go off the deep end. His uncle Al was in police custody and hopefully that would only be for show. This shit needed to be contained in Brooklyn.

"Sticks is asking after Miller," another soldier said.

"They're not bringing the bodies out yet." My chest constricted at the thought. Sticks and Miller were like brothers. I was telling myself that I assigned him to Griselda because he was club security, but the truth was I still didn't want him around Bianca. "It's going to take a while." I sighed. "I'll respond to him." My phone just buzzed with the same question from Arnie, who I was certain was trying to keep Sticks calm. And now I was worried about Bianca because old reliable Sticks was getting rattled too.

I caught sight of Nico and Trevor making their way through the crowd. When Bianca's dad asked his daughter to stay with the De Luccis, I almost gave in. But Bianca wanted to do her part for our organization. I couldn't keep her behind the De Luccis safety net because that would mean I didn't trust her enough to handle herself.

But I wouldn't reject their help. This wasn't a competition for Bianca's affection.

My phone buzzed again. The Toronto Albanian fixer.

I answered the call. "You played me."

"I didn't," the fixer answered.

I moved out of earshot of everyone. "Really? You told us we got every one of Doku's loyalists."

"I hope you're not suggesting we double-crossed you."

"The evidence is proving otherwise."

"I don't have all the evidence, but I would look into your man, Crowe Miller ."

Dread knotted in my gut, and acid churned up my throat. "You're reaching."

"That's the best lead I have."

I ended the call and walked toward the detective Tommy was talking to.

"We need to go in there and identify the bodies."

The detective glowered at me with a trace of incredulity. "That's not gonna happen. Look around you for Chrissakes. Everyone's on their damned phone, filming this circus. I can't risk jeopardizing the investigation. Who are we looking for?"

"Detective." A uniform rushed towards us. "The ambulance got hit."

That knot of dread twisted into fear and fury. The familiar mist of red whenever Bianca was in danger crowded my mind and bled into my eyes.

"What?" the detective and Tommy growled.

"Our officers are down and…"

"My wife." But my years as an assassin taught me restraint. Otherwise, I would have grabbed the cop by the collar and gotten thrown into jail for assault. Still, I crowded him, close enough that I was in his face. "My wife was in that ambulance."

"Jesus Christ, Rossi." The detective shoved me aside. "Are you lookin' to get arrested? Cool it, huh?"

Nico and Trevor appeared by our side. I pivoted away from the cops and tried to call Bianca, but it went to voicemail. I checked her proximity dot, and it wasn't pinging. Chills crawled all over my skin and my pulse pounded in my ears.

"The ambulance got hit," Nico said.

"I know," I clipped. "Bianca's not answering."

The detective exhaled heavily. "Goddammit. I should throw every single one of you into jail for your own goddamn sake."

"Then let's go," Nico snapped. "Or I'm gonna leave your ass here."

"You guys can't interfere," the detective yelled after us, but he had his own shit to handle as other uniforms vied for his attention.

"Try to stop us," I muttered. I called Sticks. Nothing. "Fuck!"

A blacked-out Nissan Armada was waiting for us. I didn't realize Tommy was following me until he spoke, "What do you want me to do?"

"Identify the dead." I got into the SUV.

"Griselda…" he choked out.

But my thoughts were only focused on Bianca. "I'll call you when I have news."

I shut the door and leaned against the headrest. My temples

were throbbing, probably from all the jaw clenching and teeth grinding I'd been doing. I inhaled a couple of calming breaths before I said, "Any luck trying to get through to Bianca?"

"No," Nico answered. "Matteo is putting our men on standby. Do we know who would hit the ambulance? Albanians—"

"My Toronto contact is pointing to Crowe Miller."

"Miller?" Trevor spoke up. "Huh…"

"That *huh* better mean something." I went through my contact list again until someone fucking answered.

"I did a background check," Trevor said.

"I'd expect you to."

"It passed from what I could tell, but something seems cagey about him."

I replayed every interaction with the man. When the club started rebuilding, he'd become more of Griselda's security than Bianca's. But Sticks trusted him, and that was why I allowed Miller to guard Bianca sometimes.

I continued trying to call Bianca, Sticks, and Arnie, but no one was answering. But it wasn't long before I had my answers. And the worst scenario greeted our eyes.

An overturned ambulance.

Two cop cars were facing the wrong direction of traffic with bodies of the cops sprawled on the ground.

The Expedition Sticks was driving was riddled with bullets and the front tire was flat. Bulletproof glass could only withstand so much. Jesus. Whoever did this had an arsenal.

Nico and I ran toward the ambulance. My mind went through a reel of things I should have done with Bianca. Should I have left her with the De Luccis? Should I have forced her to divorce me?

Should. Should. Should.

I got to the ambulance first and ripped open the door. Blood splatter was everywhere. Sirens howled in the distance. The EMT at the scene was slumped over, probably dead.

No Griselda. No Bianca. But there was too much blood.

My heart pounded as my lungs pumped out more ragged breaths. "She's not here."

My body sagged against the vehicle, suddenly sucked of strength, but my mind vomited all possibilities. "She's not here," I repeated.

Relief.

No.

Anger.

No.

But someone was going to die.

My eyes zeroed in on the skid marks that could have belonged to their attackers.

"We need to leave," Trevor said. "Cops are two minutes out." The sirens were getting closer. "I got Sticks and Arnie in the back of the Nissan."

"He's right," Nico, who'd been a quiet ball of tension beside me, finally said, "let's get out of here."

We regrouped in one of our Harlem warehouses. Arnie and Sticks were being treated for gunshot wounds. I called Sloane because the mob doc was on duty in the ER and couldn't get away immediately. I trusted her more anyway.

But we had confirmation that the mastermind was Crowe Miller.

Sticks had a hole through his side and a concussion. He hit his head on the pavement when he got shot. "I can't believe it, brother. Even if he had a mask on, I could tell it was Miller leading the bunch of men who attacked us."

"Who was with him? Recognize anyone?" I asked.

"All were wearing masks," Arnie gritted as Sloane extracted bullet fragments from his upper shoulder. "But I heard some of them shout at each other. Albanians, boss."

Nico was pacing behind us like a jungle cat, casting us glares every few seconds as he brooded.

Trevor had fired up his laptop and was digging into more information about Miller.

Tommy and Divina arrived with a bunch of our soldiers. "They're transferring the bodies to the morgue." Tommy looked at me. "No Miller."

"Is that even a question here?" Nico snapped.

"What's De Lucci doing here?" Tommy moved toward him.

"You want to question why I'm here?" Nico headed him off. "My sister is fucking missing."

"So is mine," Tommy snarled.

And my wife is missing, I wanted to yell at them, but this wasn't a pissing contest, and someone—me—needed to keep his head in the game and make sure no one went off half-cocked resulting in a bunch of us getting arrested. Because if that happened, I was really going to lose my shit.

"Now is not the time." I stepped in between them and addressed Tommy. "We have seven dead. One in police custody. And these two are injured." I nodded at Arnie and Sticks. "Trevor is the best I know at gathering intel." I didn't need to add that Trevor had access to government databases the mob couldn't touch. "We need to find out Miller's true identity."

"You think he's not this Crowe Miller?" Sticks asked. "We did his background check and he's kosher—"

"There's something I'm looking into," Trevor interrupted brusquely.

My phone went off with an unknown number.

My breath snagged as I answered, "Rossi."

“Calling you back with a video call.” The line went dead and rang again. I gripped my phone so hard it was a wonder it didn’t shatter in my hand.

Miller’s face filled the screen. It was as if a snake had shed its skin and I could see its malevolent, serpentine stare.

“Hi, boss.”

“Where’s my wife?” I shouted, keeping my head on straight be damned.

“Oh, she’s taking a dip.” He turned the phone away from him.

The roar started in my head. Loud and so full of rage, it pressed against my eyes. If I thought I was living in a nightmare, it was only the beginning. Life and death meant nothing to me. I chose life only because of Bianca. The world would cease to exist if she wasn’t in it. Because if she wasn’t in it, I would take myself out. I wouldn’t live in a world without my Sunlight.

“Bianca…” I said her name with ragged anguish.

She was in a swimming pool with her wrists cuffed above her head. The water was at her neck level, but there was a commercial hose gushing water into the pool.

My eyes blinked.

I couldn’t even speak after I choked her name. It took all my strength to remain upright and not crumble in front of the fucker.

“You fucking asshole,” I snarled. “I’m going to kill you. I’m going to end your miserable life.”

The phone switched back to Miller. “I’m fond of Bianca, but unfortunately, she was too precious not to use for my ultimate payback.”

“For what? Tell me what for? Do you want money? I can give you money.”

He laughed again. “I have enough. Why don’t you ask Divina?”

My eyes whipped around, and Divina shook her head and whispered, “I was going to tell you.”

Did Divina betray the family too? My head swam with fucked-up thoughts. Nothing made sense, except one: "Exchange me for Bianca. It's me you hate. Take me. Don't hurt her. Whatever I did to you, she doesn't deserve this. Please. I'm begging you. Take me instead and do what you want."

"The great Alessandro Rossi is begging?"

"I won't fight you. Do whatever you want with me. Set me on fire. Mutilate me. Dismember me. Anything. Just…spare her…"

"Well, see, I would love to see you beg on your knees and crawl over hot coals before I tear you apart. But you'll just die in a few days." His smile was cruel. "But seeing your loved one die before your eyes and you're helpless to stop it? That image will torment you for the rest of your life."

"Don't do this!" I roared those three words and could feel my neck muscles seizing. My hands wanted to reach into the phone and strangle the life out of that miserable fucker.

"Ask him why," Trevor said.

"Oh, why?" Miller asked, hearing his question. "Are you trying to find out my motive, Rossi? Isn't drowning one of your favorite methods as a hit man?" He made a funny face. "Oh, wait, you murdered too many people that way to remember."

My hearing went in and out of focus like a faulty radio. Rage like I'd never experienced locked every sinew of muscle because Miller was right. Once I'd established my mark deserved to die, they ceased to exist to me as a person. I erased most of them from my memory and they became a number.

I remembered some of them. Like the arms dealer I killed the night I crashed into the frat house, but that was largely because of Bianca. Miller would forever be etched in my mind as someone I couldn't wait to rip apart. Once I got my hands on him, his death wouldn't be easy. Because the only person I loved was being tortured with drowning. It had become my worst fucking torture.

More than the time I was strung up in a Russian prison, my back shredded with a whip. No torment could compare to this…watching Bianca fight for her life.

Nico had been shouting for a while, but my men had held him down.

The cogs in my brain started turning. If it was one of my jobs… How long ago? Did he team up with Doku loyalists? That meant he knew about my Doku kill.

"This is about revenge."

"I'll let you stew on that. Meanwhile, I'll text you the website where you can watch your wife drown. Enjoy your life."

The screen went blank.

"Miller," I gritted. A text message came and there was a link.

My thumb hovered over it.

Could I bear to watch Bianca die?

CHAPTER
Thirty-Eight

Sandro

"Don't click on it," Trevor said behind me. "Forward it to me and I'll make sure it's legit."

I shook off my tunnel vision, but even for two seconds, it was like my brain had ceased functioning and couldn't respond to a simple command. I sent the link to Trevor, then turned to my men, who were holding Nico down.

"Let him go."

His countenance was ravaged, eyes red, and tears tracked down his face. But he seemed to have pulled himself together because he silently joined me behind Trevor. He understood there was time for blame later. In-fighting would get us no closer to finding Bianca.

I was rusty when it came to tech, but I recognized the safeguards Trevor was taking. "I'm quarantining it through a secure browser." The wait felt like an agonizing drive through Manhattan traffic. Finally, he asked, "Ready?"

"Yeah," Nico and I said.

The screen came on and my world descended into hell.

A suppressed sob sounded beside me.

Bianca was staring straight at the camera. An emotion-filled hitch caught in my throat. My wife was trying to be brave. She was trying to work her wrists free from the cuffs attached to the ladder. Then she would slip and part of her head would submerge in water. Those shoes. She was stepping on a ladder rung. It was giving her a few inches above the water.

"Can she get out of it?" Nico asked.

"It appears to be double-latched," Trevor responded. "So no."

Someone was crying behind us. Divina.

I prowled toward her and grabbed her shoulders. "Talk."

"Hey, get your hands off my wife!" Tommy came between us and shoved me aside. "It's not her fault." If circumstances were different, he would have probably punched me.

I jabbed a finger at the scene playing out on the screen. "Bianca took her place in the ambulance. If she'd known something then, she should have spoken up!" My voice rose to a roar.

"I didn't have time," Divina sobbed. "I just found out this afternoon, and I hadn't connected all the dots."

"What did you find out?" I asked.

"Griselda was embezzling the money that was funneled through the club. I think they killed the accountant because he was being hounded by Gian about the shortage."

"Griselda? They? Did she stage this? She was working with Miller?"

"I didn't know about Miller then, but Gian was confronting her. Gian told me that someone from the club was helping her, but he was keeping that to himself."

The puzzle was falling into place, but I was having trouble wrapping my mind around it. Griselda and Miller?

"That was why I didn't get into the ambulance. I didn't know who to trust except Tommy. I didn't know Bianca was going to get in."

"You should have said something!" I shouted.

"That's enough," Arnie said. "She should have, but she didn't know this"—he tipped his chin at the screen—"was going to happen."

"What else?"

"That's all I know."

"Goddammit!" I lost it and kicked a box that was on the floor. Flashes of all the people I killed ran on a reel through my head. They deserved to die. But if I had known Bianca was going to pay the price for those jobs, I would have remained the dumbest foot soldier in the mob. I turned myself into the deadliest hit man, learned all the skills so I could protect Bianca, thinking her father had enemies. But it was my past that became a danger to her.

Rage like I'd never felt before reverberated deep inside me. Anyone who thought to calm me down was going to get punched in the face.

"Wait, I know where that is." It was Sloane who spoke up.

I whipped around and saw her standing behind Trevor.

"Where?" Nico asked.

"That's twenty minutes from here. It's owned by the Albanians. It's one of their interrogation houses. I cleaned it a couple of months ago." Sloane screwed up her face in disgust. "Last time I'm doing it for sure. They stiffed me on payment."

"Tell us where it is."

"It's better if I show you."

My jaw clenched.

"You don't have time," Sloane said. She pointed at the screen. "She doesn't have time."

"Fuckin' aware. You better be damned sure, Sloane."

She glanced at the screen and then back at me.

"I'm sure."

"Then let's go get my wife." I turned to Nico, but before I could say anything, he said, "I'm coming with you."

"I'm not wasting my time saying no. You drive. I ride shotgun. Sloane and Trevor behind me. Tommy, follow our vehicle, but do not engage until I say so."

I didn't wait for anyone to contradict me and headed for the exit. My Expedition with its own veritable armory was parked outside. I tossed the keys to Nico. It was only when we were on the road and our plan was set that I clicked on the link again.

The video came up. Tremors shook my body and I whispered hoarsely, "Sunlight."

The water had risen and she kept slipping and sputtering.

"How is she?" Nico asked from beside me.

"She's hanging in there. Your sister is a fighter."

"She is."

I wished I had a pill that would numb me through all emotions so I could remain clear-headed to execute this task. I was too close to this, but I wouldn't trust anyone else to get it done.

"Miller is Kaz Doku's bastard son," Trevor said behind us.

Fuck. My first kill. The Albanian mob boss that cemented my place in the Rossi crime family as their assassin-for-hire. The Rossis awarded me that Harlem kingdom. It would explain why Miller went after it. Most of the puzzle had fallen into place.

"He's planned it for a while."

"He was using his mother's last name. That was why we couldn't link him immediately to Doku. From what I can tell, he landed in Iowa after his father's death and assumed the identity of an army veteran named Crowe Miller.

"The Albanians run a stolen identity ring. They keep track of returning veterans who join support groups for PTSD." Trevor's voice grew progressively sharper, angrier, but I could see where he was going with this. "Veterans who've been abandoned by family and friends because they can't cope. So when they go missing, nobody questions it."

"Someone has access to government databases and changed the fingerprints and pictures?" Nico asked.

"Yeah, so they have connections to the FBI's fingerprinting system," Trevor said. "The Office of Personnel Management holds all information of government employees. They might have changed current details like photos. That is why I dug up the archives."

"That's fucked up," Sloane said.

Nothing surprised me anymore. Everyone had a price. And the Albanians were ruthless. They targeted veterans because they would have enough combat experience to infiltrate an organization's security regardless of what background check was done. When Miller joined, it was for the security of the club.

As I continued to keep my eyes on Bianca, details about Miller's secret life emerged. Did I think my life as an assassin wouldn't catch up with me? There was never any association between my kill list and myself except that very first job. Raffa was the last one alive who knew about it.

"Right here." Sloane pointed at the street coming up.

The Expedition turned into a narrow road. That was when Bianca slipped again and went underwater. "How many more minutes? Bianca is almost outta time!"

Panic warred against my ability to stay coherent. She was bobbing under water but coming up just enough to suck in air.

It was a four-lane road that narrowed into two lanes until houses with acres of land between them surrounded us.

"We're coming up on it, right?" Nico said.

"Yes. Next property after the crossing, but you might want to set up on the street over," Sloane said.

"I wish I had my drone and shit," Trevor said.

Nico parked. He grabbed his phone and called someone.

"I have two sniper rifles with infrared scopes," I said. "A couple of pistols."

"I can work with that," Trevor said.

I turned to Sloane. "You don't have to come."

"Tell me what you need."

I was used to working alone, but I was learning to trust the people in my family. And Sloane was family. I handed her my phone and a gun. "Keep me sane. Tell me how many minutes I have."

Nico was still talking on his, but I gestured we were moving out. Tommy and his crew were waiting at the cross street for my signal to go in.

The plan was for Trevor and me to take out the night guards.

The house was in front of a swath of undeveloped land, which provided perfect concealment for our approach. We trekked the short distance to the spot parallel to the front of our target house. I crouched and then shifted to crawl on my belly and studied the structure with night-vision goggles. According to Sloane, the backyard where the pool was located had ten-foot-high concrete fencing and would need someone on the inside to open the metal gate.

When the house was occupied, the Albanians frequently spent time in the living room or the kitchen. Both areas were at the front of the house.

"Nico is asking where you want him," Trevor asked.

"The rear of the property by the gate. We'll let him in. We got the front and sides covered."

"I've got two guards in sight," he said. "Someone is in the living room."

"We take them out simultaneously. Stat on Bianca?" I asked Sloane.

"You're good. You're going to make it… Just take the shot in the next two minutes."

I froze and slowly turned to her. "Why?"

"Head in the game, Sandro. She's fine."

"I got the guy on the right," Trevor said.

I cracked my neck before lining up my sights on the rifle. The two guards were not moving and just sitting on the steps chatting and smoking.

"On three," I told him. "When I say one, shoot."

"Glad you clarified that."

"Three."

"Two."

"One."

The two men flew backward.

I spied Tommy's crew moving in. We dropped the rifles and sprang to our feet to join them.

A man stepped out of the house, but one of our soldiers took him down.

Trevor and I rushed inside, with Tommy and his crew following behind us.

"Sloane!"

"I'm here."

"Stay behind me."

Where the hell was that motherfucker? Footsteps stampeded down the stairs, but I left my crew to handle them.

"Turn right," Sloane shouted.

With my gun raised and leading the way, we moved through the maze of the house.

Just when we passed a crisscrossing hallway, a blast sounded behind me.

"Shit," Sloane cried.

I whipped around to look at her and spotted a man on the floor cursing her.

Dom.

Fucking fuck.

"You fucking shot me," Dom groaned.

"You surprised me!" she screamed.

I tipped my chin at Trevor. "Check on him." And told Sloane and a couple of soldiers behind me, "Let's go."

We passed the kitchen and could see the pool.

My wife's head was submerged.

Motionless. Her hair floated in a mass around her.

"Bianca!" I roared and tore through the kitchen exit. A force knocked me to the side, but my forward momentum sent me into the water.

The lining of the pool was dark. I could still see bullets streak past me. A dark cloud rose and in the back of my mind I knew I was hit.

But I didn't feel any pain.

My life had always been preordained.

I did not save Bianca from the pool when she was five years old, only to have her die in one eighteen years later.

Nothing, not even if they riddled me with bullets, would stop me from saving her.

I reached her motionless body and lifted her up just in time to see Nico sliding to his knees and working on the cuffs securing Bianca's wrists.

"We got Miller. He's alive, but I shot him. He was waiting for you."

Shudders wracked my body and I was slightly lightheaded.

"You're shot!" Sloane appeared beside us.

"Bianca first."

The second the cuffs fell away, I heaved her out of the pool. Nico grabbed under her armpits and dragged her to the ground.

I hoisted myself out of the water and shoved Nico aside, and started mouth-to-mouth.

I blew once.

Twice.

Three times.

Bianca remained motionless.

~

Bianca

I was getting tired.

Exhausted.

My shoes kept slipping, and I continued to swallow more water. My throat had never felt more raw.

I couldn't keep my eyes on the camera anymore. Sandro was watching. I didn't know how he could save me this time. But no matter what happened, I wanted him to know that I fought hard to have the life I wanted with him. That I didn't simply give up. I fought until it wasn't humanly possible anymore.

It appeared our story would begin and end with the pool, only this time I couldn't hang on long enough for him to save me.

I'm sorry, Sandro.

I tried.

I really tried.

I love you.

And I'll love you until my last breath.

A burning sensation pierced my chest, and I panicked. I kicked and I took in more water, but relief was beyond my reach. Excruciating pain crushed me and then suddenly, there was peace. The tranquility of calm water surrounded me.

I am at the bottom of the pool. Frankie Rossi pushed me. He was an asshole, so I punched him between his legs the way Nico taught me.

A big splash fills the pool with light and then strong arms scoop me under my arms.

It's Sandro!

He's carrying me up and up!

He's my superhero.

Well, Dad too. And my brothers.

He lays me down beside the pool, but wait, who is that woman? It's not me.

Why is Sandro crying?

Why is Nico crying?

Bianca!

You wake up, wife!

Don't you dare die on me.

Wife?

My chest expands and I can't breathe. I start to choke. I swallow my tongue.

I'm yanked to a sitting position and vomit and it won't stop.

Strong arms hug me against a hard chest, and I can't breathe again. I push him away. The arms loosen and I look up into the fierce gaze of my beloved husband.

Sandro?

"Sandro?" I croaked, my voice scratchy, throat burning. His eyes were red, face pale, and his mouth was stretched into a thin line before he gave me the slightest kiss.

Then, gingerly, he scooped me up. He staggered forward.

That was when I saw Sloane and Nico.

Sloane reached out. "Sandro…"

"I got her."

"I can carry her," Nico insisted.

"I. Got. Her," Sandro gritted.

My mind swirled in a daze, trying to rewind what happened as Sandro carried me into a house. I was in a pool. How did I get into a pool? Then events came crashing back. Swallowing water. Trying to keep my head above water. My shoes. I was thankful for the platforms. But how…Miller! That fucking son of a bitch! He and his men ambushed the ambulance. They shot the EMT. Grabbed Griselda and me.

Griselda!

"Where's Griselda?" I whispered. My throat was so raw, it hurt to speak. No one answered. Sandro continued moving. "Sandro," I pushed out. "Where's Griselda?"

Still, I received no response. Growing alarm spiked inside me. Men seemed to converge around us in a protective formation, but I heard a man's wailing somewhere.

That was when I saw Tommy.

I squirmed in Sandro's arms. I spotted Tommy kneeling over a body. His hand was at the back of his head and his body was shuddering. "Oh my God. Is she dead?"

"Don't think about that right now." Sandro's voice was strained. Was it my imagination, or did he stumble? Nico was hovering, and I could feel the rumble of a growl in my husband's chest. My thoughts spiraled. Did they have to trade me for Griselda? I couldn't remember much other than Miller saying that Sandro was going to pay.

My whole concept of time and space was whacked. We moved from room to room but finally made it to the outside.

"How is she?!"

Dad.

My heart pounded. Apprehension seized me. Would Dad take me from Sandro because he thought this was all his fault?

"She's okay," Sloane said.

"I wasn't asking you."

Sandro stopped walking and Dad's face came into view. "Bianca…"

"I'm really fine, Dad."

"You're bleeding," he said.

"No, I'm not," I responded.

But that was when I noticed he was addressing Sandro.

"I'm fine," Sandro clipped.

"No, you're not," Sloane said.

"Shut up, Sloane," Sandro hissed, but the strain in his voice grew more pronounced. Things started making sense: His uncharacteristic quietness despite the relief that I was safe. The lack of answers to my questions. The single-mindedness of getting me out of that house became his singular purpose.

I scrutinized my husband's face. He was almost white beneath his tan. Sweat trickled from the side of his face despite the chilled air. It wasn't from the water of the pool.

"Sandro," I whispered.

He swung me into an SUV, relinquishing his hold on me. And that was when I saw it. The track of blood that followed him.

"You're hurt!" I shrieked, unmindful of the burning in my throat. That was the reason he wasn't all over me. He had channeled all his remaining energy into getting me safe.

"Yes, and he's a stubborn fucker," Sloane said. "Now, will you let me look at you?"

"Not now, Sloane. I need to get Bianca to the hospital."

"You know what, you'll be the one they'll be admitting if I don't stop the bleeding," she retorted.

I was so thankful for Sloane doing the talking because all I could mutter was, "Do it, Sloane."

I glared at Sandro to make my point.

He returned my glare for a beat, still breathing heavily from his exertions in his weakened condition. "You're going to the hospital."

Because I was tired of speaking, I clutched my throat to make my point and then twirled my finger for him to turn around and face Sloane to make a further point.

Sandro looked like he wanted to argue but did as he was told.

Stubborn, overprotective man.

The door on my other side opened, then Dad got in. "Are you really okay?"

I smiled at him, and clasped his hand and gave it a squeeze, then croaked, "Help him."

Dad's mouth tightened. I knew he wanted to grab me and run, but he also knew I wouldn't forgive him if he did.

Sandro and I were in this together.

In sickness and in health.

And despite how we said our vows, we were upholding them now when they mattered.

CHAPTER *Thirty-Nine*

TWELVE HOURS LATER

Harlem house basement

Sandro

My wife was safe. She was safe in the arms of her family. As for mine? It was in shambles, shredded, and burned to the ground.

Raffa, Gian, and Griselda were dead. She died of internal bleeding from beatings sustained from Miller.

The Scavos were in mourning. Tommy was inconsolable, but he had Divina. He had Arnie and Al.

The man in front of me instigated all this chaos. He was sitting in a chair, with his hands bound behind it.

Crowe Miller, aka Andrey Tanush, but his real name meant nothing to me. I wanted to know why he fixated on me. He ended the life of a military veteran before he had the chance to claw out of PTSD. Then he assumed his identity.

Miller followed my movements with dead eyes. Nico had done a number on him; his features were barely recognizable. He was also bleeding from a gut shot that was looking infected.

I had Sloane give him a blood transfusion to keep him alive. No morphine. I wanted him to suffer until I decided to end his pathetic existence. Gave him enough Adderall so he would stay coherent enough to give me answers.

We were in the basement of a Harlem house.

No one else was with us.

Miller's last breath belonged to me.

"You robbed me of my relationship with my father," he started to speak. I'd been leaning against the wall watching him. I didn't need any information from him except his reason for wanting to take revenge. The bastard had asked me to shoot him in the head when he saw me lay a gun on the desk beside him. I told him I would if he told me his reason for going after me, going after Bianca.

"He ignored me for almost nineteen years, but he was finally ready to bring me into his organization. He said he had enemies, including his own sons, and he was keeping me safe."

He gave a scornful laugh. "But you had to kill him. Drown him in his own fucking car with his hands tied against the steering wheel. I saw you that night. Not clearly. But you emerged from the woods." He continued to ramble. "It was the night I was meeting my father. You robbed me of my right to be in my father's organization."

"If you saw me emerge, you might have saved him," I said.

"I tried. I went into the water, but I saw…" He broke off. "I saw how you tied him to the steering wheel."

Layers of wire wound tightly around his wrists.

"He was bleeding with the effort to break free." Anger manifested briefly in his deadened eyes.

"You watched him..." And that was why he made me watch Bianca die.

"So you see, it's justified retribution."

I laughed scornfully. "Are you trying to make me feel guilty about shooting you right now?"

"End me, Rossi. Finish this madness now."

"Your father was a butcher."

"And you're not?"

"I am," I said. "But I'm not the one in that chair, am I? Your father deserved that kind of death. Bianca? You don't even deserve to speak her name. Your father had done nothing but deny you your existence until he needed you...until his sons turned on him. Bianca..." I caught myself.

"She was everything to you." A malicious grin formed on his deformed face. "When I looked at her with lovesick eyes...I was just testing you. I prefer women like Griselda. That bitch thought she was in control, though, but I was manipulating her. The money had gone to her head. She said she was wasting her time in the family when they never gave a damn about what she wanted. She said you're overprotective of Bianca only as a sister. But I know jealousy when I see it. And I proved how you were obsessed with her after you killed Raffa's men and the aftermath."

"You were the leak, weren't you? You were the one who planted the jammer, so I couldn't call Sticks to warn him of Raffa."

His grin widened if possible, confirming he was the mastermind behind it all.

He continued his confession. Burning the club pissed off Griselda, but the accountant was getting leery of helping them embezzle money because Gian started asking questions. He filled in the gaps of what happened in Raffa's house. Gian thought Griselda's accomplice was Sticks. He was going to blackmail Raffa in his office to reinstate him as boss before he revealed what he knew. But Miller had corrupted one of Gian's soldiers who shot Gian first. When Griselda started screaming, and since Miller was her bodyguard, he broke her jaw and continued to beat her. Al came running down the steps and it was Miller who shot him. He had already let the Albanians in and a shootout ensued. He kept Griselda alive in case he could use her as bait, knowing she couldn't speak because he'd broken her jaw.

It was Miller's cohorts in the Albanian mob who shot up Jabbin' Java. They wanted the Rossis and De Luccis to be on a collision course.

Miller slowly lost coherence. The gut shot was poisoning him.

But I wanted him writhing in pain before I sent him to hell.

I straightened from the wall, walked to the opposite corner, and dragged a trolley to his side.

Miller looked at me in confusion. "What?"

I smelled his fear. He didn't fear dying; he feared pain. His screams were going to be the soundtrack in this basement.

"You really think I'm going to make it easy for you?" I removed the canvas covering my instruments of torture. "We're going to have hours of fun, fucker."

CHAPTER *Forty*

Another six hours later

De Lucci mansion

Cesar

If I had gotten hold of Sandro before they found Bianca, I might have shot him on the spot. He promised to protect my daughter and failed. He let a man on the inside betray him. He didn't know that his ex-fiancée was making moves to hurt him. My mind calculated how to capture this overgrown ape and get rid of him. It was easier said than done, but I would expend all my resources to make that happen.

But when I pulled up to the Albanians' house and received the news that Bianca was safe and it was all over, all my rage leaked out and transformed into crippling relief. The fucker actually did it.

Saved my daughter from the psychopath who was torturing her with a slow drowning.

Nico refused to send me the link to the video footage even when I threatened to cut him out of my will.

Sandro emerged from that hellhole, carrying my daughter, and it was a sight I would never forget. Because it was at that moment when I finally saw him as a man who deserved my daughter. It might have been an amalgamation of everything he'd done since the morning he sat at my breakfast table. The morning after he had the audacity to sneak into my house, and when I bitched about it to Ava, she reminded me I did the same once upon a time.

When Sandro stubbornly refused to relinquish my daughter to anyone until he got her to the safety of the SUV, my first caustic thought was he was dumb as fuck. I mean, he could have dropped her. He had two gunshot wounds, and one of them was a bleeder.

But in his dogged determination, I saw my hypocrisy, because I would have done the same if our situations were reversed.

I saw a man who would bleed to death just so my daughter could live. I saw a man who would always put my daughter first.

And that was what Sandro did.

The Rossi crime family was a mess, but he made sure Bianca went to the hospital and had every test done to ensure she was okay. He didn't leave her side or have anyone look at his injuries until Bianca was given a clean bill of health. At that point, Sandro was in more danger of complications than she was.

He asked us to look after Bianca while he took care of the other problem.

We all wanted to take our shot at Miller, but in the end, Sandro didn't allow it.

He said there wasn't enough of Miller to go around and satisfy his bloodlust.

So here I was in the kitchen, trying to calm my daughter down. She kept checking her phone for a message from her husband.

I was making frittata, and I asked Bianca to help me. She was annoyed, but I didn't give her a choice.

"What if he's passed out somewhere?" she argued. I assigned her chopping duties because that was the most soothing to absorb her anxiety.

"He's fine."

"I should be with Divina," she muttered. "She has so many funerals to prepare for and I should help her."

I sighed. At that point, I put my hand on her arm to stop her chopping motion, and then put my hands on her shoulders to turn her to face me. "Divina insisted you should rest. She said it was time for her to show some spine." At Bianca's furrowed brows, I continued, "Her words, not mine. The Scavo brothers are helping her, and so is Sloane. But the Rossis are banding together to show support for their boss…"

"But Griselda…"

"She betrayed the family, *carina*," I said softly. "She would have been exiled. Her death is a blessing…"

"Dad…!"

"Listen to me." I gave her shoulders a light squeeze. My daughter needed to lose some of her empathy to survive being in her new position. I gnashed my teeth because ever since she was old enough to understand right and wrong, Ava and I had taught her to be sympathetic to the plight of others in less fortunate situations. But all that had changed. She needed a touch of ruthlessness inside her. When she returned after her forced marriage, I already noted a difference in her. I was just too stubborn to acknowledge it. "She would have caused friction between Sandro and Tommy. The Rossis are at a critical point in rebuilding the crime family. Those opposed to Sandro are gone. Your husband needs Tommy's unwavering support. Sandro has a lot of rage in him. He might've killed Griselda after what happened to you, and he'd be justified. She betrayed the crime family. Her death is the cleanest break for everyone."

Bianca dropped her gaze to the chopped vegetables. "I know that. I'm still worried about Sandro." She glanced up. "Won't the police be all over this? He's not in jail, right? You're not shielding me from this?"

"No, *carina*." My voice softened. "That's all taken care of." Matteo and Dom had a meeting to clean this up as part of Archer business. They were going to recover the money Miller and Griselda embezzled and keep things quiet. Law enforcement didn't want this headache either, because we could counter-sue at the negligence in transporting Griselda to the hospital. This was going in the books as gang violence and retaliation. The carnage at the Albanian house never happened.

Bianca's eyes hardened before she dropped her gaze again to the chopping board and continued prepping the vegetables. I grieved the remaining remnants of my daughter's innocence, but with it came a conviction that she was going to be okay. That I had to let her go and be the woman she was meant to be.

Footsteps outside the kitchen drew our attention. I narrowed my eyes when Ava appeared beside the simmering mountain that was Bianca's husband. My wife had always believed in Sandro, which had historically irked the fuck out of me.

But this fucker was growing on me.

"Look who's here!" Ava announced just as Bianca dropped everything and rounded the counter to fly into her husband's arms.

My chest and throat tightened. Seeing Sandro's face lose its hard edges and his eyes take on an adoring gaze was difficult to take in. But I stood transfixed as I witnessed his brawny arms wrap around my daughter. Then they drew apart and Sandro cupped Bianca's face.

"Are you all right?" Bianca asked.

Sandro dropped his forehead to hers. "I should be asking you that."

Again, it was hard to watch such love and devotion emanate from the pair as if they were the only two people in the world.

Ava came to my side, clasped my hand, and gave it a tug. I glanced at my wife and gave her a reassuring smile.

"Bianca." I cleared my throat. "Why don't you show Sandro to the west wing?"

She turned to me. "Are you sure, Dad? Don't you need help?"

"Your mom and I have got this," I said. Sandro and I exchanged a look. In the half a second that transpired, I knew the job was done.

Crowe Miller was dead.

I lowered my chin in acknowledgment. "I'm sure you and Bianca have some catching up to do. I told my boys to give you guys a break…"

"Oh, Dad." Bianca looked unsure, then she glanced at Sandro. Something passed between them and it was Sandro who responded, "Bianca and I want them here. It's a new beginning for all of us."

"I'll call them." Probably have them pick up more food. "Go. Go get ready. You know your brothers are eager to see you, too."

When Bianca dragged Sandro out of the kitchen, Ava turned to me. "That wasn't too hard."

I shot off a text to our family group chat and leaned a hip against the counter, a smile playing at my lips. "What do you mean?"

I knew exactly what she meant, and Ava knew this. She rolled her eyes and said it anyway, "Finally accepting Sandro."

"It wasn't a question about Sandro himself but the family he represented. That problem doesn't exist anymore."

Ava stepped into me and hugged me around the waist. "Agree. But admit it, you had a difficult time letting our little girl go."

"I still do, but a wise fucker once told me that to do what's best for my daughter, I have to love her less."

Ava laughed. She'd heard me grumble about Sandro's words before. But hearing my wife laugh and seeing her eyes twinkle lightened the somberness of the thought of letting Bianca go.

I dragged Ava into my arms. "Don't think it's going to work with you," I muttered.

"What?" she teased. "Loving me less?"

"Yeah." I searched her face. "I love you more and more each day. You know that, right?"

"Thirty years," she whispered.

"That's ten thousand nine hundred fifty days, give or take," I informed her.

Her eyes flashed as our faces grew closer. "Wow, I'm feeling warm."

A strangled groan rumbled up my throat before I crushed her lips and tasted the sweetness that had fueled the addiction for my wife day after day, year after year. After four children, and one grandchild, with another on the way, my life with Ava was only getting better.

I swept her up in my arms.

"Cesar! We can't," she scolded, knowing full well what I was up to. "The kids will be here any moment, and we have to cook."

"Cooking can wait," I muttered, marching out of the kitchen. "I told Matteo to pick up something from Eamonn's."

"And the frittata?"

My eyes crinkled at the corners. "That can be a snack. I have a feeling our family is going to stay up past midnight catching up."

"Or play Monopoly."

"You have cookies in the freezer?"

"Of course."

"Then we're set," I told her. My heart was getting overwhelmed. My daughter was safe. And I finally trusted Sandro to look after her. I was devoting my time to *my* obsession.

Ava De Lucci.

My wife.

Epilogue

One year later

Bianca

"You look beautiful, *carina*."

I turned to face my dad. The first man I loved with all my heart. He stood at the entrance of the parlor room of my childhood home, the row house on Tenth Street. Handsome in a tuxedo, he held my attention with his eyes. They were glassy with emotion—of pride and the bittersweetness accompanying a day in which he was symbolically letting me go.

He stepped into the room. "The day I held you in my arms for the first time, the way you stole my heart was different from what I had experienced with the boys. With them, I couldn't wait to teach them to be strong and fiercely protective of family. I didn't fear the day they would marry because I knew Ava and I would teach them how to be good husbands and how to cherish their wives."

"Oh, Dad." I started crying.

"The second I held you in my arms, there was so much love and joy, but also fear. I dreaded this very day. I had convinced myself no man was good enough for my Bianca. No man could treat you better than me, love you better than I ever would." Dad was in front of me now. And his tears finally escaped his eyes.

"And now?" My voice hitched. It was a rhetorical question. Ever since Sandro rescued me from drowning, it was like a switch had been flicked. An understanding had been forged between them, born from a mutual goal of protecting me.

"You couldn't have picked a better man."

I gave a brief laugh through my tears. "I did pick him, didn't I?" I couldn't believe my prophecy had come true. That I was marrying Sandro in the wedding of my dreams. No expense was spared. He and Dad argued about who was paying. Dad won. We were marrying in the same cathedral where all the De Luccis said their vows, and were having a wedding reception of eight hundred guests.

Dad reached into his pocket, and when he opened his palm, antique earrings were nestled in it. They belonged to *Nonna*, Dad's mom, who I'd never met because she died before I was born. "Ma would have wanted you to have these." He started fixing one in my ear. He cleared his throat. "It was meant to go to the daughter of her oldest son." After clasping on the second one, he stood back. "You really are a gorgeous bride." He compressed his lips together briefly, as if not knowing what to say next. Or maybe he was trying not to make me cry too much so I wouldn't have puffy eyes for the wedding.

"Thanks, Dad," I croaked. The features of his face became

blurry. "Our bond will always be there." Dammit, I made myself ugly cry.

Dad cupped my face and pressed a kiss to my forehead. He inhaled a ragged breath, trying to suppress a sob.

"Oh, that's perfect," a voice said beside us.

Throughout our father-and-daughter moment, we forgot the photographer was in the room. He was a friend of the family and knew how to be discreet.

I swiped at my eyes. I might have ruined my makeup.

"Cesar, I told you not to make Bianca cry," Mom admonished, coming back into the room with an entourage of McGraths and De Luccis. Despite how Sandro and Dad got along, Dad was still having the hardest time with the wedding, so they gave us the privacy without the videographer. I was sure Dad would say part of what he said to me during the father-of-the-bride toast.

"Nothing I can't fix." My aunt Kelly moved in front of me. I realized how this wedding had come full circle. Kelly was half McGrath and half Rossi and this wedding reunited not only two, but three families. And as Kelly repaired my makeup, I thought back to how the past year had been a year of healing. It started with many funerals and continued with Sandro's hard work, stepping up as the boss of the Rossi crime family.

Dom recommended a new manager for Club Aristos. The Rossi mansion had sold. There was a bidding war, and the buyer paid fifteen percent more than its original asking price. More soldiers had joined the family and more legitimate businesses had replaced the revenue streams from the toxic assets. But we were a crime family, after all, so the illegal was still there. My eyes fell on my bouquet sitting on the side table. A bouquet made mostly of sunflowers, but their varied faces made me smile. In the mix were the regular bright yellows, while some were streaked darker with black tips. Sandro knew what they meant to me. To live with my husband in the shadows and understand him, I had to be a little dark, a little gritty. I would forever be the sunlight he needed so we could support each other and thrive.

Sandro and I bought a Victorian-era revival residence in Brooklyn's Prospect Park South. Too small to be called a mansion, yet too big to be called a house. We found the property eight months ago and, being that it was in a historic district, we had to abide by regulations when making upgrades and renovations. It was all worth it. We'd been living there for three months now.

I was still Bianca, just a little tougher. Who was I kidding? I'd become a little gangsta.

"What's holding everyone up?" Aunt Lottie strutted into the room. "Oh, did Cesar make you cry?"

"She's ready," Kelly singsonged. "Uncle Cesar's children are four for four and married already. When will you be the mama of the bride or groom?"

"Tell me about it," Lottie grumbled. "I'm the one who loves to plan these things. Maybe I should stop."

My aunt continued her lament. "What is it about your kids, Cesar? By the time Bianca gets married again to Sandro, three of your children would have been married twice to the same person."

Everyone laughed because it was true. Renz married Liz twice. Matteo and Sera divorced before getting married again. And now, me and Sandro.

Suddenly, I was eager to see my husband.

On our way out of the house, I caught my reflection in the full-length mirror. My face was glowing, and Kelly was really a genius with makeup. One wouldn't imagine I'd been sobbing half an hour ago.

"Quite a difference." Renz appeared behind me. He was one of the groomsmen.

"I don't look like the bride of Dracula anymore?" I teased.

"You look like the princess of fairy tales." His eyes gleamed as he crooked his elbow. "Shall we, sis?"

Oh my God. My heart was bursting with giddiness, and despite the voluminous skirts of my wedding dress, I'd never felt more lighthearted in my life.

Full circle.

Renz led me to the waiting limo.

Dad slid in beside me and we exchanged looks of contentment and happiness.

When we arrived at the church, the crowd was a blur of golden yellow. I was eager to reach the top of the steps and Dad had to slow me down.

Finally, at the entrance to the cathedral, the man at the end of the aisle commanded all my focus and the air pumping in my lungs. Sandro cut an imposing figure in his tuxedo. Even with the length of the church between us, I could feel the heat, his yearning, and his impatience. We hadn't seen each other for twenty-four hours. He was still worried that my dad would whisk me away to parts unknown, so much so that he texted me constantly. And that was saying something because Sandro hated texting.

The bridal march started, and I made my way to *him*. The world receded to just us. And as I moved closer, I could see all the love emanating from his eyes, drawing me to him, and I couldn't wait to start our life together.

His eyes locked with Dad's as the priest asked who would give me away.

I didn't know why I held my breath. I think Sandro did, too.

But when Dad said, "I do," I breathed easily again. He put my hand into Sandro's and said, "Take care of her." Then he leaned in closer. "Or I'll make you disappear." I was sure Dad worded his threat mildly for the priest's benefit.

Sandro emitted a brief chuckle. "I will, and I expect nothing less."

I rolled my eyes, but did I expect anything different from the two most important men in my life?

Sandro led me to the altar, and we exchanged vows in front of friends and family. I married the man I'd loved for most of my life for the second time.

And when he kissed me?

It exceeded my dreams.

~

Two Years Later

Sandro

"You're so beautiful when you come." I had Bianca up against the headboard, giving her a third orgasm. I would have given her more, but she begged for my cock.

And she knew every time she said *please*, I was a goner.

I powered in for one final thrust before I emptied inside her.

Still, sometimes she'd be a bad girl, but I learned quickly enough that was when she wanted to be edged and fucked hard. Delaying her gratification was a game we played, but I hadn't sunk into her warm pussy in two months.

I was rabid for my wife.

"I missed that so much," she breathed. "We should do it again."

"Are you sure, baby? Don't you have to wake up early tomorrow to help Carlotta with something?"

"Oh, you're right." She laughed briefly. "She's so excited to finally plan a wedding for one of her kids."

I nuzzled her throat. "I'm finally glad your doctor gave the go-ahead for us to have sex."

"You've been such a good sport."

"Our daughter kept us busy enough."

As if on cue, a baby's cry broke our stolen moment.

Bianca sighed, but a chuckle rumbled deep in my throat. "I got her." My wife didn't object and instead stretched languidly and sank into the mattress.

I left the bed and headed to the adjacent room that we converted to a nursery. When I entered the room, I could see our daughter's arms and legs moving. She was growing too fast. She was responding more to voices and sounds.

It had been a sleepless six weeks. More so for Bianca, because I wasn't a traditional husband with regular working hours. I couldn't take a paternity leave. A brief chuckle escaped me at the thought. Tommy and Divina also welcomed a boy six months ago and the poor man had been nodding off at sit-downs. He grumbled we needed to rewrite the family's code and include paternity leaves. Good thing I functioned on very little sleep.

I walked over to the crib and picked up our daughter. "Hey, baby girl."

Her cries subsided to gurgles and cooing. I doubted she was hungry, but parenthood had been a learning experience. My throat tightened with emotion as I picked up my daughter.

Admittedly, when Bianca told me she was pregnant, I had the weirdest response. I was the one who couldn't wait to put a baby inside her, but when it actually happened, a stabbing feeling gored my chest that I was going to have to share my wife. I spent enough time away from her running our organization that I didn't want to share the time that was devoted to just being with her.

But all that changed the second they put Camilla Rossi in my arms. I'd fallen head over heels in love with the adorable bundle swaddled in pink. It was different from the way I loved Bianca, but the same in a way I wanted to find an isolated island so I could bask in the love of my family of three. Camilla and Bianca's light shined so fucking bright, my chest rolled each time when I thought of the gift fate awarded me after I'd felt undeserving for thirty-two years.

Not anymore. I wasn't going to waste the belief Bianca always had in me. I might have lost her faith a couple of times, but I earned it back.

I sensed her before her arms wrapped around my torso.

"I thought you were going to bring her to me," Bianca murmured.

"I don't think she's hungry, baby."

"Oh, ha!" She moved beside me and stared at Camilla, who had her eyes focused on me. "She's just fussy now, is she?"

"Yeah."

"I think she has you wrapped around her finger."

"I'm understanding Cesar now and I'm dreading the payback when she grows up."

Bianca laughed and walked over to the dresser. She had brought the carved box of things I'd given her into the nursery. She said she wanted to tell our daughter about our history. Bianca opened the box and retrieved the silver bracelet from its depths. I knew that was one of her favorites.

She nudged me to the rocking chair.

"Do you want to hold her and see if she wants to eat?" I asked.

"No, she's quiet right now and is enjoying Daddy time."

Fuck, those chest twitches.

I eased myself into the rocking chair, and Bianca kneeled in front of us.

"I polished this silver cuff today." My wife held up the shiny trinket. I didn't have money then to buy her expensive gifts, but that tiny diamond that was set in a gold-plated sun reminded me of what Bianca meant to me. Speaking of expensive, I was thankful my wife kept that huge-ass diamond ring I bought her. She said it marked her rebirth and the night I breathed new life into her. I didn't gnash my teeth anymore when I thought about the time I almost lost her. It only cemented our bond that had been there since the first time I rescued her in the pool.

Camilla tried to grasp it. Her grip wasn't strong yet, but she loved to reach for things.

"Did you know the day your dad gave me this was the day I decided I was going to marry him?" Bianca told our daughter, but she was looking at me like I was her entire universe.

Our beautiful love story. It was one for the ages and meant to be shared with the next generation.

"I love you so fucking much," I rasped with an emotion that choked me.

My wife rolled her lips together, but her throat worked convulsively, as if suppressing the overwhelming feelings that came each time we recalled the hard-fought journey we went through to reach this point.

She stood and hugged us. Father and daughter.

"You've always been mine, Sandro." She pressed a gentle kiss on my mouth. "You have my heart forever."

"In case you didn't know, you've always been mine, too."

Forever.

~

Sign up for my newsletter for Renz and Liz's POV during the time when Renz went missing including a flashback into their meet cute.

Dom's book is next in Scorned Beauty

Haven't read the other books?
Matteo and Sera's book is Scorned Heir,
Luca and Natalya's is Scorned Vows.
Nico and Ivy's in Scorned Love
Cesar and Ava's is De Lucci's Obsession

Thank you for reading Scorned Obsession! If you enjoyed this book, I would appreciate it if you could leave a review on any platform of your choice. Every one counts!

Love,
Victoria

Afterword

Ever since the bonus stories from De Lucci's Obsession, readers have been clamoring for a Sandro and Bianca book. But writing a childhood-friends-to-lovers was tricky, especially involving an age-gap. I'm not a fan of friends-to-lovers trope that much, so I added the enemies part to make it interesting. With characters already known to each other, flashbacks were unavoidable, but since I dislike reading them, I limited them to two major turning-point moments in their relationship. And the rest of their backstory unfolded naturally, like one would when remembering a memory.

This book wouldn't be possible without my amazing team.

Thank you to my developmental editor, Kara. I'm so happy to embark on this journey with you. Your insightful notes and suggestions were so helpful to the overall flow and emotional impact of the story. I can't wait to work on my next book with you.

Sue, I enjoyed going through your real-time reactions and comments as you read the manuscript, pointing out which part made you emotional, but also the sections that needed more detail. I'm thankful for your continued support, and your knowledge of my characters helps me maintain consistency.

Thank you, Becca aka The Fairy Plot Mother. You always ask me the right questions to fuel my intellection process to solve plot and character issues.

Erica, thank you for being a rockstar editor. I love working with you. And to have you say that this was the smoothest childhood-friends-to-lovers evolution you have read buoys my author's heart. We need those energy pennies when doubts set in, and you never fail to provide them after each manuscript when I wonder if it was good enough.

Judy, Thank you so much for your eagle eye and quick turn-around time.

Mandy, thank you for your drop-in hellos and chats at random times during the week. I love talking J/P heroes and audio book narrators with you and the random recipe you find for the air fryer.

To Shauna & Becky of The Author Agency, thank you for your excellent support, easy communication, and execution of building up excitement for the Scorned Fate series that culminated in the release of Scorned Obsession. It enabled me to keep my focus on writing the next book.

Shaye & Lindsey of Good Girls PR. I've never seen such meticulous methods in the marketing and building of an author brand. You have the pulse of the book community and know which readers would love my words. Thank you for connecting me with them and guiding me every step of the way.

To my Very Important Paige readers, booktokkers, bookstagrammers, book bloggers, and all my loyal as well as new readers … special mention to Suny for your stunning edits, thank you so much! It wouldn't be possible for me to do what I love without your support.

And finally, to my wonderful hubby who has the patience to deal with my mood swings whenever my characters piss me off, and Loki, a girl's best friend who makes sure I keep moving with our daily walks. Thank you for your understanding and loving support so I can live my dreams.

Connect with the Author

Find me at:

Facebook: Victoria Paige Books
Website: victoriapaigebooks.com
Email: victoriapaigebooks@gmail.com
FB Reader Group: Very Important Paige readers

facebook.com/victoriapaigebooks
tiktok.com/@vpaigebooks
instagram.com/victoriapaigebooks

Also by Victoria Paige

Scorned Fate

Scorned Heir

Scorned Vows

Scorned Love

Scorned Obsession

Scorned Beauty (Fall 2025)

Rogue Protectors

The Ex Assignment

Protector of Convenience

The Boss Assignment

Her Covert Protector

The Wife Assignment

Forced Protector

Guardians

Fire and Ice

Beneath the Fire (novella)

Silver Fire

Smoke and Shadows

Always

It's Always Been You

Always Been Mine

A Love For Always

Misty Grove

Fighting Chance

Saving Grace

Unexpected Vows

Standalone

De Lucci's Obsession

Deadly Obsession

Captive Lies

The Princess and the Mercenary

* All series books can be read as standalone

Printed in Dunstable, United Kingdom

80946569R00241